Blood-Borne Series

~BOOK FOUR~

Of Blood & Fire

C.R. QUINN

Designed by C.R. Quinn
Cover created by C.R. Quinn
Front cover photo by Thawat Tanhai /123rf.com
Back cover photo by from Mykhailo Shcherbyna /123rf.com
Spine photo by Butterfly Hunter/Shutterstock.com

Printed in the United States of America

Library of Congress
ISBN-10: 0-692-19964-0
ISBN-13: 978-0-692-19964-0

Of Blood & Fire

For Maddie, the mashed potato monster

Prologue

Devin - February 1549

The innkeeper easily divulged Garrett's whereabouts when faced with losing his thumb. He was, however, surprised when I still sliced it off. To me it was a promise of continued silence after I finished the task Father had entrusted to me - killing Garrett the Archer. He had been born in battle, and was deadly accurate with his bow. He was also my Warrior brother, one of nine made by Victor, and he would be my first kill, a test from Father. If I was successful, I would become Father's primary assassin. I coveted the title and was prepared to make whatever sacrifices necessary.

The wood of the second floor creaked under my feet as I approached the last of the sleeping quarters. The door to the room was cracked open, meaning my elder brother was expecting me. My dagger was drawn, its double-edged blade deadly sharp and dipped in silver in order to kill any vampire who crossed its path. When I pushed the door open, I found Garrett sitting in a chair in front of the fire.

"Ah, Father has sent the wee Devin for me," Garrett said keeping his back to me disrespectfully.

As I stepped closer, I noticed the fire casting a shadow on the head of a crossbow lying across his lap. "You know why I have come?"

"Devin, son of Henry…"

"I do not recognize my mortal family…"

"Now tell me, how did an Englishman like your father come across a Spanish whore?"

"Victor is my father," I growled through my clenched teeth. I could not rebuke his claim. My mother was a whore and Henry never let me forget it.

"Victor is your maker and he would sooner cut off your head if your breath vexed him."

My hand clenched Garrett's hair, pulling his head back and pressing my blade against the skin of his neck. "The only head you need to worry about is yours."

Garrett clicked his tongue at me as the silver blade burned into his skin. "My wee Devin, a true assassin would have taken my head from my shoulders by now. Father would be disappointed."

"As long as I kill you, he will not be."

"Then why am I still alive?"

"You have betrayed our coven and our father, and must therefore…"

"I…have done…nothing wrong," he grunted as he struggled against the blade cutting deeper into his throat.

"You continued your affiliation with the wolves against orders. You initiated battle against our kind and placed hundreds of humans in danger."

Garrett's fangs pierced through his bottom lip as he grabbed his crossbow and aimed it over his shoulder. Just as the arrow snapped out of its holding, I drew my blade across Garrett's neck. The small arrow pierced through my clothing and disappeared easily into my stomach. I let go of Garrett's head, causing him to fall to the floor.

In the moment it took to remove the arrow, Garrett rose from the floor and stumbled toward the open window. I leapt in his direction at the same time he lifted his crossbow and fired an arrow directly into my throat. The impact caused me to fall back and watch as Garrett fell backwards out the window. Running to the window and clawing the arrow out of my throat, I bent over the ledge of the wooden window frame and saw no sign of my traitorous brother.

I had failed. Father would never trust me again. I would never become the Warrior Assassin. Father required proof of the kill. What was I going to do? This could not be the end of being a Warrior, I had only just begun.

When I turned from the window, something next to the fireplace caught my eye. Garrett's bow - a tight wire stretched across beautifully curved wood, with grooves for his grip carved in the center. Garrett's bow was an appendage, only death would keep it from him. Hopefully it would be enough proof for father. Better yet, hopefully Garrett would truly die and never come to retrieve it.

A Book of Beckett

Chapter One

"The library will be closing in ten minutes," the automated message rang.

Shit.

I'd spent two hours in the library thinking it would somehow inspire me to research my latest Anthropology paper, but all it did was prove that I really hated Anthropology, didn't really know how to use the Dewy Decimal system, and when left to search online I ended up looking up useless questions that somehow lead me to other useless questions like why do we have wisdom teeth if they only need to be pulled out? Answer, we needed them thousands of years ago in order to chew animal meat. Hey, Anthropology! Sadly not what my report needed to be on.

I closed my laptop and took the books I'd started looking through and brought them up to the front counter to get them checked out. The attendant behind the counter glared at me for waiting until the last minute and took the books over to the other side of the counter.

While I waited for her to scan the books, a girl came up next to me and placed several books on the counter. I didn't pay too much attention to her until she cleared her throat the second time. I glanced over at her and she immediately looked up at me and squinted her eyes.

"I'm sorry, did I cut in line?" I asked.

She shook her head and glanced over my shoulder for a split second and then back at me. "Do you know those men over there?"

I turned my head in the direction she'd jutted her chin and saw two men standing near one of the stacks. "Um...no. Hey, aren't you in my English Lit class? Tish, right?"

"So, you don't know them?" she said in a bit of a bitchy tone.

"Uh, no, I don't know them. Should I?"

The girl, we'll call her Tish since she wasn't telling me, pulled her messenger bag over her head and across her chest, suddenly making it a point not to make eye contact with me. "They've been following you since you came in here."

"Following me?"

"Shhhh!" she hissed and grabbed my arm to stop me from turning around. "Keep your voice down. Do you know what they are?"

"What they are? What do you..."

"I know what you are, do you?"

"I'm a Junior," I replied.

"Not your grade, idiot, what you *are*."

Since she was whispering, and I assumed having some kind of mental episode, I whispered back, "I'm not sure what's happening here."

"Obviously," she replied and rolled her eyes. "Whatever you do, don't let them follow you home. If you feel you're in trouble, call this number. They'll help you."

She took a card out of her bag and handed it to me. I took a look at the front which said *Facility West* with a San Francisco number.

"Are you sure you don't need this?" I asked. She was obviously disturbed.

"I'm giving you the card, why would I need it?" she replied annoyed. "Just...watch out for those guys."

I looked back over my shoulder and noticed that the two men were gone, and when I turned back around, the crazy girl was walking out the front door.

"Mr. Dawes," the library attendant said and held out my student ID. "The books are due back next Wednesday."

I nodded and took my ID from her. "Thanks. It's...uh...Beckett."

"I don't care," she replied flatly.

Looks like I wasn't scoring any points with the ladies tonight. Not that that was any different than any other day. But honestly, what did I have to offer? Community college student who lived at home and was going to fail Anthropology. Talents were limited, initiative was lacking, and future career was unknown. But I was cute. At least that's what my Grammy always used to say, and she was never wrong.

Although I didn't believe the strange girl in the library, I'll admit I looked over my shoulder as I made my way across campus and to the parking lot. There was a little adrenaline pumping as I approached my car, wondering if the mob or the FBI was really following me. Maybe they were scoping me out for recruitment. Yeah right. But like I said, I was cute. Maybe that was the draw.

I laughed at the thought and started my car, happy that it started at all since it was a piece of shit. Hell, the front bumper was held together with duct tape and the engine made a terrible squealing noise whenever I slowed down. Yep, total chick magnet. It was a wonder I was single. Maybe I should ask that crazy girl out. Tish, right? Something like that. She was sort of like one of those goth chicks – always in black, covered up even when it was warm outside, standoffish all the time. She didn't wear all the dark make-up though. She'd be pretty cute if she didn't always have that I'm-better-than-you look on her face. Plus, she was a bit of a show-off in Lit class. She was one of the few people that actually read everything we were supposed to and would openly debate the professor in class. I was usually counting the minutes until I got to go home.

She was a little bit crazy, wasn't she? What was that whole thing in the library – did I know what I was. *What* I was. What the hell was that about? And why was the car behind me flashing its lights? My headlights were on. I was going above the speed limit. What the hell? I slowed down in case they wanted to pass, but they slowed down with me. Finally, I pulled off the side of the road, cringing at the sound my engine made as I slowed to a stop and waved the car around, but instead it pulled in behind me.

This was it. This was where the man with the hook came up to me in my car and killed me, but I was also the asshole not driving away just in case it really was the scary man with the hook, and honestly, I wanted to see if it was true. Loser.

Stupidly I rolled down my window as a man approached my car and shined a flashlight in my eyes. The fact that he had both arms was disappointing, but a cop without lights or sirens? No way.

"Are you Beckett Dawes?" the man asked as he lowered the flashlight and I could see that it was one of the men from the library.

"Who's asking?"

"Are you Beckett Dawes?" he said again.

"Can I see your badge or something?" I said, suddenly having that eerie feeling something wasn't right.

"Get out of the car," the man said and took a step away from the car door.

"Show me a badge first."

Suddenly the man lunged for my car door at the same moment I slammed on the gas. He must have gotten a good grip on my door since it ripped off its hinges as I sped away, swerving in and out of the lanes before my tires could get a good grip on the road. My door, my fucking car door was just ripped off. I was literally driving without a driver's side door. What the...

"Fuck!" I shouted as I swerved around a giant...dog? The beast took up half the lane. When I swerved, my tires lost their grip sending me airborne off the side of the road and landing upside down in the ditch. The airbag hit me in the chest, taking the breath out of me and causing my ears to ring. Two hands reached into the car, grabbed my shirt, and pulled me out seatbelt and all. Once I was thrown to the ground I looked up to see the man I had just tried to outrun.

"Stupid kid," he said and picked me up with one hand. "Daddy wants to meet you."

"Put him down," a girl shouted from somewhere I couldn't see.

"This don't concern you, little girl," the man replied.

"I said put him down."

Abruptly I was dropped to the ground and I painfully rolled over onto my stomach. Standing a few feet away was the girl from my English Lit class, goth girl, crazy chick, standing with a knife in one hand and a long shiny whip in the other. I must have hit my head pretty hard, or inhaled toxic fumes while in the car. This just didn't make sense.

"It's against your laws to harm a human," she began. "Violation of that law..."

"And who's going to report me?" he growled. "You, little girl? Are you going to report me to the Warriors?"

"I am," she replied, the whip in her hand starting to shake.

"You can't report me if you're dead."

"And I can kill you in self-defense," she replied and snapped the whip in front of her.

The man turned around to run but goth girl snapped her shiny whip and it wound around his neck. The man screamed and fell to his knees, smoke oddly rising from where the whip was strangling him. Like a wild animal he lunged in my direction, growling and clawing at me as I tried crawling backwards. When he lunged for me again, he suddenly froze and then fell forward on the ground. I looked up just in time to see goth girl pull the knife out of his back.

"What the fff...."

"Can you walk," she shouted as she unwound the shiny whip from around the man's neck. "Come on, we have to get out of here!"

"But you just...just," I said and pointed at the body that was now slumped at my feet.

"You're a master of words," she groaned as she helped me to my feet and walked me over to a black sports car. Once inside she reached in front of me and opened the glove compartment, pulling out several napkins and placing them on my forehead. "Keep the pressure going. Do not get blood on my car."

"I'm bleeding?" I asked as she slammed the car door and ran around the front. I pulled the napkins from my head and saw that they were soaked with blood. "Makes sense, I guess."

"What makes sense?" she asked as she sank into the driver's seat.

"I'm totally trippin'. It's got to be a head injury."

"Yep, that must be it," she replied dismissively and pulled her car onto the road as she dialed her phone.

"Wait, I can't leave my car here. Don't we need to wait for the police?"

"In less than fifteen minutes your car won't be there."

"Huh? What do you..."

"Connor!" she shouted into the phone. "It's Tosh, I'm in trouble."

Chapter Two

My head was pounding and my fingers were sticky and stained with blood. I assumed I was going to a hospital, but instead I was taken to a castle-like mansion and put on a bench with a hulking guard standing next to me. He hadn't said a word in the ten minutes I'd been sitting here, wouldn't even look at me. But honestly, that was ok. It wasn't like my brain could process anything right now, everything was a little hazy. Thankfully the bleeding from my head had stopped. Tish had made a big deal about wiping away most of it before we stepped inside the mansion. Was she afraid I'd bleed all over the walls?

"Is this a museum or something?" I asked to the stone-faced guy next to me. He didn't answer. "Shouldn't we be calling the police? My car's still there, they'll think I did this…"

"Is she still in there?" a woman said from down the hall while dragging a little girl with her.

"Yeah," the guard replied. So he could talk, he was just being an asshole to me. "Cameron's really giving it to her."

"I would have been here sooner, but someone got gum stuck in her hair and her brother decided to cut her hair off in order to get it out," the woman said, bringing the little girl to stand in front of me. She was a pretty little girl, but her black hair was chopped off in all different directions and different lengths. "Do you mind watching her while I go in there?"

"Where's Jackson?" the guard asked.

"With Kyla so that I don't kill him," she replied and stepped into the room next to me.

As soon as the door closed, the little girl began to climb up the guard like he was a tree.

"Little girl…" I said quietly, "…little girl, that's probably not a good idea."

"It's ok," she replied as he cradled her with his right arm. "Connor always lets me climb so I can get the gum."

The little girl patted his front pocket and then held out her hand expectantly.

"If your mother finds out I gave you that gum she'll kill me. Look at your hair, Livy."

"I won't tell, I pwomiss," she replied. Connor, as I knew now, couldn't be that much of a badass since he gave in to this little girl and put a new stick of gum into her palm.

"Let's try and keep it out of your hair this time, ok?"

"Fank you, Connor," she said before kissing him on the cheek and then somehow doing a backflip out of his arm and landing perfectly.

"You're showing off, Livy," Connor said, but she merely smiled and curtsied.

"What's your name?" she asked as she brushed a section of bluntly cut hair out of her face.

"Beckett Dawes, and you?"

"I'm Wivy Burke. Why are you here?"

I shrugged. "I'm not really sure."

"What happened to your head?"

My hand instantly went to my forehead. "Oh…um, I was in an accident."

"Did Toshy save you?"

"W-who?"

Connor groaned. "Tosh. The girl who almost got herself killed tonight because she helped you."

"Tosh?" No wonder her name wouldn't stick in my head. "Is it short for something?"

He didn't answer.

"What's your twick?" Livy asked as she jumped onto the bench next to me and began looking intently at my head.

"My trick?"

She nodded. "Your hybwid twick."

I looked up at Connor and he didn't offer any explanation. "I'm not sure what you're…you mean like a car? That kind of hybrid?"

She laughed. "No, siwwy. A hybwid like Toshy. She's a Healer."

"Um…a what?"

"A Healer."

"No, uh, I'm not anything. Just Beck, plain old Beck."

She shook her head and tapped my head with her index finger. "But I can see your wight, it's red. That's a hybie wight, that's what I see. Jack-Jack sees the vampys, their wights are white."

I blinked and looked up at Connor who was expressionless. "I think I have a head injury."

"How can you tell?" he said with a smirk.

"I can't understand what she's saying, it sounds like…I don't know. I think my head is messed up."

"You're fine," he replied and pulled Livy off of me. "Olivia, let's leave him alone."

Livy crossed her arms and stamped her foot on the floor. "But I wanna know his twick!"

Connor crossed his arms, stamped his foot on the floor, and stared Livy down. "I doubt he has one!"

There was an insult in there somewhere, I was sure of it. I still didn't know what kind of trick they were referring to, but I certainly didn't want to be dismissed entirely. I could have a trick. Yes, I could certainly have a trick, or a brain injury, that was more likely. I looked up to see Connor throw the little girl high, like really high in the air, and then catch her with one hand. One hand! My brain was playing tricks on me, it wasn't working right. I definitely had a brain injury.

"Beckett?" the dark-haired lady asked as she opened the door. "Why don't you come inside?"

Blood rushed to my head as I stood from the bench and I reached for the wall. The dark-haired lady was suddenly in front of me, her hands holding me at my chest and back.

"Take it slow, there's no rush," she said kindly.

"Tell that to your husband," Connor laughed smugly next to us.

"Quiet, you," she replied firmly. This lady had balls. "Can you watch Livy for a few more minutes?"

"Sure, it's better than having to watch this nightmare," he replied and jutted his chin in my direction.

"How am I…"

"That's enough, Connor, thank you," she interrupted and released her supportive hands when I stood on my own. "Feel ok to go in now?" I nodded although my body was starting to make my other injuries known to me. "Good. I'm Brianna, by the way."

"That's my mama," Livy said proudly as Connor lifted her up onto his shoulders.

"Yes, baby girl, I'm sure he figured that out," Brianna replied as she wrapped her arm around my back and guided me toward the open door.

"Bye, Beckett. Have fun wiff my Ada and Devy," Livy said as I stepped through the door into a very large study. There was a roaring fire with a fancy couch to my right and two desks directly in front of me, I assumed one for each of the men that were scowling at Tosh who was standing in the center of the room.

"I was just trying to help," Tosh said to the floor.

"You were being cocky," the muscular guy spat. "You could have been killed."

Brianna cleared her throat, causing all three of them to look in my direction. Tosh's eyes were glassy, almost on the verge of crying.

"You must be Beckett," the skinny tall guy said as he stepped over to me and extended his hand. "Welcome, I am Cameron Burke. I see you have met my wife, Brianna."

I shook his hand and couldn't help but notice how cold he was. Weird.

"And this is my brother Devin," Cameron continued and gestured behind him to the muscular guy who had been yelling at Tosh a moment before. But what I didn't understand was why he was glaring at me. "Brother? Are you all right?"

"What did you say your name was?" Devin said through his clinched teeth.

Such a simple question made me want to piss my pants.

"Um…Beckett? Beckett Dawes."

"Who is your father?" he asked and stepped forward so aggressively that Cameron put a hand in his chest.

"Brother, calm down," Cameron said in my defense. "He is a victim and our guest."

Devin ignored Cameron and his eyes were wild as he shouted, "Who is your father!"

"Richard!" I shouted. "Richard Dawes, that's my dad. What the fuck?"

Apparently that answer didn't make him very happy because he stormed out of the room. Cameron glanced at his wife and they shrugged in unison.

"Beckett, would you like to sit down?"

"Yeah, please, my head is pounding."

"Of course. Natasha, would you please bring over that chair for our guest," Cameron said and gestured to one of the tall chairs in front of the fireplace.

She gave me a dirty look before dragging the chair over and pushing me down into it. Why was she so mad?

"Now, Beckett," Cameron started as he leaned back on one of the desks and crossed his arms in front of his chest, "your father, Richard Dawes, is he your birth father?"

"Yeah," I replied, but really confused.

"And you are sure of that?"

"Uh, well, yeah. He knocked-up my mom in college, shotgun wedding, that kind of thing. They moved back here to be closer to her side of the family. What does that have to do with the accident?"

"That is what we are trying to figure out. Now what I am about to tell you is generally the toughest part to understand and accept. So please, just be patient and open. Ok?"

"Ok," I answered nervously.

"Beckett, you are what we call a hybrid. Has anyone ever said anything like that to you?"

"Wait, your daughter did. I thought she was talking about a hybrid car or something."

Tosh snorted next to me.

"Natasha," Cameron warned. At least someone was on my side. "What else did my daughter say to you?"

I shrugged. "I don't know, something about seeing a light? I didn't really understand what she was talking about."

"I see," he replied. "So Olivia has confirmed our suspicions that you are a hybrid. Now this only occurs when a human female, someone such as your mother, mates with a vampire."

All sound and movement ceased around me.

"Say what now?"

Cameron rose from his relaxed position on the desk. "Beckett, I know this can be jarring, and many others before you have had the same response. But vampires do exist, and we have been hiding among you for thousands of years. My brother Devin and I lead what is called the Warrior coven, a group of vampires charged with protecting our kind as well as our hybrid children like you and Natasha."

I let Cameron's comments settle in. Slowly I looked over at Tosh who was urging me to have some kind of reaction.

"Beckett?"

I turned back to Cameron. "Yeah, sorry, just…uh…look, I gotta hand it to you guys, you are committed."

"Pardon?" Cameron said tilted his head.

I swallowed uncomfortably. "Well, the whole vampire-goth lifestyle just isn't my thing, but no judgment. You guys have a solid backstory and everything, and you're totally committed to it. I give you credit, but I'm not into the whole goth-vamp-steampunk-whatever-you-call-it thing."

"Oh my god," Tosh groaned next to me. "You're such an idiot."

"Natasha," Cameron warned again but she huffed and threw her arms up in the air.

"The guy held you in the air with one hand and said your 'Daddy' wanted to see you. How can you just dismiss that?" she shouted.

Suddenly my brain went back to the moment she was talking about, and he did say exactly that. He did hold me up what seemed like three feet in the air with one hand, but…but…

"They must have the wrong kid," I replied and Tosh huffed again. "I'm sorry, I'm not a goth and…"

"This isn't a goth thing!" she shouted. "Your real father is a vampire and he sent those men after you."

"My dad is an accountant!" I shouted and my head pounded for it.

Cameron stood from his desk and put his hands up between the two of us. "Let us all calm down. Beckett, I believe you have the wrong idea about us, but I can understand your reluctance. We are truly here to help you, but it is your choice to leave our protection. I do, however, ask that you keep quiet about our headquarters here."

I nodded since no one would believe me anyway. "Yeah, of course."

Just then the study's door opened and Cameron waved in the person peeking his head in. "Beckett, this is Dr. Ryan, he will take a look at your head wound. Brianna, Natasha, let us give them some privacy."

The doctor was probably in his mid-thirties, but wasn't wearing scrubs or even a white jacket. The only thing remotely making him look like a doctor was the fact that he had a canvas medical bag over his shoulder. He seemed to be well liked since every person leaving the room either hugged him or patted him on the back. Maybe he was one of those concierge doctors who came to rich people's houses. Considering the size of this place it would make sense. I was really telling myself anything to make me feel better about trusting a perfect stranger that another stranger was telling me was a doctor.

"Hey, I'm Dr. Ryan, but you can also call me John," he said as he knelt down to the floor.

"I'm Beckett, but most people call me Beck or Dawes."

"I take it Dawes is your last name?" I nodded as he donned on a pair of latex gloves, and removed a pen light from his breast pocket. "Follow the light please."

I did as he asked, following the light to the left then right and back.

"So you were in an accident tonight?" he asked and began pressing his fingers around my eye.

"Yeah. My car flipped and the airbag hit me."

"Uh huh," he replied and began pressing my collarbone and chest which was more tender than I thought. "What about this bruising on your neck?"

"Oh, yeah, this guy choked me."

"Just some guy?" he replied with a skeptical look.

"Well, these guys…uh…Cameron and the others, think this guy wanted to kill me or something."

Oddly Dr. Ryan laughed a little. "Well, Beckett, it's been my experience that if they're telling you some people are out to kill you, you might want to listen."

"You're into this whole vampire club, too?"

He smirked before reaching up and cleaning the cut on my forehead. "I remember being like you, completely unaware that there was an entire population of monsters all around me. Ah, those were the good old days. I about shit my pants the first time I saw a pair of fangs."

"Wait, they have fangs installed?" I said shocked and then winced. "Boy that hurts."

Dr. Ryan pulled out a package of Steri-Strips from within his bag and began stretching them across my brow. "Sorry about that, we're almost done. I'm actually surprised Tosh didn't heal this for you."

"What do you mean?"

"Tosh is a Hea…oh never mind, I'll let you live in the beautiful world of oblivion for a little while longer," he replied with another smirk as he snapped his gloves off and then pulled a small packet from inside his bag. "You're pretty lucky, Beckett, just a cut above the eye and some bruising around the neck. You'll probably have a headache and some sore muscles tomorrow. Here's a couple of muscle relaxers that might help."

"Thanks, doc," I said, taking the packet from his hand and popping both pills into my mouth.

Dr. Ryan looked up from his bag just as I swallowed. "Did you just take both of those?"

"Um…yeah. Why? I wasn't supposed to?"

"Most take one," he replied. "Let's hope they can get you home before they kick in."

"This night just keeps getting better."

Slowly I pushed myself up from the chair and Dr. Ryan hovered while I made my way toward the door.

"Now listen, kid, I know you're in a bit of shock right now, and you have every right to be. But like I said before, if this group is warning you that you might be in some trouble, I'd listen."

"Thanks, doc, I appreciate the concern, but this just isn't my scene."

He patted my back and opened the door. "I do hope you get to keep living in that bubble you're in. Because once it pops…" He didn't finish his thought, but merely gestured to the group gathered in the corridor.

Tosh was propped up against the opposite wall and giving me a murderous glare as Connor leaned in and whispered in her ear. Cameron looked up from his daughter's awkward haircut as I stepped out into the hallway.

"Beckett here is fine, except he just took two muscle relaxers," Dr. Ryan said with a smirk. "I'd get him home before he turns to jelly."

"John, thank you for coming on such short notice," Cameron said and shook John's hand.

"Yeah, no problem," John replied before turning to Brianna and kissing her on the cheek, then taking a moment to pet Livy's crookedly cut hair. "Oh, Livybean, what is Aunt Re gonna say when she sees this?"

Livybean? Aunt Re? Dr. Ryan seemed like such a straight-edge that it was hard for me to believe that he was so deeply connected with this group. My head was starting to hurt again, and even though it had only been a few minutes, those muscle relaxers were starting to kick in. I rocked backwards a little which seemed to catch Cameron's attention.

"Natasha, I think it is time you took Beckett home."

Tosh's head flinched up from the private conversation she was having with Connor. I wondered if they were a couple. Maybe that's why he was such a jerk to me.

"I can take him," Connor answered, but Cameron shook his head.

"Natasha brought him here, she can take him home," Cameron said sternly before he turned to me. "Beckett, you were very lucky tonight. I know you are having trouble accepting who we are and subsequently what you are, but you were followed tonight and almost kidnapped. Do not take that lightly. If you suspect someone else is following you, connect with Natasha." Cameron looked over at her and narrowed his eyes. "She will call us for help and not handle the situation alone."

Tosh sighed and pushed herself off the wall. "Don't worry, sir, he can rot for all I care," she replied as she took my arm and pulled me away from the group. What was her problem? Why were the walls moving? Damn these pills worked fast.

When we rounded a corner I kept turning and my face was met with the stone wall.

"Just walk!" Natasha yelled and pulled me into her side, locking her arm around my back.

"Why are you so mad at me?" I said, although it probably sounded slurred since my entire body felt as though I'd had a shitload of alcohol.

"Why am I mad?" she asked and opened the front door. "You made me look like a fool."

I stumbled down the wide front steps, my sneakers squeaking as I tried catching my footing.

"I didn't mean to…"

"I saved your fucking life and you made me look like an asshole in front of Cameron and Devin."

"I didn't mean…"

"Shut up," she snapped as she continued to drag me across the gravel parking lot. A pair of lights flashed in front of us and a moment later I was sitting in the front seat of her Mercedes. Seriously, how did she afford something like this?

After she slid into the driver's seat she slammed the door. "What's your address?"

"Huh?" I answered and noticed that her face was getting fuzzy.

"I need your address in order to drive you home, asshole."

My head felt heavy and suddenly I couldn't keep my eyelids open. "Oh yeah, my...street...Natasha...Tasha, Tasha, Tassshhh-a."

"Dammit, Beckett, give me a little help," a voice said near me. My eyelids were so heavy. Why couldn't I just stay asleep?

"Beckett," the voice said again but this time my eyes shot open when I was slapped in the face.

"What the fu..." I started to shout but then saw Natasha standing over me, trying to pull me out of the car. "Wh-where are we?"

"Your house," she replied. "Now come on, you've got to push yourself up. I can't do it by myself with you as limp as you are."

"Never had that problem before," I laughed and swung my leg outside of the car, although I couldn't really feel it. While she grabbed me underneath the armpits I pushed down on where I thought my leg was. Surprisingly it worked and Natasha was able to lift me out of the car, although I quickly fell to the ground.

"This is bullshit," Natasha said out of breath.

"Sorry, I can't feel..."

"Just shut up," she hissed and then knelt down next to me. She pulled my arms over her back and held onto them high around her neck and chest. With a grunt she pushed up with her knees and began slowly walking me across the driveway. I tried finding my footing to help her, but I could barely feel my feet. When we reached the set of stone steps that led to the front door she groaned. "There's no way...I can...get you up...those things."

"Basement," I slurred. "I live in...the...basement."

"Of course you do," she replied snidely. "Where do I go in?"

"Around the back."

"You're fucking kidding me," she groaned as she adjusted her grip on my arms and pulled me higher up on her back.

"How did we...get here?"

"In my car, asshole," Natasha grunted as we rounded the corner of the house toward my basement entrance.

"No," I sighed, "how did you know where I lived."

"Your license, idiot," she said with one last groan as we made it to the basement door. "Key?"

"Nope."

"What?!"

"It's open," I said and tried clumsily to find the doorknob with my hand. That just resulted in Natasha slapping it and opening the door herself.

We stumbled inside, my feet tripping over the junk on the floor. The bed was on the far side of the room so Natasha flopped me over the side of her back onto the couch which was closer.

"This is my punishment," she said as she caught her breath and then looked around the room. "This place is disgusting. Don't you ever clean?"

I laughed. Why did that sound so funny? Clean? Clean! Clean was a funny word.

"Natasha, are you mad at me?" I asked, and then laughed at how drunk I sounded.

"My name is Tosh," she said and brushed away some junk off the coffee table so she could sit down.

"That other guy calls you Natasha? Na-tash-a...Tasha...Tasshh..."

She put her hand over my mouth and glared at me. "My name is Tosh, and Cameron can call me whatever he wants because he's my boss, the same boss you made me look like an idiot in front of tonight and now I have dungeon duty for a week for saving your stupid life."

When she removed her hand from my mouth I wanted to say I was sorry, but instead, "Na-tash-a," I laughed, causing her to roll her eyes and stand from the table. "It's fun to say."

"I'm glad you've taken all of this so seriously, Beckett. Where's your phone?"

"Huh?"

She sighed. "Your cell phone, where is it?"

I tried finding my back pocket, but somehow my hand kept slipping between the couch cushions instead. Natasha grabbed me violently by my hips and rolled me over.

"Buy a girl dinner first," I joked, but she didn't laugh and pulled the cell phone out of my pocket before letting me collapse back over.

"Say cheese," she said and suddenly a flash of light hit me in the eyes.

"What was that for?"

"Evidence for when you come out of your stupor," she replied and placed the phone down on the table. "Now lay flat and close your eyes."

"Buy a girl dinner…"

"It wasn't funny the first time, Beckett, just do it."

I shifted my weight on the couch to be what I thought was flat and closed my eyes. "What are you doing?"

There was a soft gasp before she replied, "Giving you medicine. Now keep your eyes closed."

I did as she asked but flinched a little when she touched my forehead with something warm.

"What is that?"

"Something to make your feel better."

"Did Dr. Ryan give you that?"

She laughed lightly. "No. It's something of my own concoction. Don't worry, it works really well, you'll see when you wake up tomorrow."

"Will you be here?"

"You really are delusional, aren't you?"

"A boy can dream."

"Go to sleep, Beckett."

"Go to sleep, Tasha."

"It's Tosh."

Chapter Three

My alarm was going off somewhere. I tried swatting my hand to find it but my arm hit the back of the couch. The couch? When did I...oh shit!

My eyes flew open and I shot up from the couch, only to have my head start pounding from the rush. Damn it! My head hurt, my neck hurt, damn even my ribs were sore. Then the memories started to flood into my head. I was pulled over but the guy was shady. I tried to drive away, swerved to avoid the ginormous dog in the road, and flipped my car. Natasha! The girl from my English Lit class helped me...wait, no. The shady guy attacked me, choked me. My hand went to my throat and I winced from how tender it was. Then Tasha came, she...she killed that guy.

No, that couldn't be right. She was just the girl in my English Lit class, not a...hybrid? Where did that come from? Natasha was a hybrid...they called me a hybrid. The goth club, the vampire wannabes. Yes! That was it. Natasha saved me and then took me to the vampire club thinking I'd join. Then there was the whole 'your dad is a vampire' speech, and you're a hybrid which is a child of a vampire. Well, it was creative. But there was still a guy dead. Did anyone call the cops? Would Natasha be hauled off in cuffs? Maybe that was part of their schtick, like role playing, all just to get me to join. I hoped it was all fake, otherwise I saw a man die. Fuck.

The alarm was still going off so I stood from the couch and once again got a head rush. My eye! My hand flew up to my eyebrow and picked away one of the Steri-Strips that was already falling off. It was soaked with blood. This wasn't going to look pretty, and it would certainly freak out my parents.

I went to step toward the bathroom when I realized there was something terribly wrong with my room – it was clean. There wasn't a shirt, a pair of underwear, or even a lone sock on the ground. What the…Natasha was here, she brought me home. Did she clean my apartment? Where was my shit?! I spun around the room and saw nothing but bare carpeted floors. Was I still asleep? Damn it! This was just too weird.

Quickly I stepped into the bathroom and immediately splashed my face with warm water and seeing it run a little red. I grabbed the towel from the rack and carefully dried my face, steering clear of my left eye. When I stood from the sink I took a deep breath and slowly removed the towel to look at the damage. I blinked and decided to splash my face again, but this time with cold water. It was obvious I wasn't awake yet. I dried my face again and stared at myself in the mirror.

What the fuck? My eye was fine. There was only a thin red line above my brow. But…I remember the pain, I remember there being blood. Hell, my neck was stained with it. The doctor...Dr...uh...Ryan! Dr. Ryan cleaned the cut, put the Steri-Strips on it, but that was it. It wouldn't have just healed…healed!

A fuzzy memory hit me – Natasha stroking my eye. I was out of it, but I remember her putting something on my eye. Medicine! She said it was medicine! What is this miracle medicine! What the fuck was going on?! Why do I keep forgetting to turn the damn alarm off!

I took a breath, threw the towel down on the floor, and went to my nightstand to turn off the alarm. Right next to it was my phone, although I wasn't sure how it got over here, the couch was twenty feet away. When I picked the phone up, underneath was a piece of folded notebook paper addressed to me. I turned off the annoying alarm and picked up the note. I didn't recognize the handwriting, but when I unfolded the note I looked to the bottom and saw it had been signed by "Tosh." I still thought it was an odd nickname.

Dear Asshole,

Hopefully you remember everything that happened last night – the men following you, the accident, my SAVING YOU. My back will remember dragging your sorry ass into your pigsty, which you can thank me for cleaning. You're welcome, and you're gross.

I know last night was a lot to take in. I know you don't fully understand all that was thrown at you, but you ARE in danger. Those men were there to kidnap you, they said "your daddy wants to see you," in case you forgot. Those who don't accept what they are end up dying or getting someone else killed. Don't be that person. You need to accept what you are. You are a hybrid, like me. Your parents both have blue eyes, I saw the picture on your nightstand. It's impossible for you to have brown eyes with two blue-eyed parents.

If you still don't believe me, look at your eye in the mirror and then look at the pictures I took with your phone. There's a reason I'm called a Healer. Want to know how I did it, come find me. If not, good luck out there.

   -Tosh

   The note fell to the ground as I swiped open my phone. Staring at me was a photo of my face with a bloody gash above my eye. I swiped through the rest of the photos of different angles of my injured eye. But now my eye was completely healed. These pictures proved I had been injured. How did she...a Healer? What the fuck was that? Could they be more than some vampire enthusiasts? What if...no. If I admitted that vampires were real, I might have to admit other aspects of my night.

   I looked at the clock and realized I was going to be late for class. Shit! I didn't have a car. Damn it, Becks, what the fuck are you going do?

   "One thing at a time," I said out loud, trying to calm the panicky voice in my head. "You're going to take a shower...and then...find Natasha."

Maybe Natasha could only heal eyes, because my throat still had a bruise in the shape of a handprint on it. While I showered, every ache and pain deep inside me seemed to come out. I was sore and cranky and was going to be late for class unless I got my ass upstairs. I was dreading the conversation with my parents, but it wasn't like I could fix the car in secret and hope they didn't notice. Hell, I didn't even know where it was.

It wasn't long until I realized my school bag was in my car, and therefore probably lost forever. I dug around my room looking for a spare notebook and backpack I could use for my classes today. It would have been easier to find stuff if my room weren't so clean now. I absolutely knew where everything was in my mess. After zipping up a hoodie to cover my neck, I ran up the stairs from my basement apartment into the kitchen. My mother was already dressed for work and pouring my dad a cup of coffee while he read the day's financials on his tablet. Both of them looked surprised to see me.

"Mornin'," I said as I opened the fridge and took out the orange juice.

"Becks, we didn't know you were home," my mom said. "We didn't see your car so we assumed you stayed with friends."

"Yeah, about that," I sighed as I took a glass from the cabinet and filled it with juice. "I…uh…got into an accident last night."

The spoon my mother was holding clanged loudly in the sink and my father leapt from his seat at the kitchen table, both of them speaking over each other with concerns.

"I'm fine, I'm fine," I said over them and pulled my mother's hands away from my face.

"Why didn't you call us?" my mother said with tears welling up in her eyes. "Did you go to the hospital? Where did this happen?"

"Abby, let the boy speak," my dad interrupted and pulled my mother into his side. My mom was always the panicky one while my dad was a calming force. Nothing ever got to him. I hoped this wouldn't be any different. "Are you really ok, son?"

I nodded. "Just some bruises, but the uh….car's totaled."

"Totaled!" Mom shouted and Dad started to open his mouth. "Richard, don't you dare tell me to calm down. If the car was totaled how are you standing here? Why are you not in a hospital? How did you get home!"

"Airbags," I lied. "They hit me pretty hard, but I'm fine. A friend brought me home."

"Why didn't you call us? Or wake us up when you got home?"

"Because I was tired and a little out of it," I replied and drank down half my juice.

"You still should have…"

"Mom, what I really need is to borrow your car so I can get to class."

She pressed her lips together and gave me an apologetic look. "I'm sorry, Becks, I have to run papers for your father all day. If it were any other day…"

"I'll take you," my dad answered.

"You don't mind?"

He shook his head and patted my shoulder. "Of course not. It'll be like old times. Do you need me to pack you a lunch?"

I smiled, remembering how he used to pack my lunch every morning and take me to school since mom worked the early shift until his business took off. He did it because he was my dad, he loved me and my mom. He never treated me like anything less than his son. That's because I *was* his son, plain and simple. Genetics weren't absolute, right? Mistakes could happen. Evolution! My genes had evolved to have brown eyes with two blue-eyed parents. I'm a miracle! Or a mutant.

"Becks?" my father asked and waved his hand in front of my eyes. "Earth to Becks."

"Yeah! Sorry, spaced out. I don't need a lunch, Dad, but thanks."

"Anytime, kid," he replied and gave me a hug. When he pulled back he patted my cheek and checked his watch. "We're glad you're ok. I'll meet you out in the car."

I nodded and as soon as my dad stepped away my mother put both her hands on my face and moved my head every which way.

"You're sure you're ok?" she asked.

I pulled her hands away from my face. "Yes, Mom, I'm fine. I've got to get to class."

She sighed and took a step back. "Ok, but if you start feeling sickly, call me. Understood?"

"Yeah, Mom, I will," I replied and gulped the last of my juice. I adjusted my bag on my shoulder and walked to the garage.

Dad was already waiting in the car and tapping his watch. I sank into the passenger seat and had an odd sense of nostalgia.

My dad put the car in reverse and backed out of the garage. "So do I need to quiz you on your spelling? What about your multiplication tables?"

"This is kinda weird," I laughed and then sighed. "I'm really sorry about the car, Dad."

"Becks, all I care about is that you're ok. And now that your mother isn't here, can I ask, were you drinking?"

"Of course not…"

"Son, I remember college and I did a lot of drinking in my day. Thankfully I lived on campus, so I didn't…"

"Dad, I promise I wasn't drinking. I was at the library and…" I paused, knowing I couldn't tell him everything. "There was a…this huge dog was in the road and I swerved to miss it. I must have hit some wet pavement or something because I skidded and flipped when I hit the ditch."

"Flipped? You flipped the car!"

"I told you it was totaled."

The color ran from his face as he pulled at his collar and tie. It was the first time I'd seen him like this. "How did you get out?"

"A…a classmate of mine saw it happen," I replied, thinking it was enough of the truth to be believable.

"Well, thank goodness for him."

"Her, actually."

"Even better," he said with a sly smile. "Do you know where they took the car?"

I shook my head. "No idea. I was a little out of it."

"It's all right. We'll figure it out. It's just a car. You're what I can't replace."

He squeezed the back of my neck and I flinched from the tenderness, suddenly remembering when the man had squeezed me in the same place, and what he said.

"So, Dad, I'm doing this project for a class," I began, trying to figure out how I could ask the awkward question. "It's a…a family tree thing."

He laughed. "Despite what your grandfather says about me, my family's tree does not look like a wreath."

I laughed, knowing my mom's father never hid his negative feelings about my dad.

"Well, I was wondering if there were any uh…you know, big family secrets?"

"Family secrets?" he asked as he turned down the street of my school. I only had a few minutes left to get it out of him.

"Yeah, you know like someone was married to a mobster, or a...an adoption that no one knows about?"

"Sorry, Becks," he replied as he pulled up to the main buildings, "you're the only scandal in our family."

"What!"

He put the car in park and looked at me skeptically. "Beckett Archer Dawes, you know very well that your mother was pregnant before we got married, which your grandfather has never forgiven me for."

I turned in my seat, looking my dad right in the eye as I asked, "But you loved Mom, right? You didn't just get married because of me, did you?"

"Becks, I've loved your mother since our Freshman year in college. I married her because I loved her, not just because of you. That's all. Are you sure you're ok, son?"

I nodded and grabbed my bag from the floor. "Yeah, thanks for the ride, Dad."

"Do you need a ride home later?"

I opened the door and shook my head. "Nah, I'll get a ride or take the bus if I need to."

"Ok. Call me or your mom if you need us to come get you."

"I will. Thanks again, Dad," I replied and shut the car door.

After he pulled away, I dragged myself to my Anthropology class. Honestly there had been no point in going. I hadn't finished my assignment because of the accident, I didn't pay attention during class because all I could think about was what happened after the accident, and I failed the pop quiz because I didn't give a shit.

It was a nice day outside so once class was over I sat down at one of the tables in the quad to do a little research on genetics. Situations like this was exactly why the internet was created. Among the sea of links and articles there were a few entries stating that blue-eyed parents could have brown-eyed children. Ha! Natasha was wrong. It was rare, but it did happen. There was a bunch of highly detailed scientific shit that I couldn't understand, but in conclusion, I could be Richard Dawes' son and everyone else could go fuck themselves.

"Beck!" someone called behind me. "Hey, Beck!"

I looked up and turned my head to see Chris Mackenzie jogging toward me. We'd been in the same Boy Scout troop, gone to middle and high school together, and both ended up at community college after a failed attempt at real college. But with all that in common, we traveled in very different circles. He lived in a party house and I lived in my parent's basement. He slept with every girl he came in contact with, and I was lucky if a girl gave me the time of day.

"Hey Mac," I said and closed up my phone. "What's up?"

He pulled the backpack off his shoulder and sat down next to me. "Just wanted to tell you we're having a party at the house tonight. It's going to be epic."

"Isn't that what you say about every party you guys have?"

He flinched and bugged his eyes out. "That's because they are."

"I'm not sure, man. Lots of things going on."

"Bullshit. You never have anything going on, that's why I'm always trying to get you to join the frat."

I shook my head and laughed. "Mac, you've got to stop calling it a frat. You live with a bunch of guys who throw parties all the time."

"Just come, asshole. Lots of girls will be there."

"Speaking of, do you know Natasha Cushlin?"

"Who?" he responded in shock, since he'd been with most of the girls on campus, and those he hadn't, he was working on them.

"She's in our American Lit class. Sits in the back but knows everything."

"Sorry, man, I have no idea who…"

"Shit, there she is," I said as she started crossing the quad toward the parking lot.

"Oh that girl," Mac said. "Isn't she like Amish or something?"

"What? No," I replied and stood from the table.

"You sure? She's always covered up and shit. Isn't that what they do?"

"You're an idiot."

"Wait," he said and grabbed my arm. "You're coming tonight, right? Bring the Amish girl."

"I doubt it, man. I gotta go," I said and ripped my arm out of his grip.

Natasha was halfway across the quad before I set out in a run to catch up with her.

"Tosha!" I called after her, but she didn't turn around. "Tosha!"

"That's not my name," she replied but kept walking without acknowledging me when I came to her side.

"Sorry, Natasha."

"Still not my name," she groaned. "What do you want?"

"What do you think?" I said and pulled her to a stop. She stared at me impatiently while she waited for me to speak, but suddenly I was speechless. I couldn't think of one word to say to her. She gave me one more second before she started walking again. I pulled on her arm again and said, "Tosh, right? You like Tosh."

"WHAT do you want, Beckett?"

"I want to know more."

"Why? So you can laugh at me and make a fool out of me again?"

Nervously I put my hands in my pockets and shrugged. "Look, a lot of things from last night are fuzzy. But I…I need to know how you did it."

"How I did what?"

"My eye, dammit. How did you fix my eye?"

She sighed and crossed her arms in front of her chest. "Understand that is just one piece, Beckett. You have to be willing to accept the rest."

I put my hands up in front of me. "I'll listen, that's all I can promise." She narrowed her eyes at me and took a step back. "And I'll keep an open mind to the fact that you're right about…certain things."

"Hey guys!" Mac suddenly said from behind me. He came to my side and placed one elbow on my shoulder and then his other on Natasha's. "What are you two lovebirds talking about?"

"Let go of my arm before I break it," Tosh said through clenched teeth.

"Wow, Beck, she's feisty. I like that," Mac replied and removed his elbows from both our shoulders. "You're Tish, right?"

"It's Tosh," she corrected.

"Well, Tosh, I'm Chris Mackenzie, but call me Mac."

"Yeah, I know who you are," she interrupted. "Half the female student body knows who you are."

"Only half?" he responded and waggled his eyebrows at her stone face. "Well, since you know my buddy Beck here, why don't you come to the frat house tonight?"

"We don't have frats here."

"It'll be a great party."

"I'm busy."

"Yeah, so is Beck, but maybe you two could get busy together."

Natasha turned her murderous glare on me before turning and walking to the parking lot.

Mac patted me on the back. "Sorry, man, I tried. She's a frigid bitch, just forget about her. Can I count on you tonight?"

"Dammit, man," I said and ran after her. "Natasha, wait."

"I don't have time for your bullshit, Beckett, or your slimy friends." I pulled on her arm again. Instantly she turned around and pushed me in the chest. "Pull on my arm again and I will dislocate your shoulder."

"Ok, ok. I'm sorry, he's an asshole, I know. Just please talk to me. I can't stop thinking about all of this. Just help me understand what's going on."

Tosha licked her lips and sighed. "Don't jerk me around."

I shook my head. "Nope, no jerking."

She sighed and debated within herself. "Your place?"

"Yeah, that's great," I replied and followed her to the parking lot. The walk was awkward and silent. Prior to last night, I'd never spoken with this girl before, and now I owed her my life. What did you say? When we got to her car there was only one thing I could think of. "This is your car?"

She rolled her eyes and unlocked the black Mercedes coupe. "You rode in it last night, asshole."

"I do not remember that."

"Do you remember me having to drag your ass over my shoulder into your house?"

My face fell. "No. Sorry you had to do that."

"I'm beginning to wish I'd left you on the side of the road," she responded and sank down into the driver's seat. "Get in, I don't have all day."

"Are you this pleasant with everyone? Or do I just bring it out in you?" I said as I slid into the passenger seat and closed the door. When I turned to face her, I flinched at the glare she was giving me. "So just me then?"

"I'm beginning to think so."

Chapter Four

"So why do hybrids only have vampire dads?" I asked as I opened the door to the basement and allowed Natasha to enter ahead of me. Beckett Dawes, always the gentleman.

"Because female vamps can't have children," she replied and chucked her very heavy bag down on my couch.

"Why not?"

She glared at me. "Because they can't. I don't know the science behind it. I'm sure it has something to do with the fact that they're dead."

"Yeah, but so are male vampires."

"Thank you, Beckett, for pointing out yet another example of how Mother Nature screws women over, even the living dead ones."

I threw my bag over onto my bed, but it slid off the side and fell to the floor.

"You really are a pig," she said while her head turned back and forth between me and the backpack. "Are you seriously going to leave it there?"

"No, of course not," I replied and jumped to the side of the bed to retrieve the bag. "Can I ask, why did you clean my room?"

"Because it was disgusting."

"Where are all my clothes?"

"Anything on the floor I put into your hamper."

My head flinched. "I have one of those?"

She rolled her eyes and pointed to the closet. I slid the closet doors open and was surprised at the sight of a basket overflowing with clothes.

"Some things were clean," I said and began sorting through the basket.

"If you thought any of that was clean, then you really have some issues."

"You've only known me for twelve hours. That's not enough to know my issues."

"I beg to differ," she muttered under her breath and sat down on the couch. "So, do you believe me yet?"

"You said you'd show me how you did it? How you healed my eye."

She huffed loudly and went digging in her bag. "Fine, sit down."

I did as she asked and sat on the corner of the bed. A moment later she pulled something out of her bag and walked around the couch toward me.

"Like I said in my note, I'm a Healer," she began and from behind her back she pulled out a small knife. She clasped her left hand around the blade and then jerked the knife out. When she opened her palm, blood was dripping from the gash she had just made.

"What the hell!" I shouted and pushed myself back further on the bed.

"Will you calm down," she shouted back and held her palm out in front of her. "Just wait for it."

Wait for it? Wait for what? What the hell was I...holy shit! Just then, right in front of my eyes I watched as the gash began to mend itself. It was as though there were tiny little elves stitching her hand back together.

"Wh-what...the...fuck?"

"My body can heal itself, hence, Healer. So, do you believe me now?"

I woke up face down, the right side of my face smooshed up against the corner of the bed. What happened? Slowly I lifted my head, hearing the sounds of someone panting in the distance. When my eyes finally focused, I saw Natasha kicking and punching the air. I didn't know anything about that kind of stuff, but she looked like she was really good at it. She could definitely kick my ass.

She whipped herself around again, kicking her back leg high behind her and then punched her arms in quick succession. With a loud sigh she bent over to catch her breath. When she rose, she lifted the bottom of her shirt and began fanning it up and down to cool herself. I squinted my eyes at the sight of thick, swirling red scars covering her torso. She was a burn victim?

Wait, wasn't she a...a Healer? That's what she called herself, a Healer, and she cut her hand in front of me and then...and then....

"Hey, you're awake," she said and tucked her shirt back into her pants.

"What happened?"

She gave me a smirk. "You fainted."

"No. I did? No. Really?"

"Yep. Fainted and then slid down into the floor. That's the second time I've had to pick up your limp ass. You're not as light as you might think."

I sat up slowly and swung my legs around the edge of the bed. "Sorry about that. I...why did I faint?"

"My guess, you're a wimp when it comes to blood."

"You cut your hand." She nodded and held up her hand. There was no cut, there was no blood, hell there wasn't even a scar. "I'm not sure what happened after that."

She cocked her eyebrow. "You watched the cut heal and then you fainted."

I shook my head. "No, I...that's impossible."

She pulled a small knife from her back pocket and proceeded to walk toward me, giving me a sense of eerie déjà vous. "This hurts every time I have to do it, by the way?"

"What?" I asked right before she took the knife to her forearm and slashed her skin four times. She held her forearm out in front of her and I watched the four cuts sew themselves together.

I woke up to the carpet pressing uncomfortably into the side of my face. Slowly I lifted my head and realized I was on the floor next to my bed. I looked to my left to find Natasha sitting on the couch with her back turned.

"Did I faint again?"

"Yep," she replied without turning around.

"Didn't want to lift my limp ass again?"

"Nope."

Pushing my elbow down on the corner of the bed, I slowly rose from the floor. My head was pounding even worse than last time and it made me stumble back. Suddenly Natasha was at my side and guided me to sit down on the bed.

"Go slow," she said. "You'll be lucky if you don't have a concussion."

"Could you heal that?" I asked and looked up at her.

"Does that mean you believe me now?"

"I believe the healing part."

She rolled her eyes and stepped away from the bed. "You can't believe one part and not the rest, Beckett."

"That's easy for you to say," I laughed. "If I believe all of this, then my parents have been lying to me my entire life. It means my dad isn't my real dad and instead it's some monster. Can't you remember how you were when you found out?"

She turned around and leaned against the back of the couch with her arms crossed in front of her chest. "I've known all my life. I didn't have the luxury of denying what I was. My sister and I are both Healers and we've had the gift since we were born."

I stood from the bed. "See! You've been able to deal with this your whole life, I've had less than twenty-four hours. You have gifts, I don't. You've been around vampires, I haven't. I almost died last night, you didn't. Just give me a fuckin' break."

"You don't get a break, Beckett!" she yelled and threw her arms up in the air. "You could have died last night if I didn't save your ass. Nut up and accept what you are!"

"I am NOT a vampire!"

"No shit. You're a hybrid! Get that through your thick skull! It's people like you that get people like me killed!"

"Becks?" my mother suddenly said from the stairs that led down to my room. "Is everything ok down here?"

"Mom, what are you doing home?" I asked as I stepped over to the stairs and nervously petted down my hair.

My mother stepped slowly down the stairs and eyed Natasha over my shoulder. "I was out delivering papers for your father and I stopped home to get my phone charger. I heard yelling down here so I got worried. I didn't know you had a guest."

"Oh…yeah," I said and looked between the two women. "Mom, this is Natasha."

"It's Tosh, actually, Tosh Cushlin," she said and extended her hand over the railing. "Nice to meet you, Mrs. Dawes."

My mother took her hand. "Please call me Abby," she began but suddenly gasped and ripped her hand out of Natasha's grip.

"Mom? Are you ok?"

Fear streaked across my mother's face as she stepped down the remaining stairs and came around to me. "Wha-what were you two arguing about?"

I shook my head. "It was nothing, Mom."

"Tell me!" she shouted and when I didn't answer she stepped past me toward Natasha. "What did you tell him?"

"You know what I am, don't you, Abby?"

"Tosh, shut up," I growled.

"NO," she yelled and stepped closer to my mom. "Abby, your son is in trouble. People tried to kidnap him last night. We need to know who his birth father is…"

"Natasha, shut the fuck up! My mother doesn't know anything." Slowly my mother turned around to face me, tears filling her eyes and falling down her cheeks. "Mom?"

"Becks, I'm so sorry," she cried and reached for my hand, but I pulled away.

"Sorry? Sorry for what?"

"Please, honey, let me explain…"

"Wait, are you saying it's true?"

"Becks, just listen…"

"It's true?! It's fucking true?"

"Let me explain."

"Explain? Explain what? That you've been lying to me all my life!"

"Beckett, calm down and let her talk," Natasha said and touched my mother's shoulder.

"Haven't you done enough?" I growled at her.

"Mrs. Dawes, we need to know the name of Beckett's birth father."

"What?" I yelled, seeing my mother's bottom lip tremble as she went to answer. "I don't want to know, I don't want to hear his name. I don't want any of this! Just go, Natasha!"

When she didn't move, I walked over to the door and opened it for her. Her lips went thin as she angrily stepped over to the couch, grabbed her bag, and walked to the door.

"You're making a really stupid mistake," she said.

"Well, I'm really good at making those," I replied and looked over at my mother who was shaking where she stood. "It must run in the family."

"Asshole," she said under her breath and walked out the door.

"Becks, please just sit down and let's talk about this," my mother begged.

I shook my head and held onto the door for stability. "I…I can't even look at you right now, Mom."

"Honey, please. Your birth father, Gar…"

"I *don't* want to hear his name," I shouted.

"Becks, he was a bad man…"

"He wasn't a man, Mom! He was a vampire! A fucking…fang-wearing…blood-sucking…vampire!"

"Yes, he was and I got away from him…"

"And you never once thought to tell me about this?"

"How?" she cried. "How in the world could I have told you? Since you were born I've worried you would find out. But then after all these years I honestly thought we were safe and he'd never find you."

"I've gotta get outta here," I said and whipped around the door.

"Beckett, please just hear me out."

"You've had over twenty years for me to hear you out, now just stay away from me!" I could hear my mother yelling for me as I slammed the door shut. I needed a drink, a lot of drinks, actually. And I knew exactly where there would be an enormous supply.

Chapter Five

"And she has the balls to call *me* an asshole? *She's* the asshole. *She's* the one who started all of this," I said to the guy next to me who I was calling Owen. I wasn't sure what his name was, but he didn't correct me when I called him Owen so I was just going with it. He was stoned as shit and hadn't blinked in a while, but he was a sounding board to my drunken rant. "Am I right?"

"Sure, man," Owen replied but then paused and looked off in the distance. When he looked back I could see my reflection in his enormously dilated pupils. "Who are you talking about?"

"Natasha! Jeez, Owen, keep up," I whined and finished the backwash that was left in my cup. "I need another beer."

"Oh good," Owen said and shifted in his seat, "cuz you're totally killin' my buzz."

I sighed and even though I couldn't completely feel my legs they somehow pushed me up from the couch and walked me over to the keg. Just as I started filling my cup, a hand came down on my shoulder.

"Good to see you're still standin', man," Mac said next to me.

"Thanks for letting me come over early."

"Ain't no thing, Beck," he said and patted my back. "Thanks for helping us set up."

I nodded and stopped the flow of beer when the foam hit the lip of my cup. "You sure it's cool that I crash here tonight?"

"Of course," he responded and began pouring a beer for himself. "You know, if you were part of the frat, you'd be home already."

I sighed and took a large gulp of my beer. "Sorry, Mac, it's just not my thing. And you gotta quit calling it a frat."

"You know I'm going to keep trying."

"And I'm not entirely sure why."

"Because you're a good guy, Beck," he began and took a big drink. "Always have been. Makes me sick."

I laughed and the two of us chugged our beers. "Another?" I asked, and Mac handed me his cup. Just as I topped my beer off, Mac hit me in the arm causing some of it to spill.

"Holy shit, she came!"

"What? Who?"

He hit me in the arm again. "The bitchy girl from today."

My head flinched and I turned around to see Natasha walking into the living room. Or was it? Her dark hair was down, it was surprisingly long. And she had legs! Well, of course she had legs, but she never showed them and that was a shame because they were sexy. Damn, they were sexy. She should wear skirts more often. Although her shirt was long and loose, it exposed her shoulders and was relatively low cut. It was a complete change from the black on black on black outfits she wore every other day. It was…nice. Really nice.

When she finally caught me staring at her she gave an awkward smile. Mac hit me in the chest and waggled his eyebrows, it was his usual signal before trapping a poor, innocent girl and luring her into activities she'd most likely regret in the morning. I didn't think much of it, I'd seen it a thousand times, but then he started moving toward Natasha.

I took a step forward to stop him when I remembered that she had turned my life upside down. I was mad at her, no, furious at her. She couldn't soften me up with her long legs and what were probably really soft shoulders, especially that place where they curved up to her neck, just behind her hair…what the fuck, Beckett! You are mad at her! But she was about to be devoured by Chris Mackenzie, the man whore. She didn't belong here, she needed to put those black pants back on and go back to her goth-vampire-hybrid mansion in the hills.

After a big gulp of my beer I walked over to where Mac had pulled her over against the wall.

"What can I get you," he asked as I approached. "There's light beer in the keg, but we also have our famous bath punch."

Natasha raised her right eyebrow as she replied, "Bath punch? Do you make it in the bathtub or something?"

"They do," I said, making her glance away from Mac. "But it'll kill ya."

"Don't listen to Beck," Mac groaned. "You'll love it, all the girls do."

I shook my head, trying to warn her that she really shouldn't drink it. It was gallons of alcohol with a hint of juice. They made it because girls would get drunk faster and their inhibitions would loosen.

But Natasha flinched her eyebrow at me and looked back at Mac as she replied, "Sounds great."

"That a girl," he cheered and ran off to get her some alcohol poisoning in a cup.

"What are you doing here?" I asked once Mac was out of earshot.

She narrowed her eyes. "I was invited, remember?"

"Yes, and you laughed at it. You don't belong here, Natasha. Go home."

She crossed her arms in front of her chest. "Who the hell do you think you are telling me what to do? You're the one who keeps saying I'm all sheltered in my little goth world, so here I am in your world instead. I'm dressed like the other girls, I'm going to drink and flirt with guys and dumb myself down and laugh at what they say because that's what girls do in your world, right?"

"Oh aren't you all high and mighty," I replied, it wasn't my best comeback but I'd had a lot of alcohol. "You are way out of your league here, sweetheart. Go home before you get into something you don't know how to get out of."

"What is that supposed to mean?"

"The fact that you don't know is a sign that you need to go home."

"Go home?" Mac said next to me with a red plastic cup filled with the poison that would drop a body-builder let alone a girl who weighed a hundred pounds. "No way she can go home now, the party just started."

I gave her a warning look, but instead of taking my advice she raised a challenging eyebrow and took the red cup out of Mac's hand.

"That a girl, Tish," Mac cheered and snaked his arm around her shoulder.

"It's Tosh," she corrected and took a big drink. A second later she was coughing and gasping from how strong it was.

I gave her a nod and a condescending laugh. "Have fun playing with the big dogs, Tosh."

I turned away and walked back to the couch, choosing to drink the rest of my beer on the way and then throwing the cup on the floor. When I sat down on the couch I couldn't help but glance over across the room. Mac was already putting the moves on Tosha – little touch there, a nudge of the cup to keep her drinking, a whisper in her ear. I was watching a predator and doing nothing. But hey, that's what she wanted, right? She came in here and wanted to play with fire. Well, she would get what she wanted and would get burned.

At the thought, an image flashed in my head. It was from today, but foggy. Natasha in my room, fanning herself with her shirt exposing angry red skin, like burn scars. I wondered what she'd been through to get them.

Wait…what she'd been through? Damn it, Becks, you're an idiot. The girl ruined your life! Yesterday you were oblivious that monsters existed, and that you were half one. Oh, and the man you've known as your father your entire life really wasn't.

"Fuuuck," I growled and fell back against the couch with my hands rubbing my face roughly. Natasha Cushlin had ruined my life, why the fuck did I care about her fucking scars?

"Bad night?" a girl said next to me.

Slowly I pulled my hands from my face to find a girl with short black hair staring at me. "Uh…you could say that," I replied and then looked over once again just in time to see Mac kiss Tosh.

The girl next to me shifted her weight on the couch and followed my gaze across the way. "Oh, I see. Ex-girlfriend?"

"Wh-what? No," I stuttered and pulled my eyes away. "No, not an ex-girlfriend."

"Someone you liked then?"

"Uh…no. Just…a…you know how when you give someone advice because you absolutely know better than they do in the current situation, but they don't listen to anything you say, even though they came in and turned your life completely upside down and didn't even apologize and then comes in here dressed all cool and goes right up to the pariah, even though you…"

"Even though you warned her?" she interrupted and I realized I was being a dick.

"I'm sorry," I sighed and rubbed my face again.

"No need to be," she replied and placed her hand on my arm. Her fingers were so cold that goosebumps formed on my arm. "I'm Delia."

"Beckett," I replied.

"Beckett? That's unusual," she said and moved herself closer to me.

"Most people just call me Beck," I replied and once again glanced over at Mac who was now pressing Natasha up against the wall while his nasty tongue assaulted her mouth. "Look, Delia, it's nice to meet you, but I'm not good company for anyone right now."

Delia followed my gaze again and shifted completely into my side. "You know the best way to make a girl jealous?"

I turned my head and found her very big, and very black eyes staring seductively at me. The hairs on the back of my neck stood on end. My brain was telling me to run, telling me those eyes meant something, but my head was foggy and slow from alcohol. I didn't stop her when she pressed her lips against mine. Like her hands, they were cold and caused a shiver to go down my spine.

"What the fuck!"

I ripped my lips away from Delia's and looked across the room in time to see Mac pull up Natasha's shirt and reveal the massive scars on her stomach. The commotion caused everyone to stop and look, and worse, they started laughing. She pushed Mac away and started to run, but he kept his grip on her shirt causing it tear around to her back.

"Holy shit," Mac laughed and pointed to the scars on her back, "what a fuckin' freak."

I stood from the couch just as she back kicked him in the stomach causing him to fall backwards on the floor.

"Tosha!" I shouted as she ran toward the front door. Immediately I ran after her, but just as I reached the door, hands came around both my shoulders and turned me around.

"Dude!" Mac shouted, still hunched from the kick in the stomach but somehow halfway laughing. "Did you see her stomach? It was like…like melted cheese or some shit. What a fuckin' freak."

My fist balled up and punched him right across the face. His dumbstruck expression was priceless as he spilled into the floor.

"You're the freak, you piece of shit."

I didn't wait for a snappy comeback and ran outside. To my left I caught sight of Natasha running across the lawn and I went after her.

"Natasha!" I shouted, but she didn't even turn around. "Tosh, wait!"

I stretched out my arm and caught her shoulder. Suddenly she reached behind her, grabbed my arm, and flipped me over onto the ground, knocking the breath out of me.

"Don't touch me!" she screamed and then just stepped over me.

Painfully I rolled over onto my side and pushed myself up to a standing position, although my back was doing everything it could not to straighten. When I looked up, Natasha was walking to the parked cars on the side of the road when the lights of her Mercedes flashed.

"Tosha, wait," I called to her, watching her grab at the ends of her torn shirt to cover the scars on her body.

"Go away, Beckett," she yelled behind her as she walked around to the driver's side door.

"Tosha," I began and she gave me a wicked eye across the roof of the car. "Sorry, I meant to say Tosh. Are you ok?"

"Are you shitting me?" she responded in a snarky tone. "No, I'm not ok, asshole. You saw what he did to me in front of everyone! That is the perfect example of why I stay in my little world. You win, Beckett, happy? Now you can go on living your stupid little denial kind of life, see if I care."

She opened the driver's side door and sank inside, slamming the door so hard that the car shook. But I wasn't happy, the exact opposite. I opened the passenger door, slid down into the seat, and closed the door.

"What are you doing?" she shouted.

"I never meant for that to happen, Tosh."

"Get out," she snapped.

"I did warn you."

Any type of violence is bad, but in that moment I would have rather she hit me than have to experience the murderous glare and angry silence she was giving me.

"Let me try that again."

"So because you warned me, I deserved what he did?"

"Of course not! I just know what he does to other girls and I didn't want him…" but I stopped when her head fell into her hands and she began to cry. Tentatively I placed my hand on her shoulder, but she slapped it away.

"Don't!" she shouted. "I don't need your sympathy."

"It's not sympathy…"

"When I drink, I forget," she said and began wiping away the tears that had leaked down her cheeks. "I forget I'm a freak."

"Tosh, you're not a freak."

She groaned and laughed. "You're full of shit."

"Tosh, come on..."

"Look at me," she shouted and lifted her shirt to expose the scars on her abdomen and back. "Go ahead and get a good look at them, go ahead. Take a look at the freak!"

"I've seen them, Tosha."

She squinted her eyes in confusion and lowered her shirt. "What? When?"

"Today when you were...uh...doing your thing. You were fanning yourself with your shirt and I saw them."

"Do you want a freaking medal or something?"

My foot slammed into the floor, my god she was aggravating. "No," I yelled. "I just wanted you to know that I had seen them and point out the fact that I didn't have the fucking reaction that Mac did and that maybe you should give me a little credit."

"Credit!" she shouted. "You have done nothing but be a whiney, ungrateful bitch. The Warriors were just trying to help you and you treated them like they were some kind of joke. Today you had a freaking tantrum instead of listening when your mother was trying to explain things to you. People like you get people like me killed or...or hurt so badly they wish they were dead."

"I have done *nothing* to you, let's get that straight," I said, not wanting to take her bullshit for another second. "YOU tore my life apart today and I still followed you out here to see if you were ok. *That's* the kind of person I am. So don't go blaming your hang-ups on me."

She swallowed harshly and wiped her face. "Are you done?"

"Uh...yeah, I guess I am."

"Then get out of my car before I drag you out of it," she said flatly.

"Fine," I growled and opened the car door. "You are a piece of work. Goodbye, Tosh."

I slammed the car door behind me before Tosh could say anymore. She was messed up, probably because of all the time she spent with those Warrior people and their creepy vampire-goth ways. It was all a bunch of horseshit and I was done with it.

Realizing I was still standing in front of Tosh's car, I pushed myself away and started walking back to the party, but then wondered if I'd be let back in. I'd punched Mac in the face. I was surprised the other guys weren't lining up to kick my ass. In fact, the only person out here was the girl from the couch and she was walking right to me.

"Well, you know how to make an exit," she said as she came to stand in front of me.

"Hey, Delia, sorry about that."

She shrugged and took my hand, her frigid fingers giving me a chill. "No, it was sweet, sticking up for your friend like that."

I looked back over my shoulder, surprised that Natasha's car was still there. "She doesn't see it that way."

Delia put her finger under my chin and turned my head back around to her. "How about we finish that kiss?"

Before I could even respond, Delia was pulling me over to the side of the house. She didn't seem too concerned with privacy, not that there was anyone in the immediate vicinity. Delia stood with her back up against the house and pulled me into her. Her lips were as cold as her fingers that were scratching at the base of my neck.

"Would you rather go inside," I asked as I pulled her arm down and tried warming her hands between mine. "You're freezing."

"Oh, aren't you sweet. There's actually only one thing I want."

I placed my hands on her hips and lowered my head into the crook of her neck. "Oh yeah? And what is that?"

Suddenly there was a sharp pain on the side of my neck. I bolted upright and my hand instantly went to my neck, my fingertips coming back with a little blood. I looked up at Delia who was sucking her index finger seductively.

"Did…did you just scratch me?"

"You'll have to forgive me," she said with a smile that made the hairs on my arm stand on end. "But you see, I'm going to need a little bit more than that."

"Wh-what?" I stuttered just as she flashed me a smile and displayed two long, sharp fangs coming down from the top of her mouth.

I took a step back, but Delia waved her finger at me. "Now, now, Beckett, I have to be sure."

"Tosh!" I screamed and turned to run. "Tosh!"

Delia grabbed me by the shirt collar and threw me backwards into the side of the house. She leapt at me, holding me against the house and forcibly tilting my head to the side. I gasped at the feeling of needles in my throat. Delia's lips sucked at my skin, drawing the blood out of me. My hands limply tried pushing her away.

Delia lifted her head from my neck, her bottom lip and chin stained red with blood. "You taste even better than your daddy," she said before licking her lips clean.

"Wh-who?" I panted, feeling the warm blood trickling down my neck.

Before Delia could answer, a loud crack came from behind us. Suddenly a thick shiny rope snaked around Delia's neck and she instantly reared her head back, hissing and exposing her fangs while she pulled at her throat. A second later she was yanked backwards and spun down to the ground as the rope around her neck unfurled. I slumped against the house and in front of me stood Natasha, still in her skirt but with boots on and a black shirt, standing with two long silver whips extending from her hands.

"Run!" she shouted at me, but my legs wouldn't budge.

Delia quickly rose from the ground, bright red marks around her neck from where Tosha's whip must have been. She hissed and crouched down before launching herself in Tosha's direction. Tosha spun her whips gracefully around her head and cracked them across Delia's face and chest. She wielded her whips around again, but Delia caught one of the ends and pulled Tosha off her feet. Tosha scurried toward one of the whips that had flown out of her hands, but Delia grabbed her and twisted her arm behind her back so hard I heard the crack of her bones. Tosha screamed and Delia stood with a look of satisfaction and victory.

"Don't you know it isn't polite to interrupt things that are none of your business, little girl?" Delia said as she grabbed the top of Tosha's head and began pulling her painfully across the lawn.

"Let her go!" I shouted, my body barely holding me up.

"I'm just having a little fun. I'm only here for you anyway," Delia replied and released her grip on Tosha. "Now are you going to be a good boy and come easily? Or am I going to have to hogtie you."

As Delia stepped forward I could see Tosha clutching her right arm to her chest as she slowly reached with her left for the whip on the ground.

"The only person going anywhere is you," I growled. "Right to hell!"

Apparently my timing was a little off. In my mind I had pictured that once I said that, Natasha would swing her whip around and kill Delia instantly, damning the demon to hell. I'd seen it in movies enough times.

"I'm sorry, what?" Delia said with her face scrunched up in confusion.

Seeing that Tosha was steady on her feet and had lifted the whip up into the air, I felt it was safe to say, "GO TO HELL!"

The shiny whip cracked across the back of Delia's knees causing her to scream and fall forward. Tosha circled the whip around her head, but before it could make contact with Delia again, she suddenly disappeared. Literally disappeared into thin air with only black wisps of smoke remaining.

"Wh-what just...where'd she go!" I shouted as Tosh stumbled toward me.

"We've got to go," she said and pulled me to my feet, although I had to put most of my weight onto her. "Just try to walk."

"Why am I so weak?" I asked as we crossed the front lawn.

"You're weak because she fed on you," Tosha replied and brought me to the passenger door of her car. "Get in."

I opened the door and sank into the seat. Tosha ran around the front of the car, her right arm still folded into her chest and hanging at an odd angle. When she sunk down in the driver's seat she reached back for the seatbelt, only able to pull it across her, but not click it into place.

"Do you want me to drive?" I asked as I took the seatbelt from her and accidently knocked her injured arm.

"Damn it!" she screamed and let her right arm fall onto the console.

"I'm sorry, I'm sorry!"

"Just give me a second," she shouted and placed her left hand over her face while her breathing became very fast.

Her right hand was mangled, three of her fingers broken and crooked while her shoulder hung low and loose.

"You can't drive like this."

"Just start the car for me," she said before taking in a big breath and holding it.

I didn't know what was going on until I heard the cracking of bones and looked down to see Tosha's three broken fingers untangle themselves. When they were perfectly straight and the cracking has ceased, Tosha exhaled and panted. "I said start the car!"

I flinched and reached across to push the start button. The engine hummed and the dashboard lit up at the same time Tosha began panting loudly through her teeth and banging her head back against the headrest. A moment later there was a loud pop, she screamed, and her shoulder had magically moved back into the place.

When her breathing became relatively normal, she pulled her seatbelt over her chest again, this time successfully locking it into place.

"Sorry about that," she said in a low, exhausted voice. "Are you ok?"

I touched my neck where Delia had bitten me and came away with blood on my fingertips. "She got me good," I said and showed Tosha my fingers.

"She didn't close the wounds," she replied and forcibly tilted my head away. "This means nothing, by the way."

"What?" I asked a split second before she ran her tongue across the tender spots on my neck. When she was done, she wiped her mouth and chin, and put the car in gear. I just stared out the windshield, uncomfortable with the fact that a girl just licked my bloody neck. I wasn't sure what you said after something like that happened.

Tosha pulled the car out into the street and took off so fast that my body was pressed back into the seat.

"Are you taking me back to that place?" I asked and clung to the door handle as we turned a sharp corner.

"The manor is the safest place for you. They'll be able to protect you."

I shook my head. "I need to go home first."

"That's not..."

"I'm accepting what just happened. Everything I've ever known is shattering around me. So give me a break and let me go home to get some things I'm gonna need. Please!"

I didn't mean to yell and Tosha certainly didn't appreciate it. The tension inside of the car became uncomfortable as we pulled onto the highway.

"Did you know Delia was going to be there tonight?"

"Why would you say that?"

"Because you had those whips. You seemed a little prepared."

"I'm always prepared," she replied and gestured to the backseat.

I looked back and saw a duffle bag with clothes hanging out of the opening. When I tilted the bag toward me there were also several more whips and knives tucked inside.

"I was changing my clothes when I heard you scream."

"Why were you changing?"

"Because your asshole friend ripped what I had on. Ok? Do you have any more stupid or uncomfortable questions?"

"Just one."

"Oh my god," she answered with a groan.

"Why did you lick me?"

Chapter Six

"Ok, we only have a few minutes," Tosha said as she slammed the gearshift in park. "Pack only the essentials, probably a week's worth."

I got out of the car and started up the walkway. "What about school?"

She shrugged. "We'll talk to Cameron and Devin, but my guess is they won't let you go."

"But if I miss class…" I started to say, but Tosha pulled on my arm.

"Miss a few classes and stay alive, I think it's a good trade."

"You're right, sorry."

"You should get used to saying those words," she said and followed me to the back of the house. "Now you've got to hurry. Get in, get out."

"Well that could be hard," I replied as we approached the backdoor. "My lights are on, that means my parents are in there waiting."

Tosha sighed and pulled out her cell phone. "Ok. I should call Connor anyway. Don't take too long in there."

I nodded, although I wasn't sure how much of it would be my choice. When I stepped inside my basement apartment my parents were sitting on the couch in their pajamas. My mother instantly looked up from her magazine while my father quickly turned the TV off and threw the remote on the coffee table.

"My god, Becks, what happened to you!" my dad shouted as both of them stood from the couch.

I looked down and realized I had dried blood all down my shirt. "Oh this, well you see, my birth father sent this hot chick to seduce me and then attack me. Funny thing though, until this afternoon I didn't know my dad and my birth father were two different people."

My dad went pale. I looked past him at my mother whose eyes were red and swollen from crying.

"How much did you tell him, Mom?" I asked.

"Honey, your father knows everything," she replied and wiped her nose with a tissue.

"I doubt that," I said in a snide tone.

"Beckett, sit down and let's talk about this."

"I can't," I replied, and gestured toward the door. "I have someone waiting to take me to some freaky commune to hide from the bloodsuckers that are chasing me."

My dad creased his brows and shook his head. "Commune? What are you talking about?"

"See, I knew Mom didn't tell you everything."

"Beckett, please," my mother begged. "Give us a chance to explain everything. It's not as simple as you might think."

"Really? Let me give it a try. Mom, did you sleep with another man beside Richard Dawes and get pregnant?"

Tears gathered in the corners of my mother's eyes as she replied, "Y-yes, but..."

"Dad, did you know that when you married her?"

"It's why I married her, Becks," he answered.

I paused for a moment to catch my breath. "So you knew I wasn't your son."

"You are my son, Becks."

"My blood apparently says otherwise."

"I don't care what your blood says," he said angrily. "I have been with you since you came out of your mother. I have raised you and loved you every day of your life."

"And you've lied to me every day of my life!" I shouted just as the door opened and Tosha stepped inside. All shouting instantly stopped and Tosha definitely felt the awkward tension.

"I'm sorry to interrupt," she said tentatively and stood next to me. "Connor told us to wait. They're sending an escort here."

"Escort to where?" Dad asked and then pointed to Tosha. "Who is she?"

Tosha stepped forward. "Mr. Dawes, my name is Tosh Cushlin. For whatever reason, Beckett's birth father has sent people after him. The

Warriors feel that the manor is the safest place…"

"The-the who?"

"The Warriors, sir," Tosh replied. "They are vampires bound to protect…"

"Vampires?" my father groaned as his hands wiped down his face. "Not that again."

"Richard," Mom said as she stood from the couch and pulled on my dad's elbow, "listen to what she has to say. Beckett's in trouble, just look at him!"

My father flinched and looked angrily at my mother. "There are no such things as vampires, Abby!"

"Not true," I replied and pointed to my neck. "Do you think I did this to myself?"

"Son, I'm sure you've had a lot to drink tonight, and whatever these two have put in your head…"

"I didn't imagine a girl's fangs ripping into my throat!"

"Everybody calm down," Tosh said with her arms extended out in front of her. "Mrs. Dawes, since we know Beckett's birth father is after him, it's really important that we get his name and anything else you can tell us about him."

"No!" Dad shouted. "No! We agreed we would never mention his name again."

"Damn it, Richard," my mother shouted. "You never believed me, just listen for once! If Garrett's coming, then we're all in trouble. Don't you see that?"

My mother tightened her robe and jetted up the stairs. My father called after her, but she slammed the upstairs door behind her.

He took a step toward the stairs, but rocked back and pointed his index finger at me. "We are not through with this."

"I'm leaving when the…the whatever they're called get here."

"No," he replied, red color rising from his neck to his face, "I'm telling you to stay put until we work through this."

"Well hey, you're not my real dad so you can't really tell me what to do."

My dad's head flinched like I had punched him in the face, but in a way I had. He didn't say a word when he turned and went up the stairs. When I turned back around, Tosha was giving me a judgmental expression.

"What?"

"Nothing," she replied and walked toward my dresser.

"Your eyes seem to be saying something different."

"Connor's team will be here soon."

Tosha started rummaging through my drawers while I pulled a travel bag from within the closet. When I put it on the bed, she spread it open and placed several pairs of my workout pants into the bag. I just stood and watched her pack my bag, not even having the energy to help her or tell her to stop. I'd made a mess of things, and I was bad at acknowledging it.

"I didn't mean what I said to him," I said finally.

"I know," Tosha responded as she closed one drawer and opened another. I stepped toward her and reached inside, filling my arms with socks and underwear. "You're not the first hybrid to be lied to."

"Is that your pep talk?" I asked and dumped everything into my travel bag.

"God you're frustrating," she groaned and shut the dresser drawer.

"So I've been told," I replied and sat on the edge of the bed. At the same time shouting could be heard from upstairs. I could count on one hand the number of times my parents ever argued, let alone yelled at each other.

"That doesn't sound good," Tosha said, looking up at the ceiling.

"Yeah, that should be just great for his heart."

"Your dad has a heart problem?"

I nodded. "He was in the hospital just last year."

"I'm sorry," Tosha answered and began to fidget. "Do you have a weapon you can bring?"

"A wh...a weapon? Like a gun?"

"It could be anything," she replied. "A gun, knife, anything you could use to defend yourself."

"No, I don't have..." I began but then got up from the bed and went digging into the back of my closet. "Actually, I do have something, but I haven't used it since I was in Boy Scouts."

"I'm not talking about a slingshot," Tosha said snidely.

"What about this?" I asked and pulled out the old bow and quiver.

Tosha scrunched her brows. "It looks like a child's toy."

"You asked if I had a weapon, this is all I have. I was pretty good at it, actually. Best in my troop. So do I bring it or not?"

Just as she was about to answer, a loud crash came from upstairs followed by the sound of my mother screaming. When I went for the stairs,

Tosha put her hand in my chest to stop me, and gestured for me to be quiet. I went to push her hand out of the way when I heard what sounded like elephants walking above us.

Tosha quickly stepped over to the wall and shut the lights off. Through the darkness Tosha's face was suddenly illuminated by the glow of her cell phone as she frantically sent a text. In the next second she grabbed my hand and pulled me toward the door.

"Wait!" I said too loudly and she hit me in the chest for it.

"Shut up," she whispered and pulled my arm again, only I slipped it out of her fingers.

"We need to help my parents."

"Do you hear all those footsteps? I am one person, I can't take them on. If we run for the woods we might have a chance. Connor and his team are on their way."

I shook my head and darted for the stairs. Just as I stepped up on the first step, the door from upstairs opened. Quickly I ducked behind the dresser. Light spilled down the stairs and a loud thunk sounded from the first step, and then the second. Whoever was coming down the stairs either weighed a thousand pounds or it was Frankenstein's monster. The thunks were loud and slow, and my heart was starting to race.

Thunk.

Thunk.

Shouts could still be heard coming from the upstairs, but I couldn't move to do anything about it.

Thunk.

Thunk.

Don't breathe, don't breathe.

Thunk.

Why is this person going so slow? I'm going to suffocate.

Thunk.

Whoever it was, was finally halfway down the staircase, the light from upstairs backlighting him in such a way that he didn't even look human. There were bends and humps where there shouldn't be, making my brain unable to form any real shapes.

Just then Tosha came out of the shadows with a knife, slid her hand through the space between rungs, and stabbed it into the top of the man's foot. He howled and fell forward, sliding down the stairs until he hit the landing, breaking the railings around it. Only he wasn't a *he*, he was an *it*.

An enormous animal, an impossibly big animal. It growled and started moving toward the final steps.

My left arm flinched and held the bow in front of me. The quiver in my right hand fell to the floor, a single arrow threaded between my fingers. In a split second, I was stretching the arrow back across the bow and setting it free. The arrow went into the monster's chest, causing it to growl and gurgle as it slumped down the remaining steps, and then it went quiet.

Tosha pulled at my arm, but I couldn't take my eyes off of what I had just done. I just killed someone…no, something. A big something. Tosha didn't seem to care so much and forcibly pulled me across my apartment and out the door.

"My parents," I said, though I was already panting and Tosha wasn't letting go of my arm.

"Our only chance is to get into the woods," she replied as we darted across the back lawn, but it was too late. Two men started running at us from the edge of the woods. Tosha slid to a stop and turned around, pulling me with her to face the house where there were suddenly two more men coming toward us, trapping us like prey. "Shit."

"Please tell me you have a plan," I whispered, making the men around us laugh.

"I've already called the Warriors," she shouted. "They will be here any minute. All of you will be punished if you touch a hair on our heads."

"Did you hear that, boys?" the man in front of me said. "Don't touch their hair." The other men laughed and continued to close in. "Bring the boy inside, kill the girl."

The two men closest to Tosha leapt for her, one grabbing her chest while the other went for her legs. I lunged toward her attackers, but hands came across my chest. My feet dragged on the ground as they pulled me backwards across the lawn, all the while watching as Tosha fought with everything she had only to be thrown violently up against the house as if she weighed nothing. I screamed and thrashed against the men who were dragging me around the corner of the house, but their grip was like iron, their bodies hard like rock. They didn't even flinch or struggle when I kicked my legs up in the air trying anything to get them to let me go.

When we got to the front of the house, the two men stepped up on the front steps, kicked the door open, and threw me inside. I landed on the living room floor, my head and knees taking the brunt of it. When I looked up I saw my parents in the center of the room on their knees, hands tied behind their backs. My mother was sobbing into her chest while my father bleed from a wound on his head. A man was standing in front of my mother and looking at him gave me chills. It was like looking in a mirror, or at least a picture of an eerily similar-looking brother, except that he had two long incisors hanging from the top of his mouth.

"Ah, Beckett, so nice of you to join us," the man said and put his index finger under my mom's chin and tilted her head up. "He looks so much like me, don't you think, Abby?"

My mother's bottom lip trembled as she answered, "Please, Garrett, don't hurt him."

"Hurt him? Hurt my own son?"

Holy shit. No wonder we looked so much alike. This man, this was Garrett, my birth father. A vampire.

"He is *my* son," my dad growled.

Garrett knelt down in front of him, tilting his head like a dog. "Richard, is it? Or do you prefer Dick?" Garrett's men laughed, and my dad grinded his teeth. "You see, Dick, that boy over there is my son, taken away from me by your very selfish and uncaring wife. Just look at him," he said and forcibly turned my father's head to look over at me, "the resemblance is uncanny. And to think, your wife had to look at that face and be reminded of me every day. That must have been torture for her, or perhaps it was a pleasure."

"Stop it, Garrett," my mother cried.

Garrett kept his back to my mother, his hand still holding my father's face. "Quiet, Abby. I'm talking with Dick."

"What do you want," I finally found the courage to say, but before he could respond, the other men who had stayed behind with Tosha came through the door.

"Where's the girl?" Garrett asked as he rose from the ground.

"Dead," one man replied.

"NO!" I shouted and tried standing from the floor, but was pushed down and kicked in the back. "You son of a bitch!" I panted and rolled back up on my knees. "She didn't do anything! You fucking bastard, I will…"

The rest of my rant was cut short because Garrett backhanded me across the face. My cheek exploded in pain, and I could feel blood dripping from my nose down to my lip.

"Garrett, sir," one of his men said, "she said she called the Warriors and they were on their way."

"Vincent!" Garrett yelled toward the kitchen. "Find your brother, we need to go."

First came the soft pounding of something heavy padding through the kitchen, and then my mother's screams. My eyes finally began to focus just as another creature stepped from the kitchen and into the living room. It seemed similar to what had come down my stairs, but now in the light I could see the hair of an animal, the body of a big man, and the head of a wolf. A werewolf. There was seriously a werewolf standing in my living room. He smelled, there was drool dripping from his mouth, and long vicious claws growing from his hands. I clenched my insides so that I wouldn't piss all over myself.

"Vincent, where's your brother?" Garrett asked as the other team members pulled my parents and I to a standing position. The wolf shook his head and held out an arrow, my arrow. So not only had I killed a werewolf, but it was this guy's brother. I was dead, I was a dead man who was struggling to keep from pissing himself.

Garrett took the arrow from Vincent's hairy paw and looked at me with a mix of curiosity and pride. He stepped over to my mother once again, grazing the back end of the arrow down my mother's cheek.

"Abby, you have no idea how proud this makes me. You never forgot, did you?" My mother only answered with a whimper. "Very well, take her with us."

"NO!" my father shouted, but in an instant one of Garrett's men picked her up and ran her out through the sliding glass doors. My father ran forward just as Vincent's lethal claws swung down through the air. I struggled against whoever was holding me as my dad fell to the ground and rolled onto his back with bright red blood pouring out from three gashes that stretched from his left shoulder diagonally across his chest.

Suddenly a loud crash came from behind us. I fell to the ground and scrambled over to my dad. Garrett's men and Vincent the wolf fled from the house, not bothering to open the sliding glass doors, but simply crashed through them and the walls on either side.

"After them!" someone yelled and black shadows whipped past me.

I ripped my shirt off and held it against my father's bleeding chest. When I looked up I saw Garrett standing only a few inches away with a devilish smirk.

He placed his fist over his heart. "The wee Devin, say hello to Father for me," he said and then disappeared into black smoke like Delia had earlier.

I whipped my head back to see Devin, the one who had yelled at me last night. "You know him!?" I shouted over my father's groans. "How do you know him!" I shouted again.

He locked eyes on me. "How do you," he growled.

Just as my balls crawled up inside me someone came around Devin and I thought I was looking at a ghost.

"Tosha?"

"Oh my god," she replied as she ran and knelt down beside me. She caught me staring at her and snapped her fingers in front of my face. "Beckett!"

"I thought you were dead," I finally said. "They said they killed…"

"They were lazy and assumed I was," she replied and pushed up her sleeve.

Just as she raised a knife to her wrist, Devin grabbed her arm and shook his head. "You can't do that, Tosh."

"What? Why?" I shouted.

Devin released Tosha's arm as he said, "Were your father's wounds inflicted by Garrett or the wolf?"

"Uh…the wolf," I replied as my father moaned. "Why does that matter?"

Devin pulled Tosha up to a standing position by the collar of her shirt. "If a wolf inflicted those wounds, your father has most likely been infected. It doesn't take much. Their claws and teeth are crawling with the disease."

"Disease? What disease?"

"Lycanthropy," he replied. "It is what turns a man into a werewolf."

"You're saying my dad is now…a…a…"

"Connor," he said over me, "anything?"

Connor shook his head as he stepped through the hole in the wall. "No sir. We followed the wolf's scent as far as we could. We found some tire tracks near a path in the woods, but nothing else left behind."

"Abby," my father groaned.

"Dad, don't move," I said, and pressed my shirt back into his wounds. "Those guys have my mother, you have to find her."

"We will," Devin replied. "Connor, take Beckett back to the manor. We need to debrief him immediately."

"I'm not going anywhere without my dad."

"It was not a request, and I am not used to having to repeat myself."

"Are you just leaving my dad here to die!"

"Of course not," Tosha answered and placed her hand on my arm. "We'll get him help, I'll stay with him, Beckett, I promise. You need to go before they stop asking nicely."

I saw the trust I needed to find in Natasha's eyes. "He has a heart condition, make sure they know that."

She nodded. "I'll tell them. Dr. Ryan will get his records."

I took my father's hand and squeezed it tightly. "You're going to be ok, Dad. I'll come find you as soon as I can."

He didn't answer, but squeezed my hand back. It was all I could ask for.

"Tosh, find something to cover your hands with, his blood could be turning toxic. Connor, you'll want to hose Beckett down before you take him to the manor."

Connor pulled me from my father's side and out the front door. Neighbors were peeking out their windows to see all the commotion. I'm sure to them it looked like I was being arrested with how Connor was dragging me around to the side of the house.

"Any particular reason you're being so rough with me?" I asked as he turned on the spigot to the hose.

"You couldn't leave well enough alone. Now look at the mess you've gotten Tosh into."

"Does it matter that she came to me?"

"No," he replied and sprayed me with freezing cold water.

This guy was a dick.

Chapter Seven

The ride from my house to the manor wasn't just an awkward silence, but an uncomfortable, squirm in your seat kind of deal where you wanted to cut your wrists to get some kind of relief. It didn't help that I was soaking wet. My world had collapsed in on me, and Connor was being a dick.

Once we got to the vampire mansion Connor dragged me to the library and shut the door. Honestly, it wasn't too bad. The couch was comfortable, the fireplace was on which was helping me dry out, and it was quiet. There was no screaming or crying, just peace to let my mind catch up with everything that had happened.

Yesterday I was a regular college student, a little bit of a slacker who still lived with his parents, but just a regular guy. Today my real father was a vampire, my mother had been kidnapped, the man I'd known as my dad could be dying or possibly becoming a werewolf, and I smelled bad. I guess I needed a stronger deodorant in order to stand up to this kind of stress. Did they make that? Complete Shit Day Deodorant, made to withstand the shittiest day of your life, guaranteed.

I laughed to myself, and Connor groaned behind me.

"It's been an hour," I said and sat up from the couch. "How much longer do I need to wait around? I'd like to see my dad."

Connor sat stretched out in a window seat at the far end of the library, his arms crossed and giving me an annoyed look. "We wait here until they're ready for you. That's all I know. Now…shut up."

I sighed and flopped back down on the couch just as the library door opened. I sat up quickly and turned to see a girl coming through the door. She was thin, had dark hair, and had lines that cut into her face from a frown that seemed permanent.

"Is she ok?" she said in a panic and walked quickly across the room toward Connor.

"She's fine, Nikki," Connor replied and got up from the window seat.

"I heard she was attacked by a dozen vamps."

Connor shook his head. "More like two. She said she lost about fifteen minutes of time, but the doc checked her out and she's fine."

The girl, Nikki, seemed distraught, but in the next second she was angry and turned a dirty look on me. "Is this the guy? The one she keeps getting in trouble for?"

"Wh-who are we talking about?" I asked, admittedly sinking a little behind the couch.

Connor rolled his eyes and smirked. "Tosh, you idiot. Unless you're risking the lives of other girls in our coven. This is Tosh's sister Nikki."

Nikki, now also known as Tosha's sister, was definitely added to the list of people in this place that didn't like me. Her arms were crossed in front of her while she glared at me. Finally she said, "Has anyone looked at your face?"

My hand immediately went up to my cheek which was slightly swollen and tender. Nikki came around the couch and roughly took my face in her hands, tilting it at different angles and pressing her thumbs in the sensitive areas.

"Uh...I've already been licked once tonight. I'd really rather not..."

Nikki pulled my face still. "I wouldn't say that in present company."

"She licked you?" Connor said behind me.

"You're fine," Nikki said and released my face.

"Nik, I'll tell Tosh to come find you when she gets back," Connor said.

"Don't bother," she replied and left as quickly as she had come in.

"Is she always in a bad mood?" I asked.

"Yes," Connor responded and sat back down in the window seat across the room.

"Is she a...one of you guys?"

"If by 'you guys' you mean a Warrior, then no. She only sleeps with one."

"She and Tosh aren't much alike."

"Thank god for that," he groaned, but then suddenly stood up when the library door opened again. "Hey, Alex. Please tell me they're ready for him."

I turned around and my jaw dropped at the sight of a man who must have been over seven feet tall and shoulders that almost spanned the doorway. My eyes kept darting back and forth between him and the floor as he stepped over to me.

"You must be Beckett," he said and extended his hand that was as big as a catcher's mitt.

"Yeah, you can call me Beck," I replied. My hand was swallowed by his as I shook it.

"I'm Alex. Sorry it's taken so long, but Cameron and Devin are ready to see you now." Alex put up his hand as he looked over my shoulder. "Sorry, Connor, just Beck."

"What? Why? This was my mission until Devin trumped it and came along. I should be there while they debrief him."

Alex shrugged. "I'm sorry, man, take it up with them. Beck, come with me."

Alex gestured toward the library's door and I turned quickly in response. The less time I had to spend with Connor the better. As I followed Alex down one hallway and to the next, I couldn't help but steal glances at him. I'd never been next to a guy so tall.

"Do you want me to stop so you can get a good look?" he asked and I froze.

"I'm so sorry...I..."

Alex held his hand up. "I was being serious, Beck. People can't help their curiosity, and I can't help how big I am. I'd rather you take a nice hard look so we can prevent any more awkward glances."

I was a piece of shit. "No, I'm good."

Alex nodded and we continued through the mansion to an area that looked faintly familiar.

"Where are we going again?"

"To see Cameron and Devin. They are the co-leaders of our coven."

"Ha!" I said proudly. "That's the one thing I know."

Alex gave me a smirk. "Hopefully you know a little more than that. They are eager to get all the details about this evening's events."

"Am I in trouble?" I asked as we rounded the corner and I saw the bench in the hallway I'd been on last night.

"Should you be?"

"Well, I did kill that wolf."

Alex slowed to a stop and looked at me. "*You* killed the werewolf?"

I nodded nervously. "But I didn't know what he was when it happened, I just…"

Alex patted my back and pushed me forward. "Beck, in this place, killing a werewolf gets you a medal. You'll be fine."

My heart was still racing when we entered the same study I'd been in last night. Cameron was standing in the middle of the room obviously expecting me.

"Ah, Mr. Dawes, thank you for joining us," Cameron said but then his face creased with concern. "Your face, I was unaware you were injured. Do you need medical attention?"

I shook my head and pulled nervously at the collar of my shirt. "No, I'm fine. Tosh's sister gave me a once over, too. And please call me Beckett, or even Beck is better than Mr. Dawes."

Alex released a soft laugh. "Good luck with that."

"Thank you, Alex," Cameron said with a bit of annoyance. "While we speak with Beckett can you ensure we are not disturbed? You can handle any updates coming in from the teams and we can gather afterwards."

Alex nodded and backed out of the room.

"Beckett, perhaps tonight we can sit. There is a great deal we need to discuss," Cameron said and gestured to the far end of the room where Devin was sitting next to the fireplace glaring at me. Had he been there the whole time? Glaring at me the whole time? Or maybe he was glaring at the other guy that was sitting on the couch opposite him.

"Beckett, I would like to introduce you to our father," Cameron said as the other guy stood from the couch and barely came up to my shoulder. But it wasn't his height that bothered me, it was the incredulous look he was giving me. "Victor, this is Beckett Dawes, the young man we were…"

"This is Garrett's son?" Victor shouted and began pointing angrily at me while looking over at Devin. "This boy came into my manor and stood in front of you, and yet you did nothing. For goodness sake, he is a clone of his father!"

"He is not…" I yelled over him but stopped myself in order for my brain to catch up with my mouth and speak in a more respectful tone. "I'm sorry. Can we please stop calling Garrett my father? My father is Richard Dawes, and right now he's fighting for his life because some fucking werewolf ripped him to shreds. So I'd really appreciate it if we could call

Garrett anything other than my father. Please."

Apparently the please didn't help all that much. There was at least thirty seconds of full silence before Cameron cleared his throat.

"Beckett, we can certainly understand your feelings toward Garrett, and will refer to him by name or as your birth father. Will that suffice?" I nodded and breathed a sigh of relief. "Very well, shall we sit and discuss all that happened this evening?"

Victor chose to sit on the couch while Devin and Cameron sat opposite me in two high-back chairs on either side of the fireplace. I relayed what happened at the party, and in probably way too much detail when it came to Tosha kissing Mac and him making fun of her, and then the resulting revenge kissing with Delia.

"Now if my opinion means anything, Tosha was awesome. Whatever training you're giving her, it's working. She saved my life…"

"She lost the target," Devin said flatly. "I wouldn't say her effort was a complete success and she fought a vampire where there were witnesses."

"Brother," Cameron said, "Natasha's efforts are to be commended, even if there was a little more exposure than we would like. Now, Beckett, can you tell us more about Delia?"

"Uh, well, she was a little shorter than me, short dark hair, really dark eyes."

"Anything else?" Devin huffed. "Something useful perhaps?"

"I'm sorry, I was drunk and honestly paying a little more attention to Tosha than Delia."

"It is fine, Beckett," Cameron said, coming to my defense yet again. "What happened next?"

"Oh! Delia just vanished. She disappeared into this cloud of smoke."

Cameron gave a smirk. "Yes, that is called a Projection. It is something vampires can do by disappearing from one location and appearing in another."

"Seriously?" He nodded. "Cool."

"Yes it is. Now what happened after Delia disappeared?"

My hands began to sweat as we headed into uncomfortable territory. "Tosha brought me home so I could pack some things and come here, but my parents were waiting for me. We argued and that's the first time I heard Garrett's name."

"What was your mother able to tell you about him?" Cameron asked and caused Devin to shift uncomfortably in his chair.

"Nothing," I replied and caused Victor to sigh loudly next to me. "My dad started freaking out, I said some...horrible things. I went back to packing my stuff when we heard the crash upstairs. A couple minutes later this...well, I know now it was a werewolf, but at the time it just looked like this beast coming down the stairs. Something kicked in and I just shot it."

"You had a firearm?"

I shook my head at Cameron and replied. "No, not a gun. It was arrow."

Victor turned his head slowly, drawing my attention toward him and then making me want to piss myself with how his eyes were boring into mine. "An arrow? As in you shot it from a bow?"

I nodded slowly. "Yes, sir."

"And you have had extensive training with this bow?"

I shook my head slowly. "No, sir. I hadn't touched it since I was in Boy Scouts. Tosha said I should bring a weapon with me. I'd just pulled it from the closest when Garrett broke in."

"Yet you were still able to take down a wolf," Victor said. "So it appears that the apple doesn't fall far from the tree."

"Can we get to the part when you actually see Garrett?" Devin said impatiently. "Perhaps we could get something useful out of this."

"Patience, Brother," Cameron said to Devin, but then gestured for me to continue.

"Well, uh, Tosha grabbed me and we were running toward the woods at the back of my house, but Garrett's men surrounded us. They took me around the front and they said they were going to kill Tosha. I tried to fight against them, I did. I couldn't get around them..."

Cameron put his hands up to stop me. "Beckett, there is no need to defend yourself. These were vampires and we certainly believe that you did your best."

I nodded and sighed with relief.

"So they took you into the house," Devin began, his patience with me was getting very thin.

"Yeah," I began and wiped my sweaty hands on my pants again. "They brought me into the house, my parents were on their knees and Garrett was standing over them."

"And? What did he say?" Devin pressed. "Why was he after you? What were his plans?"

"I...uh...I don't know. He didn't say."

"He had to have said something!" he shouted.

"I'm sorry, he didn't. He just kept making jabs at my parents, then the other wolf...um...Vincent! That was his name. Vincent came up from downstairs, I guess the other wolf was his brother. I thought he was gonna kill me, but Garrett kept him back. Honestly, he seemed kind of proud that I'd done it.

"That's when the other guys came in and said they'd killed Tosha. I lost it, and that's when Garrett said he needed my mother to keep me in line, and then they took her away. My dad tried to follow and Vincent clawed him down the chest, and that's when you guys came bursting in."

Devin fell back in his chair. "Well that was pointless."

"Brother, please," Cameron warned again. "He cannot help what Garrett did or did not say in his presence."

"Well, I will tell you this," Victor said and stood from the couch, "the two of you will need damage control once it's revealed who Garrett truly is. The Warriors have been under your leadership for less than a year. Everyone is looking for a weakness. If Garrett Archer has made himself known after all this time, there is a reason and there is going to be trouble."

I turned in my seat as Victor left the study. "What did he just say? Garrett who?"

"Archer," Cameron replied confused. "Also known as Garrett the Archer. Why does that seem to upset you, Beckett?"

Because I was Beckett Archer Dawes. Archer! My mother knew she was having another man's baby and gave me his name. Was it a reminder for her? A way to always remember her former lover, the man she knew was a vampire. I could taste the bile rising in the back of my throat. "No reason, just that my lying mother decided it was appropriate to name me Beckett Archer, as in the name of the guy she knew was my birth father, so the whole time putting her dirty little secret out there in the open." I rubbed my face roughly before looking back up at them. "Do I get to ask some questions now?"

"Of course," Cameron replied but gave Devin a worried look.

"Ok," I said and sat back against the cushions, "how do you all seem to know Garrett and why does it seem that everyone is mad at me?"

Cameron looked over at Devin and when it was obvious that he wasn't going to speak he said, "Garrett Archer is a former Warrior."

"That's you guys, right? The Warriors?"

"Yes, we are the Warrior coven," Cameron replied. "Garrett was one of the original ten Warriors, and was sired by Victor over five hundred years ago."

My head flinched. "Five…five *hundred* years ago?"

Cameron nodded. "He is only a couple of years older than Devin."

"So that's why he called you brother?" I said to Devin.

Devin's face was completely void of emotion as he replied, "He was no longer my brother the moment he betrayed us."

"You see, Beckett," Cameron began, "there was a time when vampires lived without established covens. The elders of our kind realized we needed to change the rules on how we conducted ourselves and those rules needed to be enforced. There was a major gathering of vampires and those that wished to create various covens were formerly recognized. However, the elders stated that there should be one coven, and only one, that maintained order and discipline.

"Victor and his ten Warriors were up against one other coven. One of the decision points was how each coven felt about dealing with werewolves. The other coven was firmly against any kind of truce or peacemaking efforts, however, Victor was on the fence mainly because of Garrett."

"Garrett has a thing about wolves? I thought vampires and werewolves were enemies."

"It is unnatural to be otherwise," Devin replied. "But Garrett had other feelings. He believed that we could foster the wolves to do our bidding. We would be the monsters who had their own powerful pets. When our father realized we would lose the vote if we had any affiliation with the wolves, he dismissed all of Garrett's ideas.

"What we didn't know was that Garrett had already made an alliance with a very large pack. Since all the major figures of our kind were in one place, Garrett coordinated an attack. But he significantly underestimated us, and it turned into a massacre of wolves. It was then I was contracted to kill him."

I swallowed uncomfortably, but still couldn't stop myself from saying, "But…he's not dead."

"You don't miss much," Devin growled.

Cameron cleared his throat. "This is where the scandal begins, Beckett. We have all been under the impression that Garrett was indeed killed by Devin. Killing Garrett was also a test for him to receive the Warrior Assassin position within the coven."

"I have killed thousands of others, but that doesn't seem to matter to father," Devin said directly to Cameron. "One kill went wrong in five hundred years and father treats it as though I betrayed him as badly as Garrett did. It is ridiculous."

"Brother," Cameron said calmly, "father is upset because you lied about your first kill."

"His injuries could have very well killed him, so I assumed he was dead when he didn't resurface. Why should my reputation be tainted because of one kill at the beginning of my career?"

"Um…do you want me to leave?" I asked quietly.

Cameron shook his head. "I apologize, Beckett, this is all still very raw for all of us."

"So this is why everyone hates me."

"Yes," Devin answered.

"Brother!" Cameron snapped and then shook his head again. "Beckett, no one hates you. Your presence, however, is creating a unique and uncomfortable situation."

"I think that's just a nice way of saying you want me to leave."

"Not at all. My brother and Victor need to get past the fact that Garrett is still alive and move forward on figuring out why he is coming after you."

I sighed and rubbed my eyes, exhaustion starting to come over me. "What happens now?"

"Because it is painfully obvious that your life is in danger, the safest place for you to be is here. You are technically a Warrior by birth which means you are under our protection."

"How can that be?" I asked and Cameron tilted his head. "The Warrior by birth thing. You said yourself that Garrett is a *former* Warrior."

"Beckett, you are connected to this coven through your blood. Although Garrett is considered an enemy, he was still sired by Victor like the rest of us. You are part of our family, Beckett, and we protect our family."

"Unless they betray us," Devin added and narrowed his eyes at me. "If we find out that this is all a hoax and you really are working with Garrett to get inside our walls, I swear that I will…"

"What my brother is trying to say," Cameron interrupted, "is that you must tell us if Garrett contacts you in any way."

I nodded. "Yes, sir. So, can I ask what's happening with my dad?"

Cameron sighed and Devin shifted uncomfortably in his chair. This wasn't going to be good.

"Beckett, let me be frank," Cameron began, "your father's condition is very serious. The virus that the wolves possess is easily transmittable through bites, scratches, and through blood. With the injuries your father sustained, it is most likely that he has been infected."

I swallowed hard. "So you think my dad is a werewolf now?"

"Time will tell. We will not know for sure until the full moon. His body will have no choice but to phase. Your father is currently at Facility West, which is a residential training facility for hybrids like yourself. Dr. Ryan, the physician you met last night, he is personally treating your father, and in many ways at great risk to himself."

"My dad isn't going to bite anyone," I snapped.

"Wolves can rarely control themselves," Devin growled back. "If your father begins to show signs of phasing, we will need to remove him from Facility West. Hundreds are at risk by his mere presence."

"Beckett, your father is receiving the best care, I assure you," Cameron said in a more calming tone, "but there is a lot we do not know about lycanthropy. Because of the risks, we are being precautious with everything we do."

"Why don't you know more about lycan...lycanth...that wolf thing I can't say."

Cameron smirked. "Vampires and werewolves are very much like cats and dogs. We do not necessarily know why we are enemies, it is simply engrained in us. Most things we do know are assumptions, maybe even myths. The wars and massacres thankfully stopped centuries ago. Since then there has not necessarily been peace, but more of leaving each other alone. They do not bother us, we do not bother them. Of course you hear of a scuffle every now and then, but nothing like our early history together. That is why we need to handle this situation carefully. Know that we are actively looking for your mother, but we are also being cautious in order to prevent another war. Can you understand that, Beckett?"

I nodded, but he could see my disappointment. I wanted these guys, these vampires, to knock down doors and pull out fingernails in order to get the information about where my mother was.

"I know it is a difficult message to hear, Beckett. But my brother and I have centuries of experience dealing with the wolves, you need to trust us."

I nodded again and rubbed my face in order to keep my eyes open.

"This is all going to take some getting used to. Is there a place I can crash for a few hours? I didn't think I'd be able to sleep, but suddenly my entire body is exhausted."

Cameron stood from his chair and called out to Alex who came back inside the study. "Alex, can you take Beckett up to the human wing? I believe his room is ready."

"Wait, my room?" I asked and stood from the couch.

Cameron nodded. "Yes, Beckett. Like I said before, you are under our protection. This is the safest place for you to be and we will do whatever we can to help you until we resolve this. No go and get some sleep, anything further we can discuss tomorrow."

I sighed, feeling the exhaustion sink into my muscles. With an awkward wave goodbye, I walked to Alex who ushered me out of the study.

"So is there a map or something I can get to find my way around here?"

Alex laughed and pulled me through a crowd of guys all dressed in black holding various weapons and heading in the direction we had just come from. "It's not as bad as it seems. There's only a couple places you'll ever really need to go, but we'll make sure someone takes you around tomorrow morning."

"Cool. Um…were those guys at my house tonight?"

"No," he replied and steered me toward an enormous spiraling staircase that cut into several floors above. "They're another team that was patrolling the area."

"Do you think they found anything?"

Alex shrugged as we began trudging up the stairs. "It's possible."

"But you don't have much hope."

"Don't worry, kid, we're good at what we do. We'll get your mom back."

I followed Alex up to the second landing where he turned to the right and began walking toward a long hallway of doors. It looked like a medieval hotel.

"When you come up the stairs there is a very important distinction. Everything to the right is the human wing, that's where you belong."

"What's to the left?" I asked and looked curiously around him seeing a similar hallway of doors.

"That's the vampire wing. I'd steer clear for the time being."

"No problem," I answered confidently. "Stay to the right, got it."

He laughed and stopped in front of a wooden door marked 205.

"This is your room," he said and opened the door. The room was small, similar to a small dorm room. A twin bed was pushed up against the left side of the room next to the only window. On the opposite side was a chair, dresser, and a small desk with a TV sitting on top. "I know it's small, but you probably won't spend as much time in here as you think."

"Now, you should really get some sleep. I'm sure my brothers have plans for you tomorrow."

"They're your brothers too?"

Alex turned to the door and closed it softly. "Not biologically, but a pure blood coven like ours is a family. We're not all best friends, but we would still protect each other to our deaths because we are all connected by Victor's blood. Just as you are."

Nervously I put my hands in the pockets of my jeans. "You heard all of that?"

He nodded. "I've been protecting the office door all night. Now I know that all of this has just been laid on you tonight, but you need to understand that Cam and Devin have only been leading the coven for less than a year. There are those around us that are waiting for them to fail so they can pick at their carcasses.

"What I'm trying to say, Beckett, you have absolutely no reason to, but if you were to keep who Garrett truly is to yourself for a little while, I know we would all be grateful. It is all going to come out eventually, and when it does everyone will concentrate on the fact that Devin has lied for half a century and what should be done to him rather than on missions trying to capture Garrett."

"Meaning they won't find my mom," I sighed. "And once they find out I'm a traitor's son..."

"It won't make your time here easy. It is still up to you, of course."

"Yeah, seems like there's a lot of choice."

"Well, I'll leave you now. Try and get some sleep."

"Thanks," I replied and watched him bend his way out the door.

My head was swimming, but the bed was calling my name. I peeled my damp clothes off and climbed into the bed. My eyes closed as soon as my head hit the pillow, but the sights and sounds of the night began flashing before my eyes. My mother screaming as they dragged her away, my father lying on the floor bleeding, Garrett touching my mother's cheek.

My eyes shot open. The clock on the dresser showed 3:08AM.

I punched the pillow underneath my head and pulled the blanket under my chin. When I closed my eyes again, my father's blood was soaking through my shirt, my mother was screaming, and Garrett was calling me his son. My eyes shot open again, the clock on the dresser displayed 3:09AM.

Fuck.

Chapter Eight

"Hey, asshole, wake up," a girl said and shook me awake.

"What time is it?" I groaned and stretched my eyes open to find Natasha leaning over me. "What time is it?"

"Almost 7:30, now get up," she said as she dropped a duffel bag on the floor. "I brought you some stuff from your house. Most of it you packed before everything happened, but I threw in your toothbrush and stuff."

"Thanks, I appreciate it," I replied and rubbed my eyes. "But uh…why am I getting up? I finally got to sleep an hour ago."

Tosha sighed and plopped down in the chair on the other side of the room. She looked as exhausted as I felt. "They want you to start training this morning. So get up and get going or else you're going to make me late, and I if I'm late I'm going to kick your ass."

"Training? What kind of training?" I asked stupidly and received a dirty look from across the room.

"I don't know, Beckett," she said in a condescending tone, "maybe it's for poise and etiquette. Now get up before I kick your ass out of bed!"

"Ok, ok," I said and swung my legs around to the edge of bed and realized I had major morning wood. Quickly I pulled the pillow over my lap and saw that Tosha's eyes were closed, but I still couldn't get up and walk to the bathroom like this. "So, do you want to come back in a few minutes or…"

"Unlike you, I haven't even had an hour of sleep because I was at the Facility with your dad, gave a butt load of blood in case they think it'll help, was taken back to your house to get your crap, interrogated for over an hour, and then back here for a full day of training. So, while you take what's hopefully at least a fifteen-minute shower, I can close my eyes in this chair."

"You were with my dad? Did he pull through ok?"

Tosha opened her eyes, but her face was frozen with annoyance. "If he hadn't pulled through, don't you think we'd be having a different conversation?" She caught sight of the pillow I had in front of me and scrunched her face in confusion.

"Hey, if you wake me up from a dead sleep, you have to deal with what I can't physiologically stop from happening. So, my dad?"

Tosha looked at her watch and sighed. "Beckett, I promise I'll tell you everything about your dad when we walk down to breakfast. But for now, I'm begging you to get ready so I can close my eyes and not be late for training. So please, can you and your pillow go take a shower?"

I leaned down and grabbed the duffle bag with my right hand while my left pressed the pillow uncomfortably into my crouch as I stood from the bed. With my head held high, even though Tosha was holding her mouth trying not to laugh, I shuffled over to the bathroom. Once the door was closed I dropped the bag and the pillow to floor.

"Dude," I whispered to my erection that was stretching out the front of my boxers, "worst possible time."

I kept cursing him as I stepped into the cold shower. It still took a good minute for him to go away, he was determined today. Since I had no idea what was in store for me today, I went for sweatpants and a T-shirt. I was also happy to see that Tosha grabbed most of the other toiletries I needed, although it made me nervous that she was rummaging around in my drawers.

When I finally left the bathroom, Tosha was still in the chair with her head propped up on her hand. I wondered if I just climbed back in bed that we could both get the sleep we needed.

"Stop staring at me," she said sleepily and stretched her eyes open.

"I was just debating whether or not to wake you."

"Good thing it isn't up to you," she said as she pushed herself up from the chair and headed toward the door. "Come on, we still have time to get a bite to eat as long as you don't mind shoveling down your food."

I shoved my feet into my sneakers and ran after her into the hallway. "So my dad, how is he?"

"He's in recovery," she began as we approached the big spiral staircase. "Dr. Ryan worked on him for hours and he has a ton of stitches."

"What about his heart?"

"Dr. Ryan said they'll monitor him closely, but the injuries he sustained last night don't seem to be causing problems, but the uh..." she paused on the stairs and lowered her voice, "...but the Lycan virus is what could cause some trouble because of the strain that it may put on his heart. But since none of us really know anything about the virus..."

"Right, but he could be fine," I interrupted which caused her to turn her head and look at me bewildered.

"Fine, live in denial, but you should prepare yourself for the fact that he might be infected," she said. When I didn't answer she pulled me into a large dining room. "We need to eat and then get outside for training."

"I don't usually eat breakfast," I said even though I followed her to the buffet line. These people were serious about food. There were large trays of eggs and bacon and mounds of muffins and fruit.

Tosha began piling eggs on her plate. "This isn't your normal day of dicking around and maybe going to a class or two. You'll be doing actual physical activity today, something I'm sure you're not used to."

I rolled my eyes and sighed as I took an apple and a blueberry muffin. "Will you ever lay off of me?"

"Probably not," she replied before slipping a piece of bacon into her mouth. "I hope you know that muffin is not going to cut it. You're going to burn through it pretty quickly."

"I told you, I'm not a breakfast person. I usually just drink some juice, so this is a step up."

"It's your funeral," she said flatly. "We have to eat fast, we only have a couple of minutes."

I nodded and followed her to an empty table where we sat down and she went to town on her scrambled eggs and bacon. Just as I bit into my muffin, three guys stepped over to our table. Their stances and expressions clearly displayed they were marking their territory. Between Connor and these three assholes, I wondered if everyone had a stake in Tosha.

"Hey, Scarecrow," the tallest one in the middle said to Tosha and then eyed me once again, "who's the newbie?"

Tosha didn't even lift her eyes away from her plate while she continued to shove eggs in her mouth. "Not a newbie," she said between bites. "Just a hybrid who got attacked last night. Beckett, this is Nub, Bush, and Princess."

"Those are nicknames, right?" I asked, trying not to laugh.

"You should talk, *Beckett*," the one in the middle who I assumed was named Bush replied. "Why are you here instead of the Facility?"

Tosha finally looked up from her plate, and it was nice to see she gave her look of disdain to others beside me. "Because he was attacked by werewolves last night, Bush. The sirs want him to get some training. Is that a good enough reason?"

"Actually, we both got attacked," I added. "Tosha saved my life last night."

"No way," Nub groaned skeptically. "Scarecrow against a wolf?"

Tosha dropped her fork on her plate loudly. "No, Beckett killed the wolf, I didn't do anything."

I looked at her confused. "You saved me from that vampire at the party."

"You killed a vamp last night?" Bush said with a mix of jealousy and astonishment.

"No," Tosha answered flustered and gave me a dirty look. "I just injured her enough to where she had to Project to get away."

"You still saved me," I replied, not understanding why Tosha was so upset.

"Guys! Scarecrow! Get a move on," another guy about my age shouted from the dining room entryway.

Everyone jumped to attention, the guys bolting from the dining room first. Tosha scooped up the last bite of her eggs and stuffed them in her mouth as she stood up from the table. I grabbed my apple, put it in my pocket, and went to step away from the table when Tosha suddenly grabbed my arm and whipped me around.

"Get this straight, I don't need you to make me sound better than I am," she said angrily.

"What? I didn't mean…"

"I have to work twice as hard in this program because I'm a girl and because I haven't been activated. I am where I am off my own sweat. I don't need you stretching the truth to try and impress those assholes. Got it?"

"Not really. You haven't been activated? What does that mean?"

She growled in frustration. "A vamp and a human have sex and create a hybrid – mostly human, but can have some extraordinary gifts."

"Like how you heal."

"Right," she nodded. "Most hybrids have to be activated in order for their gift to really come out. To be activated, a hybrid has to drink his or her father's blood. Doing that brings out more of the vampire traits in the hybrid."

"And you didn't do that?"

"No, and I have my reasons," she snapped.

"Ok, but you've made my point for me. You didn't do this activation thing, and you've still saved my life multiple times, and that isn't stretching the truth. Can we at least agree on that?"

She exhaled loudly and let go of my arm. A second later she was bolting out of the dining room and I was trying to catch up.

"Who was that guy that came in?" I asked as we stepped back into the main hallway.

"That's Roberts," she replied. "He's another trainee."

"How come he doesn't have a nickname?"

"What?" she said and pushed me around the corner.

"Well, there was Nub, Bush, and Princess. So why is Roberts just Roberts?"

"Trevor Roberts is the best trainee in the program, so I guess he doesn't have to have one."

"Oh. Why is Nub named Nub?"

"He has a really small pinky finger, it's like a nub."

"What about Bush?"

She sighed knowing I wasn't going to stop. "He fell into the bushes during practice one day, and I don't know why Princess is called Princess. The boys don't always share their inside jokes with the only girl."

"And why are you Scarecrow?"

"Don't worry about it," she replied and steered me down a small set of stairs which brought us outside to a big courtyard.

"Tosh! Over here," a guy called from the far side of the courtyard and waved us over. He looked to be my age, maybe a little younger, thin but muscular upper body. Although it was odd that he was wearing a winter cap, a hoodie with the hood up, and gloves. Once we were in front of him, he extended his gloved hand and I shook it as he said, "Hey, you must be the new kid. I'm Jared Ranger."

"I'm Beckett Dawes, but Beck is fine."

"Jared will train you while you're here," Tosha said.

"Cushlin! Let's go!" someone yelled.

I glanced over my shoulder and saw Connor waving his arm. Just the person I wanted to see. With the glare he gave me, he felt the same way.

"Well, you two have fun," Tosha said before she broke into a run and joined the other trainees in laps.

"You're a Warrior?" I asked.

"Yep. And you're friends with Tosh?" Jared responded as he pulled me over to a table where a sophisticated-looking bow sat with a dozen or so arrows.

"I'm not really sure," I replied. "I'd like to say yes since everyone else here seems to hate me. Even Tosh's sister despises me and I saw her for two seconds."

Jared slid on a pair of sunglasses. His entire outfit confused me. It wasn't cold out, so I wondered if he was in hiding or something.

"You met Nikki?" he asked.

"Yeah, last night when they brought me in. Talk about sisters being complete opposites of each other. I mean, Tosha's a little high strung, but her sister is kinda crazy. Good luck to the guy that's her boyfriend. Connor said it was one of the Warriors here."

"That would be me," Jared replied stone-faced.

"Please don't kill me," I said terrified, but then Jared started barreling over in laughter.

He squeezed my shoulder painfully and pulled himself up to standing. "The look on your face…classic! Damn, that was funny."

"So you're not her boyfriend?"

"Oh no, I am," he replied and my face fell. "And yeah, she's totally insane. After five years together I just can't bring myself to break up with her, although my life would be much easier. But Tosh, she's definitely the sane one. The training program has hardened her a lot, not sure I like that, but it's what she wants."

"Were Tosh and Connor ever together?"

Jared smirked. "Not according to either of them, but no one believes that, and Connor helps her out way too much without any kind of benefit."

"Well, he certainly hates me and the fact that Tosh even talks to me. I seriously thought he was going to kill me last night."

Jared patted me on the shoulder. "Meh, he wouldn't kill you, maybe just take a finger, or…now that I think of it, he does have an affinity for ears."

"Oh dear god…"

"Calm down," he laughed. "Connor can't hurt you. You're mega protected."

"I am? Why's that?"

Jared smirked and turned toward the table. "I think you know I can't say it out loud. Come on, let's get started with weapons training."

"Wea-weapons training? I thought..."

"Whatever you thought, I'm sure it's wrong. You were attacked, you've got some bad people after you, we might as well skip to weapons training since you showed some skill last night. Good work, by the way."

I sighed and looked uncomfortably at the ground. "I didn't know I was killing some guy."

"You weren't, you were killing a werewolf. When they're in wolf form, all bets are off. Now, can we get to shooting? I'd really like to see the arm that killed the wolf last night."

"I don't remember what I did. It just happened."

"Raw talent, I love it."

"What's this?" I asked as I pointed to the bow on the table that looked incredibly complicated.

Jared picked up the metal bow which had a wheel at each end and several bow strings threaded throughout. "This, my friend, is the best compound bow on the market. Weighs less than five pounds, beautifully synchronized binary cam system, flexible draw length, and perfect for big game."

"I don't know what any of that means," I replied truthfully. "Why exactly am I training on a bow?"

"Uh...well, you used one last night," he answered and then lowered his voice, "and considering who your birth father is..."

"What does that have to do with it," I said defensively.

Even from behind his sunglasses I could see he was raising an eyebrow at me. "Dude. Garrett *Archer*. Archer. Garrett was an archer. He was the best back when Dad turned him. With that, and what you did last night, it only makes sense to train you on it. Besides not wanting to train on the same weapon as your dear-old-absent-dad, is there another reason you keep stalling?"

"No, that's pretty much it," I admitted. "But this thing is just way too intense."

"What did you want, a bow that looked like a stick with a string stretched across it?"

I shrugged. "That's what I had before."

"Look, you pull this out and the wolves will run back to their dog houses. Now, I put a target out there for you, so let's see what you got."

I looked down the courtyard and about fifty feet away was a round foam archery target. With the trainees doing laps around the courtyard, Connor staring me down from across the way, and Jared shoving this intimidating bow in my hands, the pressure was pushing me into the ground.

"So how exactly do I use this?" I asked as I held the bow in my left hand and raised it up to my eye where there was a small sight gage sticking out from the center.

"Uh...thought you knew."

"I used a stick and a string, remember? You haven't used a bow like this before?"

"Never shot a bow and arrow in my life."

"Then why are you training me?"

He shrugged and dug his gloved hands into his pockets. "There are no archers in the Warriors anymore, and I'm a sharp shooter. I guess I'm the closest thing we have. Bow and arrows are so old school."

"And there was no one else available," a man with a raspy voice replied behind us.

When I turned around I found the short guy from last night walking toward us. Victor, that was his name. He seemed to be in a much better mood than he was last night. At least he wasn't yelling this time.

"Come on, Dad," Jared said, "he didn't need to know that."

"You mean the truth," Victor replied and then looked curiously at the bow in my hand. "What in the world is that?"

Jared stepped forward and took the metal bow from my hand and displayed it in front of Victor. "This is the best bow I could find. State-of-the-art."

"It looks ridiculous," Victor groaned with a deep rasp.

Jared shook his head and pushed the bow back into my chest, causing me to barrel over slightly. "Just wait, Dad. Once you see how accurate this thing is, you'll change your mind. So come on, Beck, let's see what this thing can do."

"Um...now? In front of everyone?" I said nervously. "We haven't even figured out how to use it."

Jared handed me an arrow. "Just thread it and pull it, you'll be fine.

Don't worry about anybody else, no one's paying attention to you. Oh! I almost forgot, you'll need this," he said and handed me a black with a clip on the end.

"What is that?" Victor asked as Jared strapped the bracelet around my wrist and then stretched the clip over the center of my palm.

"Once you put the arrow in place, you hook the clip to the back and pull."

Victor shook his head. "I'm sorry, child, why is there a need for such a contraption?"

"It's..." Jared sighed loudly, "...it's not a contraption. It's going to be a weapon of mass destruction. Now, Beck, let's show him how awesome this thing is. Give it a whirl."

With another heavy sigh, I notched the arrow between the two plastic holds on the pull line, and with help from Jared, clipped the bracelet's handle to the back of the arrow. After taking my stance and raising the bow to eye level, I pulled back the arrow and aligned it with the target in the distance. I took a breath in, and when I exhaled I released the arrow. But instead of flying gracefully in the air, somehow the entire bow flew forward.

The other side of the courtyard burst into laughter. Connor was literally holding his sides. Just what I was worried about, making an ass out of myself. Mission accomplished.

"How is that even possible," Jared said flabbergasted. "It's supposed to be foolproof."

"I'm sorry, Jared, this just isn't me," I said and took the bracelet and clip off my wrist. "I'm not like you guys, I'm more of the guy who hangs out on the sideline while everyone else does their thing."

Jared shook his head and retrieved the bow from the lawn. "Don't worry about it, kid, we'll keep trying."

As he held the compound bow out in front of me, I found myself unable to take it from him. Victor cleared his throat and pulled a thin wooden longbow from around his back.

"Dad, are you serious?" Jared huffed and placed the compound bow on the table with the arrows. "You think your string on a stick can beat this masterpiece?"

Victor waited a beat before saying, "Humor me."

I shook my head, the echoes of everyone's laughter still ringing in my ears. "I think I've embarrassed myself enough for one day."

"If you continue to embarrass yourself, I will cut your suffering short. Can we agree on that?"

Cautiously I extended my hand and took the bow from Victor. Instantly I could feel the difference. It was lighter to begin with, and even with a second's glance I knew how to use it. There were no wheels and multiple pull strings or even a bracelet to shoot from. Plain and simple, a string on a stick.

I took an arrow from the table and notched it between the string. With a nervous sigh, I lifted the bow and pulled the arrow back toward my cheek. As I exhaled, I released the arrow and watched as it glided past the lower left corner of the target. Damn it.

"Just because he could shoot it, doesn't mean it's one hundred percent better than the bow I got," Jared grumbled as he pulled on the strings of his hood to tighten it around his face.

Victor sighed and extended his hand towards me. "Beckett, may I see the bow for a moment?"

I handed him the bow and watched as he rubbed his thumb against the wood, filing two notches near the top and bottom where my grip would be.

"Let's see what that will do," Victor said and handed the bow back to me.

Once again I lifted the bow to eye level, the notches effectively catching my thumb and pinky causing the bow to tilt a slight bit to the right. I pulled the string and arrow back, grazing the side of my cheek before exhaling and releasing the arrow into the dead center of the target.

"No fucking way," Jared said angrily and threw his expensive compound bow onto the ground. "How...what the hell, Dad?"

Victor shook his head as he placed his hand on my arm, and gently began twisting my wrist back and forth. "There is a slight defect in his wrist that causes a slight over rotation. By adjusting the grip, the alignment fixes itself."

"But how did you know that would fix it?" I asked, remembering having the same problem when I was in Scouts.

Victor patted my arm as he replied, "Because your birth father has the same defect."

The statement hung in the air. More of Garrett was coming out in me. This sucked.

"Well don't just stand there, kid," Jared said and handed me another arrow, "let's get some Robin Hood shit goin' here."

Chapter Nine

There wasn't an inch of my body that didn't hurt and wasn't covered with an icepack. My stomach was eating itself I was so hungry, but I couldn't bring myself to move a muscle, let alone go downstairs.

"Beckett? You in there?" Tosha said from the other side of my door.

"Yeah, come in," I replied.

Tosha opened the door and my stomach jumped at the sight of the pizza box she was carrying and the smell of the garlicky, cheesy goodness that was inside it.

"I will give you all the money I have if you give me that pizza."

"I've been through your wallet, you don't have any money," she laughed and placed the pizza box on the corner of the bed by my feet. "The uh…ice packs? A little excessive, don't you think?"

"They're not helping much anymore. Now I'm just damp," I replied and rolled to my side, letting the bags of water fall off of me and onto the floor. "Please don't judge me on what I'm about to do."

"Well, since you said that," she replied sarcastically, but I didn't care and moaned loudly as I pushed myself up to a sitting position. The blood rushed down to my hands and arms, making them pulse and pound which somehow caused a high-pitched whining noise to come out of my mouth. "Wow, is there a little girl stuck somewhere in your throat?"

I groaned as I turned my body in her direction. "I asked you not to judge."

"But I'm really good at it," she said and then lifted the lid of the pizza box. "I hope you like bacon."

"There could be turnips on there and I would eat it," I said as I stretched my arm over to grab a slice and then flinched at the pain. Tosha pulled a big slice of pizza and held it out to me, yet my fingers couldn't even close enough to take it from her.

"Are you seriously in that much pain?" she asked annoyed and shaking the pizza for me to take it.

"Maybe you could feed it to me?"

"You're kidding, right?"

"Or maybe just put it on the edge of the bed and I can sit in the floor and try and eat it…"

"Beckett! What the hell is your problem," she shouted and threw the slice of pizza back into the box.

"I can't use my hands," I said and held them out in front of me. "They're numb except for the blisters that have their own pulse."

"Why didn't you say something," she sighed, placing her palm under mine and painfully stretching my fingers out straight. "I can help with this," she said and stood from the bed.

"You're not going to lick me again, are you?"

"You wish," she huffed and ducked into the bathroom. A moment later she returned to the bedroom with a wet washcloth hanging from her hand. Once she sat down on the bed she pulled a small knife from one of the pockets on the side of her pants. "I have to cut myself, you're not going to faint again, are you?"

"I fainted because I saw you heal, not because…" but I didn't finish because at the same moment she cut the inside of her palm open and the blood drained from my face. Could there be one moment where I didn't make an ass out of myself in front of this girl?

With a wince, she squeezed the blood from her palm into the wet washcloth. Carefully she took my hand again and wrapped the washcloth around my fingers.

"You didn't have to do that," I said, although I was thankful that the throbbing in my fingers was beginning to stop.

She shrugged and squeezed the washcloth tightly, making me flinch for a second and then once again the pain began to subside. "You have to train tomorrow, don't you?"

"Not sure I have a choice."

"Well, you could either train tomorrow with painful blistered fingers, or let me help you so you can get through the day."

"Yeah, but I feel bad when you cut yourself," I replied as she removed the washcloth from my fingers and wiped away the residual blood.

"It only hurts for a minute or two," she said, opening her palm and showing that the cut had healed leaving only a thin red line. She took the washcloth and waved for my other hand. "You were looking pretty good out there today towards the end."

"Really?" I asked skeptically as she wrapped the bloody washcloth around my palm where my bow had rubbed the skin raw.

"Wouldn't have said it if it weren't true." Tosha stopped pressing the washcloth in my hand and looked up at me with a little bit of guilt in her eyes. "I didn't mean for that to sound harsh. I know I can be intense sometimes, but it's this program. There's no room for bullshit. It makes you hard."

I laughed to myself, as any guy would have just hearing someone say the word hard, but it took several seconds before it hit her.

"Oh my god, not like that," she laughed and removed the washcloth from my hand. "You know what I meant. You have to put all emotions aside, there's no room for it."

"Jared said you had changed since you got in."

"You could say that about anyone. He probably changed after he joined the military, we all do. It's harder for girls because we're judged when we're not feminine enough."

She rose from the bed and went back into the bathroom. The skin on my fingertips and palm was tender and slightly numb, but pink and painless.

"You should donate your blood to science or something. You could save so many lives."

Tosha stepped back into the bedroom as she replied, "I do already. Give blood, that is."

"You do?"

She nodded. "I give blood at the Facility every week. Dr. Ryan has been doing research with it."

"Dr. Ryan…why do I know that name?"

"He's the guy who treated you the other night. He's also treating your dad, remember?"

My shoulders fell and suddenly reality came rushing forward. "Oh my god, all I've been thinking about is how much pain I'm in that I didn't even…how is he?"

"He's doing better from what they told me, but still in a lot of pain from all the stitches. They did some bloodwork, and uh

"He's infected, isn't he?"

"They did find a virus they've never seen before, so they're assuming it's the Lycan virus."

I swallowed hard at the news. "So that means he's a werewolf now?"

"From what they told me the transformation won't be complete until the first full moon."

"The next full moon is like a week away."

"I know," she replied and then took a piece of pizza from the box. "He's in a secured area in the medical wing at the Facility, but once he starts phasing, they'll probably have to bring him here."

"Why can't he stay where he is?"

After she took a bite of her pizza she replied, "Beck, he's not going to be able to control himself and he could hurt someone. The fact that he's even at the Facility has a lot of people upset."

"Are we sure he has it? You said they were assuming."

"Dr. Ryan found an anomaly in your dad's blood, and it is starting to alter his cells. Because there's no research or data on the actual virus, there's nothing definitive he can compare it to, but considering the circumstances he's pretty sure."

"What about his heart?"

Tosha shrugged. "They didn't tell me anything to the contrary. I'll be sure to ask next time. You should eat, Beckett."

She slid the pizza box in front of me and the smell was killing me. Reluctantly I took a piece and took a bite. "Wow, I think this is the best pizza I've ever had."

"It's from my favorite place that's conveniently located between here and the Facility. And don't think that just because I'm a girl, that I won't eat this whole thing. You better eat faster or you're going to be shit out of luck," she said and took another piece.

"Believe me, Tosha, after everything I've seen you do, I don't underestimate you in the slightest," I replied, finishing off my slice and taking another one. "Have they heard anything about my mom?"

"They deployed some search teams, but it's too soon to hear anything."

"And why's that?"

She finished off her pizza's crust and replied, "They want to search for your mom and Garrett, but not start another war with the wolves, remember? So the searches have to be done carefully and quietly."

I finished off my second piece of pizza and threw the crust into the box. "Which means my mom is missing longer because they don't want to ruffle any feathers."

"More like fur," she replied with a laugh, but sighed and rolled her eyes when I didn't laugh with her.

"I'm sorry, I'm not the best company at the moment."

"Are you ever?"

"Hey," I whined and then finally laughed. "These last few days don't count. Generally, I'm incredibly fun, we've just never hung out before."

"Yeah, that's because you hang out with jerks like Chris Mackenzie."

I sighed. "You're right, but technically he's not a good friend, we've just known each other since high school. About that, are you ok?"

"I'm fine," she replied flatly.

"Really? Most girls would…"

"I'm not most girls, Beckett."

"You don't have to pretend with me, Tosha. I think we've been through enough together that…"

"He's not the first person to ridicule me about my scars, and he certainly won't be the last."

"I won't. Ever."

"Sure," she replied skeptically and finished her last bite of pizza crust.

I shook my head and grabbed another piece. "Why do you do that?"

"Do what?"

"You'll be open for a second and then just shut down. You dismiss everything I say when I'm being honest with you."

She sighed and rubbed her eyes. "Beckett, I can count the number of people I trust on one hand, and that doesn't even include my sister. I've been too naïve in the past, I can't make those mistakes anymore."

"But making mistakes is part of life, Tosha. That's kind of the point."

"Sure, Beckett. I'll start making mistakes just because you told me to. That will certainly help me become a Warrior."

"I'm sure they've made a ton of mistakes through the years."

"Yeah, but they're already Warriors. I'm fighting tooth and nail to become one, and every day I'm reminded that I'm second best compared to Roberts. This is all I've ever wanted to be, and if I don't get inducted I…" she stood from the bed and quickly turned her back on me, "…I don't know what I'll do."

"Well, you'll kick ass somewhere else," I replied. "At least you know what you want to do. I still don't. I've switched my major three times, have no real interest in any kind of career, and now I'm shooting an arrow in a courtyard at a vampire mansion. Oh, and everyone around me knows so much more about my birth dad than I do and how much I'm like him."

"What do you mean?"

I stood from the bed, picked up my bow, and held it up in front of me. "See these notches?" I said and pointed to the areas that Victor had filed down. "My aim was off, Victor filed these notches into the bow and then boom, I was dead on. And why? This is how Garrett does the grip on his bow. Apparently, I have the same defect in my wrist. And hey, they called him Garrett the Archer, guess what my middle name is? Archer. My mother did that. She knew what she was doing and never told me, never told my dad. It's bullshit. Everyone knows this guy but me. It sucks."

I lowered my bow and propped it up against the wall. My stomach growled, so I picked up another piece of pizza.

"How are your hands?" Tosha asked.

"Great. They feel fine, wow. Thank you."

"Do you feel good enough to go downstairs?"

"I guess so, why?"

She shrugged again. "If you're curious about Garrett we could go to the library and do some research on Garrett. We could even look for some books about werewolves if you wanted to."

"Really? You don't have some Warrior thing?"

She shook her head. "Not tonight. Usually Connor and I do some extra training, but he's out with the scouting party looking for your mom."

"Are you sure he knows it's my mom?"

"Yes, of course he does. Don't be a jerk."

"Me! He's the one…"

"Do you still want to go to the library?" she interrupted.

"Yes," I answered like a scolded child.

"Then shut up. Connor's my friend and he goes out of his way to help me, so lay off."

"I'll give him what he gives me, that's all I can promise."

"That's fair, I guess."

"Funny that we met in a library, and now we're having a date in one." Tosha narrowed her eyes, making me clear my throat. "Ignore me, I'm uh…delirious, remember?"

"Well this one's a bust," Tosha said and tossed the thin tattered blue hard-cover book on the floor. "I swear there were more books about wolves in this place."

I laughed and turned the page of my book which was also pretty much a bust. "Maybe they hate wolves so much that they don't want anything about them in their library."

"You'd think they'd want everything known about their legendary sworn enemy of all time."

"Maybe they had people pull them out already," I replied and closed my book when it began describing another coven called the Cleaners. Seriously? I should have read on to know who they were, but all I kept picturing was a group of vampires scrubbing floors somewhere all looking like Mr. Clean.

"Any luck?" Tosha asked and took my book away.

"Nope. Garrett's name is mentioned as a founding member, but then was the first to be killed by Devin. How do these books even exist? Seriously, is there a vampire publishing company that only distributes to other vampires?"

Tosha scrunched her eyebrows together. "You know, I don't think I've ever thought about that."

"That's because all of this is normal to you."

Tosha rose from the fort of books we'd made in the corner of the library. She took a few of them in her arm and began searching for the shelves they belonged to.

"I don't think you can say that any part of my life is normal, Beckett."

Slowly I pulled myself up, my body groaning from sitting so long on the floor. "You know what I mean. You're not twenty-two and trying to play catch-up with all of this."

"Yes, yes, you're overwhelmed, we're all well aware," she said and came back to our fort to gather a few more books. "Honestly there are days I wish I could have been oblivious to all of this like you. I wouldn't have minded being in the dark, but with a gift like mine there's no way."

"Yeah, how have you never gotten caught? You must have hurt yourself around other people at some point, especially at school."

"Who said I didn't," she replied and shelved her last book.

"Really? How...uh...what happened?"

Her mouth opened to respond, but in the next moment she caught herself and her protective wall went up once again. I shook my head as she came back over to me, wondering if she would ever bring that wall down.

"You know, I bet there's something in the vaults," she said and pulled me toward a bookcase on the other side of the room.

"Vault? What do you mean vault?"

Quickly she typed in a code on a small keypad, and then the bookcase next to it opened slowly.

"That is. The coolest thing. I've ever seen."

Tosha laughed next to me and pulled me into a dark tunnel. The only light came from the library, but the bookcase was slowly closing behind us. Tosha pulled out her cell phone and used it as a flashlight.

"Why aren't there any lights in here?"

"They're vampires, they don't need it. Plus, we're really not supposed to be in here."

"What!"

"Shh!"

"Sorry," I whispered, "what?"

"Just be quiet and no one will find us," she replied and pulled me over to one of the vault doors.

"If we're not supposed to be in here, then how did you know the code?"

"Jared's given me the codes for a couple of the vaults," she replied while she examined the keypad next to one of the vault doors, "but this one is Victor's and I probably only have two attempts until someone comes and throws us in a cell for trespassing."

"What!"

"Shh! I'm kidding," she whispered harshly.

"So we're ok then?"

"Of course not," she replied and typed in a four-digit number. The small light on top of the keypad flashed red. "Shit."

"Come on, Tosha, this isn't worth it," I said and tried to pull her arm, but she slipped it out of my grip.

"You don't know that," she replied before she typed eight digits into the keypad. My body flinched to run but the light above the keypad turned green and the vault door released. Tosha's smile radiated through the darkness. "I told you. And my name is Tosh, for the millionth time."

"Lead the way, then," I replied. "But if we get caught, I am totally telling them you forced me in here. Ok, *Tosh?*"

"Fine," she said as she slowly pulled the heavy vault door open.

"So uh…what was the code?"

"Month, day, and year the Warriors were established."

"Which was?"

She smirked. "Guess you'll need to find that out for yourself."

"Are you always such a know it all?"

"Yes," she replied and stepped inside the vault.

Thankfully it was fully lit and inside was a very long, very organized treasure trove. Slowly we walked down the aisle, gazing at the historical trinkets, paintings, and even small sculptures. While I marveled at some ancient weapons, Tosha continued down the aisle.

"Hey, Beck," she said halfway down, "I think you should see this."

I put back the mace I shouldn't have been holding in the first place and walked down to her. My head flinched when I realized what had caught her eye. In front of us hanging on the wall was what looked like a painting of me, but the medieval clothing gave way to the realization that it was Garrett.

"I'm guessing that's him?" Tosha asked, unable to stop herself from looking back and forth. "That's Garrett?" I nodded. "No wonder Devin and Victor freaked out."

"Um, yeah. It's a little unnerving."

"Why is his picture up there?" I asked.

"They're all fallen Warriors," Tosha replied and pointed down the aisle seeing that there were other paintings hanging down the line. "But it's all of them, anyone killed by Devin or during battle."

"Why would Victor have the ones Devin killed up on the wall? Devin was all about how they'd betrayed them."

Tosha shrugged. "They're still Victor's sires. I guess he can't throw them away as easily as everyone thinks he can," she said and pointed to a glass case underneath the painting that held a simple wooden bow with notches filed near the center grip. "That must be his bow. It has the grooves just like yours."

"Yeah, sure does," I groaned.

Tosha stepped forward and pulled a box down from the shelf underneath the bow. "These must be some of his things," she said as she opened the box and picked through the rest of the contents. "A few arrows, some clothing…oh wow."

"What? What did you find?"

From deep within the box Tosha pulled out a gold medal or maybe it was a coin. Her eyes sparkled when she held it up.

"It's a Warrior pin," she replied as she began taking in all its details. "I mean it's bigger and not as defined, but that's definitely the Warrior seal."

"Pin? Seal? What are you talking about?"

She glared at me from underneath the lids of her eyes. "Every coven has a seal, it's like a coat of arms. When a Warrior is inducted, they get a pin that has the Warrior seal on it. This must be one of the originals. I guess they were medallions before they were pins."

"Cheaper too."

Tosha rolled her eyes as she stood from the floor. "Make fun of it all you want. This circle of gold is sacred to everyone in this place. It means you're a part of something important. Having this means you protect others above your own life." She stepped toward me, pulled my hand out, and placed the gold medallion in my hand. "Whether you like it or not, you're part of that legacy, but go ahead and keep making jokes. We're stronger than your insecurities."

When she brushed past I tried taking her hand, but she pulled away from me and kept walking toward the vault door. I looked down at my palm and found the gold Warrior medallion staring back at me, laughing at me and telling me I was douche. I shoved the damn thing in my pocket to shut it up and packed up the other items. Just as I slid the box back on the shelf there was a loud crack from the tunnel. Tosha flinched and looked out into the tunnel before waving me quickly toward the door. Without a second's hesitation I ran to her and together we slowly pushed the heavy vault door shut. Of course the tunnel was now pitch black, but you could hear someone coming from further down in the mysterious tunnel.

Thankfully Tosha could find her way using the thin sliver of light coming from the library and pulled me with her along the wall. But when the sound of someone whistling echoed through the tunnel, Tosha lost her nerve and bolted to the library door. Once we pushed the faux bookcase shut, the two of us burst into laughter.

"Oh my god," she huffed breathlessly, "I thought we were goners."

She smiled, and it was a real smile. She didn't give those often, and it looked really good on her.

I shoved my hand in my pocket and pulled out the gold medallion. "So what do we do with this?"

"You took it!"

My hand froze with the circle of gold suddenly burning a hole in my palm.

"I thought…well, I thought that's what…"

Just then the faux bookshelf flew open and I quickly slid the gold medallion in my pocket.

Jared walked casually into the library from the tunnel behind the bookcase. "Oh hey, guys. Whatcha doin'?"

"Nothing!" we replied loudly.

Jared pursed his lips and nodded skeptically. "Uh huh. Looks like nothing. How ya feeling, Beck? I know today was a little rough."

I held up my hands, showing my healed fingers. "I'm good thanks to Tosha."

"Tosh," she corrected.

Jared laughed. "Do I want to know how she healed your fingers?"

"It's not what you think, Jared," Tosha groaned. "What are you doing in here?"

"I live here."

"You don't live in the library."

"I could."

"You can read?"

Jared whistled before he replied, "Ouch. That is why I love ya, Tosh. I was just taking the long way around in order to avoid your sister."

"Oh good, you two at it again?"

"When are we not these days. Anyway, I'll leave you two to it then. Whatever *it* might be." Jared headed toward the door but turned back before stepping through. "Oh and Tosh, I'll delete the vault entry logs as long as you tell your sister you never saw me."

Tosha's eyes grew wide as she watched Jared walk out the door. "Yeah, ok."

Once the door shut, the two of us breathed a major sigh of relief.

"How did he know about the vault?"

"Jared may act like a punk, but he's very smart. He was Army Ranger at one time."

"Really?"

"Mm-hmm, before he became a big-time hacker. That's how Victor found him. Being a Ranger and a marksman was icing on the cake."

"Damn," I replied as we left the library.

"Thought he was just a punk, huh?"

I nodded. "Yeah, kinda. Why is he avoiding your sister? I thought they were together."

"Depends on the day. They'll hate each other, then screw like bunnies and get back together, then hate each other again. Shows you the true power of really good sex."

"Can't say I've had that kind of experience."

She didn't reply. We walked up the spiral staircase in silence, the awkwardness building between us as we reached my room.

"Hey," I said as I touched her arm and stopped her from walking past me, "did I say something that hurt you?"

She looked up at me and I could see the wall was up. "Of course not."

"If I did…"

"I said you didn't," she snapped.

I sighed knowing there wasn't much I was going to be able to do to get through her defenses. "Do you want to come in? We could watch a movie or something."

"I can't," she replied and looked at the floor. "I've got things to do."

"Like what?" I said softly, moving my hand from her arm down to her hand.

For a split second her fingers curled around my palm, but then she shook free and looked up at me. "Just things, ok? And remember to hide that medallion, by the way. If they know it exists and can't find it, they could come looking for it and Jared will put it together. Got it?"

"Yeah, I got it." She nodded and turned to leave. "Oh, and thanks."

"For what?"

"The pizza, the fingers, the felony."

She laughed and looked over her shoulder. "Let's keep that last part to ourselves. I'll come get you for breakfast tomorrow morning."

"Sure thing," I replied and watched her until she disappeared in her room a couple of doors down. Reluctantly I went inside my room, plopped down on the bed, and pulled out the gold medallion from my pocket. Just remembering how in awe Tosha was by this circle of gold made me wonder how Garrett went from Warrior to traitor.

A whole night of research and nothing to show for it. Except a smile. I got a smile from Natasha Cushlin. I did it once, I could do it again.

Chapter Ten

"You seem chipper this morning," Tosha said as we started down the hall, she with her bag of whips, me with my bow and quiver. If there was some music, we would have an awesome slow-mo video.

"Yeah well, this girl totally stood me up last night so all I could do was go to bed."

Tosha stopped and whipped her head around. "I did not..." she said loudly but when it echoed throughout the stone hallway she switched to a whisper, "...I did not stand you up. There was nothing to...stand you up...on."

"Could have fooled me," I replied and stepped past her to the big spiral staircase. "We had a great adventure last night which you cut short."

"Keep your voice down," she scolded as she ran to catch up with me.

"Who's listening?"

"Everyone! Vampires are all around, they can hear everything."

"So?"

She sighed loudly and rolled her eyes as we stepped off the stairs and headed into the dining room.

"Are you going to eat today? Or die from hunger like you did yesterday," she asked rhetorically as we grabbed plates at the buffet.

I didn't answer her snide comment but loaded my plate with eggs and bacon, fruit, toast and even potatoes. Once we sat down at a table I noticed it was a lot less crowded than yesterday, but maybe that's because it was Sunday. Maybe everyone else got to sleep in but us. Lucky bastards.

"What did you do last night?" I asked and shoved a strip of bacon in my mouth. Tosha didn't reply and just kept her eyes on her plate. Today, I wasn't having it. "Tosha, why is it so hard to have a conversation with you sometimes? It was just a simple question."

"I didn't do anything, ok?" she snapped. "I watched a movie and did some yoga. That's it, why are you making it such a big deal that I wanted to have some time to myself? And since you seem to keep forgetting, my name is Tosh, not Tosha."

"Morning," the trainee named Roberts said before sitting down across from us. Tosha immediately snapped her mouth shut and concentrated on her plate. "Don't mind me, I just didn't want to sit with the morons."

I sighed and had to ask. "By the morons, you mean…"

"The wonder triplets over there," he replied and pointed with his fork over to where Nub, Bush, and Princess were sitting. "But uh, you guys were arguing, so don't stop on my account. I just need to eat."

"Cool," I replied and looked to Tosha. "So seriously, you're the one who wanted to hang last night, so why run away from me just to go and do nothing? I thought we were…"

"He wasn't serious, Beckett!" Tosha said loudly and glared at me with eyes so big and full of rage I swear my face was melting.

"Calm down, Scarecrow, I totally meant it," Roberts replied without looking up from his plate and continued to eat.

Tosh stood abruptly from the table. "Oh my god, I'm not talking about this." When she stepped away from the table I got up from my chair to follow and she planted her hand in my chest. "Don't."

Without another word she turned and left the dining room. Roberts was laughing softly through the eggs stuffed in his mouth. I sighed in defeat and took my bow from where it hung on the back of the chair.

"I have to hand it to ya," Roberts said once he'd swallowed his eggs, "you've got balls going after her."

"Why do you say that?"

He laughed again. "Because she's a hard nut to crack, that's all. The first thing the Warriors teach us is to keep our guard up. When it's down, people get hurt. Tosh takes it to an extreme. But she's been that way since her accident, it's just gotten worse since she's been in the program."

"You knew her before this?"

He nodded. "Yeah. We were both at Facility West. Before her accident she was friends with everyone, but after? Well, you see how she is. And it's a shame really," he said and plowed into the remainder of his breakfast.

"What's a shame?"

Why did I keep asking questions?

With his mouth half full he replied, "It's a shame she's banking on getting inducted."

"Why wouldn't she? Aren't you all?"

He shook his head. "I've heard they're only inducting one of us, and well, it's going to be me."

This guy was an ass.

"Yeah, well, we'll see about that," I said and hurried out of the dining room. It wasn't the strongest comeback, but I couldn't stand looking at his smug face a second longer.

After I stepped out of the dining room and rounded the kitchen it hit me that I wasn't exactly sure how to get out to the courtyard. When I came to the front doors I knew I was close, but thankfully I heard a voice I knew.

"Hey kid," Jared said behind me and placed a hand on my shoulder. "Thinking of bailing?"

I laughed and shook my head. "Oh no. Just lost."

He patted me on the shoulder and lead me down a hallway that looked vaguely familiar. It struck me that he was once again wearing thick sweats and gloves, with sunglasses in his hand.

"I thought Tosh would bring you out."

"Yeah well, I pissed her off so…"

He groaned over me. "The Cushlin sisters are very volatile, this I know very well. Tosh is definitely better than Nikki, but when either of them flips that switch it's just best to walk away."

"Is that why you were hiding from Nikki last night?" I asked as we stepped out into the courtyard.

"I hide from Nikki on a regular basis," Jared replied. "Sometimes a relationship needs space."

Similar to yesterday, there was a table lined with arrows and a target standing roughly fifty feet away. Nerves started to settle in my stomach, especially with the trainees warming up on the opposite side of the courtyard.

"Hey kid," Jared said and shook me back to the present, "you gonna start shooting? Or just have a stroke? I really can't tell."

I shook the nerves away and twirled one of the arrows around in my fingers.

"Let's do a few warm-ups, nice and easy," he said as I took my stance.

As I stretched the arrow and string back, I took a deep breath in, holding both the arrow and breath in until my sight zeroed in on the bullseye. Three, two, one, release.

Failure. The damn thing hit the right side of the target and ricocheted off toward the trainees who had just started running around the courtyard

"Shit."

"Yeah, that sucked," Jared laughed. "Let's try another one, and remember what we talked about yesterday. Imagine a clear blanket of silence coming up over you, helping you tune out all the noise. Now shake it out, and take a deep breath. Come on now, shake it out."

"Do I have to?"

"After that horrible shot, yes, you have to."

Reluctantly I shook my arms and legs, doing the shake dance that for some reason made Jared laugh. Once done, I laced the second arrow and as I pulled it back I breathed in deeply and imagined it draping an invisible force field around me, silencing all the other activity around me. It wasn't perfect, but I couldn't hold my breath anymore and released the arrow. This time, it at least hit the target, the outer edge, but at least it was a hit.

"Better," Jared said and handed me a third arrow. "Now speed it up, don't worry so much. Just make it a fluid motion from start to finish. In battle, you won't have time to think it through."

"In battle?"

"You never know. Just try it. I'll give you a count of three before I hit you in the balls."

"Wait, what?"

"One."

"Wait a second," I said and quickly laced the arrow.

"Two."

I pulled the string and arrow back and didn't hear whether he said three or not before I released the arrow.

"Boo-yah!" Jared shouted when the arrow sank into the bullseye. "That's what I'm talking about it. Now do it about a hundred times."

I laughed and saw Tosha looking over at the target with a smile on her face.

"Stop ogling my girlfriend's sister," Jared groaned and handed me another arrow.

"I wasn't...ogling," I replied, but he raised a skeptical brow.

"Ok, one more warm-up before we really get into things."

"Like what?" I asked as I took another arrow from his hand.

He shrugged. "Just some defensive training, nothing intense."

"Cool," I replied and pulled the last arrow back to my cheek.

"So what did you steal out of Victor's vault last night?" Jared asked just as I released the arrow in a panic causing it to go flying beyond the target's right side and bounce off the stone wall.

I lowered my bow and turned away from him as I answered, "Steal? I didn't steal…"

"Dad knows every inch of that vault and everything that's in it. If one speck of dust is missing, he'll know. It's better you tell me what you guys were doing in there last night so I can defend you."

My heart was racing as I pulled the gold medallion of out my pocket and opened my palm. "Just this. It was all my idea. Tosha didn't know I had taken it until we were out of the vault."

Even from behind his dark sunglasses I could see that his eyes were wide in shock over the circle of gold. After only another second or two he closed my fingers over my palm and said, "Where did you find that?"

I swallowed and lowered my voice as I put the medal back in my pocket. "It was in a box with Garrett's things. His bow is even there in a glass case."

"Well don't let anyone catch you with that. Those were the first Warrior pins ever given out. If anyone sees that, you'll be in a shitload of trouble."

"I was just trying to find out more about Garrett, that's all."

"Well here's a solution that doesn't require breaking and entering. Just ask."

"Ask what?"

Jared scratched the back of his neck impatiently. "Ask Victor about him, hell, ask Devin. The two of them were very close from what I was told."

"Devin won't talk to me."

"Then talk to Victor."

I shrugged uncomfortably. "I wouldn't even know where to find him or even what to ask. Besides, he kind of scares me."

"Yeah, he's pretty intense," Jared replied with a wide smile. "But you're technically family, and he's very serious about family. If you go to him, I think you'll be surprised."

I sighed and put a few arrows in my quiver. "I'll think about it. Have you heard anything about my dad?"

He shook his head. "I think Tosh is keeping tabs on that."

I sighed again and pulled an arrow from my quiver. Like Jared had instructed, as I stretched it back I imagined an invisible blanket coming over me and shrouding me in silence. With an exhale, I released the arrow and it sank into the target just left of center.

"What about my mom? Did they get any leads?"

"Sorry, kid, not that I know of, but there's another team going out tonight. Don't worry, we'll find her. But for now, let's work on speed. You're taking way too much time. I need you to shoot three arrows from your quiver within the next fifteen seconds, or I hit you in the balls."

"What is with you and hitting me in the balls?"

"Because it's the only way to get you to move faster," he said and looked down at his watch. "Are you ready?"

"No!"

"Great. Ready in three, two…"

"Jared, wait!"

"Go!"

Damn it! Don't hit me in the balls, don't hit me in the balls, I kept repeating in my head as I pulled the first arrow from my quiver and shot it without the slightest bit of concentration and it hit the very edge of the target.

"Seven seconds left," Jared announced and I pulled the second arrow out from the quiver and quickly stretched it back. When it too hit the edge of the target Jared announced. "Four."

I pulled the last arrow from my quiver.

"Three."

I threaded and stretched the arrow back.

"Two."

I looked down at the target, I wasn't going to miss it again, and released the arrow. Whooofpt.

"One!"

Dead fucking center.

"Hell yeah!" I screamed and punched the air. In response, Jared pulled my bow forward causing it to whip between my legs and catch me in the balls. I keeled over and landed on my knees, unable to breathe while shocks of pain radiated out from my groin.

"Why…I…made it!"

He pointed forward toward the target. "Yeah, but look at those first two."

"I fucking hate you," I groaned as I slowly pushed myself back up.

"Yeah, but sometimes hate means love."

"Not this time," I replied and adjusted myself.

"You can't hide your feelings from me," Jared said and handed me three more arrows. "Let's try that again, and then we'll work on some defensive work. Ok?"

"Do I have a choice?" I groaned.

"Not really. Fifteen seconds on the clock. Ready, go!"

"Beckett," someone said in my ear, "Beckett, wake up."

"Hmmm?" I whined and reluctantly stretched my eyes open to find Natasha leaning over me. "Tosha?"

"I'm just going to stop arguing with you about my name," she sighed and rose up. "Are you ok?"

"What?" I asked confused, my head still foggy.

"You're sleeping on a bench in the middle of the hallway."

I looked around me and was a little confused. "I finished training with Jared and just sat down for a minute. What time is it?"

"It's a little after five," she replied and picked up my bow from the ground. "Not used to any physical activities, huh?"

I shook my head and painfully stood from the bench. My back and hip hurt from the hard surface, but my hands, arms, legs, and somehow even my hair hurt from Jared's defense training. "Jared kicked my ass."

"Yeah, I saw," she replied and my entire chest caved. "Come on, Sleeping Beauty, we can't be late for dinner."

"Yeah, sorry," I said and began to follow her down the corridor. "Um, why can't we be late for dinner?"

She looked over her shoulder and handed my bow back to me. "Christine made mashed potatoes."

"Should I know what that means? Why are we walking so fast?" I asked, trying desperately to keep up with her pace even though my quads and calves were burning.

"Christine runs the kitchen and tonight she made mashed potatoes. We have to get a good seat," she replied.

A moment later we stepped into the dining room and it was packed, which was a vast difference from this morning. When I stepped toward the buffet line, Tosha pulled on my elbow and pointed over to where Jared was sitting and waving us over.

"You save me a seat and I'll get us food," she said and stepped away. I had yet to see this side of her. She was excited and almost giddy, but I had no idea why. Was there a show? The Warrior choral singers?

"Hey man," I said and sat across from Jared. "What's going on?"

"Christine made mashed potatoes," Jared replied with a wide smile.

"Yeah, I've heard that. What the hell does it mean?"

Jared was almost bouncing in his seat as he replied, "Well, my niece and nephew, for whatever reason, go insane when it comes to mashed potatoes and it always ends up with one of them getting a face full. It's awesome, especially since neither Bri or Cameron seem to be able to ever stop them."

"And that's why everyone's here?"

He nodded with wide eyes. "Oh yeah. It's highly entertaining. Oh, here they come," he said excitedly and hit me from across the table just as the two kids ran into the dining room with Cameron walking in behind them.

"Uncle Jared!" the little boy called and ran over.

"Jack Attack," Jared cheered and picked him up off the floor. "Where's your mom?"

Once his feet were back on the floor he replied, "She went with Auntie Kyla because she said we were driving her nuts."

"I'm sure that's true," Jared laughed. "Ok, love you. Go eat."

"There's tatoes tonight," he said happily and ran toward the small table where his sister was already sitting.

When Jared turned around, his eyes were large. "This is gonna be good."

"Why's that?" I asked just as Tosha put a plate down in front of me. I was happy to see two big pieces of chicken, a small bundle of green beans, and a mound of creamy mashed potatoes complete with brown gravy. "Hey, thanks, this is perfect."

"You're welcome," she replied as she sat down next to me, her portions heavier on the green beans and only a dollop of potatoes. "I figured you for a potatoes kind of guy."

"You figured right," I smiled and dug into them.

"Jer," Tosha said softly as she began cutting her chicken, "is Cameron all alone?"

Jared nodded vigorously, a soft squeal coming out of his clinched teeth. "The kids'll definitely take advantage of that. Don't get me wrong, I would give my life for both of them, but they can be little monsters when they want to be. Let's hope they'll deliver for my friend Beckett here."

I swallowed my potatoes and answered. "Ah, thanks, man. If you hadn't tortured me for hours on end that might have actually brought a tear to my eye."

He laughed for a moment, but then quickly stopped when Nikki sat down next to him with a full plate. He must have known he was in for it just from the bitchy expression she had on her face.

"Thanks for waiting, Jer. I'd like to think you're here to eat with me, but since there are mashed potatoes and the kids are here, I seriously doubt that," Nikki said nastily without even the slightest glance in Jared's direction.

"I thought you had a class tonight," he replied.

"Whatever," she hissed. "Maybe if I threw mashed potatoes everywhere like the kids you'd actually want to see me."

Jared groaned and let his head fall down on his forearm. "Not now, Nik."

"Nikki, what are you going to school for?" I asked, trying to take the heat off of Jared.

Slowly she raised her eyes to look at me from underneath her brow. "Nursing."

"Oh," I replied, trying to nod confidently, "I...I can see that."

Suddenly a calm came over the room as Cameron stood over the children's table with two plates in his hands.

"Olivia, Jackson," he began as he placed a plate down in front of each of them, "you will eat like good, well-mannered children. All your food will go into your mouth. You will not touch it with your hands and you certainly will not throw it at each other. Is that understood?"

"Yes, Ada," they replied in unison and picked up their forks.

"Let the games begin," Jared said and rubbed his hands together excitedly. "Tosh, how has training been going these last few days?"

"Good," she replied and wiped her mouth with her napkin. "I finally got one over on Roberts today."

I laughed. "I knew I was right."

"About what exactly?" Tosh asked with a questioning look.

"Well," I shrugged dramatically, "he made some asshole comment about how there's only one spot for the Warriors and that he was going to get it. So I basically challenged him and eluded that it would be you. And then you kicked his butt. So overall, I was right. Point, Dawes," I said and shoved the delicious mashed potatoes into my mouth.

"You said that to Roberts?"

I nodded. "Of course I did."

"You get a couple more over on Roberts and the spot will definitely be yours, Tosh," Jared said which for some reason made Nikki snarl and roll her eyes.

"Thanks," Tosh replied shyly. "At least you guys are behind me."

"Is that some crack against me?" Nikki said nastily and threw her fork down.

Tosha shook her head and looked around for anyone who might be watching. "Nik, no, I didn't mean you…"

"Bullshit," Nikki hissed. "Just because I don't want to lose my only remaining family member, I'm the bad guy."

"Nikki, please not here."

"Just kill yourself now rather than wait for them to do it."

"Nikki!" Jared shouted, causing those around us to turn around and look. Even Cameron and the kids stopped what they were doing and looked over.

Tosha quickly pushed her chair back and stepped away from the table. I looked over at Jared who was glaring at Nikki and whispering harshly at the side of her face. Nikki didn't look the least bit remorseful over the terrible thing she had just said to her sister.

"Olivia, do not even think…" Cameron began and leaned in toward his daughter as her hand dropped near her mashed potatoes. Unfortunately, the distraction didn't allow him to see the flying blob of potatoes coming from the other direction until they splattered on the side of his face. He flinched once they hit, but then slowly turned to see his son with a joyous smile.

The entire dining room erupted in laughter, and if I wasn't still in shock over Nikki's statement I probably would have joined them. With a sigh I pushed my chair back from the table and grabbed my plate as well as Tosh's.

"See you tomorrow, Jer."

"You're leaving?" he asked.

"I'm gonna take Tosha her food."

"Good idea. Tell Tosh that Nikki will apologize to her later."

"Don't tell me what to do," Nikki said loudly and I didn't bother staying around for the rest.

I made my way out of the dining hall and headed toward the spiral staircase with plates in hand. The walk gave me time to calm down and gather my thoughts. What in the world could have happened to cause Nikki to wish death on her sister? Why does Tosh always just seem to take it? She certainly had no qualms about yelling at me, so why didn't she stand up against her sister?

When Tosh's room was only a few feet away my stomach started to flip nervously. She was vulnerable right now, and I pictured her as a caged animal in the corner of her room. I placed her plate on my forearm and knocked on her door. There was a murmur from the other side, but I couldn't make it out.

"Tosha, it's me," I said to the door and heard a reply that sounded like she said to come in, so I opened the door and stepped inside.

"What the!" Tosha shouted loudly before she turned her back to me. She must have been changing her shirt since she was clinging it in her hands trying to get it over her head. With her back to me I could see in more detail the extent of her scars curling and swirling deeply around her. "I said hold on!"

"I thought you said come in," I replied and kicked the door shut.

She whipped her head around at the sound of the door shutting. "I didn't say come in, and I certainly didn't say you could stay. Get out!"

"Tosha, your sports bra covers more than most bikinis, it's no big deal."

"It's not...the bra I care about," she said as she angrily pulled her shirt down her waist.

"Is it the scars?"

"You don't just barge into someone's room like that."

"Tosha, I've seen the scars. You showed me, remember?"

"What. Do. You. Want."

Although she was still glaring at me I could see that she'd been crying.

"Two things. One, I brought up your dinner," I said and placed her plate down on the corner of her bed. "And two, Jared said to tell you that Nikki will apologize."

She laughed and relaxed her glare. "I doubt Jared could get her to cross the street, let alone apologize to me."

"She should still apologize," I said and sat down on the floor, putting my plate on the edge of the bed near hers.

Tosha sighed and looked at her plate on the bed, her face showing the debate that was going on in her head of whether she would sit down or not. Thankfully with another sigh she gave in and sat down on the floor.

As she picked up her fork she asked, "Why did you bring my plate up?"

I swallowed my potatoes and looked at her curiously. "Well, I figured you were hungry, and...well...who else am I going to eat with? Certainly not Jared and your bitchy sister."

"Thank you," she said quietly.

"You're welcome. But you should know that you missed Jack getting Cameron right in the mouth with mashed potatoes."

"What!" Tosha shouted and spit a bit of chicken out of her mouth. "I missed that?"

I nodded. "You did, it was pretty awesome."

"Damn Nikki."

"Got that right," I replied and cut into my chicken. "Can I ask you something without you biting my head off?"

She raised her eyebrow and put her forkful of chicken back down on her plate. "Generally if you have to ask, it means I will probably bite your head off no matter what."

"Yeah, but I've put it out there, so that means you can't."

"I'm not sure it works that way."

"I am," I replied with my most charming smile and I was happy to receive a smirk in reply.

"Fine. What do you want to ask?"

"So, what did Nikki mean?"

"I think telling me to kill myself was pretty self-explanatory."

I shook my head. "No, no. She said do it before they do it for you. Who was she talking about?"

Tosha scrunched her face and tilted her head, seemingly astonished by my stupidity. "Uh, the Warriors."

I shook my head again. "What about them?"

She stared at me blankly. I was definitely an idiot in her eyes. "What do you think will happen with the trainee the Warriors pick to become one of them?" I shook my head. "They Turn you."

"I don't know what that means."

"It means they turn you into a vampire. They drain most of your blood and then make you drink their blood. The vamp blood takes over your body, and eventually stops your heart. That's why Nikki said it that way."

"And that's what you want? To be…a…a vampire?"

"I wouldn't be in the Warrior Training Program if I didn't."

"Yeah, but you're…"

"Young? I'm a year older than Jared was when he was Turned."

"Well, that's part of it."

"Oh, is the other part because I'm a girl? Because that's bullshit. There are other female Warriors."

"Yeah, but can't you just be a hybrid Warrior?"

"There's only been one other hybrid Warrior, and that was Brianna. I'm not near as powerful as she was. Besides, I don't want to stay human."

"So…you *want* to be a vampire."

"Of course I want to be a vampire," she shouted and threw her fork down on her plate. "Why wouldn't I? I get to help people and be a part of a coven with a tremendous history. I'll be surrounded by family for eons who will support me, which I certainly don't have now. And I hope to god that when I'm Turned, the vampire blood takes away these goddamn scars. So yes, Beckett, I want to be a vampire."

I nodded slowly, but the stupidity just continued to come out of my mouth. "And you don't want to get married? Have kids?"

Tosha's eyes flared, as did her nostrils before she replied in a very pointed tone, "Not all women dream about getting married and having kids. And not that it's any of your business, but I can't have kids. I want different things for my life. Is that ok with you, Mr. Dawes?"

"Uh…sure," I replied and looked down at my plate. "It was just a question, Tosha."

"Will you ever call me Tosh?"

"Sorry. You just don't look like a Tosh to me."

"Good thing it isn't up to you."

A silence fell over us while we picked at our plates. When the silence became uncomfortable, I asked, "Why do you let Nikki treat you that way?"

Tosha's eyes widened and I kept a cool expression as I put the chicken in my mouth and causally began to chew. I wasn't going to let her hide from me anymore.

"Why do you care?"

"Because no one, especially your sister, should talk to you that way."

"But why does it matter? It doesn't affect you."

"But it does," I replied sternly and put my fork down. "Tosha, I like you. There, I said it." She didn't yell, she barely reacted at all. "And since you're not freaking out right now, I don't think it's much of a surprise, and I think that you might like me too." She raised her eyebrow ever so slightly. "Maybe just a sliver, but it's there."

"And that's another reason why you brought me dinner?"

I shrugged and looked down at my plate. "I wanted to be with you."

"Is that why you're asking all these questions?"

"You know my family's deepest, darkest secret, I figure it's only fair that you finally start opening up a little more about yourself. So I ask again, why is Nikki always so nasty to you?"

Tosha lowered her eyes and began to open her mouth to answer, but then shook her head.

"Tosh, I'm not here to hurt you," I said and gently touched her hand. "Why can't you open up to me just a little bit?"

Her lips tightened as she raised her eyes to look at me. "I don't open up to anyone because I don't want it to be used against me later."

"I would never do that," I replied defensively.

"I don't know that, Beck."

I slid closer to her. "Then give me a chance, Tosha. That's all that I'm asking for."

She swallowed slowly and looked at her plate as she said, "Nikki blames me for our dad leaving."

"Oh."

"Yeah, oh," she replied and picked up a forkful of potatoes. "My dad was a solitary. He didn't belong to a coven, he didn't have a vamp family or other sires. He liked the freedom of roaming around the world seeing and doing things he could never have done when he was human. But one day he met my mom and there was this instant connection.

"He would stay for a few weeks and then get antsy. So he'd go wandering, that's what my mom called it. He'd leave for a little while but always come back. It wasn't normal, but they loved each other. A couple years later they had Nikki, which my dad certainly wasn't prepared for. According to my mom he struggled a lot when Nikki was a baby, and his wandering would last longer. It was tough on my mom, but she loved him so much she was willing to deal with it."

She sighed and tightened her arms around her chest. "A few years later they get pregnant with me, and he tried to do better, but he was gone months at a time. Nikki would totally monopolize Dad's time whenever he was home, so I was always closer to my mom. Nikki would cry for days whenever Dad would leave."

"So she did have feelings at one time," I said snidely.

"Shocker, isn't it?" she laughed. "When I was about four years old, Mom had gone out for some reason and Dad was watching us, which didn't happen very often. I'm playing out in our yard and he asks me to come inside. I come running in from the yard and trip on our cement patio face down."

"Ouch," I replied. "But you must have healed quickly."

"My healing ability wasn't as fast as it is now. When I fell, I broke my front teeth, scraped up my whole face, it was just a bloody mess. My dad ran out and brought me back inside. While he was trying to help me, I guess the blood was too much for him and he bit me."

"Bit…you?"

She nodded and began to play with a green bean on her plate. "He almost killed me. Thankfully Nikki was there and she ran to our silver drawer and hit his arm with a piece of silver chain. The pain was enough for him to pull his fangs out and then he realized what he'd done. He was so guilty about it that he decided he couldn't trust himself around two kids and left for good."

"Wait, so you never saw him again?"

She shook her head sadly. "We got cards on our birthdays, but even that stopped after a few years. It took a real toll on my mother, and even though he never came back, she couldn't bring herself to move on. She got depressed and started drinking more and more. One night she took us for a drive, but she'd had a few. She ended up flying over a guardrail and rolling our car down an embankment. Nikki and I survived, obviously. But, uh…you never forget the sound of your mother's last gurgling breath."

I stopped eating and put my fork down on the plate. "Tosha, I'm so sorry."

She shrugged. "If it had been a few years earlier, Nik and I may not have been as lucky. The first responders thought we were some kind of miracle coming away without any injuries. If they only knew, right?"

"What happened?"

"Well, we didn't know how to find our dad, he wasn't even on our birth certificates. So they had no choice but to put us in foster care, which was really hard for Nikki. She kept throwing fits that would cause the foster families to send us back. I think it was after the fourth or fifth family they decided to separate us. They sent me to a great foster family, but Nikki stayed behind. So while I was flourishing, she was getting sent to the worst places to get her problems under control."

"Lot of good it did," I teased, and thankfully she laughed a little. "It's not your fault that you went someplace better than she did. Nikki is fully responsible for what happened to her because of her behavior."

"I know," she said with only a hint of confidence. "Doesn't make the guilt any easier."

"I can understand that. So how did you go from foster care to that hybrid place?"

"You mean the Facility?" I nodded. "You should really remember that. Facility West will be able to help you once all this nonsense is over."

"Yeah, yeah. Facility West, I'll remember it. How did you get there?"

She narrowed her eyes at me, but then finally replied, "I was with my foster father and we were climbing this big tree they had in the backyard. I was near the top when my hand slipped and I fell and broke my arm."

"I think I can see where this is going."

She nodded. "My forearm was hanging from my elbow, and by the time we got to the hospital it had started to heal. They kept bringing in all these doctors to try and figure it out, they were taking gallons of blood. My foster family was claiming a miracle, they were talking to news outlets and everything. Then the next day a very pale man walked into my hospital room, told me he knew what I was and that I was in danger of exposing the vampire race."

"Who was he?"

"He was what we call a Gatherer. It's basically a group of vamps that find and help hybrids and bring them to the Facility. It was around the same time when hybrids were being hunted, so I was lucky I wasn't found by the other side. When I got to the Facility I told them I had a sister with the same gift and they sent out another Gatherer to try and find her.

"What they didn't know, was that Nikki's Gatherer, a man by the name of Aidan Pierce, was actually working for the woman who was hunting hybrids. He took Nikki, brainwashed her, and got her to do terrible things for him. So, the reason Nikki hates me is because if I hadn't tripped over my damn foot when I was four years old our dad may have stuck around longer, our mother wouldn't have died, we wouldn't have been separated in foster care, and she wouldn't have been taken by a maniac."

"Well, when you put it that way, it really is all your fault," I laughed.

"I tried to tell you," she replied with a smile and began cutting the last half of her chicken.

"So how exactly did that guy Aidan get Nikki to do bad things for him?"

She smirked. "He convinced her he was our father."

"What?!" I shouted, almost knocking my plate off the bed. "How? I mean, did he at least look like your dad?"

"Not really. But he was a master manipulator. He found her weakness right away and preyed on it. She was so desperate to believe Aidan was our dad that even when they tortured her, she was actively convincing herself to ignore the truth."

"But why didn't your actual father come back? Don't they have some kind of vampire calling tree or something?"

She licked her lips and sat back. "There's a lot we don't know when it comes to that. Jared and Alex did some digging, looking for any kind of trail and everything stopped right before Aidan took Nikki. We know he was alive when my mom died, but no idea if he knew about the accident. But Aidan knew so many details about my dad and our lives that we think Aidan found him first, learned everything he could, and then killed him."

Her statement hung in the air, not so much the words, but the lack of feeling stating that her father had been killed.

"I'm sorry, Tosha."

She shrugged and leaned back on her hands. "I barely knew him. Losing my mother was harder because we were much closer. She's the one who actually always called me Tosh."

"Now everything makes sense."

She smiled and rolled her eyes. "I know I'm a pain in the ass about my name. But Natasha sounds like a Russian spy. Nik calls me Nat because our dad always called us Nik and Nat, or just NikNat. So it's either a spy, a bug, or Tosh. I choose Tosh."

"I didn't know. I'll do better, I promise."

She sat up but kept her eyes on her hands. "It's not that I…hate…what you call me."

"I'm sorry, Miss Cushlin, could you repeat that?"

"Stop being a jerk," she said, giving me a stinging look from underneath her lashes. "Tosh or Tosha, that's it."

"Yes ma'am," I replied and sat at attention.

She gave me another smirk and leaned back in toward her plate. "Did you actually say that stuff to Roberts?"

"I meant it, too. Roberts' is an ass."

"Got that right," she replied and finished off her green beans.

"He told me that he knew you when you were at that Facility place." She nodded and wiped her mouth with her napkin. "He...uh...said he knew you before the accident."

She nodded again. "He was Ty's best friend."

"Who's Ty?"

"My ex," she replied. "He died, and I was left like this."

"So how exactly did you get your scars?"

"You're pushing it, Dawes."

I shrugged. "A man has to try."

A shroud of darkness settled across Tosha's face.

"Actually, no you don't," she said and rose from the floor, being sure to keep her back to me. "There's no point, Beckett."

Slowly I stood from the floor and stepped up behind her. Gently I touched the back of her arm and braced impact, but after a couple of seconds I realized she was letting me touch her. Maybe the wall was crumbling.

"Tosha," I began and moved even closer, her back only inches from my chest, "I'm just asking you not to shut me out."

She shuttered and went to take a step away, but I stupidly squeezed her arm to stop her.

"I can break your fingers."

"I know you can," I replied and released my grip on her arm. "Just give me a chance."

She shook her head. "I can't."

"At least say it to my face then."

With a sigh she turned stiffly around, her lips pursed and twitching while trying to keep her composure. "You're a distraction."

"I'm just standing here, no way am I a distraction. Got another excuse?"

"It's not an excuse," she snapped. "They are weeks away from choosing one of us to become a Warrior. I need to put all my focus on winning that spot, and you keep getting in the way."

I shook my head. "Sorry, Tosha, you keep rescuing me and bringing me into secret vaults, that wasn't me. You keep flipping this switch on whether you have the time of day for me. Just keep it on for a little longer before you get scared and shut it off again."

The edges of Tosha's nostrils were flaring while the rims of her eyes became glassy. "Please stop."

"I've seen you heal, I now know about your parents, hell, I've seen the scars. I'm still here, Tosha. I'm right here."

With a slight shake of her head she cleared her throat and the wall was rebuilt.

"Beckett, you've been through a very traumatic event," she said in an even tone. "It's not uncommon for you to form a bond with a someone who shared that event with you. That's all this is. Once all of this blows over, these feelings will pass."

I blinked slowly. "A traumatic...event?"

"It's perfectly natural," she replied and took a step away from me.

"Well, that's the first time I've heard that one. You could have just said you weren't interested, Tosh. Considering the traumatic event we've been through, the least you could do is be honest."

"I can be your friend, Beckett, that's it. I have nothing to give to you, or anyone for that matter. That is me being honest, happy?"

I took a step forward to close the gap between us and Tosha's chest began to rise and fall quickly. Slowly I touched my fingertips to her forehead and traced them down the side of her cheek.

"You neglected to say you weren't interested," I said softly and leaned into her. She didn't pull away, she didn't flinch, instead her lips parted ever so slightly while her eyes were inviting me to come closer.

"Cushlin!" someone shouted and banged on the door.

"Shit," Tosha hissed and immediately stepped around me.

When she opened the door, Connor was standing in the doorway with an irritated look on his face. I was only half an inch away from kissing Tosh and he had to interrupt. Did he have some kind of radar?

"I thought you wanted to train tonight. What's he doing here?" Connor said and jutted his chin in my direction.

"He brought me some dinner because Nikki was being a bitch to me and I got upset. That's all. I'm ready though..."

"Look, Tosh, you're the one asking me for help. If you can't take this seriously…"

"No, no! I am. I'm ready, really I am," Tosha replied nervously. Connor really knew how to manipulate her.

When she bent down to grab her plate I leaned down to stop her. "I'll take it back down to the dining room. Have a good practice."

"I'm sorry."

"No need to apologize," I replied and enjoyed the relief I saw in her.

"You should call your dad," she said and pulled her bag up onto her shoulder.

"I can do that?"

"Yeah, they said he was doing well enough. So uh…see you tomorrow."

I nodded and she stepped out of the room. Once she disappeared around the doorway I held up my hand and waved to Connor. "Connor, always a pleasure, man."

He growled, literally growled, before turning and following Tosha down the hall.

"Dick," I said under my breath. I assumed it was quiet enough since he didn't come charging back into the room to kick my ass.

Tired and a little weary from the last couple of minutes I sat on the corner of Tosha's bed. If only that fucker had waited two more seconds I would have kissed her. Maybe then she wouldn't have left so quickly. She let her guard down tonight and I was there with her. Tomorrow was another day, but I knew very well I'd have to start from scratch and slowly removed one brick at a time.

With a sigh I took my phone from my back pocket and called my dad. After only the second ring his face came up on the screen.

"Becks," he said with a big smile, but then flinched in pain.

"Oh my god, Dad, you look good!"

He laughed but then flinched with pain. "Oh, don't make me laugh. Thanks, though, I don't feel all that good, but at least I look pretty."

"No, Dad, you look so much better than I thought you would."

"Well I have to give credit to the doc," he said and tilted the phone up to show Dr. Ryan just over his shoulder. "Say hi, doc."

"Hey Beckett," Dr. Ryan said and waved. "I was just finishing up with your dad. He's healing pretty well."

"How's the heart?" I asked.

Dad shrugged. "Haven't had a heart attack yet."

"Dad," I groaned. "Doc? How's his heart?"

"He's doing well, Beckett, we're keeping a good eye on him. Don't keep him up too long, he does need his rest."

"Thank you, doc," I said and Dad tilted the phone back down. "Hey, Dad."

"Hey, Becks. I miss you, son. I wish you could be here with me."

"I know, Dad, me too. I'm hoping they'll let me leave soon to come see you. They're afraid Garrett is watching me."

My dad's face flinched at the sound of Garrett's name. "Have you heard anything about your mother?" he asked nervously.

I shook my head. "I know they have people going out and trying to find where Garrett's hiding, but nothing's come of it yet. Dad, I'm so sorry," I said with sudden emotion tingling my nose and eyes.

"Becks, come on now. You have nothing to be sorry about. We'll get through this. We just need to get your mother back."

"I know," I nodded and tried shaking the emotions away. "So…uh…I don't know how to ask this, but uh…"

"Am I a werewolf?" he interrupted.

My breath caught in my throat. "Well, yeah. Do they know?"

Dad lowered his eyes as he answered, "They took my blood. You'd think it was radioactive with the way they were acting. Anyway, Doc Ryan said they found an unknown virus. Although they can't say for sure, considering what happened, they believe I've been infected."

I froze. Even though everyone had already told me that it was inevitable, it was still hard to hear. My dad, the nicest, kindest man that had ever lived, a man who sacrificed and raised another man's son, didn't deserve this.

"I'll get him, Dad," I said angrily. "I will make him pay."

"Becks," he warned, "let the professionals do their thing. I mean, I'm guessing they're as professional as you can get for this kind of thing."

"I know," I replied and rubbed my face in frustration. "I'm going to let you go, the doc said you needed rest. I'll call you again tomorrow."

"Ok, son," he replied and then his expression turned very serious. "And remember, you are my boy, my son."

Tears instantly formed in my eyes at my father's intensity and I found it hard to answer. "And you're my dad."

He nodded, fighting emotions of his own. "Ok. Just so we're clear."

"Yeah, Dad, we're perfectly clear."

"Love you, Becks."

"Love you too, Dad. I'll call you tomorrow, get some rest."

When the screen went dead, I found myself needing a moment to compose myself. When did this nightmare end? With a deep breath I stacked the dinner plates on top of one another and headed out of Tosha's bedroom back down to the dining room. I was impressed that I could find my way back and forth so easily now. Just as I approached the dining room Cameron came out holding a child in each hand by the back of their shirt. Both children were covered in food.

"Did I miss the food fight?" I asked and Cameron looked up in my direction with an exhausted expression.

"If these children are ever allowed to eat again, I will be surprised," Cameron growled.

"But I wike to eat!" Livy shouted.

"Really? It appears you like throwing it at your brother more than you like eating it," he replied sternly and then looked back at me. "Beckett, when I saw you leave I was hoping you were going after Natasha?"

"Yes sir. She was pretty upset."

"Toshy was upset?" Jack asked sweetly.

"She was," I replied, "but she's practicing with Connor now. I'm sure it'll get worked out."

Cameron nodded. "Indeed it will. And you? How are you holding up?"

I swallowed and had to take a second before answering, "I just talked to my dad. He looks good, but uh...it's not all good news."

Cameron nodded again and understanding what I couldn't say out loud. "Remember we are all here to help you with whatever you need."

"Yes sir," I replied and realized I had finally started to believe it.

"Well, Beckett, if you will excuse me, I must hose down my unruly spawn."

"We're not spawn," Jack yelled and squirmed in his father's grip.

"You are absolutely my spawn," Cameron replied. "My very dirty, willful, and unruly spawn."

Chapter Eleven

"Well, Beckett," Victor began behind my shoulder, "you are certainly improving."

"Thanks," I replied, enjoying the sight of my last arrow in the bullseye of the target.

My morning session with Jared had been another session of defensive training. I never thought I'd be so happy to have my bow back in my hand. Jared was unbelievably patient with me. If I were him, I would have given up within the first hour. Target practice was much more my speed, and it was certainly easier without the trainees in the courtyard today.

Apparently, Monday was usually a day off for the trainees, one where they could go to work or in Tosh's case go to school. But since we were both told that we couldn't attend classes for the time being, I wondered what it was she was doing since I hadn't seen her all day. Considering last night's events, I doubt she even gave me a second thought.

"You said this was just a warm-up. What torture are you two going to put me through now?"

"Torture, you say?" Victor said critically behind me. "You have no idea what I define as torture. Jared, move the target out of the way."

"That sounds ominous," I said and turned around only to find Victor standing a little closer than I had expected and was narrowing his eyes at me. "What?"

"Is something bothering you?"

I shrugged. "Just a lot of things on my mind."

"Such as?"

Nervously I pulled an arrow from my quiver and began rolling it between my fingers. "I'm worried about my mom. Dr. Ryan's pretty sure my dad has that wolf virus, I'm tired and sore from all this training, and...and the last one is embarrassing."

"Beckett, for all intents and purposes you are my grandson, you can tell me anything, and believe me I have heard almost everything."

I twirled the arrow around and put it back in my quiver. "Just girl trouble."

"Miss Cushlin, I presume." I nodded. "I wouldn't be too disheartened."

"Why? Do you know something I don't?"

"I know many, many things, Beckett, many things. You need patience with that one, trust me on this. I am sorry about your father. I wish there was more we could do."

At this point Jared had placed the target against the stone wall. I still couldn't get over the fact that he was in a hooded sweatshirt, gloves, a hat on underneath the hood, and sunglasses.

"Why does Jared always look like he is in witness protection in Alaska?"

Victor looked at me curiously. "Because he will burn, child."

"Burn?"

Victor shook his head. "Forgive me if I assumed that you had seen a vampire movie or read a book."

"Well...I mean, I have. They're just not my thing."

He laughed. "There is a bit of irony there. So what are some of the rules about vampires you saw in the movie."

"Um," I answered uncomfortably and thought back, "you keep vampires away with garlic."

"Not true, it is just uncomfortably odorous. Next?"

"You don't have reflections."

"False."

"You drink blood."

"At least you have that one right."

"Can't touch silver."

"Correct again."

"You can't be out in the sunlight." Victor raised his eyebrows and watched as the gears turned in my head. "Wait, how are you guys out here right now?"

He sighed. "Sometimes I do worry about you, child. So yes, most

124 ~ C.R. QUINN

vampires have a sun sensitivity, but that lessens over time. Jared can be outside during the day now, but he can still burn if he is exposed to sunlight for too long."

"You said most vampires."

He smirked. "Yes, we have just recently found a formula for creating sires without the sun sensitivity."

"How's that?"

"Oh child, in no way do I trust you enough to divulge that information," he said and pointed down at the target. "Now, when in battle your targets are not going to just stand there and let you shoot them. As an archer you need to anticipate your target's movement and speed. Jared is going to go out into the field and begin to run different patterns."

"I will?" Jared shouted from the middle of the courtyard.

Victor turned his head slowly to look at Jared. "Yes, child, you will."

"But I'm a little weak today."

"You should have fed last night rather than argue with your girlfriend all night."

"It wasn't all night," Jared corrected. "I played computer games the rest of the time."

Victor sighed. "It is a good thing we need you to go slow at first."

"So you're just going to let him pummel me with arrows?"

"That is the idea, child. You're lucky that I am no longer running this coven. If I was, I would be sure that these arrows were silver tipped with the way you and your girlfriend have been acting."

Jared groaned and pulled the drawstrings of his hoodie down tight. "Love you too, Dad."

"Now, Beckett, as I said before, one of the biggest parts of being an archer is anticipating your target's movements in combination with the elements around you," he said and stepped behind me. "Jared, let's start running away from him."

Jared growled and then began slowly jogging further away from us. "I'd like to go on record that I hate this."

"Yes, yes," Victor replied with an annoyed tone. "Ok, Beckett, let's aim for his heart."

"I heard that!" Jared shouted over his shoulder just as I raised my bow and pulled the string back near my cheek. When I released the arrow it soared forward and bounced off of Jared's shoulder.

"Beckett, you are not going to hurt Jared. These arrows won't even pierce his skin. Now let's try it again and actually put some power behind it, shall we?"

After grabbing a new arrow from my quiver I exhaled and lowered my bow to start fresh. As I inhaled I lifted the bow once again, pulled the string back, and looked down the arrow's straight edge to narrow in on Jared's back.

Pfffhhtt!

"Hit!" Jared shouted and in a split second was back in front of us. "I felt it in the center of my back. The only way to make dad happy is if you hit a little more to the left."

"Thank you, child," Victor groaned in his raspy voice. "But he is right. Beckett, again."

It only took nine arrows to effectively hit Jared in the back where it would go through to his heart. After that, Victor instructed Jared to start running sideways in various patterns. With the first three arrows I hit the courtyard's stone wall, a bush, and Jared's foot. But thankfully after a dozen or so more I seemed to get the hang of a moving target.

"Very good, Beckett," Victor said after my arrow hit Jared in the upper chest. "Jared, let's speed it up."

I reached back for an arrow and found an empty quiver. "Guess I need to round up a few first."

Victor nodded and I began to walk the courtyard for my arrows. I enjoyed the break, as did Jared who ran back inside to…I swear he said to drink a bottle of blood. What had my life become?

After collecting a couple of arrows I heard a familiar voice behind me.

"Hey," Tosha said causing me to turn around. She was wearing a tight jumpsuit which made her look incredibly sexy. It wasn't something I'd seen her practice in before, but when I saw Roberts in the distance wearing something similar I realized it must be some kind of uniform.

"What are you doing out here?" I asked and continued my search for arrows. "I thought you had the day off."

"We did," she replied and from the corner of my eye I saw her pick up an arrow from the grass. "But we have to do a demonstration for Devin and Cameron in a few minutes. That's um…why it was important that I have a practice with Connor last night."

"Uh-huh," I replied and took several steps away from her to pick up an arrow near the stone wall.

"Looks like you've had a successful day."

I shrugged. "I'm starting to get it, I think. Now that you all are coming out here I'll probably make a fool out of myself."

Tosha squeezed my arm and turned me around to face her. "Hey, you're doing great. You've barely had three days of training. Give yourself a break."

"I will if you will," I challenged and bent down to pick up two more arrows from the ground. "So, what did you do all day?"

"I have been working on a surprise for you."

"Me?"

She nodded and handed me two arrows she'd collected. "Yeah. I wanted to do something to make up for last night."

"No need. You had things to do, I understand," I replied.

"Yeah...but some of the things I said were wrong."

"Beckett Dawes!" Victor shouted from the other end of the courtyard. "This is not social hour."

I nodded and waved that I was coming, but in that split second I took my attention away from Tosha she had turned and walked away.

"Wait!" I said to her back. "Which things?!"

But I didn't get an answer and instead had to trudge back over to Victor with a handful of arrows. Jared stepped back out in the courtyard with a bottle of what had to be blood. It seriously came in bottles? Where did it come from? How did they get it in the actual bottle? How did they clean the bottles afterwards? Did they recycle?

"Beckett?" Victor said and nudged my side.

"Yeah, sorry," I replied, still eyeing the red-stained bottle Jared placed on the table. "Do we have to do this in front of so many people?"

Victor looked around and then returned a curious gaze. "There are only two people, Beckett, I'm not sure I understand."

I groaned and shoved the arrows I had into the quiver. "Yeah, but it's who those two people are, and there will be more in a few minutes."

"Oh nonsense," he replied and waved his hand dismissively. "Jared, child, surprise us this time."

Jared gave a nod and began zigzagging across the courtyard. I watched his pattern carefully and stretched my bow's string back by my cheek. Looking down the line of my arrow, I released it just before Jared came in line with it and hit him in his waist.

"Again," Victor said firmly before I could even put my bow down.

I pulled another arrow from my quiver, tracked Jared once again, and released, this time hitting him in the upper back.

"Again."

Quickly I pulled another arrow from my quiver and just shot. No thinking, no overanalyzing, just breathing and aiming and hoping it hit something.

And it did. Bullseye right in Jared's chest.

"Hit!" he shouted from the far corner of the courtyard.

"Yeah, Beckett!" Tosha cheered from the ground where she was stretching. She even gave me a few claps and a thumbs up. Her approval made my chest swell a little.

"Do not rest on getting one hit," Victor said sternly. "Again."

Jared started running toward us from the right corner. Quickly I pulled another arrow and laced it in the string, watching Jared carefully and waiting for the perfect time. Just as he swerved and turned back to the other corner, I pulled my arrow back and hit him just to the left of the center of his back.

"Hit!" Jared shouted again, but rather than wait for Victor to tell us to do it again, he spun around quickly and started running directly at us.

I took a breath before threading another arrow, taking the time to focus my aim.

Phhfff!

"Hit!"

"Woo!" I shouted and punched the air with my bow. "Hell ya!"

Victor patted me on the back and gave me a little nod. This time even Roberts joined in and gave me a few claps. It felt good to finally do something right.

When I turned to put my bow down on the table I noticed Devin strolling toward us.

"Child, you just missed Beckett's demonstration," Victor said happily.

"No, Father, I saw," Devin replied flatly.

"You were not impressed?"

Devin raised his left eyebrow and tilted his chin down. "Impressed by three hits on a slow-moving target with no real distractions? How well could he do in an actual battle?"

"I believe he would do well."

Devin smirked and shook his head. "Father, have you lost all your hard edges now that you are retired?"

"Then by all means, child, tell me what we can do better."

"You need faster targets. He needs to be making split-second decisions with more distractions in his environment."

"Beckett has shown great improvement in just a couple of days. I believe he could handle anything you throw at him."

"Uh, Victor, I'm not sure…"

"Fine, Father," Devin interrupted, "let's see what he can do with a real target."

Shit.

"Perfect, child, are you volunteering," Victor asked.

Why was this happening to me? What was Victor thinking?

Devin stepped away from the table and walked over to the group of trainees, and unfortunately Connor had joined the group at some point. Could this get any worse?

"Just remember your training, Beckett. The breathing, the focus, the aim and anticipation. Don't be intimidated by my eldest child."

I laughed. "That last one is a little hard."

A moment later Devin walked away from the trainees and Connor, and took Jared's place out in the middle of the courtyard. With a deep exhale I pulled an arrow from my back and threaded it in the string. Devin darted to the other end of the courtyard in the blink of an eye. I swallowed hard and pulled the bow up to eye level, stretching the arrow back by my cheek.

Devin darted back across the courtyard and then started coming at me. It was a perfect shot. Three, two…"

"Beckett, help!" Tosha screamed off to my right.

My head whipped around to find her and I lost my grip on my arrow causing it to fly crookedly into the ground only a few feet away. When I finally found Tosha she was standing with Connor's arm draped around her shoulder and chest. I turned my head back to find Devin standing toe to toe with me.

"You're dead," he said and flicked my forehead.

The trainees, including Connor, burst into laughter at my expense, although Tosh wasn't joining in.

"It was a trick?!"

"It was a distraction, and you failed," Devin replied and started stepping back across the lawn.

My heart started to beat out of my chest. I was embarrassed and angry and couldn't stand the sound of Connor's overdramatic laughter. Victor looked less than please since I'd embarrassed him too.

"Are we through?" I asked and Victor narrowed his eyes.

"You have one failure and you're ready to quit?"

"I made an ass out of myself, I'm done."

Victor pulled my chin down to look him in the eye. "You will have failures all your life. It is how you move forward is the real test of your character. Don't stand there and let them laugh at you. Show them the Warrior you can be."

I pulled my chin from his grip and stood up straight. "Can I go?"

Victor sighed in defeat and waved me off. I was in no mood to hear inspiring speeches. I just wanted to go home and play video games. Was that too much to ask? Well, I guess it was since my house was abandoned with a big hole to the outside. Was there still a dead werewolf on the steps of my basement apartment?

"Beckett, wait," Tosha called from behind me.

"Go away."

Just as I stepped through the archway to make my way back inside, Tosha's hand squeezed my shoulder and turned me forcibly around.

"Beckett, I'm sorry."

"You're sorry? I thought you were hurt and you made me look like an ass in front of everyone. For a second there I thought you were my friend, stupid me."

"I was given an order, Beckett."

My head flinched. "So that makes it ok?"

"Cushlin!" Connor yelled.

"Coming," she responded over her shoulder but then turned back to me. "I was given an order to distract you, I had no choice. Regardless, it was a good lesson."

"The lesson being I should ignore you if you need help?"

Tosha bit her bottom lip. After a breath or two she was finally able to reply, "You should have handled Devin first. You lost your focus which in a real battle could mean we're both dead. That's the lesson."

"Natasha Cushlin!" Connor yelled once again and this time Tosha ran back out to the courtyard.

Victor passed right by her, almost as though she was tagging him in.

"She's a smart girl," he said and went around me to the small set of stairs to go inside.

"Victor, wait," I said but he didn't stop so I had to run to catch up with him inside.

"What is it, Mr. Dawes."

"Mr. Dawes? You're resorting to the last name already?"

"I thought you were going to go pout somewhere."

I lost a step at his comment and had to catch up to him again. "I wasn't pouting, I just needed a moment…"

"To cower."

"Not to...no! I...I just...you saw how fast he went. There's no way I will ever be able to hit a vampire. I will never be able to shoot that fast."

"With an attitude like that you'll never amount to anything. I would like my medal back."

My hand instinctively went to my pocket where the Warrior medal was hiding. "Wha-what medal?"

Victor raised an eyebrow. "The medal you stole from my vault. I would have been happy to give it to you, but now I see your true colors. Perhaps Devin is right, I could be trying to see something that isn't there. Your uncanny resemblance to Garrett is clouding my judgement in regards to your potential. If you are willing to walk away so quickly, then you don't deserve that medal."

Victor held out his hand and slowly I put my hand in my pocket, rubbing the circle of gold between my fingers. I found myself struggling to pull it out of my pocket. Victor folded his fingers into a fist and held it at his heart.

"This is the Warrior salute, it is a sign of respect and honor. The medal you have is a symbol of our family, our sacrifices, and our responsibility to protect those who might be threatened by our kind. You need to decide whether you can rise to our level, or simply hide under our protection. So I ask again, will you give me Garrett's medal or not?"

"No," I replied and squeezed the medal tightly. "But do you really think I can do better?"

"Beckett, no one in this entire coven has ever had dedicated training from me. Why do you think Devin is behaving like a petulant child? If I didn't think you had potential then I would have left you to Jared. But I am not training you just for fun. I truly believe you will be in battle in the near future. You do have some deficits that are detrimental in your current circumstance. I believe you really need to be activated. I have seen the glimmers of your real talent. Activation will bring out your powers, and help you with what is coming."

"Activation, that's where I drink your blood or something, right?"

He nodded. "It's very simple."

"But it means I'll be more like Garrett. What if I become evil like him?"

Victor squeezed my shoulder. "You have a goodness in you that Garrett never had."

"I don't want more of him to come out in me."

"I understand your concerns, but please understand mine. By not being activated, you will not improve in the time we have to work with."

I sighed and released the gold medallion in my pocket. "I hear you, I do. I just need to...I know this sounds crazy, but I need to talk to my dad about this. I don't want him to think I'm becoming less of his son because I'm activating more of Garrett."

Victor nodded slowly. "I can understand that, but we cannot wait too long."

"Yeah, I get it," I replied and turned to walk back up to my room.

"Oh, and Mr. Dawes," Victor said loudly, "do not let Connor's antics deter you from pursuing Miss Cushlin. Connor has never had a real relationship in the sixty years since I Turned him."

"Thanks, Victor."

"I will see you bright and early tomorrow."

I took a step away but then turned back around to face him, formed a fist, and put it to my heart. "Is this right?"

Victor cleared his throat and turned quickly away from me. "Perfect."

"Hey, how did you know I had the medallion?"

With his back turned he replied, "Child, I told you I know many, many things."

Chapter Twelve

"Come in," I said from my bathroom.

After a shower and some clean clothes my head was clearer and my anxiety down. I'd found a button-up shirt in my bag, which was nicer than the T-shirt and sweats I'd been sporting the last few days. I didn't feel as grungy and that was somehow improving my mood.

"Tosha? Is that you?" I asked as I brushed down my hair.

"How did you know?" she replied from inside the bedroom.

"You're the only person who comes to see me."

"Oh, well…uh….did a tornado come through here?"

I stepped out of the bathroom and found Tosha looking cautiously around my room. There were a couple shirts on the floor, a sock, not sure where the other sock was, honestly it wasn't that bad and I didn't deserve the look she was giving me.

"What?"

"You're a pig," she said and picked up the shirts from the floor and threw them onto my bed.

"Feel free to clean my room again."

She cocked an eyebrow at me, but I didn't mind, it was cute. She looked nice too. Her hair was loose and hung down past her shoulders. I liked when her hair was down, she didn't do it often, but it softened her a little. She had on jeans, really nice tight-fitting jeans and a loose sweater that hung off her shoulder. How had I never noticed how nice her shoulders were? Was it bad that I really wanted to kiss that shoulder? She'd probably slap me.

OF BLOOD & FIRE ~ 133

"Are you having a stroke?" she asked and looked at me strangely.

"What? No, I...you look really nice."

"Thanks," she replied and looked down at the floor.

"So uh, I want to apologize for today. I didn't mean to yell at you."

"Apology accepted," she replied with a smile. "I'm sorry Connor and the others were acting like assholes."

"They're really good at it," I said and sat down on the bed to put my shoes on. "Does this mean you'll have dinner with me?"

"Actually, I'm taking you out," she said and began folding the shirts she'd thrown on my bed.

"Out? Like outside of the manor?"

She nodded. "I told you I had a surprise for you."

"Ok, let's have it."

She smiled. "Well, I spent my whole day off working with Dr. Ryan to help me convince Cameron and Devin to allow you to have dinner with your dad."

I stopped tying my shoe and sat up instantly. "I get to see my dad? In person?"

"It took a lot of work, but we were able to compromise on a neutral location, one meal, and a couple of hours of visitation. Not a bad deal if I say so myself."

"Not a bad deal?" I said as I stood from the bed and hugged her tightly. "Thank you, Tosha."

Awkwardly she patted me on the back, making me think the hug was a little forward. But when I released her there was a look in her eye, one of wanting. Slowly I leaned down to kiss her and for a moment I swear she tilted her head up a little to meet me, but in a split second it was as if the string bringing us together was cut and she stepped out of my arms.

"We need to get going," she said and walked toward the door. "Everyone's waiting for us."

"Oh wait," I said and grabbed my bow and quiver.

"Um, why are you bringing your bow?"

"I'd like to show my dad what I've been doing the last couple of days."

Tosha shrugged and opened the door. "Whatever floats your boat. Just don't shoot anybody, ok?"

"Very funny," I replied and gestured for Tosha to go into the hallway. "You said everyone was waiting? Who is everyone?"

"Brianna and Cameron are going to escort us along with Alex and

Kyla, just to make sure no one is following us."

"They don't mind? I feel bad that they have to hang around."

"Well, we're actually meeting at Brianna's grandfather's house," she said as we started down the spiral staircase. "We're just kinda crashing their time together."

"Brianna's grandfather? She has family?"

She nodded. "The only Warrior with family left, actually. Ollie, her grandfather, lives with my friend Maddy. I can't wait for you to meet her. Honestly, she's like a surrogate mother to me. She was the person that got me through recovery after the accident, she stayed with me almost every day."

"Then I can't wait to meet her," I replied and we made our way toward the massive front doors. "They all know that uh...about my dad, right?"

She nodded, but she seemed a little hesitant. "Just don't be offended if people seem..."

"Scared?"

"I was going to say apprehensive," she said kindly.

"Toshy! Catch!" a little girl yelled from down the corridor.

Tosha quickly turned around and in an instant she caught Livy Burke in midair.

"Gotcha!" Tosha said and had a smile from ear to ear. It was a smile of pure joy I had yet to see, and it continued while she bounced Livy on her hip. Livy's hair was still crooked and oddly cut in places due to the gum incident. One of the few things I remembered from sitting on the bench that night. "Where's your brother?"

"Wiff Mama and Ada," she replied and pointed down the corridor to where Brianna and Cameron were walking with Jack in between them. "He's still grounded."

"I am not!" Jack shouted. "Am I?"

"Of course you are," Brianna corrected.

"What's dis?" Livy asked as she touched the tip of my bow.

"It's a bow, Wivy," Jack answered for me. "You shoot arrows wiff it."

Livy whipped her head around. "Are you going to shoot arrows at Da-e-O's?"

"Who?"

"She means my grandfather," Brianna said. "And no, baby girl, Beckett will not be doing any shooting tonight."

"Why?"

"Because he doesn't need to."

"Why?"

"Because we're just going to Daddy O's, honey."

"But he could," Livy said hopefully and Brianna sighed.

"Beckett, I'm sorry we're crashing your visit with your dad. The kids haven't seen their great-grandfather in a couple of weeks."

"No, of course," I replied. "I'm just happy to get to see my dad in person. Thank you."

"Do not thank us," Cameron said and pointed to Tosha. "Natasha coordinated everything. She was very adamant about letting you see your father tonight."

"It wasn't just me," Tosha said embarrassed and even tucked her head down to hide her blush.

"Yes, heaven forbid Natasha take a compliment," Cameron replied and took Livy from Tosha's arms. "Remember to go out the back driveway, Natasha. Alexander and Kyla will be waiting."

"Yes sir," Tosha replied formally with her chest high.

"Back driveway?" I asked as I followed Tosha out the front doors.

"It's a precaution in case we're being watched. Cameron and Brianna will go out the front and scan for any vamps along the way. We're going out the back with an escort in case anyone starts to follow us."

"This is kinda intense," I said just as we came to Tosha's Mercedes, the lights flashing as she unlocked the doors.

"It has to be in order to keep you safe, Beck."

I smiled at her calling me Beck. She made it sound like a new word. No one said it like she did. I slid down into the passenger seat, letting the expensive leather seat cup my legs and back. She really did have a sick car.

After she started the car it was only seconds before she squealed out of her parking spot and tore down the gravel driveway. Fighting the centrifugal force that was pushing me into the car door as she sped around the corner of the manor, I struggled to click my seatbelt into the lock and may have released a slight whimper.

"You're such a baby," Tosha said with a huge smile on her face.

"You talk about keeping me safe and then you drive like a maniac in the freaking driveway!"

"Oh please, I could do this with my eyes closed."

I clung to the door handle when she swung out the backend and then pulled onto a narrow dirt road that had a canopy of overgrowth.

"I take it this is the back driveway?"

She nodded as her eyes sparkled while twisting down the road until we swerved onto a regular street.

"Oh thank god," I sighed with relief. "Please don't ever take me down that again."

Tosha laughed and turned up the music. The fast beat rock music seemed to only make her drive faster. When I glanced in the side mirror I noticed a big SUV pull out behind us.

"I think we're being followed," I said and whipped around to look out the back window.

Tosha glanced in the rearview mirror and smirked. "It's Alex and Kyla."

"Should I know them?"

She rolled her eyes. "Alex is the really big guy you met your second night here. Kyla is his wife."

"Someone married that enormous man?"

Tosha gave me a quick cautious glance. "Be careful who you say that around. The only person in the coven everyone loves more than Alex is Kyla."

"Another woman Warrior?"

She shook her head. "Nope. Kyla belonged to another coven, but before that she was a solitary."

"A solitary, like your dad," I said feeling proud that I was finally starting to understand the lingo.

"You were listening," she replied and turned down another road that would take us to the outskirts of the city.

"Despite what you might think, I do listen to everything you say. For example, how was your demonstration today?"

She shrugged and turned another corner so fast that I was pushed into the door again. "I did ok," she answered right before a call came through. "Hey, Alex."

"Tosh, I know you love your car, and you know these streets very well, but maybe you could slow down in order to not bring attention to yourself?"

Her shoulders fell. "Yes sir."

Alex let out a deep laugh. "No need to call me sir, I'm not Cameron. Just slow down."

"Yes si…Alex," she laughed and the line was cut off. It was a nice sight to see the speedometer go down. "It doesn't matter, we're almost there anyway."

"My prayers have been answered," I laughed and she hit me in the chest. "That hurts you know."

"It's supposed to."

"Ok, so seriously, how did your demonstration go? You have to have done better than I did in front of Devin."

"Anyone could have done that better than you," she replied with a smirk. The cute little smirk was becoming pretty common around me. "Like I said, I did ok. I kicked Nub's ass and put Princess into the ground."

"That sounds more than ok."

"I didn't get to go against Roberts. He's the one I need to beat in order to get that spot."

"You'll get him next time. You seem to be such good friends with everyone, I can't see that they would make him a Warrior over you."

She shook her head. "That's just it, they may pass on me *because* I've gotten so close to them. I'm afraid they won't want to show any kind of favoritism, and then this whole year was a waste."

"Not true, you met me," I said trying to sound charming, but I only got a quick side glance in response.

The rest of the conversation was cut short when Tosha pulled into a driveway of a small ranch-style house. We were very much in seclusion with woods surrounding the house on three sides. From the outside you could tell the warmth that filled the inside. Maybe it was the smell of food wafting toward me or the soft glow coming from the windows, but either way it seemed more like home than the manor did.

Alex's enormous truck pulled in behind us. Considering his size, I supposed there weren't a lot of options in the vehicle department where he could be comfortable. The giant man stepped down onto the driveway as a woman with long red hair came out of the passenger side.

"Goodness, Tosh, are you training for NASCAR?" Alex laughed.

"I wasn't going that fast," she replied.

Alex shook his head. "I'm surprised you didn't take flight."

The woman with red hair came to stand in front of me and extended her hand. "Hi, I'm Kyla, Alex's wife."

"Oh, cool," I replied, not quite sure why I answered that way. Maybe it was because I couldn't imagine this tiny woman with a giant as a husband. "Um...I'm Beckett."

"Oh, I know," she said with a sly smile. "Believe me, I know a lot."

"Kyla," Alex warned, "leave the boy alone."

"But what's the fun in that?"

Alex put his arm around his wife's shoulders and pulled her across the driveway toward the house. We filed in behind them and as soon as we stepped inside the children squealed for their Toshy. With Livy in her arms and Jack wrapped around her leg she introduced me to Brianna's grandfather.

"Welcome, Beckett, please call me Ollie. Can I getcha somethin' to drink?" he asked in a really thick Southern accent.

"A beer if you have it," I replied. "You're not from around here, are you?"

Ollie winked at me. "How could ya tell?"

"Could be the accent."

He smiled. "Where I come from, ya'll are the ones with the accent. I'll getcha that beer. Now go on and make yourself at home."

Ollie turned away and I was happy to see Dr. Ryan approaching me. "Dr. Ryan!"

He smiled and shook my hand. "Hey, Beckett, just call me John."

"Uncle John," Jack said looking up from the Tosha's leg, "where's Wills?"

"Sorry, Jack-Jack, he's sick with a cold. Your Aunt Rene is home taking care of him."

"Wills is sick?" Livy said with a pout and then tapped Tosha on the cheek. "Toshy, can't you make Wills better?"

Tosha gave an awkward glance over to Dr. Ryan before she replied, "I'm sorry, Livy, I can't fix colds, but I'm sure Wills will be better soon."

"We need to draw him get-better pictures!" she shouted and leapt out of Tosha's arms, somehow doing a full layout-twist before she hit the floor.

Livy quickly grabbed Tosha's arm and began to pull her toward a kitchen table in the back corner, all while Jack laughed with glee as Tosha tried walking with him still clenched to her leg.

"They're pretty cute."

John nodded. "Yeah they are until their fangs comes out."

My face fell. "Come again?"

"You haven't seen them?" he laughed. "Guess I'll let you experience that on your own."

"Thanks. So, how's my dad doing?"

John closed his mouth and nodded cautiously. "He's healing a little faster than humans, but they're still giving him some pain."

"And his heart?"

"It's beating," he said trying to make a joke of it, but then changed his tone when I didn't laugh. "So far so good, but we're keeping a close eye on him."

"And the uh…wolf…thing?"

Dr. Ryan sighed and shrugged. "To be honest, I'm figuring it out as I go. There's just not enough information for me to really look at. The main worry is how his heart will hold up over the next week."

"Full moon?" He nodded and I took a step back. "Thanks, doc."

He patted my shoulder and when I turned around I found Ollie standing with a beer. It was exactly what I needed in that moment.

"Whoa, slow down, youngin'," Ollie said when I drank roughly half the bottle in only a few gulps.

I wiped the corner of my lips with the cuff of my sleeve. "Sorry, just too much reality for a second there."

He nodded and pulled me over to the kitchen where an elderly woman was working hard around her stove.

"Beckett, this is Maddy. Madelyn, this is Richard's son Beckett."

Maddy wiped her hands on her apron and then squeezed me tightly in a hug. "Beckett, we are so happy to be able to bring you and your father together for a little visit."

"Me too," I replied even though she was squeezing my cheeks tightly between her hands.

"And don't think I haven't seen a change in my Tosh. She's practically been a different person these last few days. I've never seen her so happy."

"Um…we're talking about Tosh? Natasha. Cushlin."

Ollie tried stifling his laughter behind his hand, but Maddy didn't bother. "She's tough, I know, but she can't hide anything from me. I've seen her at her absolute worse, and I'm finally starting to see the light coming back in her eyes. And considering your name keeps coming up I have to believe you have a lot to do with that."

"Now come on, Maddy, let the boy go. He's already been here ten minutes and hasn't even seen his daddy yet."

Maddy released my cheeks and shoed Ollie away, similar to how my grandma would dismiss my grandpa on a daily basis. "Now you go on outside and visit with your father. Dinner will be ready in about fifteen minutes. I hope you brought your appetite."

"Always," I replied and gulped down most of what was left of my beer and slid open the sliding glass door.

The backyard was narrow but spanned the length of the house. On the small patio in front of me were two lounge chairs and my dad was laying out in the one on my right. When I closed the sliding glass door behind me, my dad turned his head slowly and looked up at me from behind the chair.

"Becks," he sighed and I knelt down next to him. His arms were already outstretched and waiting for me. My head started to fall toward his chest when I stopped myself.

"Where can I...I don't want to hurt you, Dad."

He wrapped his hand around my neck and then pulled me down into the crook of his shoulder. When his other arm wrapped around my shoulders and his cheek rested on my head, I didn't even try and hold in the tears that were burning my eyes.

When I lifted my head I quickly wiped my eyes with the back of my hand. Dad did the same with the palm of his hand, and then we laughed when we caught each other.

"Oh that still hurts," he said and placed a hand on his chest.

"How are you feeling?"

"Every day is better. They say I'm healing faster than most people which is probably linked to the...you know."

"I do," I replied and realized he was having as much of a hard time verbalizing what he was becoming as I was hearing about it. "Can I uh...see the scars?"

My dad lifted the bottom of his shirt up to reveal three thick scars rising from his stomach and leading up to his chest. Three claw marks branding and infecting him for life.

"It is what it is, Becks."

"I didn't say anything."

"I've raised you, I know what's fishing around in that head of yours."

I sighed and pulled the other lounge chair closer to him to sit down. "John told me there's a full moon coming this week."

"Yeah," he answered and smoothed his shirt back down. "At least we don't have to wait too long to really know. I guess I might start having some changes...what did he call it?"

"Phasing, I think they call it phasing."

"Yes, that's it, phasing. I'm trying not to think about it too much. Have you heard anything about your mom?" he asked with hopeful eyes.

I shook my head just as the sliding glass door opened and Tosha walked out onto the patio.

"Hey guys, dinner is almost ready," she said as she walked around the lounge chair. "Hi, Richard."

"Richard?" I asked, wondering when they had gotten so informal.

"What do you expect her to call me? Mr. Dawes?"

"Well I did until you yelled at me and told me that if I was going to see you in that condition I could at least call you by your first name," Tosha said and sat down next to me.

"That I did," my dad laughed, but then caught himself and rubbed his chest.

"You're looking better even since this morning."

"Wait, how often are you going and seeing my dad?"

"Don't make it seem like I'm keeping something from you, Beckett. I saw Dr. Ryan for some tests, and I just looked in on your dad while I was there."

"Tests? Are you ok?"

Tosha's eyes grew wide and looked awkwardly between me and my dad. "Yeah. Fine. Um, have you told your dad what you've been doing at the manor?"

"Oh!" I shouted and shot up from the lounge chair. "My bow! I wanted to show you my bow. Do you mind staying here for second so I can run and get it?"

"I'm not planning on going anywhere else. This'll give Tosh and I a few minutes to talk about you behind your back."

I nodded and leapt over the lounge chair before I realized what he'd really said. "Yeah, please don't do that," I said and ran around the side of the house to where Tosha's car was parked.

Just as I pulled my bow from the backseat, my back pocket started to vibrate. The feeling was so jarring that I jerked up and hit my head on the roof of the car. Holding my head, I slowly backed out of the car and pulled out my cell phone. I almost dropped the phone when I saw that it was my mom calling. My hand was shaking as I put the phone up to my ear.

"Mom?" I said tentatively.

"Hello, son."

"I'm not your son," I replied and instantly wanted to crush the phone.

"Your mother says otherwise," Garrett said with a slight laugh. "You must be as angry as I am about being lied to for over two decades. I have certainly spoken to your mother about it."

"If you so much as breathe on my mother, so help me..."

"I do what I want, Beckett," Garrett shouted and then sighed loudly into the phone. When he spoke again his tone was oddly calm. "I know I don't have long until you run to my former brothers-in-arms, but I have a proposition."

"I'm listening," I replied and started slowly back around the side of the house.

"An exchange. You for your mother."

"I want to talk to her. I need proof she's still alive."

"I'll meet you in one hour at the park down the street from your house."

I rounded the corner to the backyard where Tosha and Dad were laughing. "I want to talk to her now!" I shouted, causing their conversion to quickly end and Tosha to stand.

There was a quick shuffle of the phone and suddenly, "Beckett? Honey?"

"Mom!" I shouted and Tosha came running to my side.

"Honey, I'm ok, don't..."

"There's your proof," Garrett interrupted. "One hour, and no Warriors. If I see one Warrior, I will kill her. Understand?"

"I'll be there, but if you..."

The line went dead.

Tosha placed her hand on my arm. "Was that..."

"It was Garrett," I said and pushed past her to get to my dad. "Mom says she's ok. We're going to go get her."

"Beckett, wait!" Tosha called after me as I rushed into the house.

"Cameron!" I shouted in the crowded house causing instant silence. "Garrett just called me."

Cameron put his son down on the floor and stepped toward me while Tosha helped my father inside.

"Beckett, slow down," Cameron began calmly, "tell us what happened."

"I got a call from my mom's cell phone. She must have had it on her when they took her, but it was Garrett. He said he wants to do an exchange – me for my mom. I don't have long..."

"Slow down, Beckett," Cameron interrupted again and put his hands up in front of him. "We need to get a team together and scope out the location. Where does he want to do the exchange?"

I shook my head. "No, he said no Warriors."

"Of course he did," Cameron replied and then looked behind him. "Alex, we need to load up and get back to the manor. Call Jared on the way to see if he can get a trace on Mrs. Dawes' phone. Beckett, the location."

"But he said he would kill my mom if he saw any Warriors."

"Beckett, this is what we do. If we get a team together now, we can beat him there and scope out the location. It is not safe for you to go and it is obvious he wants you but for reasons unknown. Let us do what we do best. We will get your mother and Garrett, and all of this will be over. The location, please."

I looked over at my father who suddenly looked pale and weak. He needed my mom more than he needed me. If they wouldn't let me go, I'd do it myself.

"There's a park outside of the city, I used to play soccer there. He said to be there in two hours."

Cameron nodded and began barking orders. "Call Jared, I want satellite pictures of this park and all entry points by the time we get back to the manor. Then call Connor and tell him wheels up in twenty minutes. I will call Devin and have him put the manor on high alert."

"Cam, what about the kids?" Brianna asked quietly.

Cameron looked to Ollie. "Da, would you mind taking the children for the night?"

Ollie nodded. "Absolutely, son, but what about Mr. Dawes?"

"I can take him back to Facility West," Tosha replied. "The worry was someone following us from the manor. Going to the Facility from here shouldn't be a problem."

Cameron nodded. "Very well. Mr. Dawes, we will do everything in our power to get your wife back."

My dad nodded nervously and everyone in the house dispersed in various directions. I shook hands with Ollie and thanked Maddy for her hospitality.

"Hospitality? You didn't even eat. Why don't you stay and have a bite?"

"I want to get back to the manor so I can at least know what's happening." Because I was running out of time, I finished in my head.

Maddy patted my cheek and wished me luck. Tosh received a tight hug from Maddy while everyone else filed out the front door and into their cars. I took the opportunity to place my arm around my father's shoulders and carefully led him out of the house.

"Becks?" he asked softly in a tone I knew very well. Just in saying my name he was asking for an explanation since he knew I was lying.

"I know what I'm doing, Dad," I said as we came to Tosh's car. I opened the passenger side door and helped my dad slide down into seat. By the time I started walking around to the driver's side, Tosh was next to me. "How long will it take us to get to this Facility place?"

She shrugged. "Fifteen, maybe twenty minutes. Why?"

"I just want to get back to the manor," I replied as I ducked into the narrow backseat, pulling my bow and quiver across my lap.

Eventually Tosh revved her car to life and headed back through the winding roads, thankfully at top speed.

"Well, Miss Tosh, you have got quite a car," my dad said, trying to make small talk.

"So your son keeps telling me," she replied, looking at me through the rearview mirror, trying to get some kind of response from me, but all I could do was look away and nervously stroke the grip of my bow.

Time was ticking away to get to my mom, and I somehow had to steal Tosh's car. I was going to get my ass kicked, that is if the Warriors ever found me again. Maybe that would be Tosha's incentive to come rescue me, so that she could kick my ass for stealing her car.

"You ok back there?" Tosha asked, once again looking back through the rearview mirror.

"Yeah, fine. Shouldn't you be looking at the road?"

She narrowed her eyes at me and then looked back out the windshield. The rest of the ride to Facility West was uncomfortably quiet, but I welcomed it. It allowed me to think through what I was going to do once I got to the park. But before I knew it we were pulling up to a tall gate and I still had no real plan. A guard waved us through and Tosha sped up the driveway to a massive modern-looking concrete and glass building. Tosha drove right up in front where the entrance was an entire wall of glass.

Tosha got out of the car and I about spilled out onto the driveway from the cramped backseat. She left the car running, which was perfect, and walked around to help my dad get out of the front seat. Slowly the two of us helped my father up the half dozen concrete stairs and once we reached the top, the wall of glass slid open to a large lobby full of leather chairs and couches. Once we stepped past the receptionist's desk I released my dad's arm and stopped abruptly.

"Dammit," I said, "I have something for you, Dad. I left it in the car. I'll be right back."

He gave me a concerned look and squeezed my hand. "Becks, I..."

"It's fine, Dad. I'll be right back, no need to wait for me. I'm sure someone can tell me where the medical wing is."

Before either of them could object I casually ran back through the whispering glass doors, but once I hit the stairs I took two at a time and raced to the car. Quickly I opened the driver's door, slid down into the seat, and slammed the door shut. A few seconds later I put the purring car in gear and sped around the half circle that would take me back around. Just as I was about to turn onto the driveway, Tosha came running across the center gardens and jumped in front of the car. I slammed on the brakes and pulled the steering wheel to the right causing the car to skid to a stop and coming so close to Tosha that she hit the hood of the car with her hands.

Both our chests heaved with adrenaline.

"Are you kidding me?" she screamed. "What are you doing?!" I didn't respond. "I'm not moving, Beckett. Either run me over or put the car in park." I didn't move. "Beckett, I will call security and the guards down there won't let you out. Now put the fucking car in park and get out!"

Reluctantly I put the car in park and angrily opened the door, leaving it between us to protect me from her.

"They have my mom, Natasha! They told me no Warriors or they'll kill her. What else am I supposed to do?"

"Not this! You can't just run off to play hero..."

"That's not what I'm doing," I shouted. "I'm giving Garrett what he wants, I'm just exchanging myself for my mom."

"And then what?" she yelled and stepped up to the car door, getting right up in my face. "You'll just leave her alone in the park to find her way home?"

"Then come with me and bring her back."

She exhaled loudly and tightened her lips before saying, "And what if you get there and she's not, then your father loses both of you."

"Another reason to come with me."

She shook her head and walked around the car door, pulling me away and reaching inside for her cell phone. "I'm calling Cameron."

"No!" I shouted and reached for her phone, but she pulled away.

"Beckett! This is not a game, we need them and they're leaving for another location. We have to stop them."

"Tosha, please!" I shouted again and successfully grabbed the phone from her hand. "I just want my mom safe and if that means giving myself to Garrett then that's what I'm going to do. All I'm asking is for your help."

Tosha was breathing hard, her eyes suddenly glassy. Without another word she took her cell phone back and slid into the driver's seat. When I didn't move, she looked up at me and snapped, "You didn't think I'd let you drive, did you? Get in!"

With a jump I ran around to the other side of the car. I barely had the door closed before she put the pedal down and squealed the tires. Once they got traction we sped down the driveway, barely getting through the gate at the bottom.

"Thank you," I said.

"Shut up," she replied. "I can't believe I'm doing this."

"I appreciate it."

"Shut up," she snapped, being sure to keep her focus on the windshield.

"Did my dad give me up?"

"He said you never played soccer. I should have known. You playing any sort of sport is laughable."

"That's a bit harsh."

"You have no idea how harsh I'll be if this all goes to shit."

Chapter Thirteen

The park was pitch black except for the security light beaming down on the small dirt parking lot. Tosha switched off the headlights before turning down a side path where her black car couldn't easily be seen by any cops. I only knew the path existed because I had hidden here many times with my past girlfriends before taking them home for the night. Thankfully Tosha didn't ask how I knew about it. Honestly, she hadn't spoken since we left Facility West. I was putting her in a tough position, but she could have just let me steal her car.

"Ok, now what," she said as she put the car in park.

I shrugged. "I guess we wait."

She sighed, and I assumed she rolled her eyes as she did so often. "No. We're not going to be sitting ducks. Let's get out and take position so we can see them wherever they decide to come out."

I nodded and opened my door just as she did. Quickly she stepped back to the trunk of the car and removed a black bag. When she returned to the front of the car she placed the bag on the front seat and pulled out a black utility belt. After she clicked the belt around her hips she attached two silver whips on either side, and pulled out an aerosol can.

"Give me your arrows," she said and snapped her fingers.

"Um, ok," I replied and reached back for my quiver which only had three arrows in it. "Why?"

"Three arrows? That's all you brought?"

"I wasn't expecting any of this to happen."

"Idiot," she muttered under her breath and took the three arrows out of the quiver. She held the first arrow out away from the car and pointed the aerosol can at the tip. A thin mist shot out of the nozzle of the can and coated the top four inches of the arrow in a silver film.

"What is that?"

"Aerosol silver," she replied as she coated the second arrow.

"Will that help?"

She laughed nervously. "Let's hope so. Here," she said and handed me three silver-coated arrows.

With a nervous exhale I strapped my quiver around my shoulder. I held my bow loosely in my left hand and began walking slowly around to the front of the car. My stomach started to spasm and I found it a little hard to breathe. Tosha came up behind me on my right side and together we walked onto the park's playing field.

As the nerves took over, my right hand started to shake. Tosha's fingers curled around my hand and the gesture took my attention away from my nerves. I twisted my hand open to surround hers and squeezed.

"What are you doing?" she asked and pulled her hand out of mine.

"I...I thought you were holding my hand."

"I just wanted you to stop shaking."

"Just the rejection I needed right before all this shit goes down. Thanks, Tosh."

She squeezed my arm and violently turned me to face her. "Get your head in the game, asshole. This is as real as it gets. Right now I'm trying to deal with you just giving yourself over to Garrett, getting your mom back, and somehow explaining this all to the Warriors to where they don't kick me out of the program."

I took her hand and squeezed it, pulling it back toward me when she tried to pull it away. "I'm sorry. Thank you for everything you've done for me. You keep sticking your neck out for me and I have nothing to give you back. Just know I appreciate it."

Tosha's nostrils flared and her lips pursed ever so slightly. Her breath quickened and just when I thought I might get away with giving her the slightest, softest kiss, a stick broke in the distance. Tosh immediately went on the defensive, pulling her hand out of mine and unraveling the whips from her hips. In reflex I lifted my bow and laced an arrow in the string.

From the wood line on the opposite side of the field two hulking shadows emerged and glided to the middle of the field. Werewolves. Tosha's whips shook either from nerves or preparation. My bow was definitely shaking because of nerves, especially when Garrett stepped out of the woods with three others behind him, one of which was Delia, the girl from the party.

"It warms my heart to see that bow in your hand, boy," Garrett began, "but I specifically said no Warriors."

"She's not a Warrior," I shouted just as Garrett pulled his own bow over his head. "It's not like you came alone, either. Now where's my mother."

From across the field I could see his smirk as he raised his bow to his chest.

"Shit," Tosha groaned next to me, "she's not here. Run!"

Before the word run was even out of her mouth I heard the familiar sound of an arrow flying through the air. Pfffht!

I looked to my left and gasped at the sight of a thick arrow sticking out of Tosha's left shoulder. The force with which it hit her whipped her around. The shock on her face caused a fury to burn inside of me. I pulled my arm back by my cheek, and as I had been taught, pulled an invisible shield of silence to block the noise around me. The wolf to my right growled and leapt toward me just as I released my arrow. Pffht!

The wolf went down instantly as the arrow hit him in the chest. The other werewolf leapt forward, but Tosha pulled a knife from her belt and threw it, letting it cut through the air and sink into the wolf's head right between the eyes. The wolf immediately slumped to the ground, exposing a vampire who was running right at us with amazing speed. Without even thinking, I pulled my second arrow from the quiver, threaded it, pulled it back, and shot. Pffht!

The arrow went right through the vampire's neck, knocking him back and causing him to writhe while he bled out.

Pffht! Pffht!

Two arrows soared through the air, but they weren't mine. Terrified I looked to my left again and saw two more arrows sticking out of Tosha, this time one sticking out of her thigh, another in her stomach. Tosha slumped and skidded to the ground. Quickly I rushed to her side, but another arrow whizzed by my face, nicking my cheekbone.

"That was a miss on purpose, boy," Garrett yelled from across the field, now with only Delia and one other vampire behind him. "You are outmatched, Beckett. You only have one arrow and I have a dozen. It will only take me one to kill her, do not force me to do it. Now put your bow down and step toward me."

"Screw you, we had a deal," I shouted as Tosha fell against the hood of the car.

"Deals change," Garrett replied.

Suddenly the vampire to Garrett's left bolted from behind him. His fangs were exposed as he leapt toward me. His fingers stretched out, only inches away from me when an arrow came through his back and directly through the left side of his chest. Instantly he fell to the ground, unmoving and dead, like for real dead, not just vamp dead.

The fact that he had hit Tosha three times in different parts of her body, and then hit the vamp directly in the heart meant only one thing – he needed me alive. Which is why he killed the vamp who had obviously strayed from his orders. I pulled my last arrow from the quiver and Garrett quickly responded, "Don't be so stupid, boy. There is no way you'll hit me before I've killed her."

"It's not for you," I replied and held the point of the arrow to my throat. "You're going to let us leave."

"You don't have the balls to hurt yourself," Delia laughed.

Gritting my teeth, I swiped the arrow tip and sliced my wrist. "You think I'm joking?" I shouted. Delia took a step forward, but Garrett put his bow in front of her. "Take one more step and I swear the next will be in my throat."

Neither Garrett nor Delia made another move so I took the opportunity to pull Tosha's arm across my shoulders and painfully get her around the car, all the while holding the arrow's tip at my throat. She screamed in pain as she sat down in the passenger seat, the arrows sticking out of her getting caught on various parts of the car.

As I ran around the front of the car, Garrett took a step forward so I gave my throat a superficial swipe, which made Garrett freeze. "If you follow us, I will flip the car or plunge this thing in my throat, do you understand me?"

"It's not like we don't know where you're going," Delia shouted as I opened the driver's side door.

"Then come there and get me. I dare you," I said and slid down into the driver's seat. The headlights shown on Delia and Garrett just watching us as I sped backwards out of the park. As I turned the wheel, the lights flooded on the three dead heaps lying on the ground. What a fucking mess.

Tosha groaned next to me as I sped down the street and headed back to the manor, being sure to keep an eye in the rearview mirror. "I'm sorry, I'm so sorry, Tosha."

"Just drive," she moaned through her clinched teeth and then gripped the arrow sticking out of her leg and yanked it out. "Shiiiiit! Holy shit, shit, shit!"

"What are you doing?!" I shouted and swerved the car back onto the road.

"I'm...healing...around them," she panted and reached for the arrow in her left shoulder. "Got to...get them...out." She tried pulling on the arrow, but it didn't budge and only caused her to grunt in pain.

"Stop, Tosha, stop!" I yelled and grabbed her hand. "Put pressure on your leg to stop the bleeding. Someone else can take out the other two."

When she didn't respond I glanced over at her to see that she had passed out. Worried that she was still bleeding from the hole in her leg, I pressed my palm down on her wound. She jolted awake and grunted in pain. Her body tensed and relaxed and tensed again as I weaved through traffic. My hand was covered in warm, sticky blood, and after another minute Tosha pushed my hand away.

"It's almost healed," she slurred, the pain she was in very much in her voice. She pressed a button on the console and then said, "Call Brianna."

The phone rang through the speakers and after only the second ring it was answered.

"Are you on your way back?" Brianna asked without saying hello.

"Brianna, it's Beckett. Tosh is hurt."

"What do you mean Tosh is hurt?"

"Bri," Tosha said in a teary voice, "I screwed up. I should have told them."

"What? What is happening? Beckett?"

"Brianna, I'm sorry. This is all my fault," I said as I turned up into the hills. "I lied. Garrett was here and not where I told Cameron. Tosh got shot and needs help. I didn't...I'm the one that screwed up. I didn't mean for this to happen."

There was silence on the other line.

"Brianna?"

"How far out are you?" she said tersely.

"Five, maybe ten minutes."

"We'll be waiting," she replied and hung up the phone.

"No doubt she's mad," I said and pressed the accelerator down. The

Mercedes just roared and glided up through the winding roads.

"That's her Warrior voice," Tosha groaned as she shifted in her seat. "We're in trouble."

"Just stay still, ok?" I said and squeezed her bloody hand in mine. She didn't fight me this time and when I looked over she had passed out again. "We're almost there," I whispered, mostly to make myself feel better.

It took only another six minutes before I was squealing onto the manor's street. I could see that the tall black gate up ahead was already open and several men were standing guard in front waving us. Once I pulled up to the front of the manor I slammed on the brakes and skidded to a stop.

Devin, Brianna, and Alex's wife Kyla were already waiting for us on the front steps. As soon as I cut the engine Devin opened the driver's side door, pulled me out of the car, and threw me up against the side. I was sure a little piss came out of me from the sight of his fangs only an inch away from my face.

"I'm sorry, I had to."

"Dear god!" Brianna shouted as she opened the passenger door.

Devin grabbed me by the back of the neck and dragged me toward the front steps. Behind me I could hear Tosha crying out in pain as they pulled her from the car. As we came through the door, Brianna flew past us with Tosha in her arms, the arrows sticking up over her shoulder.

"I'll get Nikki," Kyla said to Devin and ran away in a blur.

"Perfect," he grumbled and pushed me forward, the tops of my sneakers dragging and squeaking across the stone floor. "Like we need to add that nut job to this whole situation. Can you even fathom what you've done?"

"I didn't mean…"

"If you want to go and get yourself killed, go ahead. But you dare to jeopardize the life of one of my trainees? Twice!"

"Technically the first time wasn't my fault," I replied as we rounded a corner into an area of the manor I had never seen.

"I should snap your neck," he growled through clinched teeth.

"I didn't mean for this to happen."

Abruptly he stopped and pushed me into the stone wall. "Liar!" he shouted. "As soon as you sent my Warriors to a different location you meant for all of this to happen. I just hope you both can handle the consequences."

"Wh-what?" I stuttered but he painfully grabbed my shoulder and pushed me into a large, but very sparse bedroom.

Tosha was sitting on a long table in the center of the room. Her leg had stopped bleeding but she was obviously still uncomfortable and in pain from the other two arrows. Now in the light I could see that both arrows had gone through her and were sticking out the other side. I couldn't figure out if I wanted to vomit, bang my head against the wall, or run before one of these vamps killed me on the spot for doing this to her.

"Where is she!" someone called from the hallway and a second later Nikki came running into the room. She took one look at Tosha and then slapped me hard across the face. "You son of a bitch!"

Kyla put her hands on Nikki's shoulders and pushed her toward her sister.

"Nikki," Devin began as he placed an old-fashioned medical bag on the table, "your blood could help her heal faster. Are you ok with that?"

She sighed nervously. "I am as long as no one attacks me once I open a vein."

Brianna rolled her eyes, but didn't respond. Devin handed her a pair of scissors and she started to cut open Tosha's shirt from the bottom.

"Tosh, honey, do you want Beckett here?" Brianna asked as she began cutting around the arrow in Tosha's abdomen.

Tosha nodded slightly and replied in a weak voice, "He's seen them."

Brianna's eyes rose to meet Kyla's and then both of them along with Nikki looked in my direction in surprise. Devin didn't seem to give a shit and pulled out what looked like a small set of bolt cutters from his medical bag. When the shock over the fact that I had seen her scars had passed, Brianna carefully pulled Tosha's sweater from her body. Where the arrows had pierced through her there were streaks of blood trailing below.

This was just supposed to be an exchange, me for my mom. Tosha wasn't supposed to be hurt, and I only had a couple of scratches on my wrist and neck. I wanted Devin to pull the arrows out of Tosha and jab them into my eyes because I would never get this sight out of my head.

"Ok, Tosh, here's how it's going to go," Devin said as he stood behind her, "I have to cut one end of the arrow close to your skin, and then we'll pull it out through the other side. Understood?"

"Mm-hmm," she whimpered and squeezed Brianna's hands tightly.

"Now stay very still," Devin said and then opened the cutters on either side of the arrow in Tosha's shoulder. The metal of the blades were right up against Tosha's skin and then with a sudden snap the arrow was cut. Tosha tensed again when Devin placed the cutters around the arrow sticking out her back, but with another snap the other tip was gone.

Nikki placed gauze pads on both wounds and taped them securely.

"Lay her down," Devin instructed and the women responded by laying Tosha on her back.

Tosha groaned in pain. "Beckett," she whimpered and let her hand fall to her side.

Instantly I ran to her side and gently wrapped my hand around hers. "Tosha, I'm so sorry."

"No time for that," Devin snapped. "Everyone, hold her down. Tosh, I'm not going to lie, this will hurt. The tissue around the arrow has healed around it. I will start with the arrow in the shoulder and I'll be as quick as I can. Nikki, once I pull the arrow out, be ready to help her."

No one in my life had prepared me for this moment. I didn't know what to do so I rested my lips on Tosha's wrist. She squeezed my hand in response and braced herself for what was about to happen. With Brianna at her feet and Kyla at her head, Tosh was firmly held down in place while Devin pulled the arrow from her shoulder.

The action was quick, but with the arrow came a thick layer of bloody, pussy tissue around it and a piercing scream from Tosha. There was a hole almost two inches in diameter in her shoulder. Tosha's eyes rolled back in her head and she was mumbling incoherently while Nikki cut the inside of her palm and allowed it to bleed down into Tosha's wound.

"Just leave the other one," Tosha groaned and rolled over on her side.

"What?" I replied and tried pushing her back. "Tosha, you need…"

"Nope, just leave it in," she slurred, almost as if she were drunk, but it was truly from the delirium of pain.

"Tosha, I know it hurts, but we have to get it out."

Tears streamed from her eyes. "I can't…I can't do it."

"Natasha, you are the bravest girl I know, you can do this."

"It's going to hurt so bad," she cried.

"That it is," Devin replied as he held the bloody arrow up to his eye line and brushed his index finger against the surface. "No wonder it took so much tissue. There are tiny barbs on the shaft. Talk about an instrument of torture."

"Devin!" Brianna yelled and he quickly jerked to attention. "Let's not make the situation worse than it already is, ok?"

"I was just pointing out the reason…"

"And you've done that," Brianna snapped. "But it's not helping."

Nikki came around and pushed me out of the way. "Nat, the longer you wait, the more tissue will get connected. Now lay down and let's do this."

Tosha swallowed her tears and reluctantly laid back down on the table.

Nikki grazed the area around the arrow that was about an inch above Tosha's thick scrolling scars. "Damn, Nat, you are one lucky bitch."

"How so?" I asked, and from her glare it was obviously a stupid question.

"Because she can't heal from injuries in her scars, ass wipe!"

"Nikki, enough," Devin scolded.

"No, it's not enough," she shouted. "An inch lower and she could have some real damage. So forgive me if I want to punch this asshole in the face."

"Nik, stop," Tosha said weakly.

"Let's everyone stop and get this over with," Brianna snapped.

"We'll need everyone to hold her down," Devin commanded.

Tosha started shaking as everyone held her down at their post – Brianna at her feet, Nikki at her pelvis and legs, and Kyla at her head and shoulders. I felt so helpless just holding her hand.

"Breathe, Tosha, it'll be over soon," I said and tucked her hand into my chest.

"Ok, Tosh, in one, two," Devin began but didn't wait until three and began to pull.

Tosha screamed and bucked against those who restrained her, but suddenly all movement stopped when the arrow came free, leaving a hole three to four inches in diameter in the middle of Tosha's abdomen.

"Tosha?" I said and squeezed her hand, but she didn't respond. "Tosha!"

Her eyes were wide and frozen for a moment before finally closing, and then her body went limp.

"She's fine," Nikki snapped and then cut her palm again to let the blood drip into the hole.

"It's ok, Beckett," Kyla said kindly next to me and patted my hand. "I can hear her heart, it's still beating."

I nodded and watched as Nikki dressed her sister's second wound. Devin covered both disgusting looking arrows in a cloth and closed up his medical bag.

"Brianna," he said, "contact Cameron and let him know what all has happened. I will get a unit to surround the manor. If Garrett is still in the area, we may be at risk."

Brianna nodded and looked over me to see Kyla. "Ky, can you take Tosh to her room?"

"Of course," Kyla replied.

"I'll come with you," Nikki said and licked the blood away from her palm.

"And Beckett," Devin said and I jumped to attention, "later we will be talking about tonight's events."

"Yes, sir," I replied and felt my stomach sink.

Brianna followed behind Devin and slammed the door as they left the room. The sound caused Tosha to moan and her eyes flutter. I went to take her hand again but Nikki pushed me out of the way and took it instead.

"Nat," she said and petted Tosha's forehead and hair, "can you hear me? It's Nik. We need to take you back up to your room."

"Beck," Tosha whispered before her head flopped to the side.

Nikki glared at me over her shoulder, but then patted Tosha's hand and replied, "I'm going to take care of you tonight, Nat. We just need to get you upstairs."

"Where's Beckett," Tosha moaned and her eyes stretched open a little.

Nikki huffed loudly and tossed Tosha's hand away. "You know what, Nat, you want him, you got him. Ungrateful bitch."

Nikki stepped away from her sister and slammed the door.

"Well," Kyla sighed, "this has certainly been a dramatic evening."

I looked at her guiltily. I'd only met the woman with orange hair a couple of hours ago, and even then it was just an introduction. But in this moment she seemed like my only ally.

"I really didn't mean for any of this to happen."

"Of course you didn't," she said with a kind smile. "You're just thinking like a stupid kid."

My face fell. I might have been wrong about having her as an ally.

"Beck," Tosha said again, this time with her hand floating in the air.

Quickly I took her hand and looked down at her face. She was pale and her eyes were still very heavy.

"I'm right here, Tosha," I said. "Can you sit up if I help you?"

She nodded slightly and gripped my hand tightly. Kyla put an arm around her back, and the two of us carefully raised her to a sitting position.

Tosha yelped in pain and started to fall back, but thankfully Kyla caught her and held her up.

"Maybe you could give her your shirt?"

I looked down at my button-up shirt and then at Tosha who was only in a sports bra, her scars exposed, and blood soaking through her bandages. Quickly I unbuttoned my shirt, happy that I was wearing an undershirt, and with Kyla's help carefully put her arms through the sleeves.

Kyla placed a hand around Tosha's back, the other under her legs, and lifted her from the table.

"Aren't you coming?" Kyla asked as she stood in front of the door. "She's been calling your name, not mine."

I nodded nervously and held the door open for her. "Whose room is this anyway?"

"Devin's," she replied as we started down the stone corridor.

"Really? I thought it would be more...uh..."

"Glamorous? More like a coven leader's quarters should be?"

"Well, yeah," I replied nervously.

She shook her head. "It's not like we haven't tried, but that's Devin. No non-sense, to the point. Fabi tried to add some throw pillows one time. I don't think they talked for a week."

"Who's Fabi?"

"Oh, Fabiani. That's Devin's partner," she replied as we came closer to the foyer and the areas I was more familiar with.

"Partner? Wait, you mean like Devin's gay?"

"Gay, gay, in every way," she replied with a smile. "Does that surprise Of course for some reason there were more people roaming the halls than usual and they took notice of Natasha Cushlin passed out in Kyla's arms. you?"

"Of course it does," I replied way too loudly. "Sorry. Just me being a stupid kid again, I guess."

"You're very good at it," she replied but in a very sweet tone.

Whenever Tosha woke up, she was going to kill me.

When we started up the spiral staircase Tosha stirred and groaned in Kyla's arms. Instinctively I reached for her hand.

"Aw," Kyla cooed, "you're so sweet."

"She's going to be ok, right?"

"Tonight will suck, but yes, she'll be ok. Tomorrow will be the real whopper."

"Wh-what's tomorrow?"

Kyla raised her eyebrows and I could see that in her mind she was calling me a stupid kid again. "Beckett, you and Tosh have a lot of explaining to do. You're a guest here, but Tosh is a trainee. There are consequences for the choices she made tonight."

"But I didn't mean for it to go down like this. I was just going to trade myself for my mom. I didn't mean for Tosha to get hurt, she just wouldn't let me steal her car."

Kyla smiled as we turned and stepped up on the landing. "Stupid kid."

"Yeah, that's for sure."

Once we got to Tosha's room I opened the door and Kyla put her down on the bed.

"Are you going to stay with her?" she asked.

"Absolutely. Although she'll probably kick me out once she's conscious."

"That sounds like Tosh. Well, good luck. I need to check on the twins."

"Thanks, Kyla."

"Goodnight, stupid kid."

I smiled as she waved goodbye. Tosha woke at the sound of the door shutting. With a loud groan she rolled onto to her side and then pushed herself up to a seated position.

"Tosha, please stop moving…"

"My boots," she slurred and reached down to her feet.

"I'll get them," I replied and unzipped each boot. As soon as the second boot was off she stood from the bed and unbuttoned her jeans. Her eyes were closed, almost as if she were sleep walking, or more so sleep undressing. I didn't know whether to look away or help. When she began pulling the jeans down her hips I decided helping was the better option. I pushed her hands off and pulled her jeans down to her calves. It was the first time I had seen the scars below her waist. My jaw clinched at the sight of them traveling down to her thighs.

When she sat back down on the bed I freed her of her pants completely and she fell to her side. I pulled the blankets down behind her, gently turned her over to face the wall, and tucked her underneath the covers. Now what?

There was another twin-sized bed against the opposite wall, it was either that or the uncomfortable-looking chair in the corner. With my decision made I pulled off of my sneakers and stepped toward the other bed when Tosha started groaning. When I turned around she was twitching and flipping the blankets off of her.

"Too hot," she said breathlessly. I took the blankets from her and folded them down. Tosha curled up in a ball and I couldn't help but stretch out behind her. Beads of sweat formed all over her body. She was healing, but it was painful.

"Tosha, I'm so sorry," I said, placing my forehead against the nape of her neck. All of her pain was my fault. Me, the stupid kid.

Tosha cried out loudly as her grip on my hand became a vice. Tears streamed from the corners of her eyes before she went completely limp and silent. I watched her ribs closely and breathed a sigh of relief when they raised and lowered. Her hand went lax in mine so I untangled her fingers and gently placed her arm across her waist.

Once again I rested my forehead against the nape of her neck, feeling absolutely helpless and guilty for everything she was going through. My hand rested on her hip and I felt the uneven skin of her scars. I propped myself up on my elbow and looked down at her. My shirt only covered her waist and the top of her hips, leaving most of her scars exposed. Gently I traced my fingers along the different ridges and swirls, feeling where the smooth and bumpy scar tissue met and melted together. Someone had done this to her, and now I was responsible for causing her even more pain.

I would hold her all night if she let me, and by the time we woke I would know the feeling of every inch of her scars. I prayed she wouldn't push me away because I wasn't just holding her for her sake, but also mine. I needed her. I liked Tosha a lot, it was an instant connection on my part, and tonight I could have easily lost her because I was a stupid kid in a new world he had no business being in. I couldn't lose her again, or her swirling scars.

Chapter Fourteen

"Beckett, get up," a male said as he kicked the edge of the mattress.

I rolled over, putting my hand over my eyes as I tried to pull them open.

"Jared?"

"Yeah, it's me," he replied tersely and kicked the mattress again. "Now get up."

"What?" I asked, still not fully awake and pulled the blanket off of me

"Damn, man," Jared shouted and looked away, "put that thing away."

I looked down and realized I had massive morning wood. People seriously needed to stop waking me up out of a dead sleep like this. Quickly I put the blanket back over me.

"Sorry, man, you woke me up. Wait…" I said, my brain finally starting to wake up. "Where's Natasha?"

"She's already getting hers."

"What do you mean getting hers?"

Jared put his hands on his hips. "She has to answer for the stunt you two pulled last night."

"But it was all me. I tried to steal her car and when she stopped me I gave her no choice."

"No, there were fifty other choices she could have made. She made a stupid choice and she has to answer for it. It's that simple."

"What's going to happen to her?"

He scrunched his brows together and looked at me like I was stupid. "She's out, Beck."

"Out? Out of the program?"

"Of course. What did you think was going to happen?"

"I need to talk to them," I said and stood from the bed.

"Don't worry, Beck, you're up next."

"No, I need to talk to them now," I said and pushed past him, but he grabbed my arm tightly and whipped me back around.

"Hey! You don't get a say here, Beckett. This is serious and you can't just go barging in on them because you have some mad crush."

I shook my head. "That's not what this is about. Hey man, I'm losing feeling in my arm, could you let go of me?"

"Fuck you for almost getting her killed. She's family to me, Beckett, and the fact that you brought her here with two arrows sticking out of her makes me want to rip your goddamn face off." He let go of me roughly, knocking me back a step. "But I won't."

"Well, you can't, can you?" He raised his eyebrows at me. "It's a law or something. You can't hurt humans or hybrids."

"I just can't get caught," he replied. "Seriously, when is that thing going to go down?"

Placing a pillow over me, I waddled into the bathroom to splash some water on my face. Once my morning wood went down, I stepped backed out into the bedroom and stuffed my feet into my sneakers. Once I stood from the bed, Jared opened the bedroom door and pushed me out into the hallway. He stayed right behind my left shoulder as we walked to the spiral staircase in angry silence. When we got about halfway down another Warrior was coming up the stairs and he glared at me. When it happened again with another Warrior at the foot of the stairs I looked back at Jared.

"Why are people giving me the evil eye?"

"Those two were on the mission last night," he replied. "And no one knows why you're getting to stay and Tosh is getting kicked out. Because of course, they can't. It's another reason why what you did last night makes you an asshole."

"Kyla called me a stupid kid."

"She was being nice."

Just as we turned the corner, Tosha was running out of the study. Her hand was covering her mouth while her loud sobs escaped and echoed off the walls. Unfortunately, Connor was right behind her and as soon as he saw me I thought he would be the one that would actually rip my face off.

"Tosha," I said, causing her to look up before we collided.

She stopped abruptly and lowered her hand from her face. Her eyes were red and swollen from crying and her whole body was shaking. I reached for her hand but in the blink of an eye she reared her hand back and punched me in the face. I was so taken off guard that I fell into the wall.

"Leave me alone!" she shouted and ran around the corner.

My cheek was pounding, but suddenly I was pulled up by my shoulders and pressed uncomfortably into the stone wall.

"This was all she had and you screwed her over," Connor growled in my face. His fangs were extended and dangerously close.

"That's enough, Connor," Jared said and put his hand on Connor's shoulder.

Connor shoved him back hard but Jared grabbed him by his shoulders and forcibly pulled him away. My knees failed and I slid down to the floor while the two of them kept pushing each other.

"Enough!" someone yelled.

When I looked to my right I saw Devin standing in the middle of the corridor. Both men stepped back from each other, but neither stopped glaring.

"Connor, I believe you have a session with the trainees," Devin said tersely.

"Yes, sir," Connor replied, finally breaking from Jared's gaze and turning to me. "And we're one down because of you."

"Move on, Connor," Devin warned. "Dawes, inside."

Jared bent down and pulled me up to a standing position. I brushed myself off and thanked him, but he didn't acknowledge me in the slightest. I was beginning to wonder if there was anyone left in this big place that would talk to me after what happened last night.

Unfortunately, Cameron's and Devin's study was becoming a familiar sight. The fireplace to the right wasn't lit, making the room less comforting and warm, and the looks I was getting from Cameron, Devin, and even Brianna were even colder. Once Jared closed the door behind me, Devin and Cameron sat on the edges of their desks with their arms crossed tightly in front of their chests.

"Sirs," I began nervously, "may I..."

"No, you may not," Cameron interrupted and pointed at my face. "What happened to your face?"

"Um...I ran into a door."

He narrowed his eyes at me. "Did one of my Warriors do that to you?"

I shook my head. "No, sir."

He didn't seem convinced, but continued, "Very well. We have heard Natasha's side of the story, now we have some questions for you."

"Yes, and Natasha is exactly who I need to talk to you about..."

"Did you lie about the meeting location last night," Cameron said over me.

"Yes."

"Why?"

Before I could answer, the study door opened and Victor came inside.

"Have I missed anything?" he asked calmly and came to stand next to me.

"No, Father," Devin replied, "we have just started."

"Oh good," Victor said. "As you were."

"Father, we did not invite you..."

"Beckett is my grandson," Victor interrupted. "He will need my counsel."

Cameron gave Devin an impatient glance before coming back to me and asking, "Why did you lie to us about the location?"

I sighed and looked down at the floor. Just as I was about to answer, Victor tapped my arm and gestured for me to look up. "It is important you make eye contact, child. Keep your head up."

Awkwardly I straightened up and once again saw Devin and Cameron exchange impatient glances.

After swallowing the lump in my throat, I finally responded, "I was stupid and scared."

"There you have it," Victor said.

"Father, please," Cameron warned. "Beckett, you will need to elaborate."

"Look, this is new to me. My mother has been taken and my father is a monster. Garrett called and I had a chance to get my mom back. He was specific that he would kill her if he saw any Warriors. I was afraid you wouldn't listen to me."

"Beckett, we have been doing this kind of thing for hundreds of years. We know the threats that people make, and we know how to go into a situation without being noticed," Cameron replied.

"Yes, child," Victor said, "but you are going against another person who knows the general tactics. Beckett had every right to be concerned for

164 ~ C.R. Quinn

the safety of his mother if Garrett saw any of you."

"He had a reason to be concerned, but not to lie and send our forces away from the manor, exposing all that live here to a man and his army, and severely injuring a hybrid that if she had not been a Healer would have died last night."

Victor gave a slight nod. "Yes, you do have a point there, but do not negate his reasoning. Beckett, tell them why you lied."

I looked at him nervously, a little unsure of what he wanted me to say, but I jumped when he hit me in the arm and replied, "I just wanted my mom back and I was worried about my dad. We don't know if his heart will be strong enough when the full moon comes. I needed my mom here to be with him, I didn't care about myself. Garrett wanted me for her, and that's all. I was willing to do that, and that's why I lied."

"And you were naïve to think you could confront a former Warrior and no one would get hurt. Both of you could have been killed," Devin said and stood from his desk. "I expect the stupidity from you, but Tosh should have known better."

My shoulders fell. "That's really what I wanted to talk about. Here's the deal, I was going to steal her car but she stopped me. She told me I was making a mistake and was ready to call you, but I begged her not to. It wasn't her fault, I pressured her into coming. She was really just trying to ensure my mom got back safe. She shouldn't be kicked out of the training program because of something I did."

"That is where you are wrong, Beckett," Cameron said flatly. "Natasha knew better and she made a bad decision. It was her choice to go with you and not contact anyone. You lying to us is a risk and an inconvenience. Her lying to us is a betrayal and that means expulsion from the program. It is that simple."

"No it's not!" I yelled and Devin's crossed arms fell to his sides ready to strike, but I didn't back down. "This place, the Warriors, this is her life. There is nothing else she wants but to be one of you. You can't take this away from her, not after everything she's been through. I don't think…she won't…I don't know what she'll do. She shouldn't be punished for the situation I put her in. Let me do *something*, please!"

"What did you have in mind, child?"

"Father!" Cameron snapped.

Victor shrugged next to me. "It wouldn't hurt to hear what sacrifice he's willing to make in order to save Miss Cushlin's position."

Cameron stood from his desk and pulled his fingers slowly down his face. "I cannot believe I am hearing this. Father, you would have chained us to a board or worse for doing something like this."

"And perhaps I was too harsh and too quick to judge," Victor replied.

Cameron put his hands on his hips and looked up at the ceiling in frustration for several seconds before saying, "Father you are utterly unbelievable. Fine, Beckett, what would you sacrifice for Natasha?"

"My life," I blurted out and Victor put his hand on my shoulder.

"That would defeat the purpose, child. Think of something else."

Looking down at Victor a thought struck me and I needed them to understand how much of a sacrifice it would be for me.

"What's it called when a hybrid drinks your blood?"

Victor raised his eyebrow and gave me a smile. "Activation?"

"Yeah, that. I'll let you guys activate me."

"And how exactly is that a sacrifice that benefits us?" Devin asked.

"Well, it's a sacrifice for me because it's the last thing I want to do. Since this all started I've been fighting to keep as much of my old self intact. The last thing I want is to be more like Garrett."

"I still don't see how…"

"And I'll give up the Warrior by birth thing. You don't need to protect me and I won't tell anyone who my birth father is, ever. And I won't ask for anything when this is all over."

Devin glanced over at Cameron before replying, "So you'll give up the birthright in exchange for us allowing Tosh back in." I nodded. "And I can kill you if you tell anyone who your birth father is."

I choked on my spit and Victor patted my shoulder. "He's kidding. So, are we in agreement? Activation and birthright revocation for Beckett in exchange for Miss Cushlin's reinstatement?"

This time Cameron glanced over to Devin who gave a slight nod. "Very well. Father, I am assuming you will activate him?"

"Of course," Victor said and pulled on my shoulder.

"I'll go find Tosh and tell her what's happening," Brianna said and left the office ahead of us.

"Before you go," Cameron said and held up his hand, "we also need to have an understanding going forward." I swallowed and nodded nervously. "If Garrett contacts you again, and I believe he will, you will tell us. Is that understood? If we find out that you are keeping anything from us, or if you dare to lie to us again, not only will Natasha be kicked out of the program, but you will be on your own. Neither you nor anyone in your family will have access to our resources. All efforts to find your mother and help your father will cease. Am I being clear?"

"Yes, sir," I replied and almost felt ill.

Victor squeezed my shoulder again and directed me from the study. I had forgotten all about Jared being with us until he stepped up next to me.

"Aren't you a lucky son of a bitch," he said. "Don't be surprised if Tosh isn't thrilled with your arrangement."

"As long as she's in, I don't care. What do we do now?"

"What we said, I will activate you," Victor answered.

"Now? Like right now?"

"When did you think he was going to do it?" Jared said and steered me up the spiral staircase.

"No time like the present, and we are running out of time."

"We are?"

"Dear, dear child, you have so much to learn. Garrett didn't get what he wanted and he'll be trying to find ways to get to you."

"Oh," I replied, my stomach starting to flip and spasm. The sight of my room's door made me take a large nervous breath in. Jared pushed the door open and the three of us filed in. "That's why I cut myself."

Jared's head flinched in my direction. "Was the rest of that conversation in your head?"

"Sorry," I said and sat down on the bed, "Victor said Garrett didn't get what he wanted. Last night, one of his vamps leapt at me and Garrett shot him through the heart. That's when I realized he didn't want me hurt. I only had one arrow left so I cut my wrist a little. When he didn't believe I'd hurt myself I nicked my throat. I think that's the only reason why he let us go."

Victor squinted his eyes at me, but there were a thousand thoughts running behind them.

"Well, Dad, maybe he's not as stupid as we thought," Jared said and stepped to the corner of the room.

"Perhaps," Victor replied and began rolling up his sleeve. "Now, let's get on with it, Beckett. I will pierce the skin on my wrist, and you will need to drink from me. You must be quick or else the wounds will close."

"Huh?"

"I take it back, Dad, he is as stupid as we thought," Jared groaned and sat down in the chair in the corner. "Dude, you have to drink his blood."

"Yeah, but…can't you…I don't know, put it in a cup or something?"

"No," Victor sighed impatiently. "Now open up."

I went to object but in the blink of an eye Victor bit into his wrist and placed it up to my mouth. The thick, cold blood touched my bottom lip first, but when I didn't start to drink it, Victor wrapped his free hand behind my head and pressed my mouth into his arm. The cold blood ran to the back of my mouth and I was forced to swallow. Victor didn't release his grip on me and I reluctantly swallowed again, and then again. My stomach was turning and I kept telling myself not to throw up.

Victor lowered his wrist and I took in gulps of air. "Now, that wasn't so bad, was it?"

I wiped my mouth, my thump coming away with a thin smear of blood. "If you say so. That's it, right?"

Victor nodded and Jared stood from the chair in the corner. Oddly both were staring at me intensely.

"Do I have something on my face?" Both shook their head in unison. "Then why are you staring at me?"

"How do you feel?" Victor asked.

"Besides trying not to get totally freaked out by you two, I feel ok."

Victor smiled in relief. "That is good news."

"Why is that good news?"

"I have never activated a hybrid. I wasn't quite sure how you would react."

"Now you say that!" I said and stood from the bed.

Just then my bedroom door flew open and Tosha stood in the doorway panting. "You think I need your fucking help?" she yelled. "I do NOT need you to help me."

Victor and Jared quickly stepped to their right in order to fully expose me to Tosha's wrath. Seeing her made my stomach flip and suddenly my cheeks became hot and flush. Tosha slammed the door behind her. She didn't seem to care that Victor and Jared were in the room.

"I don't need you to make deals for me," she continued to yell and stepped right up to me, putting her finger in my face. "I will find a way to get back into the program without anything from you."

"I beg to differ, my dear," Victor interrupted and a sudden chill came over my body that made me sit back down on the bed. "Devin and Cameron were very firm in their decision to release you. Beckett's deal is the only reason you are being allowed to come back."

My body started to shutter and sweat began to form on my forehead. Was I getting the flu? Was there such a thing as vamp flu?

"Why do you look like you're going to be sick?" Tosha asked.

"I don't know," I replied and shivered. "I was fine before...I...I...I think I am going to be sick."

"You cannot," Victor said and moved Tosha to the side. I flinched when he put his ice-cold hand on my forehead. "You mustn't lose any of the blood you drank."

"Blood he drank?" Tosha asked over Victor's shoulder. "Did you activate him?"

"Yes, child," Victor replied, "that was one of several stipulations. Let's hope he doesn't have a reaction like Brianna."

"What...happened?" I asked and fell onto my side across the bed.

"I suppose we should leave him in your care, Miss Cushlin," Victor said completely ignoring me.

Tosha looked at Victor and then back down at me, a cross between shock and confusion on her face. "Um...yeah, I guess."

Victor turned slightly to his left and raised an eyebrow at her. "Your confidence is overwhelming, Miss Cushlin. Can I count on you to take care of my grandson?"

"Yes, sir," she responded, her tone drastically different than before.

"And you will advise me if he takes a turn for the worse?"

"Of course."

"Turn for the worse?" I said although it was muffled into the pillow that was mushed to my face.

"Rest up, Beck," Jared said and patted me hard on the shoulder, "training only gets harder from here."

"Harder?"

"Oh yeah, you've stepped in it now," he laughed.

Victor stepped up next to me and squeezed my shoulder. "Do rest, Beckett. Those you love are depending on you."

"No pressure," I replied and heard the door shut.

I lifted my head from the pillow and found Tosha standing with her back to me. When she finally turned around I could see that her eyes were red and her face blotchy. Suddenly another shiver came over me. I was freezing even though sweat was soaking into my shirt. Tosha stepped into the bathroom and returned with a washcloth in her hand. She rolled me onto my back and sat down on the bed. I gasped when she wiped the cold, wet washcloth across my forehead.

"Sorry, but you're burning up," she said and wiped the cloth down my neck. When I started shivering she pulled the blanket from the bottom of the bed over me. After she tucked it around my sides she began wiping my forehead again. "Why did you do this?"

I pulled her hand away from my face and tucked it into my chest. "I'll do anything...for you."

"Don't say that."

"It's true, Tosha. I'm sorry," I said and began to shiver uncontrollably, "I shouldn't....have gotten you...mixed up in this."

"Stop, ok, just rest," she said and wiped my forehead again. "I can't believe you agreed to get activated."

"Among other things."

"What else? God, Beckett, what have you done?"

"I gave up my birthright," I answered and she froze.

"What? Why? Why would you do that? Beckett, you shouldn't have done that for me."

"You're worth it."

"You need to stop saying stuff like that."

"Why?"

She didn't answer right away and instead looked at the other wall. "I'm not worth this, Beckett."

"Not...true," I replied and felt as though my head was going to explode. Ice was running through my veins and making my limbs flinch and shake. "You scared me...last night. It was...all my fault."

Through the haze and ache I went to touch her cheek when a pain in my stomach made me curl up in a ball. She brought my hand into her chest and rested her cheek on mine.

"You need to fight, Becks," she said, holding me tightly against her while I shook and groaned in pain. "For your mother and your dad, you need to fight through this for them."

"And...you?"

She sniffled and took a moment before she answered, "Yes. Me too."

I lifted my head slightly causing her to rise and look down at me. Seeing Natasha with tears in her eyes was more painful than the fire that was burning through my body. I untangled my hand from hers and wiped the tears from her cheek.

"I'm glad...you're here," I said. "Don't...leave...this time."

"I need you to get better," she replied and began wiping my forehead with the washcloth again

"Don't…leave."

She shook her head. "I won't."

"Don't punch…me…again."

She gave me a little smirk. "I can't make any promises."

I flinched violently at the feeling of ice-cold hands touching my face and neck. My eyes could only open a slight amount and I could see a man hovering closely over me, lifting my eyelids and shining a light into them.

"Tosha," I said painfully through my burning throat.

"I'm here," she replied and I could see her face over the man's shoulder.

I pushed the man away when he put a freezing cold stethoscope on my chest.

"Beck, let Dr. Ryan look at you," she said.

"Oh, hey, doc," I said and released his hand. "Sorry"

"Hey, Beckett," he laughed and put the stethoscope to my chest again. "You just keep looking better every time I see you, kid."

"I try," I replied and arched my back in order to take in a breath.

Dr. Ryan laughed again and stood from the bed. "Well, besides the fever, Beckett is exhibiting the symptoms we expect from an activation, especially from someone as old as Victor. I'm sorry there's not much else we can do but let this pass."

"But he's been like this all day. Isn't there something you can give him?"

"I'm sorry, Tosh," Dr. Ryan said, "there's nothing I can really do. The cold compresses will help and be sure to keep him hydrated. If the fever doesn't break within the next couple of hours, try using some bags of ice under his arms, knees, and neck."

"That…does not…sound fun."

"Shut up, Beckett," Tosha snapped and glared at me before looking back at Dr. Ryan. "Thanks for coming."

"No problem," he replied and pulled his bag onto his shoulder. "Just call me if anything changes or gets worse. Take care, Beckett, this'll all pass soon, I promise."

"Thanks, doc," I replied and curled onto my side.

I heard the door shut and a moment later Tosha was sitting on the edge of the mattress. Softly she brushed my forehead and I tried not to flinch from how cold her fingers were.

"I feel like shit," I groaned and rested my cheek against her leg.

"Then you look how you feel," she replied and I couldn't help but smirk. "Let me get another cold compress."

"No," I said and grabbed her thigh. "Just stay here."

"We have to get your fever down."

"Just a few minutes," I begged and pushed back to look her in the eye. "Please, Tosha?"

After only a few seconds her face broke and she nodded. "But you need to drink something."

Before I could try and keep her on the bed, she was up and stepping into the bathroom. I pushed across the narrow bed until my back was pressed up against the wall. Tosha came out of the bathroom a few moments later with a glass of water in her hand. She sat down on the bed again and helped me sit up enough to take a sip of water. My fever was so high and the water so cold that I could feel it traveling down my throat, chest, and down into my stomach.

"Drink some more," she said and held the glass up to my lips.

I only took a small sip since my stomach was starting to churn. "Why did you leave?"

She looked at me confused. "Leave? Becks, I've been here the whole time."

I shook my head. "No, this morning."

She sighed and bent over to the floor. It wasn't until she lifted her foot and pulled off her boot did I realize what she was doing. After she removed her second boot she pulled both legs up on the edge of the bed.

"I didn't have much choice, Beck. They were waiting outside the door."

"But you left and went out that door."

"Fine, I was scared," she replied. "That can't be too much of a surprise."

"Scared...of what?" I said as my body started to shake again.

She stretched out next to me, her head sharing my pillow. With the narrow mattress we were practically nose to nose. Her fingers glided across my forehead and down my jawline.

"You need to get better so we can do it again," she whispered.

"I...can hold...you," I said and pulled my arm out from under the blanket, but she took my hand and tucked it into her chest.

"You can't hold anything right now, Becks."

I liked when she called me Becks, especially when she was looking at me with her big dark eyes. I wished I could soak her in without feeling like my insides were burning through to the outside.

"Can I..." I started to say, but then my head started to pound at the same rhythm as the pulsing in my stomach.

"What do you need? What can I do?"

I took a few deep breaths before I replied, "Let me...touch your scars."

She blinked several times before replying, "What?"

I panted from the burning pain in my stomach and rested my forehead against her shoulder. "I like...the way...they feel."

"Uh...when did you feel them?"

"Last night."

"When last night?"

"You were...sleeping."

"You felt me up?" she asked, her voice slightly raised.

I lifted my head from her shoulder. "No! I was holding you. Not my...fault you only...had my shirt on. I didn't sleep much...so I was feeling them...and then I named them."

She raised her left eyebrow. "You did what?"

"N-named them?"

"I...I don't even know what you're talking about."

I pulled my hand from her chest and looked in her eyes for permission before I slowly began to pull up her shirt.

"This one's the wave," I said as I traced my fingers across one of her scars in the middle of her stomach that stretched up and curled like a wave cresting in the ocean. Her body tensed and her eyes didn't move from mine. Then I reached over to the side of her waist where a scar was flat in the middle but pulled into several points. "This one is the star."

Her nostrils flared as I ran my fingers up the side of the of her thigh to her hip. Even through her pants I could feel the ridges I was looking for. "And last, the three fingers."

"Three fingers?"

I nodded. "It's like three fingers ran up your thigh."

She cleared her throat and wiped her eye. "You need to stop."

I rested my hand where the wave scar was carved into her stomach. "I like the way...they feel."

"You don't have to live with them."

"I like how they feel."

"You said that."

"They're you. It's all you," I said and nuzzled into her. "Tell me a story."

"What?" she said with a flinch.

"I'm sick...tell me a story to take...my mind off."

"A story?"

"Mmm-hmm. About you."

"Wha...why?" she groaned.

I pushed back to look at her in the face. "You could have died...last night. I feel like...I'm going...to die now..."

"You are not going to die. I haven't..." she interrupted and pursed her lips, "I've broken all of my rules for you, so don't you even dare talk like you're going anywhere. You are going to fight through this, do you hear me?"

My head shook from the fever and pain, but it was enough to make her think I was nodding. "So will you tell me...a story? About these," I said and pressed my hand against her scars.

She inhaled slowly, her face extremely tense as she exhaled. "Fine. Not like it's a secret..." she sighed again. "A year after I got to Facility West I met Ty Firino. He was wild, rule-breaking, fun, basically everything I wasn't which was why I was drawn to him. He was also a Firestarter. Do you know what that is?"

I shook my head against her chest.

"A Firestarter can create fire and control it."

I lifted my head. "Are you serious?"

She nodded. "He could create it right from his palm."

"That's awesome," I replied and put my head back down.

"Yeah well, it can also radiate throughout their body. Ever heard of spontaneous combustion?" I nodded. "Well, those are Firestarters who couldn't control their fire."

I lifted my head again. "I thought that was a myth."

"So are vampires," she replied with a smile.

I put my head back down and said, "So the less-handsome-than-me Ty was a Firestarter."

"Yes, the similarly handsome Ty was a Firestarter, and his father sent him to the Facility because he thought they could help him. Ty was a little...resistant to anything that came from his dad."

"Why?"

"His father was very all or nothing, which considering they were Firestarters is pretty understandable. Ty just wasn't that way and rebelled against everything and anything."

"And you liked that?"

She laughed lightly. "I'm allowed a rebellious period, too. Anyway, Trevor had a steady girlfriend..."

"Trevor?"

"Roberts has a first name, remember? He and Ty were best friends so the four of us were always hanging out together. Too bad he turned into an asshole when he got here."

"True."

"Anyway, things got serious with me and Ty and neither of us had ever been with anyone else. Everyone kept warning me that being with a Firestarter was a bad idea, especially when it came to sex. Of course I didn't listen. Even Trevor was warning Ty that he didn't have enough control over his powers. But what happens when you tell two stupid kids not to have sex, it only pushes them to prove everyone wrong.

"So Ty planned this whole night together, and we started to...you know." She went quiet for a moment. "He started getting really warm, which I was used to, but then it started getting uncomfortable. I told him we should stop and let him cool down, but he just kept pushing saying he was ok." She paused again and I put my hand around her waist, pulling her into me. "I started smelling something burning. I think it was the sheets or something. He was getting close to...you know...I remember opening my eyes and looking at him, he was...glowing. He looked like...it's so stupid, but for a second I remember thinking he looked like an angel. He was this golden glowing being and I pulled him closer thinking in some way that we would meld together like in some kind of stupid movie. But instead, he...that glow he had, it was like a sunburst. There was this burning hot pain that shot through me. The bed caught fire, and then the whole room was in flames. Ty's body burned me alive. The heat and the pain was...I just wanted to die.

"Finally, someone came in and put the fire out. They thought I was dead, but when they pulled Ty off of me I made a sound or something, I don't even remember. They rushed me to the medical ward, but didn't think I'd survive. I was burned down to the bone in some places. After a few days my upper body finally started to grow back, then my legs. They really had hope until everything stopped when it came to my abdomen and pelvis, but considering they had to rip Ty's body off of mine..." she sighed and cleared her throat. "That's when they tried doing the skin grafts which for whatever reason my body didn't take very well and left me like this."

"I like them," I said and squeezed her into me.

"Do you?" she asked as her index finger traced across my eyebrow.

"As much as I like you."

Her eyes suddenly became glassy and she bit her bottom lip.

"I won't...hurt you," I stuttered while another shiver went through my body. My eyes closed from the pain but a second later I felt cool, soft lips pressing against mine ever so softly. Slowly I opened my eyes halfway, which was all they would stretch. I opened my lips slightly and pushed against her, although I could feel how tentative she was.

But a second later my whole body started to spasm and cramp. My back arched painfully and Tosha placed her cold hands on my face and neck.

"Let's get you in the shower," she said trying to pull me forward, but my body stiffened making it impossible to move. Tosha didn't give up and heaved me over the side of the bed causing both of us to topple onto the floor. The action knocked the breath out of her but a few seconds later she pushed herself up to a standing position, snaked her arms under my armpits, and dragged me into the bathroom.

Tosha whipped back the shower curtain and flipped the faucet on. When she turned back to me she propped me up against the wall and began pulling my shirt over my head.

"This isn't going...to feel...good. Is it?" I asked, already shivering from the cold floor and lack of shirt.

"Just remember I'm trying to help you, so don't hate me."

I shook my head. "Never."

"You say that now. Ok, you're going to have to help a little. I can't lift you into the tub."

"No, I wanna know," I slurred.

"What?"

"I wanna know why you were scared." She didn't answer. "I won't stop asking."

She looked at me angrily. "You are infuriating."

"Won't stop asking."

"I liked waking up in your arms, ok?" she snapped. "It scared me to death. Just like having to see you like this. I'm scared, happy? Can we be done with this and get you in the tub?"

"I knew you liked me," I replied and tried telling my legs to push up. I was only able to get a couple inches off the ground, but Tosha was able to pull me into her side and walk me to the tub. My legs felt like rubber as I lifted them over the edge of the tub and practically fell down in a heap. At first the cold water only hit my toes and it was uncomfortable, but when Tosha flipped the switch to the shower, suddenly it was like shards of ice were stabbing my body.

"Holy shit," I yelled as the water washed over my face and bare chest. "Fuck! Mother-fucking-fuck!"

"I'm sorry," Tosha cried above me.

"Turn it off!" I screamed.

"I can't, Becks, please…"

"I lied, I fucking hate you right now!"

Chapter Fifteen

The sun was beating against my face. It was waking me up enough to realize my entire body was damp, but thankfully free from pain. Slowly I opened my eyes, having to turn my face away from the window to avoid the morning sun. That's when I noticed Tosha laying on the floor, curled up in a ball with her head propped up on what looked like a rolled-up hoodie. That certainly made me feel shitty.

Slowly I peeled away the damp towels from my body and slid to the edge of the bed. Tosha looked so peaceful even though she was lying on the uncomfortable floor. She needed to be up in the bed, but all the sheets were damp from the bags of ice and wet towels.

Quietly I stepped over Tosha to get to the dresser where I had seen a set of clean sheets. After I pulled the sheets and blankets from the bed, I stretched the flat sheet over the mattress and flipped the pillows over to the drier side. I knelt down next to Tosha and touched her shoulder. Instantly she flinched and her eyes flew open.

"What? You ok?" she asked breathlessly and grabbed my arm.

"I'm fine," I replied and pulled her hand off my arm. "I just want you to get in the bed."

"Are you sure..." she began, but I helped her up from the floor to the bed.

"Go back to sleep," I interrupted and kissed her hair. "I'm going to take a shower."

She looked up and touched my bare chest. "You feel much better."

"But I smell like shit. Go back to sleep," I said and leaned down slowly, hovering for only a moment before she tilted her chin up and allowed my lips to rest on top of hers. When I raised up her eyes were still closed, a small relaxed smile forming at the corners of her lips.

"You do smell like shit," she said and fell backwards on the mattress.

I laughed to myself and walked into the bathroom. Clothes and towels were strewn all over the floor. Things got hairy a couple of times last night, and even the sight of the shower made me shiver. I stepped up to the sink and looked in the mirror. My hair was sticking up in all directions, and the bags under my eyes made me look like I'd been on a binder all night. But besides that, nothing seemed different. I guess I was expecting super powers or lasers coming out of my fingers after all I went through. Great.

While I debated on whether I was the only hybrid whose activation didn't take, I flipped on the shower and turned it to the hottest setting. Although I wasn't shivering anymore, I still felt cold down to my bones. The hot water pelted me and soaked into my skin until it was a bright red and humming with warmth.

A few minutes later I was dry and donning a clean pair of underwear and sweatpants. When I stepped back out into my bedroom I had to stop and check that I was in the right room. I saw my bag on the floor, bow and arrow in the corner chair, but everything else had been neatly put away or folded. I looked over at the bed where Tosha was now curled up in a comforter, the clean sheets peeking out from underneath. How did she clean so fast? Seriously, how was it physically possible?

With a sigh I stepped over to the bed, lifted the comforter, and slid up behind Tosha. She was curled tightly in a ball, her knees pulled up high into her abdomen. My arm wrapped around the side of her waist and my hand slipped underneath her shirt instantly finding the star-shaped scar. My fingers began to trace its edges when Tosha turned around in my arms. Her eyes stretched open, even though they stayed half closed from exhaustion.

She brushed her fingers down my cheek as she said, "Feel ok?"

"Yup."

"Feel any different?"

"Nope. I'm a dud."

"Don't say that," she replied and then yawned widely. "Sometimes things just start happening"

"So, are you next?"

She scrunched her face. "After what happened to you? I think you made my case not to. Plus, Cameron and Devin aren't pushing it...well, at this point maybe they're thinking what's the point."

"Stop," I said and pressed my forehead against hers. "they're not pushing it because you're doing great without being activated."

"Unlike you, the dud," she said with a smile.

When she titled her head back my lips instantly found hers. Just a gentle kiss on her unbelievably soft lips. When I opened my mouth slightly she pulled away and looked down.

"Tosh?"

Without a response she wrapped her arms around my neck and squeezed her cheek tightly against mine. Gently I rubbed my fingers up and down her back while she sniffled in my ear.

"Tosha, talk to me."

With a loud exhale she pulled away from me and rolled onto her back. Her eyes were glassy and she quickly wiped away the tears lining her lids. I couldn't help but smile.

"I'm crying and you smile?"

"It's real, Tosha," I replied. "I've only seen glimmers of you peek through the walls around you. I'm sorry that I like when the real you comes out and not the Warrior."

"Trainee," she corrected, and wiped her eyes again. "I don't have walls."

I laughed. "Yeah, and I'm a clean freak." She narrowed her eyes at me. "Why are you crying?"

She swallowed and finally responded, "This is scary, all of this."

Suddenly she erupted in tears while her hands covered her face. Not knowing what else to do, I tucked her into my chest.

"I won't hurt you, Natasha, I promise I will never hurt you."

She lifted up from my chest and shook her head. "You can't promise that. No one can. The last guy I was with burned me within an inch of my life. What will happen to me next?"

"Happiness," I answered and she blinked in surprise.

Before anything else could be said, a cell phone alarm started going off behind me. Tosha sat up and leaned over me, her breasts brushing against my cheek. When she came back over, she had her cell phone in hand and was shutting the alarm off.

"We've got to get up," she said sleepily and rubbed her eyes.

"Seriously?" I asked and slipped my hand underneath her shirt. "I think I'm still feeling ill."

Tosha narrowed her eyes at me. "You're fine. At least you got some sleep," she said and scooted to the end of the bed. "I'm going to get my ass handed to me today. You couldn't have gotten activated the day before when I could have had a day off?"

"I'm sorry, next time I'll tell Garrett to consult the trainee schedule."

"Not funny," she replied and starting forcing her feet into her boots.

"It was a little funny," I said, rolling onto my back and lacing my fingers behind my head.

"Don't think you get another day off," Tosha said and stood from the bed. "Victor will be waiting for you."

"How do you know?"

"Because he came to see you last night."

I propped myself up on my elbows. "Really? When?"

"About the time you were speaking incoherently," Tosha replied while she secured her hair messily on top of her head.

"I don't remember that."

"I'm not surprised. You were pretty out of it. He stayed until your fever finally broke. Once it looked like you were going to be ok, he said he would expect you at practice this morning. So, get a move on," she said and stepped toward the door.

"Wait!" I said and jumped up. She scrunched her face up in confusion as I stepped up to her. Slowly I lowered my head and placed my lips on top of hers. When I pulled away her eyes were still open and looking at me questioningly.

"What was that for?"

"Goodbye kiss," I replied and then kissed her softly again.

"And that one?"

"Thank you kiss."

"Thank you for what?"

"For taking care of me and not being angry at me anymore."

"Who said that?" she said and scrunched her brows. After a second, she broke her serious face and kissed me.

"What was that for?" I asked teasingly.

"For getting me back into the program."

I shrugged. "I was responsible for getting you kicked out. It was the least I could do."

She shook her head. "No, Cameron and Devin were right. My actions got me kicked out. I just wish you didn't have to go through all that pain yesterday to get me back in."

"I'd do it again," I said and rested my forehead on hers.

"Then you're stupider than I thought."

If I thought that Tosha would suddenly be some gushy girl and want to hold my hand while we walked together down the hall or kiss me in front of everyone, I was sadly mistake. In fact, she seemed to stand further away from me instead. It wasn't until we were both out in the courtyard in our separate corners did she even give me a glance. At least when I caught her looking at me she gave me a small smile back.

While the trainees began their laps around the courtyard I filled my quiver and checked the string on my bow. Only a few minutes passed before Victor stepped out into the courtyard with Jared at his side.

"Well, good morning, child," Victor said. "You look well, how are you feeling?"

"Good," I replied and pulled my quiver up on my back.

Victor eyed me for more. "And? Any…changes?"

"Um…no," I answered and saw the disappointment in his face. "Sorry."

His expression quickly changed and he waved his hand dismissively. "Let's not give up hope yet. Jared, can you put out the target?"

"Sure, Dad," Jared replied.

"Hey, Jer," I began and waited for him to stop and look at me. "Are we…uh…ok?"

Jared waited a beat before answering, "Yeah, we're ok. It was stupid, but I understand why you did it. We've all made bad judgements when it comes to people we care about it, including me."

"To say the least," Victor said with a raspy laugh, but before Jared could respond Victor waved him away with the target. "Let us see what we're working with. At least we know you couldn't have gotten any worse."

As soon as the words were out of Victor's mouth I knew lightening was going to strike me down. Jared stood roughly fifty feet away with the target next to him. With an exhale I pulled an arrow from my quiver and threaded it in the string of my bow. With an inhale I brought the bow up and pulled the arrow back by my cheek. When I squinted my eye to look down at the target, my vision suddenly narrowed and zoomed forward.

The sight was so jarring that my grip on the arrow loosened and it went flying crookedly through the air. Thankfully Jared ran and caught it before it hit anyone.

"Sorry! So sorry," I yelled and wanted to jab myself in the eye.

When I looked down at Victor he was stone-faced and looking forward. "Perhaps I spoke too soon."

"Sorry, something…uh…weird just happened. Let me try again."

"Yes, let's try and hit the target and not the trainees."

I sighed and pulled another arrow from my quiver. As I threaded it into my bow I found myself nervous and blinking my eyes uncontrollably. With an inhale I brought my bow up and imagined pulling the invisible field around me. I pulled the string back to my cheek, and squinted my eye. As it had done before, suddenly my vision zoomed forward as if it were a telephoto lens. The target was enlarged and looked like it was only a few inches away. With an exhale I released my arrow and heard that familiar sound of my arrow cutting through the air when it's done correctly. Phffft.

When I lowered my bow, my vision returned to normal but I could see my arrow sticking out of the bullseye of the target.

"Jared," Victor called, "pull the target back."

Jared nodded and pulled the target back another twenty or thirty feet. I brought my bow up again and pulled the string back. As soon as I squinted my eye the target narrowed and magnified as if I could reach out and touch it. Phffft!

"Yes!" Jared shouted when the arrow hit right next to the one already in the bullseye.

"Jared, bring the target all the way to the wall," Victor instructed and I swallowed hard since I'd never made it that far. "You can do it, child, believe that you can."

I nodded and exhaled a nervous breath. When the new arrow was back to my cheek, I squinted my eye as I had done before, but the target looked only halfway as close as it had before. I squinted my eye even more and the target zoomed forward the rest of the way. Phffft!

"Bulls-fucking-eye," Jared shouted. "Wooh!"

"Well done, child. I knew you could do it."

"Thanks," I sighed with relief and stole a glance over to where the trainees were doing drills. Tosha was looking back at me and gave me a sly smile. Even Roberts gave me a thumbs up.

Victor squeezed my shoulder and turned me toward the manor. "Take the arrows. We are going on a field trip."

"What?" I asked surprised as I scooped up the remaining arrows that were lying on the table.

It was hard to keep up with Victor as he left the courtyard and weaved through the many corridors of the manor. By the time we passed the spiral staircase Jared had caught up with us and was looking confused when we came to stand in front of a door.

"So you're just going to go in there and say what?" Jared asked as Victor knocked quietly on the door.

Victor waited a moment before replying, "It doesn't look like I'll need to say anything since no one is in there."

Victor raised one eyebrow and opened the door as if challenging Jared that he wasn't brave enough. Jared sighed and stepped inside with Victor and I filing in after. The room was very large with a sunken living room at the front and the bed up a level several feet behind. Jared and Victor continued through the center of the room and out a set of double doors that opened up to a patio, or maybe they called it a veranda, I had no idea.

"You know Bri or Cameron are going to realize we just walked through their bedroom and they're going to want to know why."

"Considering this used to be my quarters, I could easily say it was muscle memory."

Jared laughed as we stepped out on the veranda that looked out onto a pristinely kept lawn and gardens that connected to a wooded area behind.

"Dad, just admit that by going through here you can avoid having Devin or Cameron see us from the windows of their office."

"Why would I care if they saw us?" Victor asked dismissively as he went down the steps leading to the lawn.

"Because you know they don't want Beckett outside of the manor."

"The woods are technically part of my property. I go wherever I wish, and everyone should best remember that."

"Fine, Dad," Jared sighed. "But if they come after me for doing this, I'm not taking the blame for it. I will totally say you dragged me under duress."

"Yes, yes, child, I understand," Victor replied, shaking his head. "But how come when *I* was your coven leader you would break every rule in the

184 ~ C.R. QUINN

book without even the slightest bit of urging."

"Because I was rebelling, Dad, that's what sons are supposed to do."

Victor laughed and even I smiled at their back and forth. Suddenly I missed my dad and felt a pang of guilt in my stomach. I hadn't checked in on him since we dropped him off at Facility West two nights ago. Between the meet up with Garrett, Tosha getting injured, and me being activated, I had barely given him a thought. I was a terrible son.

"Mr. Dawes, I suggest you get out of your head and keep up," Victor said over his shoulder. How he even knew I was torturing myself inside my head was beyond me.

Quickly I picked up my pace and eventually had to start running in order to catch up with them as they disappeared into the woods.

"What are we going to be doing out here?" I asked, shamefully a little out of breath.

Once we were deep in the woods, Victor turned around and had a very serious expression on his face. "Do you want to take down Garrett?"

I flinched. "Of course I do, but..."

"No buts," Victor interrupted and put his hand up. "We've seen that you're able to take out wolves, which in our current situation is a good thing. We need to get your skill up to do the same for the vampires."

"Ok," I replied and then gestured around us, "but why the woods."

"We're going to test your activation," Victor replied and turned his back to me. "Hop on."

I blinked and looked at Jared who replied, "You heard the man."

But how did one hop onto someone who was five inches shorter.

"I don't have all day, child," Victor groaned.

"Yep, sorry," I replied, and awkwardly wrapped my arms around his neck.

Victor jump onto the trunk of the tree in front of him and began climbing up at an amazing pace. The higher he went, the tougher it was to hold onto him. I tried everything not to look down, but my curiosity got the best of me.

"Holy shit," I gasped when I saw how far off the ground we were, "please tell me we're not going any higher."

"Patience, child, patience," he replied and went up another ten feet.

When we finally reached a fork in the tree, Victor pulled me up to where my feet could easily fit.

"Now, child, being up here you have the advantage, however, you must be even more precise and take into account your surroundings. What will the arrow have to go through in order to reach your target, which way is the wind blowing, how fast is your target moving. All of those things you must keep in mind within three seconds of taking your next shot."

"This is an incredible pep talk, sir."

He raised his eyebrow. "I hope you realize I don't allow anyone else to talk to me in the same manner you do. Others have died taking that tone with me."

"Sorry. I'm just really nervous being up here. What if I fall?"

"I will catch you."

"But how will I be able to hit anything from here?"

"How do we know unless you give it a try," he said and then looked down at the ground. "Jared, take a run, but start slow. Let's see how he does."

Jared gave a nod and started a slow winding run through the woods. I pulled an arrow from my quiver and laced it in my bow, but continued to watch him run.

"Don't let him get to Oregon before you take a shot, Mr. Dawes."

I sighed and pulled the bow up to my eye level. With an exhale, I pulled the string back to my cheek and squinted my eye. My vision zoomed forward, flashing through all the vegetation and then finally focusing on Jared's back. I released the arrow and watched as it bounced off a tree a few feet to Jared's right.

"Dammit," I growled through my teeth.

"Don't be so tentative, child. You have the skill, but you need to put some confidence behind your arrow. Now try again."

"You make it sound like it's something I can just turn on and off. It's not that simple!"

"You dare to raise your voice to me?"

"I'm in a goddamn tree, Victor!" I shouted. "And you want me to shoot this small moving target in the middle of the woods. It's...it's insane!"

"Then your mother is a dead woman."

My body froze, but an intense anger suddenly flared behind my eyes. "What...did...you...just say?"

Victor narrowed his eyes at me as he replied in a low, calculated tone, "You have nothing but excuses, Mr. Dawes. It's just easier to give up, isn't it?"

"Fuck you!"

He snickered. "You really are a pitiful child."

"You think I can't make that shot!"

"Please," he scoffed. "You couldn't hit Jared if he were only a foot away."

"You want me to take the shot?!" I challenged and pulled another arrow from my quiver.

"Why waste an arrow. It's not like you're really going to do anything to save anyone."

Quickly I pulled the string back, narrowed my eye down the length of the arrow which shot my vision forward to where Jared was running away from us. The feather of the arrow grazed my cheek as the arrow shot forward.

"Hit!" Jared shouted in the distance. "Right in the heart!"

My chest was burning and heaving with my heart beating out of my chest. Adrenaline was racing through me and Victor had a smirk on his face. When I could finally control my breathing, I asked, "Did you do that on purpose?"

"Do what, child?"

"Get me all worked up."

He nodded. "I have noticed that your best work seems to be when you're under great stress."

"You really are a conniving bastard, aren't you?"

A sly smirk stretched up his cheek. "I am. However, I would suggest watching your language."

I laughed. "I'll try my best. So what now?" I asked as I took a step forward, completely forgetting that I was hundreds of feet up in the air, and fell straight down. My high-pitched shriek echoed in the woods but caught in my throat once Victor grabbed me around my waist and then dug his free hand and feet down the tree's trunk. My feet dangled in the open, my brain not quite processing the fact that this small man was hanging from the side of a tree and somehow holding me with one arm.

"You stupid, stupid, child," Victor shouted as he slowly began to climb back up to our perch.

"Sorry. Will you judge me if I need a new pair of pants?"

"I will," Jared yelled up from the bottom of the tree.

"Jared, seriously, it was just a drop," I said nervously as we stepped back into the manor. "I don't need you to make it out like I pissed my pants or anything."

"It smelled like a lot more than just a drop," he replied.

"Smel...wha...bullshit."

He held his hands up. "I'm just reporting what I experienced."

"Jared," Victor warned, "leave the child alone. He cannot help his incontinence."

"What?!" I shouted and the two of them laughed. "I hate you both."

"Good work today, child," Victor said and patted me on the back.

I put my fist against my heart and lowered my head slightly. "Thank you, sir."

"You're totally sucking up," Jared said and walked the opposite direction.

"Don't listen to him, child. I like being sucked up to," he laughed. "Now don't go too far, I may need to steal you away tonight," Victor said before turning in the same direction as Jared.

"For what?"

"Patience, child, patience," he replied, keeping his back to me.

"Easy for you to say," I mumbled under my breath.

"Yes it is," he said before turning a corner.

Would I ever get used to the vampire super hearing? I shrugged and headed toward the dining room. Whatever was for dinner tonight smelled wonderful and I would eat my weight. Today had gone so well that Victor kept pushing to keep going. Again, he would say, again, again. At one point Jared threw me a protein bar and I burned through that within an hour. The only thing I wanted more than food was to see Tosha. It was hard not seeing her train only a few feet away. In some ways I wish she could have seen me today up in the trees, just something to prove I'm not a loser.

When I turned into the dining room I immediately saw Bush, Nub, and Princess sitting together at a table so I scanned the room for Tosh. When I didn't see her at another table or in line for food, I reluctantly stepped over to the three idiots.

"Hey, you guys seen Tosh?"

Nub and Princess sat back in their seats while Bush replied, "You haven't heard?"

My face fell and I swallowed the lump in my throat. "Heard what?"

"She got a mission," Nub said and then picked up his fork again.

"A...mission?"

Bush nodded. "Yep, her and Roberts. Looks like the sirs made their decision."

"What's the mission? Where's she going?" I asked.

The three of them shrugged in unison, but Nub responded, "Something big though. All the big guns are going too."

"Big guns?"

"We saw Alex grabbing some stuff from the armory with Devin. So it must be something big," Nub said and I bolted from the room.

If they were bringing out the "big guns" like Nub said, it must mean they found Garrett, and potentially my mother. But if that was the case, and Tosha had been asked to come along, that meant she was going into a very dangerous situation. The adrenaline gave me the ability to take the stairs two at a time until I reached my floor and ran down the hall to Tosha's door.

"Tosha!" I shouted and burst into her room.

"Dammit, Beck!" Tosha yelled back as she pulled a black jumpsuit up over her shoulders.

"S-sorry," I said and stumbled forward.

"Shut the door!" she shouted at me as she zipped up the jumpsuit to her neck.

I jumped and shut the door behind me. "Sorry."

"I swear you have radar of when I'm changing."

"First of all, great gift to have. Second, you're going on a mission?"

"News travel fast."

"So it's true?"

She nodded with a mix of nerves and excitement. "Me and Roberts. I can't believe it, especially after everything that happened the last couple of days. I thought for sure they'd..."

"Is it Garrett?" I interrupted and I could tell it annoyed her.

She pursed her lips and sat down on her bed where she had her boots, belt, and weapons laid out. She picked up her left boot and began stuffing her foot into it. "They think so. It's a pack outside of the city."

"You can't go out there!"

She blinked with a shocked expression and then her face settled into a nasty squint. "And why not?"

"Bec…"

"Because I'm a girl?"

"No, bec…"

"Because I'm a hybrid?"

"Not just that…"

"It better not be because we're…"

"Because it's way too dangerous and you could get hurt!" I shouted over her.

She nodded slowly with tight lips and began putting her other boot on. "You keep forgetting that I was a part of the training program way before we met. And just because we've started something…"

"Tosha, think about what happened last time."

"Because of you!" she shouted and stamped her foot on the floor. "I honestly can't believe you're doing this to me before I leave on my first mission."

"Tosha, it's just because I…"

"Sorry, Nat," Nikki announced as she burst through the door with a bag over her shoulder, but then stopped abruptly when she saw me. "Oh, didn't know he was here."

"Does that mean you'll turn around and get out?" Tosha said snidely.

"No," Nikki replied and stepped over to the twin bed on the other side of the room. "What are you two arguing about?"

"They're letting Tosha go on a mission where they're going to attack a pack of werewolves."

"What?" Nikki said, the color suddenly draining from her face. "You can't…you can't go on that. You'll be killed."

Tosha grabbed the utility belt and whips from the bed. "The confidence between you two is astounding."

"It's because we care about you," Nikki said.

"Bullshit," Tosha replied. "Why are you even here?"

"Monthly restriction," Nikki said and sat down on the bed.

"Again? It's like you're having your period every other week."

"Well at least I can have one," Nikki said nastily causing Tosha's nostrils to flare. Without another word, she stepped toward the door.

"Nikki," I shouted, "if you make another shitty remark about my girlfriend's…reproductive issues, or anything else, I swear I will punch you in the junk." Nikki's eyes flared. "Ok, well, I won't, but I will find someone else to do it. She's your sister for fuck's sake, you're supposed to love her not tear her down at every opportunity."

Nikki was speechless. When I turned around, Tosha had ducked out the door. Immediately I ran into the hallway and caught her just a few doors down. I grabbed her elbow and turned her around. Her eyes were glassy and her cheeks flush.

"Girlfriend?" she asked weakly, her bottom lip trembling.

I took her face into my hands and slammed my lips against hers. Her arms wrapped around my neck and pulled me in until I was pressing her against the wall. Our lips and tongues battled each other for control while we gasped for air.

Someone cleared his throat behind us. I rose from Tosha's lips and when she looked past me she jerked away.

"Tosh," Devin said tersely, "shouldn't you be at the briefing?"

"Yes sir," she responded and quickly ran toward the stairs.

Devin gave a smirk before walking away.

"Devin, wait," I called and he slowly turned around. "I'd like to come too."

"No."

I flinched angrily. "I have been training my ass off and even got activated which was the last thing in the world I wanted to do. I deserve to go!"

Devin just stood and blinked several times before replying, "No."

"But…"

"You are too invested," he interrupted.

"And you're not?"

Devin slapped me hard in the shoulder knocking me back into the wall. "You really are a little shit. I do hope Garrett is there tonight so we can end this and I can get you the hell out of here."

When he finally disappeared from sight I hit and kicked the wall in front of me. This was bullshit. Bullshit! I'm the one who should be going on that mission. Not Tosha, not the Warriors. Me.

I kicked the wall again and then regretted it since I had to limp back to Tosha's room to get my bow. Nikki quickly raised her head from her hands and turned away to wipe her eyes.

"Sorry, I just need my bow," I said and took it from the bed. The sound of her sniffling made me feel incredibly guilty. "Nikki, I'm sorry for yelling before. I didn't mean to upset you."

"You think I'm crying over you!" she shouted. All guilt was stripped from my body. "I'm crying because they're sending my sister out to be slaughtered, you idiot."

"We just have to have faith that she's as good as they think she is."

She wiped her eyes with the cuff of her sleeve. "You really like her, don't you?"

I nodded. "I do, I really do. I just didn't realize how hard something like this would be. Maybe I can't do this."

"Don't give up on her," Nikki said and rose from her bed.

"I'm not giving up on her, Nikki, but if she's picked to become a Warrior, I don't fit in her life anymore."

"Beckett," she began and stepped over to me, "I know I'm a bitch."

It took all my strength not to immediately agree. "Whaa-what?"

She narrowed her eyes at me. "I've always hurt the people around me before they can hurt me. It's self-preservation and it fucks up my life, but that's who I am. Nat was always the good sister, everyone loved her, she always did the right thing until she met that dirt bag Ty. He didn't just burn her skin away, he destroyed the light that was inside her. But since she met you, I've seen it start to come back. There's a spark in her that's been missing and I know it's because of you. That's why I'm begging you not to give up on her. She's going to fight this because she believes you won't stick. So if you really like her, show her you're here to stay."

"But how? No matter what I say she never fully believes me. I can't get through that wall even if I had a sledgehammer."

"Here's what you do, when the team finishes up their brief, they'll all be going through the main corridor to the front doors. Sometimes loved ones will stand in the corridor to say goodbye. If she sees you, she'll know you're serious. Show her you care and support her. She deserves to get it from someone."

"Then come with me."

She shook her head. "No, I'll breakdown in front of everyone and…well, I can't let any of those people see me cry. Now get down there, they'll be leaving any minute."

"Nikki, come with me…"

"Did I stutter? Get the fuck out."

My fingers dug into my palm as I squeezed my hand tightly around my bow. She was right, she was a bitch. Quickly I turned and left, slamming the door behind me. I ran down the hallway and skipped steps down the spiral staircase. Even though Nikki had serious issues, she was right about her sister. Tosha was waiting for an excuse to turn away from me, and I had to prove to her that she could trust me. I wouldn't hurt her like Ty, and I would stay unlike anyone else in her life.

When I headed toward the front door I found people lining the main corridor, one of whom was Kyla standing next to a small man wearing a pink suit. I didn't want to stare, I had to admire the guy's confidence. It begged the question, who the heck was he here for?

"Beckett," Kyla said and waved, "are you lost?"

"I...is Alex going on this mission?" She nodded nervously and the guy in the pink suit rubbed her arm while he made no attempt to hide the fact that he was scanning me from the feet up. "Will they come through here before they leave?"

She nodded again and gave a thin smile. "Are you waiting for who I think you are?"

"Who?" the man in the pink suit asked excitedly.

"Yep," I replied, "I just hope...honestly I don't know what to expect."

"Who!?" the man in the pink suit said again and pulled on my arm.

"Beckett, this is Fabiani. Fabi, meet Beckett."

Fabiani flinched back dramatically but then extended his hand. "Oh, so you're Beckett. I've heard a lot of scuttlebutt about you."

"I'm not sure how to take that," I replied and reached out to shake his hand.

As soon as he took my hand he jerked it down and brought me eye to eye with him. "Who!"

Kyla laughed and thankfully pulled him away. "Don't mind him, Beckett, he's a little needy."

"To say the least," he laughed just as several Warriors came walking down the corridor, one of which was Alex who quickly picked Kyla up off the floor and began kissing her. Fabi turned to me and said, "It's just best to look away when it comes to them."

I smiled and took his advice, just in time to see Roberts strutting down the corridor. He looked for someone behind him and then looked back at me before giving me an accepting nod. It wasn't until a few seconds later did I realize he had been looking back at Tosha who was walking side by side with Connor. He actually saw me first and sneered. Tosha reacted to Connor's sudden change in expression and then looked around until she locked eyes with me. Connor tried taking Tosha by the arm and pulling her forward, but she quickly pulled out of his grip and stepped in front of me. Her lips hit me so hard I thought my teeth would chip. I ignored the gasps around us and kissed her back, cupping my hand around the back of her neck. A moment later Connor pulled her away, but her eyes were locked on mine until she stepped through the front doors.

It was done. I showed her I cared and supported her. Now all I had to do was sit back the rest of the night worrying about her. When I finally came back down to Earth I realized that Fabi was staring at me with his jaw dropped.

"That's who," I said with a smirk.

"Good for you," he said and hit me in the arm. "I mean it. She's a tough one, but here you are. Oh, speaking of a tough one."

Kyla and I turned our heads to find Devin coming toward us. Without a word, or barely even a pause in his gate, Devin extended his arm and wrapped his hand around the back of Fabi's neck and kissed him. It was a quick kiss, and Devin kept walking toward the door, but it was a kiss. A kiss with another guy who was wearing a pink suit. Devin, the most intimidating person I had ever met just kissed a guy. On the lips.

"Trying to wrap your brain around that one, aren't you?" Fabi said with a smirk.

I nodded. "I mean, it's cool. I knew he was...you know...it's just...uh..."

"Unexpected," Kyla finished for me.

"Yeah, that's a good way of putting it," I replied. "Seeing it right in front of my face just made it real."

Just then the corridor was flooded with the sound of children squealing with laughter. Brianna, dressed in a black jumpsuit, was trying to make her way down the corridor, but one child was clinched around her leg and the other hanging from her arm. At the same time, Victor and Jared came in through the front doors.

"Ah, Mr. Dawes, I'm so glad we found you," Victor said and then looked down the corridor at Brianna who now had Cameron pulling Olivia from her mother's body.

"Hello, sir," I said to Victor but then jutted my head in Brianna's direction. "She's not going on this mission, is she?"

"Why wouldn't she? She is a terrific Warrior, one of our most lethal, in fact."

"Really?" I asked shook my head.

"Why are you so surprised? Do you believe that women can't be Warriors?"

Kyla gasped and her eyes became large.

"No, no," I answered quickly. "It's just that...she's a...mom."

"Babies," Brianna said while trying to pull her son from her leg, while Cameron continued to pry Olivia's arms from around her mother's neck, "I have to go...Devy...will yell at me if I don't get outside."

"Children, you must let go," Cameron commanded, but the kids just laughed.

"Burke children," Kyla shouted, "I command you to let go of your mother for there is ice cream in the kitchen that will go to waste if you don't eat it."

Both kids immediately let go of their mother and ran down the corridor toward the kitchen. Brianna and Cameron thanked Kyla as she passed, but then gave each other a worried glance. Brianna kissed Cameron lightly and then ran to the front door. Cameron watched her until she disappeared outside and from the look on his face he was scared for his wife. Cameron's shoulders slumped as he turned around to follow his kids and Kyla to the kitchen. He had much more to lose than I did. She was his wife, the mother of his kids. How did he just let her go?

"Mr. Dawes, come back to us," Victor said next to me.

I turned my head back around to face him. "Yes, sir. Sorry, sir. You were...uh...looking for me?"

"Yes," he replied and looked around cautiously at the others around us that were starting to disperse. "I'm glad to see you have your bow. You will need it."

"Oooh, secret mission?" Fabi asked and Victor nodded. "And I take it that Cameron and Devin are to be kept in the dark?"

"If you can manage, my dear Fabi," Victor replied.

Fabi patted Victor on the arm. "Don't you worry, Victor. I love knowing things he doesn't. It doesn't happen often, so I have to take the opportunity when it's presented. Are you completely overstepping your bounds?"

"Most likely," Victor answered and Fabi clapped his hands together with excitement.

"Oh I love it. Well, good luck to you all. And Beckett, I hope you survive whatever Victor is going to put you through because I really want to see what happens with you and Natasha. Good evening, gentleman, I have some stress shopping to do."

Once Fabi stepped away from us, Victor squeezed my shoulder and pulled me down the corridor toward the library.

"Where are we going?"

"Patience," Victor said quietly, yet still commanding.

Finally, we reached the library and Jared went directly to the vault's key pad and typed in a code. The bookshelf opened and Victor waved us inside the dark passageway. Of course, they could see perfectly fine while I fumbled and felt my way along the wall.

"Come along, Beckett," Victor said impatiently.

Thankfully Jared grabbed my arm and pulled me along the winding halls deep into the depths of the manor.

"So you and Tosh made it official in front of everyone?" Jared asked as we came to a steep set of stairs.

I took hold of the stair railing and slowly made my way down. "How did you hear about that? You weren't even there yet."

"You underestimate how quickly Warriors talk. Plus, I was outside and Connor made a comment."

"Do I want to know?"

"Probably not."

"Fantastic. Well, I think I should tell you that I yelled at your girlfriend."

Jared laughed. "Whether she's my girlfriend is a little up in the air, but hey, she probably deserved it."

"That she did."

"Can we stop with the idle gossip?" Victor growled before he disappeared around the corner.

"Sir, please tell me what we're doing," I said as I rounded the corner and plowed into him.

He took a step back and held a duffle bag up in front of me. "Do you want to help rescue your mother?"

My stomach dropped. "Of course."

"And do you want revenge for what was done to your father?"

"Stupid question," I replied and Jared cleared his throat behind me. "Sorry. Yes I do."

"Do you think you're brave enough to face Garrett if you had the chance?"

My breath started to quicken as I replied, "Absolutely."

Victor threw the duffle bag at me. "Then suit up."

"Suit up?" I replied, kneeling to the ground. Jared shined a light from his cell phone over me revealing a black jumpsuit and boots within the duffle bag. "Are…are we going on the mission?"

Victor shrugged. "More like a mission of our own."

"So we're crashing Devin's mission?"

"Crashing?"

Jared laughed and placed the cell phone down on the ground, allowing the light to shine upward. "Yeah, Dad, that's what the young kids call what we're doing. So, Beckett, basically we'll sneak you to where this pack is hiding, but are you willing to accept the consequences when we get caught? And we will get caught the second you release an arrow, so are you up for this?"

I stood from the hard stone floor and replied, "Abso-fucking-lutely."

"That a boy," Jared replied and hit me in the arm. "Now get dressed."

Victor and Jared also had bags packed and began to change into similar outfits, begging the question, how long did Victor know that this mission was happening? We were out in the woods all day. It was scary what Victor knew.

Several minutes later I was changed with my bow and quiver slung around my shoulder as we walked the rest of the dark underground tunnel. When we came to the end, Victor typed in a code on another keypad and the door opened to the outside. The night was cool and crisp, and the moon was fighting to shine from behind the clouds. We stepped toward a white panel van that was parked a few feet away from the door. After crunching across the driveway a few steps, someone cleared his throat behind us.

"Going somewhere, gentleman?"

Jared and I turned around quickly to find Cameron standing with his back up against the outside of the manor.

Victor smirked, slowly turned around, and then replied, "That all depends, child. How did you know?"

Cameron pushed off the wall. "Father, you once told me that there would come a time when I would know everything that was going on in the manor."

"Julian told you."

Cameron gave a single laugh. "You know Julian is completely devoted to you, but he also knows who his boss is. You're using his van, Father, and you don't drive. Don't you think that sent up a flag with him?"

"So what now, child? Are you going to stop us from going? Prevent this young man from possibly rescuing his mother? Seeking justice for what was done to his father, holding Garrett accountable for…"

"Father, enough," Cameron interrupted and held his hand up. "I am holding you completely responsible for the safe return of Mr. Dawes."

"What about me?" Jared asked, sounding offended.

"Forgive me, little brother, of course we need you to come back. Someone needs to mop the floors."

Jared laughed and turned toward the van. Victor gave a quick nod and pulled me by the shoulder, but Cameron took a step forward.

"Gentleman, if…" he paused uncomfortably, "…if you happen to see Brianna in distress or danger…"

"Bro," Jared said, "we got her. Don't you worry."

Cameron nodded. "Thank you, and please, do not tell her I asked. She will never forgive me for thinking she could not take care of herself. But she has two children to come home to…"

"Child, everyone will come home," Victor said and pulled me toward the van.

"Good evening then, gentleman," Cameron said and turned toward the door. "And good luck."

"We'll certainly need it with Beckett falling out of trees," Jared laughed before opening the van's panel door.

"It was only once," I replied and climbed in.

"Isn't that enough?"

"You have a point."

Chapter Sixteen

After an hour drive in the back of panel van, rolling side to side and continually slamming into Jared's ammo bag, we finally pulled into an empty field. The only light came from the slivers of moonlight reflecting off the tips of the tall grass.

"This is it?" I asked.

"Hardly," Victor answered and pointed to the edge of the field where the tree line began. "We'll need to run about a mile in, but don't worry, I'll carry you in. I don't need you completely out of breath."

I sighed with relief, although I wondered how exactly him carrying me would work with our height difference, but I didn't argue and climbed out of the van. Jared unzipped his ammo bag and began laying out his arsenal with a very serious expression on his face. It wasn't often that Jared was serious about anything, it honestly made me nervous.

What had I agreed to? I had no business being here. What the hell was I thinking?

"Beckett, child," Victor said and placed a hand on my shoulder, "it is normal to be scared. You just need to breathe."

"Is it that obvious?"

Victor smiled. "Fear has a distinct smell, but I have also put many a young soldier into battle. I know that nervous look very well. Just remember everything we've worked on these last few days."

"What if I hit one of our people?"

"That is a risk, but do try not to," he said and pulled out a bundle covered in a black cloth and tied with string. "Now, you will need these."

He handed me the bundle and when I untied the string the black cloth fell open on either side exposing new arrows, but these had silver tips. "These will go through a vampire, unlike the ones you've been practicing with."

My breath started to quicken as I put the new bundle of arrows inside the quiver. This was scarily real now.

"We should get going," Jared said, a long-range rifle sticking up from behind his back and ammunition cartridges stuck to various belts.

"Very well, child, I will follow you," Victor announced and turned his back to me. "Climb abroad, Beckett. The battle awaits us."

"Um, ok," I replied while awkwardly bending my knees and placing my hands on his shoulders. Quickly he wrapped his hands around the back of my knees and pulled them up around his waist. The tall field grass began to whip past me as Victor set out in a run so fast that I was having trouble keeping myself upright. I tightened my grip around his shoulders to bring my body closer to his back, although that allowed my face to get whipped by the field grass. I wasn't going to win in any position.

Ahead of us, Jared took his rifle off his back and put it up in front of him. Eventually we reached the tree line, leaving behind us a trail in the field where we had trampled down the grass. Jared's pace slowed, and he brought his rifle up to eye level and began checking side to side for targets. The deeper we ran into the woods, the darker the coverage around us became. It wasn't long before I could barely see Jared at all.

After another few minutes of running in complete darkness a soft light could be seen in the distance. Suddenly a loud, high-pitched howl broke through the night, and was soon joined by others.

"I think we found them," Jared said quietly over his shoulder.

Victor nodded and followed when Jared quickened the pace again. The light in the distance became brighter as we drew closer, the sounds of fighting bouncing off the trees around us. My hands and arms kept flinching in anticipation but also in worry that we wouldn't get there in time.

Jared stopped running and turned around, pointed to a tree to his right, and then to another one on his left. Victor nodded in understanding and stepped over to the tree on our left.

"Hold on tightly," Victor said and began climbing up the tall tree.

This was going to be our perch, and Jared was just opposite us. As Victor pulled us up higher, the farmhouse in the distance was easier to see between the thinning trees. Security lights were blaring down on the property, making the house and the land around it very visible.

When Victor reached a split in the tree trunk he stopped and placed me down. From this distance and height I felt as though I was watching a football game. Wolves and Warriors were running back and forth across the farmhouse's lawn. Immediately I pulled my bow off my shoulder, but Victor placed his hand on my forearm.

"Child, as soon as you take your first shot, they will know we are here. We need to hold out as long as possible."

I bit the inside of my cheek and lowered my bow, my entire body twitching with anxiety. The howls and wails became louder and I couldn't help but squint my eyes to zoom my vision forward, looking for any sign of Tosha. When I reached the far left corner of the farmhouse I finally found her. Initially she was standing side by side with Roberts both fighting what must have been a vampire when a wolf came running toward them, causing Tosha to turn and protect their exposed side.

Slowly I pulled an arrow from my quiver and threaded it in the string of my bow while watching Tosha's whips fly and crack in the air. The werewolf was getting angrier each time one of the whips split open his fur. My finger holding the arrow on the string twitched every time the wolf would step closer to her, but all in all she was holding her own until Roberts ran after the vampire who was fleeing, leaving her back exposed. Asshole.

Suddenly a vampire ran up behind Tosha, wrapped his arms around her chest, and swung her around. Her whips were useless since the vampire had her arms pinned down at her sides. Quickly I pulled my bow up to eye level, and Victor didn't stop me this time. Tosha kicked and flailed in the vamp's grip. They were so intertwined and moving so erratically there was no way I was going to be able to hit him without hitting her. My heart started beating out of my chest, the bow shaking slightly at the beat of my pulse from the adrenaline.

Victor placed a hand on my shoulder, whispering in my ear to breathe and calm down. I closed my eyes for a moment and took a deep breath in and then out. When I opened my eyes, I squinted and zoomed in to find Tosha. She was still squirming in the vampire's arms, his fangs out and ripping at the skin on her neck. I pulled the arrow back and with it the invisible field of focus, praying in my head to let the arrow only go into the vampire and not my girlfriend. Just as I was about to release the arrow, Tosha kicked her leg up high in the air and pulled a knife out from one of her pockets. As her leg came down she plunged the knife into the vampire's thigh, causing the vamp to drop her to the ground as he howled in pain. Tosha quickly turned around, removed the knife from his leg, and stabbed him through the heart.

The vampire froze for a moment and then sank down to his knees, finally falling forward in a heap. I lowered my bow for a moment, a relieved smile stretching across my face at her victory, when the wolf she had been fighting previously began stalking up behind her. Tosha knelt down and flipped the dead vampire over to retrieve her knife, all the while, not knowing that the wolf was behind her. When the wolf was only a foot away from her, I gritted my teeth, stretched the string of my bow back to my cheek, exhaled, and released. The arrow shot through the trees and sunk into the wolf's neck just as his clawed hand stretched out near Tosha's head. Tosha jumped up from the ground, startled by the sound of the werewolf falling down behind her. She looked down at the wolf, and then scanned the tree line. I knew she wouldn't find us, but at least she knew I was here.

"In the trees!" someone shouted, and as Victor had warned, wolves and vamps came running in our direction.

A shot rang out next to us, the flash from the rifle easily seen in this kind of darkness. Jared chambered another round and I realized my work wasn't finished. He got off another shot before my second arrow left my bow. He took out a vamp while my arrow went through a wolf's shoulder. The hit only slowed the wolf down for a second or two, but in the end another one of Jared's bullets hit him through the head causing blood and brain matter spout out of his head. It was the most gruesome thing I had ever seen in my life.

This wasn't a movie or a video game, this was real. They were monsters, but they were also men, and we were slaughtering them. Did they have families? Someone who loved them and hoped they would come home? A million guilty questions were suddenly flooding my mind.

"Remember why we are here, child," Victor said behind me. "They will not show you mercy, so neither should you."

I sighed and pulled an arrow from my quiver. While I threaded the arrow I looked down to see a werewolf digging its claws into the bark of our tree, climbing and pushing itself up. I leaned over and pulled the string back to my cheek, but I froze. The spot between the werewolf's eyes was shining like a beacon up at me, but I couldn't bring myself to shoot.

202 ~ C.R. Quinn

"Beckett? Beckett, do it now. Now!"

My right hand began to shake as the wolf continued his climb upwards, but in the next second his chest exploded. Jared had shot him because I froze. The wolf's lifeless body plummeted to the ground.

"Perhaps this was a bad idea," Victor said but I shook him off.

"No, I can do this. I haven't seen Garrett yet, have you?"

Victor shook his head and then pointed at a vamp that was running toward the tree line but then disappeared in a swirl of black smoke. "If others are Projecting, I'm sure he has as well."

"But the wolves?"

"They are disposable. Whether they know it or not," he replied. "I believe our work here is done."

"But what about my mom?"

Victor nodded in understanding. "Hop on," he said and tapped his shoulders.

I did as he instructed and placed my hands on his shoulders. He grabbed my legs and leapt from the tree in a perfect swan dive. When we were only a few feet from the ground he pointed his feet down and landed quietly like a cat. I hopped off his back just as Jared landed in front of us, his long-range rifle held tightly across his chest.

"Hey!" a woman shouted in the distance, but within two seconds Brianna came into view. "What are you guys doing here?"

"And hello to you too, Beebs," Jared said.

"Does Cameron know you're here? Devin is pissed."

"Yes, my dear, he knows," Victor answered.

"Please tell me he didn't send you to watch over me."

Victor shook his head. "Of course not, child, we are totally breaking the rules in order to get a glimpse of Garrett or possibly bring Beckett's mother home."

Brianna's lips became tight as she shook her head. "We didn't find either of them. I'm sorry, Beckett. Maybe he got wind we were coming and moved on."

My shoulders fell and I took a defeated step back. I wanted to throw something, yell at the top of my lungs, and cry.

"Thank you, my dear," Victor said and pulled on the back of my arm. "We will leave the way we came. If Devin has an issue, he can come see me when you return."

"Great, I love being the messenger," she replied and turned to leave, but gave me one last look. "We'll take the house apart looking for any clues of where they may have taken your mom, Beckett."

I nodded and thanked her quietly, not sure if my voice would crack or not. After Brianna disappeared back into the darkness, I climbed aboard Victor's back once again and we headed through the path we'd created through the tall field grass. When we had made it to the van, Victor deposited me on the ground while Jared began packing his gun away.

"We live to fight another day, Beckett," Victor said stoically and patted my arm.

"That doesn't make me feel any better," I replied truthfully.

"Are you angry?"

"Hell yeah I am."

"Good," he nodded. "We'll need that for next time."

"Next time?" I asked and hopped into the van.

"I am not giving up until we have your mother back. Are you?"

"Of course not."

"Good. Did you have fun?"

"Yeah," I replied without even thinking.

"That's my boy."

"Does that make us sick people?"

"Of course it does," Jared laughed.

Chapter Seventeen

The ride home seemed endless. My mom still wasn't safe, Garrett was several steps ahead of us, and my dad wasn't responding to my texts. Maybe he was resting. I just hoped it wasn't for any other reason.

By the time we returned to the manor my body was shot. I had trained all day and didn't get to eat before we left on the mission. My stomach was practically eating itself and I didn't feel I could trust my legs much longer. Thankfully the woman in the kitchen, I think her name was Christine, made me a sandwich and threw in some veggies leftover from dinner. The sandwich didn't even make it halfway up the stairs, but I waited until I was in my room before finishing the veggies.

After the shakes died down and the food calmed my stomach, I took a shower to wash the sweat and dirt that seemed to be ground into my skin. The tub's drain had a ring around it I was so disgusting. The hot water sank into my sore muscles, unwinding the tight knots in my shoulders and arms. When my skin was numb to the heat, I shut off the water and changed into a clean pair of sweats, although it was the last pair of pants I had. It begged the question, how the heck did I do laundry around here?

I flopped down on the bed and called my dad, but got his voicemail.

"Hey Dad, it's me…um…call me. I sent you some texts about Mom, but want to make sure you're ok too. So…call me back. Hope you're feeling ok. Call me. Bye."

I hung up the phone and tossed it on the floor. Where was he? Could I just go and see him? Probably not unless Victor snuck me out again which I was pretty sure wouldn't happen twice in one night. With a sigh I clicked the TV on just when a knock came at the door.

"It's open," I said and clicked the TV back off.

The door flew open and Tosha stepped inside, closing the door quickly behind her. She was panting which made me think she'd run up the stairs.

"You ok?" I asked and sat up from the bed.

"Yeah," she replied, but it seemed she was struggling with what to say next.

"I...uh...didn't think you'd be back so soon."

"Were you there?" she asked and threw her bag down on the floor.

I nodded. "Victor and Jared snuck me out."

She took a tentative step forward and I rose from the bed. "You...you saved my life tonight."

"No. I only had your back when Roberts didn't. You were incredible tonight."

Her chest began to rise and fall quickly before she leapt across the room and wrapped her arms around my shoulders. She pressed her lips against mine and I moaned at their softness. Her hands moved from my shoulders and wrapped around to my back. Not putting on a T-shirt after showering was the best idea I had ever had.

I rested my hands on Tosha's hips and pulled her closer. Slowly she pulled her lips away from mine, her eyes opening lazily.

"Girlfriend?" she said with a crack in her voice and even more questionable than when she had said it a few hours earlier.

"If that's what you want," I responded and grazed my fingertips down her cheek and chin.

"But...why?"

I took a step back, shocked at her question. "Why, what?"

Her eyes became glassy. "Why me? You could have anyone. Why..."

"Tosha," I interrupted and wrapped my hand around the back of her neck, "you're beautiful and smart and you fight to help others and you can kick a vampire's ass..."

"Stop," she said embarrassed and looked down at the floor.

I pulled her into my chest. "Did I mention how hot you look when you're swinging your whips around? Like, really hot." She laughed a snotty laugh and looked up at me, shaking her head. I could see the conflict and pain in her eyes and couldn't help but kiss her gently. "And don't you dare say anything about your scars. I love your scars."

She shook her head again. "You can't love my..."

I stopped her by slamming my lips on hers. She responded with a gaping breath and plunged her tongue into my mouth. I couldn't stop myself from moaning, especially when she began rubbing her hands and nails on my bare chest. My hands went to the zipper of her jumpsuit. Her kisses didn't stop so I slowly pulled the zipper down her chest, her white bra peeking out from inside.

Tosha pulled away from my lips, both of us out of breath. She didn't take her eyes off of mine while she put her hand on mine and pulled the zipper down past her abdomen. Next, she pulled at either side of the jumpsuit, yanking it down off her shoulders and pulling her arms free. With a jolt she wrapped her arms around my neck and jumped up on me, wrapping her legs around my waist.

I'd never had a girl jump on me before and the way she was squeezing her thighs tightly around me gave me an instant erection. It wasn't easy trying to walk Tosha over to the bed while my penis was being squashed in an awkward position, but when my shin hit the side of the mattress I leaned over and lowered her down onto the bed.

When she released her legs from around my waist she pulled me down between her legs. My hand instantly went around to her back to unclasp her bra but the hook wasn't there. Casually I tried feeling around, pinching here and there, feeling around for anything that would get this bra off so that I could see her fabulous breasts. Where the fuck was it!

"It's in front," she said breathlessly, popping her bra open from the front and pulling it away from her shoulders.

"How was I ever supposed to figure that out?"

She smiled and pulled my lips back down on hers. I shifted my weight to her side and cupped her left breast, loving the soft gasp she released. They were small, but perfect in shape, some might call them perky. Tosha tensed when I left her lips and took her breast in my mouth, but it was only a moment before she released another moan and dug her nails into my shoulders.

While still attacking her breast with my mouth, I took her jumpsuit and started pulling it down around her hips. Tosha tensed and her hands grabbed both my wrists.

Quickly I looked up at her. "You ok?"

"I…I don't…"

"Let's stop, then."

"No, I…" she said and rubbed her face, "…what am I doing?"

I sighed quietly knowing this was over. After adjusting myself inside my pants I sat up and reached down for her right leg. "You're right. What are you doing with your boots on? Can't watch TV unless you're completely comfortable."

Tosha pulled her hands away from her face while I unlaced her boot and pulled it off. When I pulled up her left leg to do the same she said, "TV? Really? That can't be all you want."

I shrugged and threw both her boots on the floor. "I want to do what you want to do. And if you're not ready for us to go all the way…"

"All the…Beckett, come on," she groaned, covered her chest with her arm, and rolled onto her side.

"Come on what?" I said and stretched out in front of her, but she kept her eyes tightly closed. "Tosha, please look at me."

After a few moments she finally opened her eyes, but her tone was still guarded. "Being with me is like sleeping with a freak. I don't want that for you, Becks. I'm a freak, a messed-up freak."

"Hey," I said firmly and put my hand on the curve of her waist, "I already yelled at your sister for insulting my girlfriend, I don't mind yelling at you for the same reason. You are *not* a freak, Tosha, I don't know how many other ways I can say that to you. I love your scars, hell, I named three of them. What does that tell you?"

"That you're weird," she replied.

I narrowed my eyes at her. "You keep testing me like you do everyone else, and I'm still here. I've passed, Tosha, you need to realize that."

She swallowed hard, closing her eyes once again before she answered, "You're right."

"Ok then. Can I see your boobs again?" She hit me in the arm. "What?"

"You're such a child."

"Um…when it comes to boobs, all men turn into children."

"That doesn't sound right."

"No, it doesn't," I laughed. "So, can I see them again?"

She rolled her eyes but opened her arms, flashing me her beautiful small breasts. "Happy?"

I smiled and wrapped my arm over her waist, pulling her chest against mine. "Very."

Slowly I moved my fingers down her back, going between her soft skin and bulbous scars. Tosha tilted her head down to rest on my chest, and

I sighed at the feeling of completeness.

We laid there silently for several minutes before she said, "It's not that I don't want to."

I leaned back and prodded her to look up. "Do what?"

She looked up at me with sad eyes. "I want to be with you, Becks. I haven't been this close to anyone since Ty, and I certainly haven't let anyone touch or even look at my scars. Being with you like this...I forgot what it was like to be held."

I squeezed her into my chest and kissed her hair. "And I love holding you, Natasha. What we do together is our business, and we'll do it in our own time. Ok?"

She pushed herself up from my chest. "You mean that?"

"Of course I do. Tosha, you don't need to hide who you are with me, you should know that by now. I just want to be with you."

She tilted her head down and sighed, but her eyes were looking back and forth under her lashes, seemingly debating something. When she finally looked back up at me, she placed her hand on my cheek and pulled me down to her lips. I squeezed her closer into me, pushing against the curve of her back and sliding my hand further down to pull her leg over my hip. Tosha put pulled at the waistband of my sweatpants, and suddenly her hand was grabbing at my penis. With only two motions I was hard again in her hand.

I leaned away from her, questioning what she was doing, but she responded by rolling me on my back and climbing on top of me. Tosha sat up, scratching my chest lightly with her nails and grinding her pelvis back and forth against me. When I reached up and squeezed her left breast, she placed her hand on top of mine and leaned over to kiss me. While she pressed and squeezed my hand around her breast, her pelvis continued to rub against me and I could easily see where this was going.

I released Tosha's breast, unzipped her jumpsuit as far as it would go, and pulled the edges of the jumpsuit down around her hips. My hands explored her scars before finding her hips and guiding her to grind against me harder and faster. Tosha rose up slightly, anchoring her hand behind my head while hovering over me but not stopping her pelvic motion.

"You have to tell me when you're close," she said breathlessly.

I nodded but had to admit, "I'm really close."

Tosha closed her eyes tightly and clinched her jaw. Even though she started this, she wanted it to be over. I pulled her to my chest and she tucked her head down next to mine before quickening her pelvic rhythm to a speed that caused my body to tense and then finally give a full release.

When our breathing finally slowed, Tosha pushed herself up and rolled off of me. She swung her legs over the edge of the bed and bent over herself, holding her head in her hands. I reached over and grabbed a few tissues from the nightstand, cleaning myself up as fast as I could. After I tossed the tissues in the garbage, I crawled up behind her and wrapped my arms around her.

"I'm sorry," she replied and wiped her eyes, "the moment itself still scares me."

I sighed and kissed the side of her face. "You should have warned me."

She shrugged and slid off the bed altogether. With her back still to me she asked, "Can I stay here tonight? My sister is staying in my room and I'm not sure I can deal with her."

"Yeah, of course," I replied and watched her head into the bathroom. "It'll be tight in this twin bed, though."

"I don't see a problem with that," she answered and shut the bathroom door behind her.

While she was inside I quickly straightened up the room, even though she'd already seen the mess, and pulled down the blankets of the bed. Could this night get any better?

That question was easily answered when Tosha opened the bathroom door. She had shed the jumpsuit and was only wearing a pair of underwear. She had also taken her hair out of the tight ponytail and it was hanging down straight and long, just touching the tops of her breasts. I could feel things stirring underneath my pants again just looking at her full on, her scars almost shining from her torso down to her mid-thighs.

"Do you have a shirt I could borrow?" she asked.

"Why?" I said too quickly and loudly, but thankfully she laughed. "I'm just saying that you don't have to cover up if you don't want to."

"Well, I want to," she responded and stepped toward the bed.

"Oh, um...ok," I said pathetically and handed her one of my last clean T-shirts.

She took it from me and once she had shrugged it on I leaned down to kiss her gently. She was so small that my arms could almost wrap around her twice.

When I rose up from her lips she was looking at me like she had never looked at me before. There was caring and, dare I say, love in her eyes.

210 ~ C.R. QUINN

"Maybe I don't need the shirt," she said.

Quickly I pulled the T-shirt over her head and threw it across the room. She laughed and stepped around me toward the bed. Once she was settled, I climbed into bed and pulled the blankets up around us. Having her body intertwined with mine made every muscle in my body relax.

"Did you have fun on your mission tonight?" She scrunched her face. "Victor asked me that after we left."

"What did you say?"

"I said yes. What about you?"

She shrugged. "Yeah, I guess I did."

Her response confused me. This program was her life and she had a lukewarm reaction to her first mission.

Tosha reached up and traced my face with her fingers. When she reached my jaw, she cupped my cheek. "Be honest with me."

"I'm always honest with you."

"Was...that...ok? What we did?"

I jerked my head back. "Ok? How could that not be ok?"

She shrugged. "I don't know. It's different."

"Same outcome," I said and smiled, thankfully she gave me a little smirk. "Tosha, what did I say? We'll figure out what's best for us. What we did just now was great. I also love this, this right here, just us being this close."

She gave a tentative smile. "I like it too."

"So I've finally won you over?"

"More like you wore me down."

"I'm worth it, I promise," I laughed and kissed her gently. Her eyes didn't leave mine as I gave her another kiss, and then another. "And you're worth it, Natasha."

She sighed and rolled over to face the wall. I pulled her back into my chest and she curled her legs up tightly into her abdomen. "We'll need to agree to disagree on that."

"No need," I replied and settled into my pillow, "I'm right about most things."

She laughed. "We'll definitely need to agree to disagree on that too. Goodnight, Beckett."

"Goodnight, Natasha," I said and kissed her hair. "And I'm right. There's no one more worth it than you. True story."

She didn't reply.

Chapter Eighteen

It was the nudge in the gut that woke me initially, and then the sun that shone through the windows officially pulled me out of sleep. Tosha was still curled up in a ball, she'd been that way most of the night since there wasn't much room to lie any other way. Can't say that I minded. It meant we were touching in some way all night long. It was comforting in a way and very needed.

I rolled over onto my back and stretched out as best I could. As soon as I stopped moving, Tosha rolled over as well and draped herself across me. My hand absentmindedly went to her thigh, finding the three-finger shaped scar and rubbing my fingers gently into the grooves.

"Is that one of them?" she asked sleepily into my chest.

"One what?"

"One of the scars you named."

"Mmm-hmm," I replied. "This is three fingers."

She shook her head against me. "You're so weird."

"You keep saying that to me, and yet you're laying across me naked."

"I have underwear on."

"Yes, and you should lose them."

She hit me lightly in the stomach. "You snore, by the way."

"Um, no I don't."

"Um, yeah ya do, and since you snored in my ear most of the night I believe I know what I'm talking about."

"I'm still not convinced," I replied and started to put my free hand behind my head when I jerked from peeking at the clock on the nightstand.

"Tosha! It's after nine you're late for practice."

Gently she placed her hand on my chest. "It's not a practice day."

"Oh," I replied. "I feel like every day is a practice day."

"You've forgotten already we used to attend community college together."

I flinched slightly at the thought. So much had happened in such a short time, my life had shifted in ways I never imagined. Today would have been a history class and English Lit, and a beautiful young woman named Natasha would be sitting behind me, stand-offish and shy, but all-knowing.

"I'm glad you stayed. I thought for sure you'd sneak out."

Tosha arched her back and looked up at me. "This was nice."

"Natasha Cushlin, is that wall of yours finally coming down?"

She narrowed her eyes, straddled me like she had last night and kissed me. I was certainly ready for another round, but just as quickly she slid off of me and stepped away from the bed. Looking at her from behind was still a nice view.

"Where are you going?" I called to her. "Come back to bed."

"Nope. You had to be a jerk, so the wall goes back up."

"No, Tosha," I pleaded and rolled off the bed.

When I looked up and into the bathroom I saw her standing in the doorway pulling her jumpsuit up her legs.

"Calm down, Becks," she said and slid her arms into the sleeves, "I'm just sneaking back to my room to take a shower."

"Take one here," I said and she rolled her eyes.

"How about we get some breakfast and see where it goes."

I put my arm around her waist and pulled her into me. "How about we stay here and see where it goes."

She opened her mouth to answer, but then she paused and I could see the doubt in her eyes. "We should be downstairs in case the trainees get called into anything. They captured a wolf last night."

"They did?"

"I didn't tell you that?"

I shook my head. "No. I think the kissing got in the way."

She rose up and kissed me. "I'll give it to you, the kissing was nice."

I smiled and kissed her back. "Meet you downstairs?"

She nodded, grabbed her boots, and left the room. I stood staring at the door, waiting for her to come back in, missing her. I was pathetic.

Eventually I pulled my pathetic self together, took a shower, and made my way downstairs for breakfast. The manor was unusually quiet. No one was bustling in the hallway, only a couple of humans also making their way to the dining room. What was up?

When I stepped into the dining room I was disappointed that Tosha wasn't there. Once again, I was being pathetic.

"Beckett! Come sit wiff us!" little Olivia Burke called from across the room where she was sitting at a table with her brother and Victor.

I waved and nodded, and then proceeded to fill my plate with eggs and waffles. When I sat down with the kids, I found it funny that my plate looked very similar to theirs, and even Victor gave a noticing smile.

"Good morning, my dear boy," he said, "how are you feeling?"

"Good," I replied and dug into my eggs. "Are we practicing today?"

Victor shook his head. "Not today. I am having to babysit these two since everyone is in conference."

"They caught a wolf!" Jackson said happily.

"So I heard," I said and raised my eyes at Victor. "Is that where everyone is uh…conferencing?"

"Yes," he replied, "and don't even ask if we can go, because we cannot."

"What are you guys talking about?"

"Toshy!" both kids shouted and jumped from their seats to hug her.

Once each child had their hug and kiss, she nudged them back to their seats. I smiled up at her and then said, "Victor was just about to tell me how he can get us in to see the wolf."

"I said exactly the opposite."

"You implied, you know you did."

Victor scowled at me. "Goodness sake, child, at least keep your voice down if you cannot keep your mouth shut."

Tosha smirked. "No thank you," she replied and sat down next to me.

"You seriously don't want to go?" I asked and stuffed a piece of my waffle into my mouth.

"I think I've been in enough trouble lately, don't you?"

"That is very true, my dear. You probably shouldn't risk it," Victor said and I gave him a curious look.

"So you'll really do it? You'll sneak us in?"

Victor shrugged. "We can't sneak in, but there is a way for us to still see the interrogation." Victor stood from his seat and it appeared we were

214 ~ C.R. QUINN

going right at this second. Quickly I shoved as much food into my mouth as would fit. "Children, do you want to see a werewolf?"

"Yes!" they shouted and jumped out of their chairs and then ran from the dining room.

Victor tucked their chairs under the table and stepped past me. "Come, Beckett, the wolf awaits."

I struggled to swallow my food and waved at him. When I finally got my food down I looked over to Tosha who suddenly seemed sad. "I'm sorry, I jumped at the chance without asking you. Do you want me to stay?"

She shook her head. "You don't need to ask my permission, Beck."

"I...I know, but if you wanted me to stay with you today..."

"Beckett, go. I was able to live without you before, I think I can survive not being with you for a little while."

I lowered my head, slightly embarrassed. "Of course you can, I didn't mean it to sound like that. I just wanted to keep spending time with you, that's all."

"So it's really all about what you want?"

"Oh my god," I groaned. "That's not what I..."

She laughed, lifted my head with both her hands, and gave me one kiss. "I'm kidding. Just come find me after."

"Mr. Dawes," Victor shouted from the corridor.

"I will," I replied and rose from my seat. I leaned down and gave her another kiss, loving the smile she gave me when I rose from her lips. "Want to learn how to shoot a bow and arrow?"

"Sure," she said with an even bigger smile. "Something else I can kick your butt at."

I jerked up and laughed. "Maybe I should leave well enough alone, then."

"Beckett Dawes!" Victor shouted again.

"Coming, coming," I shouted in reply, reached over to my plate to grab the remaining corner of my waffle, kissed Tosha one last time, and finally ran out of the dining room.

"It's about time," Victor said impatiently when I caught up with him. The kids were already at the end of the corridor and running around the corner. "So, you and Miss Cushlin, that is official?"

I smiled and nodded. "Yeah. I guess I finally wore her down."

Victor laughed. "We do what we must."

"Where are we going," I asked as we rounded the corner.

Victor pointed ahead just as the kids disappeared into the library at the end of the hall. "I believe you are familiar with the vaults and tunnels."

I nodded and smirked. "Just another day of sneaking around and getting into trouble, huh?"

"Yes, a wonderful morning adventure with all my grandchildren."

It was an interesting statement that hung in the air as we entered the library.

"Grandfather?" Livy asked.

"Is Beckett your grandchild too?" Jack finished. "Wike me and Wivy?"

Victor exhaled uncomfortably and closed the library door behind him. "Children, you must promise me your upmost secrecy."

They both nodded with large eyes and replied simultaneously, "Yes, Grandfather."

"Very well," Victor began and clasped his hands behind his back. "Then yes, Beckett is also my grandchild."

Jack scrunched his face and looked at me. "Ada's your daddy too?"

I shook my head. "No, different father. So we're like cousins."

"Oh," Livy replied. "Wike Wills is our cousin."

Victor shook his head. "Not exactly. Children, it is a complicated situation that we do not have time for, but it is still something you cannot talk about. Is that understood?"

"Yes, Grandfather," they answered in unison and then darted toward the bookshelf.

"Can I press the buttons this time, Grandfather?" Livy asked as she began climbing the bookshelves to reach the keypad. "Jack-Jack got to do it wast time."

"No I didn't," Jack snapped back and the squabbling began.

Victor lifted Olivia from the bookshelf and quickly typed in the code much to the twin's dismay. The fake bookshelf swung open revealing the dark tunnel and vault doors along the left side. Once we all stepped inside, Victor reached down to the ground, picked up a flashlight, and handed it to me.

"You may need this," he said and began walking forward with the twins in front of him. "It will get dark very quickly and the children can see almost as well as I can."

I turned the flashlight on and had to catch up to them. As we turned a corner the tunnel became pitch black. That's when it hit me.

"You planned this, didn't you?" I asked and caught Victor's sly look through the side of his eyes. "You planned on bringing me to see this wolf the whole time."

He shrugged. "I believe in learning experiences."

"You hate being left out," I replied with a laugh. "You're using me as an excuse."

"That is also true," he said before we headed down a set of stairs, similar to the one we had traveled down last night, but steeper. "Now we must all be quiet from here on out."

"Where do these stairs lead to?"

"The dungeons," Victor replied shortly. "Did you not hear what I just said? We are underneath the Council Hall, we must be absolutely silent."

The twins gave a single nod simultaneously. I lowered my flashlight to shine down on the ground and followed behind them through a dark passageway. The further we walked in, the louder voices could be heard in the distance. As the passageway narrowed, Victor reached down and lifted Livy into his arms, bringing all of us closer to the thin rays of light that were coming through a set of bars cut high into the wall.

Victor waved me forward before moving Livy to his shoulder and bringing Jack up in his free arm. As I peered through the bars I realized I was looking out floor-level to a large stone room. Warriors were seated on the opposite side of the room on wide concrete steps. Everyone was staring at a man in the center of the room. His hands were tied together in front of his stomach while four Warriors stood around him with long rods that each had a loop of rope connected to the tip that was secured around the man's neck.

Werewolf.

Victor gave me a side glance and nodded, as if confirming what we were looking at. I craned my neck to see around the side of the bars but only saw the side of a large chair and someone's calf. Victor placed his hand on my chest and pushed me back from the bars. Even though we were right at floor level, everyone was looking in our direction, any one of them could spot us if we got too close or made the slightest sound.

"I will ask you again," a man I couldn't see said angrily, "how long has your pack been associated with Garrett Archer?"

The man in the center of the room gave a smirk and a second later the guards yanked their poles backwards and caused the man to snap down onto his back on the stone floor. Painfully he rolled onto his side and began to cough to get his breath back.

"Things will not get any easier, Adam. I suggest you cooperate," the man I couldn't see said. "Shall we try again?"

The guards pulled on their poles once again, this time lifting him up forcibly by the neck. The wolf, now known as Adam, grunted and pulled at the ropes around his neck until his feet finally caught the ground and could relieve the pressure. He placed his hands on his knees while he coughed and caught his breath.

"How long has your pack been associated with Garrett Archer?"

"Two years," he coughed but then finally stood, though hunched slightly. "He came to us two years ago. We heard he'd been trying to get in with a couple of other packs, but they didn't want to do business with a blood sucker. I mean, the smell alone is a deterrent."

A mumble went through the crowd.

"So why was your pack different?"

Adam shifted his weight and replied, "That's above my paygrade."

"A pack suddenly doing business with a vampire must have caused some outrage."

Adam laughed and smirked. "You know nothing about being part of a pack."

"Then enlighten us."

"If my pack leader tells us to take orders from a blood sucker, we have to take orders from a fucking blood sucker whether we like it or not. There's no choice."

"And what exactly did your pack do for Garrett Archer?"

He shrugged. "I know some people helped him track that kid."

"What is that kid to Garrett?"

"I don't know."

"Why did they take his mother, Abigail Dawes?"

"I don't know."

"Weren't you there when they took her?"

Adam shook his head. "No."

"Abigail Dawes was never in your presence?"

"No," he replied. "Must have been with someone else."

"Your pack has several locations?"

"We're not the only pack Garrett's involved with."

"And where are the other packs located?"

He shrugged. "I don't know."

Suddenly all four guards lifted their poles in the air and stretched Adam's neck high enough to where he rose up on his toes. When they released him, they allowed him to fall to his knees where he gasped for breath.

"I don't know!" he shouted through his coughs. "I hope you treat the other wolf like this."

I looked over to Victor but before I could say anything, Jackson said in his full voice, "Grandfather, you said we'd see a wolf."

Victor and I both took a step away from the bars, but the man who was sitting in the chair leaned down slowly and turned to look down into vent. It took only a moment to realize that Devin was staring at us. When he narrowed his eyes, Victor turned and ran with me tight on his heels and fumbling with my flashlight.

"But I wanned to see the wolf," Livy whined as we reached the end of the passageway.

"You did, little one," Victor said and put both children down on the steps, "the wolf was inside that man. They don't always come out when you want them to."

Livy harrumphed, pouted, and began stomping her feet up the stairs.

"Shall we?" Victor said and gestured up the stairs.

I nodded and shined my flashlight upward, catching Livy already standing at the top. "Sir, did you hear when he said there was another wolf?"

"I did."

"I thought they only caught one."

"It is an interesting development," he replied, and then he ran up the stairs, leaving me at the bottom of the stairs alone, in the dark.

"Good talk, sir."

"Now pull the string back slowly," I instructed while keeping a guiding hand near Tosha's arm. She looked sexy as hell holding my bow and stretching an arrow to her cheek. "Do you see your target?"

"Yep," she replied seriously and squinted her eye.

"Ok, on your exhale, just let go. And don't feel bad if you don't make it..."

But of course, as with everything else that Tosha did, when she released the arrow it flew through the air perfectly and hit the target just on the edge of center.

She released a single laugh and then looked up at me. "What shouldn't I feel bad about?"

"I really do hate you sometimes."

She knew I wasn't serious and nudged me in the gut.

"Don't let her show you up, Dawes," Roberts shouted from across the courtyard. "Do a shoot off!"

"I'd like to keep my man-card intact, thanks, Roberts."

Tosha placed her hand on my arm. "I'll go easy on you if you want to look good in front of everyone."

I arched my eyebrow at her snide comment, but then leaned down and whispered in her ear, "You make me look good just standing next to me."

When I lifted up, I smiled at her flush cheeks.

"Beckett Dawes," someone shouted.

When I looked back toward the front of the courtyard I could see Devin standing between one of the arches and waving me over.

"It's been nice knowing you," Tosha said quietly.

I looked nervously down at her. "Yeah, we had a run."

She smiled and patted my chest. "Good luck."

I sighed loudly, tried to hold my chest up to look confident as I walked across the courtyard toward Devin. The man was just standing there, doing absolutely nothing, and he was intimidating the shit out of me. Seriously, I thought the shit was going to come out of me by the time I reached him.

"Beckett, come with me," he said and began walking toward a set of tall wooden double doors where several Warriors were exiting.

As soon as I stepped inside I realized we were in the courtroom I had seen hours earlier. Courtroom? No, what did Victor call it? Council room? Either way, it wasn't where I wanted to be.

Cameron stood in the middle of the room talking with several people who he dismissed as soon as he saw Devin and I walking in.

When I was within inches of Cameron, I wasted no time in defending myself. "Let me just explain, Victor totally forced me to do it."

Cameron flinched and Devin snickered.

"So your first instinct is to throw the former head of our coven under the bus?" Devin asked, although his tone thankfully wasn't angry.

"If it gets me off the hook, then yes," I replied truthfully. "He said it was a learning opportunity for all of us."

Cameron shook his head. "Of course he did. What is a more fitting place to bring my two children than to an interrogation. However, Beckett, that is not why we have brought you in here."

"Oh thank god," I said loudly, even hunching over with a sigh of relief. "You have no idea what a relief that is. Ok, so uh…what's up?"

Suddenly both Cameron and Devin became very serious, and my stomach sank. Cameron put his hand on my shoulder as he said, "Beckett, your father has taken a turn for the worse."

Nearly ten seconds passed before I could reply, "How so?"

"He has begun to phase."

"Phase? What does that mean?"

Devin stepped forward. "It's when the man turns into the wolf."

"Wait, no, that wasn't supposed to happen until the full moon," I said and stepped back, removing Cameron's heavy hand from my shoulder. "That's…that's days away."

"We believe your father's heart condition has weakened him," Cameron interrupted. "And in this weakened state, it is causing him to start phasing prior to the full moon. I am sorry, Beckett."

I took another step away. "Ok, so can someone take me to Facility West?"

"He's here, Beckett," Devin replied. "He was transported early this morning."

"What!" I shouted. "He's here? You mean he's been here all day and no one told me! What kind of bullshit operation are you running here?"

Cameron put an arm across Devin's chest and I realized I needed to get myself in check.

"I'm sorry," I said softly. "Can I see him?"

"He's this way," Cameron said calmly and gestured toward a door at the corner of the room.

"Where does that go to?"

"It leads down to the holding cells."

"You mean the dungeon."

Devin put his arm around my back, gently pushing me forward toward that door. "Beckett, your father cannot control his phases. We need to keep him contained until this passes."

My feet reluctantly stepped forward, following Cameron and being guided by Devin through the single door and down a twisting set of stairs. When we reached the bottom, we were met by a group of men, one of whom introduced himself as Julian.

"We are making your father as comfortable as possible," Julian said and waved us down a darkly lit corridor lined with prison cells on the right side. "He hasn't phased in the last couple of hours, but based on the patterns we've witnessed, that could mean he's due for another attack."

I slowed down, but Devin pushed me forward and around the corner. "But if he's such a danger to everyone, why are you letting me see him?"

Julian stopped and turned around. "Your father has a heart condition, correct?" I nodded. "Based on what Dr. Ryan has observed, each time your father has a phase, it is stressing his heart to dangerous levels."

I straightened up and looked at each man before I replied quietly, "You think he's going to die from this?"

Cameron squeezed my shoulder. "Beckett, we do not know what his body will be able to handle. He could certainly pull through."

"But you don't believe that," I said.

"I would like to be hopeful, Beckett, but if there is anything you want to say to him you may want to say it now."

I rubbed my face harshly, pulling at my cheeks and chin. With a sigh I took a step forward, but Julian put his hand on my chest. "A few rules," he said very seriously. "Although you may be tempted, you must not approach the bars, and you certainly cannot touch your father. Is that clear?" When I didn't respond, he pushed me in the chest. "If you approach the bars, you will be removed, is that clear?"

"Y-yes," I stuttered.

"Good," he said and began walking again. "You must also not speak with any of the other prisoners. Is that understood?"

"Yeah," I replied, not sure why I would want to speak to another prisoner until we passed by a cell that contained the man, Adam the werewolf, I'd seen interrogated earlier.

That's when it hit me. Adam the wolf had said there was another wolf here. He was speaking of my dad. Victor knew, everyone knew, and I was walking around like an asshole all day.

"Mr. Dawes," Julian said, and I picked my head up, but then I realized he was addressing the man on the other side of a set of bars. "You have a visitor."

My father was laying on a mattress on the cold stone floor wearing hospital scrubs that were dirty and ripped.

"What the hell is this," I shouted.

"Becks," my father said as he slowly pushed himself up to a sitting position.

"What the fuck! He's not a criminal. Why is he down here on a fucking mattress on the goddamn floor wearing dirty clothes? What the fuck!"

"Becks, calm down," my father pleaded, pumping his hand out in front of him. "It's easier this way, trust me. I'm fine."

"Fine?! How can you say that," I said and rushed to his cell, but was instantly stopped by Julian pushing me up against the opposite wall.

"The rules, Beckett," Julian said firmly.

I struggled under his grip, but finally nodded in frustration and pushed his hands off of me. "I get it, I get it. I won't approach the bars."

Julian stepped back, adjusted my T-shirt, and patted my chest. "I'm sorry it has to be this way, but it is for your own safety."

"Yeah, yeah, whatever."

"You can stay as long as you like," Julian said, nodded to both Devin and Cameron, then turned and left. "Do not approach the bars."

"He means that, by the way," Devin said firmly, and I nodded.

"Our search for your mother continues," Cameron said and then looked over to my father. "We are doing everything we can to find your wife, Mr. Dawes."

"I'm sure you are," my father responded weakly.

Cameron patted me on the shoulder one last time before he and Devin turned and walked away. Then I was alone. Alone and staring at the man behind the bars and trying not to see the flashes of the monster lurking inside him. I couldn't stand seeing my father like this. So weak and dirty, nothing like the man he was.

"Dad..." I said but he held his hand up.

"Tell me everything they're not telling me about your mother."

Chapter Nineteen

Having to tell my father that we were no closer to finding Mom was the hardest thing I'd ever done. What was devastating was seeing him get emotional at the realization that he may never see her again. My life kept crumbling around me and there was nothing I could do to stop it.

Eventually my father passed out from exhaustion. Even in this low light I could see he was unhealthily pale. Time was running out, and all I could do was sit on this cold, hard floor like an asshole.

"Beckett!" Tosha's voice rang from down the hall.

I looked up to my right and saw her running toward me. Painfully I pushed myself up from the floor, my joints and muscles groaning from sitting on the stone floor for so long. I took several steps forward in order to stop her from coming in front of the cell my father was sleeping in.

Tosha threw her arms around my neck and squeezed me tightly. "I just heard," she said quickly in my ear. "I'm sorry, I'm so sorry. I would have been down here sooner if they had let me."

I pulled her arms down from my neck. "You shouldn't be here."

She backed away abruptly. "What? But why? Where else would I be…"

"I can't let you see him like this," I interrupted and then clinched my jaw.

Tosha's expression changed to one of sympathy as she cupped my cheek with her hand. As soon as her hand touched my face, I was overcome by the emotions I had tried to push down into the depths of my stomach. With a gentle nudge, she pulled my head down to her shoulder

224 ~ C.R. QUINN

and wrapped her other arm around me allowing me the release I needed.

"He'll be ok," she whispered but I shook my head. "Don't be like that. He'll fight through this."

I rose from her shoulder and embarrassingly wiped my eyes. "It's not good."

"I know," she replied. "But let's not get ahead of ourselves. Ok?"

I nodded and wiped my face again. "I still don't want you to see him like this."

"And I'm not leaving you alone, Becks, I'm sorry. I'm here with you as long as they allow it." She took my hand and squeezed it to her chest. "It's your turn not to push me away."

I swallowed the lump in my throat and rocked back on my heels, pulling her with me toward my father's pathetic cell. She didn't gasp or break out into sobs at the sight of my dad like I expected. Instead she simply squeezed my hand tightly and sighed.

"I'll be right back," she said and jogged back down around the corner.

"Was it something I said?" my father said quietly.

I looked over to see that he had pushed himself up to a seated position.

"We didn't mean to wake you."

"You didn't. I've been half awake for a few minutes now. What time is it?"

"Almost four."

"Wow," he sighed. "It's been a while since anything happened. Maybe that's a good sign."

"Yeah," I nodded, hoping it was true. "It's a real good sign."

Just then Tosha came around the corner with a stack of pillows and blankets in her arms.

"What's this for?" I asked and took the blankets off the top.

"Do you want to keep sitting on the hard floor?" she said and stepped past me, placing a couple of the pillows down on the floor.

"Where did you get all this?"

She shrugged. "I've spent a lot of time down here, sometimes not voluntarily, but you learn where things are." She took one of the blankets from my arms and tossed it down next to the pillows. "Hi, Mr. Dawes."

He smiled. "Sweetie, if this doesn't constitute calling me Richard, I don't know what does."

She smiled kindly, not in sympathy, not in sorrow, just in kindness toward my dad. "Richard, can I get you anything? Are you cold?"

"No, sweetheart," he replied. "This wolf thing keeps me pretty warm."

She nodded and sat down on the pillow closest to her, pulling the blanket across her feet and legs. "Becks, come sit down."

"Yeah, Becks, have a seat," my dad said, giving me an eye I'm sure over Tosha's use of my nickname. "This feels a little like the humans looking at the animals at the zoo."

"Dad, don't say that," I snapped and pressed my back against the wall.

"Son, I'm only trying to lighten the mood."

"Well, it isn't funny."

Tosha pulled down on the edge of my shirt. "And you're making it worse. Now sit down." Her tone was almost the same as when we first met and she bossed me around. And just to spite her, I held my ground and stayed standing up against the wall. She rolled her eyes at me and turned back to face my dad. "Richard, did Beckett tell you about the mission he went on last night?"

"Yes he did," my dad said with a hint of pride, but I was in no mood.

"Not that I did any good," I groaned.

Tosha looked up at me annoyed. "I guess saving my life isn't doing any good?"

"You know what I mean," I replied. "We didn't find my mom. That was kind of the whole purpose."

Tosha looked sympathetically over at my dad. "But they're getting closer, Richard, I promise they are. I heard they got some leads from the wolf we captured."

"Then whoever you spoke to is lying because that guy didn't divulge shit."

Tosha pulled the blanket up to her shoulders and sighed. I was being a dick.

"Sorry," I said and kissed the top of her head, then looked back at my dad. "Sorry, Dad."

"It's all right, Becks, this is a lot...um, for all of...us," he struggled to say, almost like he was going to be sick.

"Dad? You ok?" I asked and pushed myself off the wall. Even from this far away I could see sweat beading on his forehead. "Dad?"

Suddenly my dad's back arched up, his head tucking tightly into his chest as he let out a painful groan. I took a step forward and Tosha stood in front of me. She placed her hand gently on my chest.

"You have to stay back, Beckett."

My father began screaming from his cell, his body contorting and clinching in different painful looking positions. His arms started turning darker from the thick hair sprouting through his skin. His fingers cracked and elongated while his nails grew into thick sharp points. He was phasing right before my eyes. His painful screams were unbearable, and sending shivers down my spine. Forcefully I stepped around Tosha, trying to get closer to the bars, but in an instant she grabbed my arm, bent it behind me, and threw me up against the stone wall.

"Let me go!" I shouted, although my face was pressed painfully up against the wall, the taste of blood leaking into my mouth.

"Beckett, please," Tosha said, pushing me into the wall again when I tried pulling out of her iron grip. "Don't make me hurt you."

My father's agonizing screams were echoing around me, ripping through my body and making me scream along with him.

"Just let me see him," I cried, finally stopping all resistance and collapsing into the wall.

Tosha released my arm but then wrapped her arms around me, pressing her weight into my back to keep me turned away. When my father's groans began to die down she finally removed her hold on me and I pushed off the wall. Tosha's lashes were wet with her tears and when she looked up at me she flinched. She reached up and wiped my chin with her thumb.

"I'm sorry," she said and licked the blood from her thumb. "Let me take care of that?"

When I nodded, she rose onto her toes and licked my bottom lip where it had opened up, and then sealed it with a kiss. Once she lowered herself back down she stepped aside to allow me to see my dad. He had collapsed down on the mattress, his arms and hands looking almost normal but shiny with sweat.

"D-dad?"

He looked up from the mattress, his face wet with sweat and void of all color. "I guess...I spoke...too soon."

"Becks hears us come home, he's got the matchbook on fire and figures that if he dumps his laundry on top of it, it'll go out."

Tosha laughed. "So did he burn the house down?"

"Obviously not," I replied, annoyed that the last hour had turned into my dad telling my girlfriend embarrassing stories about me. But it was better to laugh than talk about my dad's phasing. "You've been to my house, it's still there."

"It is, and with new carpet in your old bedroom because you burned a hole in the floor," my father said with a laugh. "You were lucky you didn't set your room on fire."

"Yeah, yeah, I screwed up, I was only thirteen."

"And a pyromaniac from the sound of it. I'm glad you got that out of your system." Tosha said with hidden meaning.

"Can we change over to embarrassing stories about you?" I asked her and she smiled.

"Sorry, Becks, they just don't exist."

My dad laughed and I shook my head. "Scary enough, that's probably true."

She shrugged and I stood from the floor. My ass was falling asleep, even with sitting on a pillow. At the same time, Julian came from around the corner with a tray in his hand. I looked down at my watch and noticed it was dinner time. Just the thought of dinner made my stomach growl loudly.

"Richard," Julian said as he came in line with my father's cell, "do you think you could eat something?"

My dad nodded, but stayed on the mattress while Julian slid the tray into the cell underneath the bars. On the tray was a plate with some vegetables and a steak, but there was something wrong with that piece of meat.

"Wait," I said, pulling on Julian's arm and getting a closer look at the plate, "that meat is practically raw."

"Your point?" Julian replied with a challenging look.

"What, because he's turning into a wolf you feed him raw meat? He's not a wild animal for god's sake."

"Becks," my father warned.

"No, Dad," I interrupted. "This is ridiculous. Just because…"

"Beckett!" my dad shouted. "Leave it alone."

"But Dad…"

"It's how I want it, son," he replied, sounding almost embarrassed. "Thank you, Julian. I'm sure it's not your job to deliver meals, so I thank you for the kind gesture."

Julian gave a nod. "We need to keep your strength up. If there's anything else you need, please let me know."

"I will," my father responded and stepped over to take the tray.

"Tosh," Julian said and looked down at Natasha, "I have been told there will be a night practice session for the trainees. You are expected to attend."

Tosha gave a worried glance up at me. "Do you know what time?"

"I was told seven o'clock, so in about an hour."

"Can I come back down tonight when it's over?"

Julian shook his head. "I am not having hybrids sleeping amongst my cells. You can come back in the morning. The same goes for you, Beckett. You can stay until your father falls asleep for the night."

"But...but what if something happens?" I asked nervously.

"Then someone will come for you," he replied sternly. "I'm sorry, but those are my rules."

"Thank you, Jules," Tosha replied, and I was surprised at her using a nickname. But like she said, she'd been down here enough I guess they had formed some kind of friendship.

Once Julian left, Tosha rose from the floor and dusted herself off. "I'm sorry I have to go."

"I understand," I replied and rested my hand on her hip. "Thank you for staying down here so long."

"Of course," she said. "Do you want me to bring you something to eat?"

I shook my head. "I'll grab something later," I replied, and my stomach growled angrily.

Tosha gave me a skeptical look. "I don't mind."

"You have enough to do. I'll eat later when Julian finally kicks me out."

Tosha sighed and kissed me. Just one soft kiss, but a perfect one.

"I'll catch up with you later, then," she said and stepped away from me. She smiled and gave my father a wave. "Goodnight, Richard. I'll see you tomorrow."

My dad smiled and waved his fork in the air. "I certainly hope so, dear."

Tosha gave me a second kiss on the lips and slowly turned away. I couldn't help but watch her until she disappeared around the corner.

"I'm happy for you, son," Dad said between bites. When I looked over at him I could see that his very rare steak was almost gone. "She's a good girl."

I stepped back and leaned up against the wall. "It's been hard to convince her of that." My dad tilted his head questioningly while he chewed his last bite of steak. "She's had a rough road. Lost her parents when she was young, practically grew up in Facility West, and then..." I paused wondering if I was telling too much, but this was my dad, the most trustworthy person I knew, "...and then she had this really bad accident."

"She told me."

"She did? When?"

"That first night, I think. Why do you seem so shocked?"

"I-I don't know. She doesn't really like talking about herself."

"She must have a crush on me then," he laughed and I joined him, but then something came over him and his laughter died. "I'm glad I got to see you happy with someone. You obviously bring her out of her shell, and she challenges you, those are good things, son."

"You saw all of that in a couple of hours?"

"Of course I did, I'm your dad," he replied and then froze. "Well, one of them."

"The *only* one," I corrected.

He nodded, but not confidently. A silence fell upon us while my father slowly finished his dinner. It was uncomfortable but neither of us seemed ready to talk about anything important. I rubbed my face with my hands when my father suddenly dropped his fork, causing it to clang loudly on the plate. I looked up immediately and stood up from the wall.

"Not again," my father groaned as he tossed his plate aside causing it to shatter on the hard floor. He positioned himself onto all fours to prepare himself for what was coming. Once again his arms became dark with hair, his fingers cracking and elongating. His cries were a mix between growls and screams sounding deep within his throat. My body was swaying back and forth, trying to take a step forward and then remembering I couldn't.

With a deafening howl my father leaned back on his knees, ripping the tattered hospital shirt down the middle and exposing his chest revealing the three thick scars. With the sound of bones cracking, his chest widened and expanded, ripping his scars open and causing them to bleed.

"Julian! Somebody help!" I shouted and ran around the corner. "Help, please!"

"Oh let him be," someone shouted behind me. When I turned around I saw Adam smiling devilishly and banging on his bars. "Come on, old man, go full phase! You can do it!"

Angrily I lunged toward the bars but at the same time, a set of arms wrapped around my waist and threw me up against the wall.

"What did I say!" Julian shouted.

"My dad," I said through the pain, "he needs help."

Julian released me and I instantly pushed myself off the wall. By the time we got to my father's cell he was back on all fours, his screams dying down to growls, and blood dripping onto the mattress from his chest.

When I stepped toward the bars, Julian's hand grabbed my shoulder. I turned my head and said, "What are you doing? Help him!"

Julian's face was hard and stern. "What is it you want me to do?"

"He's bleeding! We need to do something," I said and tried to take another step toward the cell, but once again Julian tugged on my shoulder.

"He is dangerous enough on his own, but that blood is hazardous to everyone. We absolutely cannot go near that cell. Do you understand that?"

"It's getting worse, look at him!"

Julian pulled me back to the wall and patted my shoulder. "There's nothing you can do to stop this. You need to calm down, and take advantage of the time you have left with him."

My eyes began to burn as I glanced over at my dad whose body was slowly going back to normal.

"Please don't make me leave. I'm begging you, let me stay with him."

Julian sighed and looked back at my dad before replying, "Fine, but no matter what happens do not…"

"Do not approach the bars. Yeah, I got it."

He gave a nod and looked at my dad one last time. "I will bring some bandages down for him."

"Thank you."

He nodded again. "I am sorry, Beckett. I wish there was more we could do. Like I said, use the time you have with him."

As he walked away, I slid down the wall. Dad had officially passed out. Julian's words were ringing in my ears and my brain was flooded with everything that I wanted to ask before it was too late. I couldn't get my hands around that.

"Did he make?" Adam shouted from the other end of the cell block.

"Fuck you."

Chapter Twenty

Julian kept his word and brought down some bandage pads for my father's wounds. He slid them underneath the bars like he had the tray of food earlier, although this time he behaved as though the bars were made of acid and he couldn't touch or get near them. Did he honestly think my father's blood would just jump out at him?

Even two hours later I was still angry about it. My father hadn't budged since he collapsed, but I never took my eyes off of him to make sure he was still breathing. My Warrior medallion was in my hand and I'd practically rubbed it smooth.

"Here you are," Victor said, coming around the corner. I had to blink twice to focus my eyes and believe that I was seeing Victor wearing a white Roman-looking robe. A toga? Was he seriously wearing a toga? I didn't get it, but I didn't have the energy to ask. As he came closer I realized he was carrying a large cup with steam coming up from it. "I brought you some soup."

I looked down at my watch. "It's eleven o'clock."

"Have you eaten?" I shook my head. "Then why are you questioning me? You must have something."

I sighed and accepted the cup, it was actually nice and warm on my cold hands. I took a sip, and then a big gulp. It wasn't super hot, but the chicken broth and thin cut noodles were soothing. Before I knew it, I'd eaten the whole thing.

"If I'd known you were that hungry I would have brought you a bowl," Victor said and took the cup from me.

"No, that's plenty," I replied and slowly pushed myself up off the floor. "I'm surprised Julian let you down here."

"Let me?" Victor said offended. "I erected these walls, I built these cells, I gave him his position. You think I need permission to come down here…"

"Hey, hey, calm down," I said and pumped my hands. "Having a little trouble dealing with not being in charge anymore?"

He sighed and pursed his lips. "Perhaps a little. How is your father doing?"

"He's been better."

"I expect so," he replied, taking a look into my dad's cell.

"Did you know?" I asked pointedly.

"Know what, child?"

I gave him a skeptical look. "You knew they brought my dad here this morning."

His stoic face gave him away even before he replied, "I did."

My head started shaking. "Why…why didn't you tell me? When you brought us down to the tunnels today, we were near the dungeons. Why didn't you bring me here?"

"Because it was forbidden."

"So was sneaking to watch the interrogation, but that didn't stop you."

"But I agreed with the decision that you shouldn't see him."

"That's bullshit! You should have told me."

He stepped in front of me and even with his short stature he was incredibly intimidating. "And what would you have done? Stood outside until they let you in? Waiting and worrying about him even though there was nothing that you could do. What good would that have done?"

"You break the rules you want to."

"Correct," he replied flatly. "I felt it best you waited to see your father until he was more under control."

"This is under control?"

"Perhaps the phases weren't as dramatic, but they were certainly more often. I'm sorry that you are upset, but it was for the best."

"We'll have to disagree on that one," I grumbled and leaned my back up against the wall. "Have you heard anything about my mom?"

"I have not heard anything," he replied.

"Would you tell me if you had?"

"I don't appreciate the tone."

"Well, it's the only one I have."

He took another step closer and placed his hand on my shoulder. "I know this is difficult, child. Please know that we are all pulling for your father's recovery."

"Another wolf in the world? I doubt that," I said in the same snide tone and rubbed my face roughly. When I pulled my hands down, my eyes refocused on his clothes. "Can I ask, why the toga?"

He petted the line of his toga down his chest. "My robes are part of my history, and they are comfortable."

"And you just walk around in them?"

He let out a frustrated sigh. "I do find it rather annoying that you don't have the fear or respect of me like everyone else."

"Maybe it's because you keep breaking the rules and sneaking me into places I shouldn't be."

"Perhaps," he laughed and turned to walk away. "I will come back down in a little while to check on you both again."

"The kitchen closed hours ago, how did you get soup?" I asked to his back.

As he rounded the corner he replied, "I built that kitchen and hired Christine myself! If I want a cup of soup, I shall get one."

I couldn't help but laugh a little, but then a noise came from the cell. My father slowly turned over and opened his eyes.

"Dad? Did I wake you?"

He shook his head. "No," he said quietly and painfully pushed himself up to a seated position, his torn shirt covered in blood. "Who was that man?"

"That was Victor," I replied and slid down to the floor. "He used to run the coven and has been training me. He uh...made...Garrett."

"Ah," he said and winced as he shifted.

"There are some bandages here if you need them."

He looked down at his chest where his scars were still red, but had stopped bleeding. "I think I'm good for now. Son, there are some things we need to talk about."

"Um...ok," I replied nervously. I knew that tone well, and I was usually in trouble when I heard it.

"You know the safe in my office at home?" I nodded. "The combination is one, four, four, five, seven."

"Wait, what?"

"Repeat it, Becks."

"Why?"

"Repeat it, please."

"One, four, four, five, seven. Why do I need to get into your safe?"

"Inside you'll find my life insurance policies, all the paperwork for the house, banking information..."

"Dad, no. No!"

"Becks," he pleaded, "we both know how this ends, and I don't think they'll find your mother in time. So you need to be prepared to handle things."

"No. I-I can't do it, Dad."

"The laptop on my desk has a file called 'In case of.' It has all the user ids and passwords for every account we have."

"Dad, please stop. I'm begging you."

"I need you to know that I've always thought of you as my own. I hope you never felt otherwise."

A lump caught in my throat and I looked at my dad in shock. "Of course I didn't know any different, I was blinded by all of this. What kind of world is this where you're not my dad?"

My dad struggled to keep his composure, and the staggered breathing seemed painful. As we stared at one another I was reminded of Julian's words. Whether I liked it or not, this could be my last chance.

"Dad, why did you do it?"

He looked at me curiously and shook his head. "Do what, son?"

"You could have married any other woman and had a family of your own. Why did you get mixed up in this mess?"

He gave an exhausted smile. "I was young, stupid, and madly in love with your mother."

"Yeah, but..."

"But nothing, Becks. She was my best friend. I'd been in love with her since the day I saw her at freshman orientation. When she came to me in trouble, I couldn't turn her away."

"I still don't get it, Dad."

He sighed. "Your mother and I were best friends until I came back from winter break our Junior year. She actually stayed on campus during that break and that's when she met...him. That's when we first started losing touch. She was skipping class, was hardly ever in the dorms, I never saw her. It was really hard to see her pulling away like that.

"By the time we got to finals I hadn't seen her in almost two months, and then one day she just knocks on my door." He laughed a little to himself. "Honestly, I thought I was seeing a ghost, but there she was. She looked as though she'd been crying for days, and she was terrified."

"About what?"

He shifted his position and winced again in pain. "She said that the man she'd met wasn't who she thought he was. At the time she wouldn't give me specifics, all she said was that he was a really bad guy and she was afraid he'd come after her. I told her I'd help her get home, but she burst out crying and told me that she was pregnant. She knew her dad, your grandfather, would disown her. Knowing what I did of your grandfather and how religious they were, I knew she was right."

"So, you just married her?"

"I told her I'd take her home to San Francisco, we'd tell her parents that the baby was mine, and we'd get married right away."

"Is that why Grandpa was always such a jerk to you?"

He nodded and laughed. "Yeah, pretty much. He blamed me for ruining his daughter."

I shook my head in disbelief. "But you didn't need to go through all that."

"I was young and stupid. Initially I told her we'd stay married for a year. That way I could finish school and get a job. Then after that year, we'd decide whether we wanted to stay together or not."

"Really? That whole year you never knew if she was going to dump you or not?"

He nodded. "It was a tough year. We had a newborn, I was working part-time and juggling school, and we were living with each other for the first time in our lives under her father's roof. It was hell. But to make it worse, your mother was really protective of you."

"What do you mean?"

"Well, she didn't want me helping to take care of you. She barely even let me hold you."

"Why?"

"I don't know exactly, we've never really talked about it, but I always assumed it was because in her mind we had an end date. She didn't want me to bond with you, or you with me, if we were just going to separate in a few months."

"That obviously changed."

He nodded. "It did. You were a few months old and she caught the flu. Your grandparents were out of town so I was the only one who could take care of you. It was the first time you and I had some real time together. You were being fussy all night and at some point I fell asleep on the couch with you on my chest. I woke up out of a dead sleep to your mother crying over me. I didn't know what to do, so I just held her. The three of us slept on the couch for the rest of the night and after that day everything changed.

"We were coming up on a year, and every day I thought this is the day she asks for a divorce. I was driving myself nuts worrying she'd kick me out. So on our first anniversary I just came out and asked her what she wanted, and she said she wanted to stay married. I was relieved, but I told her I wanted to know about...that other man."

"That must have been an interesting conversation."

"To say the least," he answered. "I just thought she'd found some guy that was into vampires, you know, pretending to be one. That was the only time in my life that I thought your mother was gullible and naïve."

"And you told her never to talk about it again?"

"I now see that was not the smartest move. I just didn't want...if I was going to be your father, I didn't want to hear about anyone else. It was selfish of me."

I shook my head. "You did what you thought was right. I'm sorry that I was it for you."

"What?"

"Come on, Dad, if you and Mom had had a child together, they would have been the smartest, most dedicated kid ever. You got stuck with me who couldn't make his mind up in college and has no plan whatsoever."

"Is that what you think?

"Come on, Dad, you were my age and had finished school, married, and did this unbelievably selfless act. And I live in your basement."

"Beckett," he struggled to say.

"Dad?" I asked softly, scared at the familiar signs.

He flipped on his back, his legs kicking out and his back arching painfully. He grunted and pounded the mattress with this fist, pushing himself toward the bars. Slowly he rolled back onto his stomach, his back now arching upward like a cat. When he looked at me, his eyes turned a yellowish color, his face becoming wet with sweat as his breath became staggered.

I couldn't take another minute of being apart and ran to the bars. Dad crawled the rest of the way and grabbed my arms through the space between the bars.

"You are…my son. *My* son," he shouted and then growled in pain as a wave of his phase went through his body.

"And you're my dad," I replied quickly, knowing that Julian or the guards would be coming around the corner any second. "I love you, Dad."

"My son," he said again and then suddenly his hands flinched, his nails turning sharp and sinking into the top of my left wrist.

Footsteps could be heard coming quickly down the hall so I pulled away, but in an instant, arms were around my waist and pulling me away. My father's screams increased and I could barely see him over the shoulder of the guard that was restraining me.

"Dad! Dad!" I shouted, watching as he thrashed around his cell, his skin turning dark again with hair. His chest expanded through his ripped shirt, his scars ripping open again. Julian had joined the guards and pushed everyone back.

My dad reared back on his knees, his face cracking and elongating. He howled in pain as his body continued to change, but suddenly a scream caught in his throat. He grabbed his chest and then fell face first on the ground.

"NO!" I screamed and pushed against the guard, kicking my legs and clawing at his arms. "Help him! For god's sake help him!"

But everyone stayed frozen in place, they're heads down and backs turned to what was happening to my father. Then it was quiet. My father went still and I leapt toward the cell. Julian grabbed me by my shoulders and pushed me into the wall.

"There's nothing you can do, Beckett."

"Let go of me!" I shouted in his face, but got thrown into the wall again.

"He's gone, Beckett."

"Then let me in there!"

"He is just as dangerous dead as he was alive. You can't go in there."

"Fuck you!" I shouted and pushed against him.

Julian banged me into the wall. He didn't even say anything, just held me face to face with him until my anger turned into tears. He brought me into his chest where I sobbed uncontrollably. I hit and pulled at his arms, and in response he whispered his condolences.

Julian ordered his guards to do various things while I pulled myself

238 ~ C.R. QUINN

together, finally standing on my own and wiping my eyes. I felt numb and empty, and my legs didn't feel confident under me.

Julian patted me on my shoulder. "I can have someone escort you back to your room."

"N-no, I...can do it." I looked over at my dad lying on the floor, lifeless, but slowly transitioning back to his human self. "What happens now?"

"I don't know," Julian replied truthfully. "I need to consult with Devin and Cameron."

"I'll wait then."

He shook his head. "You need to go to your room."

"But...I don't want him to be alone."

"We'll take care of him, Beckett."

I took a step away and addressed Julian as well as the guards. "Please don't treat him like a wolf. He's...he's my dad, not a monster."

Julian nodded and turned me away from my father's cell. "We will show him every ounce of respect, I assure you."

I took one last look, clinging to that small amount of hope that my father would suddenly start breathing again, but when he remained silent and frozen I turned away and pushed my feet forward.

Just as I was about to round the corner, someone clicked their tongue at me.

"The 'ole man didn't make it, huh?"

I looked over to see Adam staring at me from his cell, his bright yellow eyes shining through the darkness. My chest started to heave and in an instant I lunged toward his cell and my hands went through the bars.

"Damn, boy," Adam whistled as he jumped back, but a second later he began sniffing the air and then focused on my arm. "Uh oh, got a little close, did ya? Wanned to see what it's like on our side?"

Quickly I pulled my arms from the bars and noticed the puncture on my wrist. "You don't know anything."

"I know that smell," he said with a sneaky smile. "You better run, boy. Or else you'll be in a cell like me and your 'ole man."

Panic started to set in and I turned away from the cell. As I ran away I pulled my sleeve down over my wrist, looking nervously from side to side to see if anyone was running after me. I didn't realize I was holding my breath until I was outside in the courtyard and began gasping for air. No one was chasing me, there was hardly even a sound at all. It took almost five minutes before I caught my breath and stopped pacing. Standing there in the darkness I'd never felt so alone. My dad was dead. I thought I'd have another thirty years before I would have to say that. I didn't know what I was supposed to do now. How did I live life without my dad?

A chill went through my body which finally convinced me to head to my room. I kept my head down as I walked through the corridors of the manor. Someone called my name, I wasn't sure who, but I kept on walking and trudged up the big spiral staircase.

Before I knew it, my hand was twisting the door handle to my room and pushing open the door. When I closed it behind me I flipped the lights on and heard a moan.

"Beck?" Tosha said from my bed, turning over and putting her hand up in front of her eyes to block the bright bedroom overhead light. She stretched her eyes open and the realization hit her. "Oh my god. Beckett? He didn't…"

I collapsed down onto the bed and my body curled up into itself. Tosha draped herself over the side of my body, her tears dripping onto my face while she held me.

"I don't know what to do," I cried with a feeling of panic. "What am I supposed to do?"

"First, you just breathe. You figure out how to breathe again."

Chapter Twenty-one

My body felt heavy, and not just because Tosha was curled on top of me. Every breath took effort, every movement was painful, even my eyes wouldn't focus clearly. The one thing that kept circling in my brain was that I would have to tell my mother that her husband died in front of me, and I could do nothing.

One fucking car accident, and my life went to shit. If only Tosha hadn't saved me that first night, none of this would have happened. Garrett would have me and my family would have been left alone. I kept having to remind myself that this wasn't Tosha's fault. If only she wasn't as good as she was at being a Warrior maybe she wouldn't have noticed those men following me. My mom didn't deserve to be kidnapped, and my dad certainly didn't deserve to die.

Tosha rolled away from me toward the wall. I lifted my left arm to check the time and my forearm burned with a sharp pain. The moment when my dad's claw sunk into my skin flashed in my head. I looked over at Tosha and carefully slid off of the bed in order not to wake her. She didn't stir so I quietly stepped into the bathroom and closed the door behind me.

When I flipped the light on, I avoided looking in the mirror. I didn't want to see what I looked like. I was pretty sure it was about the same as I felt. Slowly I undressed and stepped into the shower. I placed my hands on the shower wall and let the hot water stream down my back. The puncture wound burned and almost seemed to glow and morph its shape the more I stared at it.

What did it mean? Would I turn into a wolf now? Would everyone abandon me and put me in a cell like my dad? They certainly wouldn't want to associate their coven with a wolf. Would they stop looking for my mom? This was bad. This was really, really bad. What was I going to do? Where would I go? How in the world would I live as a werewolf? A goddamn werewolf!

I slammed the shower off and rubbed the water out of my face. The shower didn't do anything but make me feel worse. I wrapped a towel around my waist and stepped out into the bedroom. My duffel bag was lying on the floor open and empty. I'd have to wear something dirty until I could do laundry. Quickly I dropped the towel and found a pair of sweats that didn't smell too bad.

"Nice view," Tosha said just as I pulled the waistband over my ass.

"Polite girls wouldn't have looked," I said and tied the drawstring.

"Never said I was polite."

I was too tired to come up with something witty in response and simply began picking up several of the dirty shirts that were on the ground, smelling them to see which one I could wear one more day.

"Come back to bed."

"Don't you have training today?"

"Doesn't matter."

"You'll get in trouble."

"Doesn't matter."

I laughed and stepped toward the bed. "Who are you and what have you done with Natasha Cushlin?"

"You're a bad influence, that's what happened."

Forgetting about the shirt, I stepped back over to the bed and crawled easily in beside her. "Tosha, if I've learned anything about you it's that no one can influence you to do anything you don't want to do."

She wrapped her leg around the top of my hip and brushed her fingers down my chest. "I want to do whatever I can to make you feel better."

"Can I feel your scars?"

She shook her head and blinked her eyes slowly before finally sighing and raising her shirt. My hand went right around to her back and tucked my head into the crook of her shoulder. We laid silently while my fingers traced over the bumpy, swirling patterns of her scars.

"Do you want some breakfast?" she asked quietly.

I shook my head. "I can't eat anything."

She sighed, but didn't push it any further. She reached behind her, pulled my hand from her back, and lifted it up to her lips.

"What happened to your arm?" she asked as she grazed her index fingers over the slim scar.

I pulled my hand from her grip. "Nothing," I replied dismissively. "I hit it up against the wall."

"Why were..."

"Julian threw me up against the wall when I tried to get to my dad, ok?" I said and sat up in the bed, shifting my legs over the edge of the bed until my feet hit the floor.

Tosha was silent for almost a minute before she hugged me from behind, bringing my back into her chest. "I'm sorry."

"No, I'm sorry. I didn't mean to snap."

Both of us jumped at the knock at the door. Tosha untangled herself as I stood up from the bed, but I hesitated opening the door.

"Beckett? It is Cameron."

I looked back at Tosha who quickly got out from underneath the blankets. Once she was done making the bed I opened the door. Cameron stood on the other side, his face already showing sympathy.

"Good morning, Beckett, may I come in?"

"Sure," I replied and opened the door fully.

Once he stepped inside he noticed Tosha standing nervously by the bed. "Good morning, Natasha. I apologize for the interruption."

"Good morning, sir. Do you need me to leave?"

"That is up to Beckett," he answered and looked over at me.

"Anything you need to say to me can be said in front of her."

Cameron nodded. "Perhaps you both could sit."

As I sat down, Cameron pulled a metal container from behind his back.

"What is that?" I asked nervously and Tosha squeezed my hand.

"Beckett, I am so sorry for your loss," he began and crossed the room to place the container on the nightstand.

"What's in the container?"

"As a matter of safety, we had your father cremated."

"Crem...cremated? He's...in there? Who said you could do that?" I shouted and stood from the bed.

Cameron put his hands up. "Beckett, your father's body, his blood, was still dangerous to everyone. The safest thing to do was cremation and we needed to do it quickly."

My chest was tight and my pulse kept pounding in my head. How could my dad be in that container? He was a man of skin and bones, not a heap of ash.

"But…he needs a funeral…a memorial, something! This is bullshit."

Tosha pulled on my arm. "Beck, please calm down."

"Calm down? Your father isn't dead!"

"Yes he is, and so is my mother, remember?" she shouted and stood up. "And I have no idea when it happened or where his body even ended up. At least you got to be with your dad in the end and everyone here is going to help you through it. So calm down and listen to what Cameron has to say, ok?"

I sat back down on the bed and my head fell into my hands. "I'm sorry."

"There is nothing for you to be sorry about," Cameron said. "I can come back later if you wish, but we do need to go over a few things."

I lifted my head. "No, it's fine. Let's just get it over with."

"Very well," he replied and straightened up. "Unfortunately, and this will be the hardest thing for you to hear, you cannot have a funeral for your father at this time."

"Why?"

"For one, your mother is still missing. Having a memorial without her will create too many questions. It would be better to do a ceremony once your mother is found."

"And then, what? What do we tell people? Certainly not the truth."

He nodded. "The cover story we have come up with is that your parents went away on a last-minute trip. Due to your father's heart condition, he suffered a heart attack and your mother acted quickly in order to bring him home."

I froze. "You guys just came up with that like it was nothing."

"I mean no disrespect, we have simply had to do this for a very long time. Shall I continue?" I nodded reluctantly. "So that we can keep the appearance that nothing has happened to your parents, we need access to any and all finances, accounts, even access to your father's business records. Are you able to help us with that?"

"Yeah," I replied with an awkward laugh, thinking about how my dad insisted that I know the combination to the safe. "I can get you any paperwork he has, and he left a file on his laptop. But all of that is at the house. I need some more of my things anyway."

"Good. I will have Jared take you."

"I'd like to go to, sir," Tosha said and rubbed my back. Only now did I realize I still didn't have a shirt on. Now I was uncomfortable and self-consciously put my right hand over the wound on my left wrist.

"I would prefer that you stayed, Natasha," Cameron replied. "You do have a long day of training today."

"But I…"

"Tosha," I interrupted her, "it's fine. I don't need you there." Her face fell in disappointment. "You have more important things to do and I'm just going back home."

"Ok," she said with a shrug, although she wasn't happy.

"I shall leave you then," Cameron said with a nod. "But before I go, I just want to make sure you know that we will help you any way we can, both emotionally and financially. I hope you know you are not alone."

I stood from the bed and extended my right hand. "Thank you, sir. I appreciate it."

Cameron shook my hand and then left the room, leaving behind him an awkward silence. Tosha started moving around behind me, prompting me to bend down and grab a shirt off the floor. By the time I turned back around she had remade the bed to military standards.

She looked up at me apologetically. "I didn't mean to yell at you."

I shook my head. "You had every right to. You've…" I had to clear my throat to push down the lump that had suddenly formed, "…you've been through this."

She stepped over to me with tears in her eyes, although I didn't know if they were for me or for her parents. I wrapped my arms around her and even snuck my right hand underneath her shirt to press my palm against her scars.

"Are you sure you don't want me to go with you to your house?"

"Yeah, go to training, we'll catch up later."

She pulled out of my arms and kept her head down. I was doing something wrong, I was sure of it, but frankly I was just trying to stay on my feet and not fall to the floor and cry. She took her hair tie from my dresser and pulled her hair back tightly. Warrior Tosh was present, wall and all.

"I have training all day so maybe we can meet at dinner or something. Or not. Whatever you want," she said quickly without looking at me.

When I didn't respond, she began gathering her things while I stood frozen in the middle of the room. She stepped over to me and kissed me lightly.

"Becks…"

"Don't call me that," I snapped and she took a step back. I wasn't sure what was worse, her hurt expression or the tears welling in her eyes.

"Fine," she said and slammed the bedroom door behind her.

I didn't stop her from leaving and I knew it hurt her. I wanted to be alone. No, that wasn't even true. My father's ashes were sitting on my nightstand and it was making my skin crawl. My wrist and arm were starting to burn and that scared the shit out of me. My girlfriend was trying to help me and all I could do was push her away.

"Fuck!" I screamed and kicked my duffle bag across the room.

I slumped down on my bed and put my head in my hands. Just then there was a knock at the door.

"What!" I shouted.

The door opened and Jared stuck his head inside. "Really dude?"

"Sorry, it's been a rough morning."

Jared stepped inside. "Yeah, I'm sorry to hear about your dad, man."

I stood from the bed and had to scratch the top of my arm. "Why are you here?"

"Uh…Cameron said I needed to take you to your house and I'm supposed to get your family's financials."

"Oh yeah," I replied, my brain was still swimming, my arm still itching. "Just let me put on a shirt."

"Sure," he said and gave a quick look down at my arm. "Is your arm ok?"

"Yeah, just stress."

He nodded skeptically and backed out the door. "I'll wait for you out here."

"I'll just be a minute."

As soon as he closed the door I pulled my arm from behind my back and saw that the puncture wound was scabbing over, and the surrounding area was red and spreading.

I looked at my dad's ashes and said, "What the fuck do I do now?"

246 ~ C.R. Quinn

Jared was coming up on my street and my stomach started to churn. It was difficult to put my head around the fact that the last time I was here my entire world was flipped upside down. For the first time in my life I was afraid to go home. Another reason Garrett Archer was a bastard. Just the thought of him made me want to change my middle name.

Jared parked on the street a few houses away. He looked cautiously up and down the street as I led him to the garage. After I punched in the code, the garage door opened loudly and the two of us ducked inside. Jared followed me through the garage and in through the inner door that led us into the back of the house. As soon as we stepped into the kitchen, I froze.

"Dude, what's the matter?" Jared said and came around me.

I pointed to the wall with the sliding glass door. "There…there was a hole there. They took out the whole damn wall…there was…just a hole."

Jared looked back at me as if I was crazy. "Did you think we'd just leave the hole there?"

"W-what?"

"Devin had a clean-up crew here in less than an hour."

"Clean-up crew?"

"Ever seen a show or movie where the bad guy makes a call to someone to come and clean up a murder and make it look like nothing ever happened?"

"Yeah."

"Same thing, except the guys we use also Glamour your neighbors who might have heard something during the night. Costs a fortune, but hey, you get a new wall and no one around you knows what really happened."

"That's for real?"

Jared rolled his eyes. "No, I just wasted five minutes of my life to make that shit up. Of course it's true. Now, where's your dad's office? We shouldn't stay here too long."

"The office is through the living room, other side of the staircase. Laptop should be on the desk, password is Dawes#1."

"That's original. You're not coming?"

I shook my head. "I can't go in there."

"It's cool, I'll get everything."

"I've got to get some of my things from downstairs. I'll meet you back here."

Jared nodded and I gave him the code to the safe before I made my way down to my apartment. As I went down each step I was reminded of the hulking sound the werewolf made when he came down each one. And then I shot him and he died and then his brother came up and tore my dad apart and now my dad was dead and sitting in a fucking urn while my mother was having god knows what done to her.

"Shut up," I growled and stepped down to the floor.

"Do you normally talk to yourself?"

I whipped around and found Delia sitting on my couch. Quickly she flipped over the back of the couch, her short black hair falling into her eyes.

"How did you get in here?"

"The door," she replied and brushed her hair back. "My god was it boring waiting for you."

"Wait," I said and took a step back as she came closer, "you've just been waiting here? Why?"

"Garrett's punishment for what happened in the park. But now that you're here…"

"There's a Warrior upstairs. Take one more step and I'll scream."

In an instant she leapt forward, pushed me back into the chest of drawers, and clamped her hand around my mouth. Suddenly she caught a whiff of something in the air and followed the smell down my left shoulder. When she lifted her head, she had a devilish smile stretched across her face.

"How did it happen?" she asked and moved her hand from my mouth.

"How did…what happen?"

She lowered her head to my chest and took in a deep inhale. "I know wolf when I smell it. It's faint, but it's there."

I flinched and she pushed me back into the chest of drawers.

"Fuck you," I said through the pain radiating in my back from the knobs of the drawers.

Delia stepped back. "You can deny it all you want, Beckett. Unfortunately, I know that smell all too well."

"You don't know anything."

"And the Warriors do?" she asked mockingly. "Did they promise you they'd accept you and help you through this?" I nodded even though it was a lie. "It's bullshit, Beckett. They know nothing about being a wolf."

"And you do?"

"Having been around them for so many years, I know far more than they do." Quickly she reached into my back pocket and pulled out my cell phone. "If you come to us, you'll be with a pack of your own with people who know exactly what you're going through. They'll teach you how to be a wolf and give you that acceptance that the Warriors will never give you. And what's better, you'll be doing it voluntarily."

"Not a chance," I said and tried swiping the phone out of her hand, but instead she quickly turned her back and started typing something with her thumbs. "What are you doing?"

"Putting in my cell number," she replied and threw the phone back at me.

"Why in the world…"

"Because you're going to start changing," she said tensely and pressed herself up again me, "and there's only one place you can go, and you know that."

I pushed against her and stepped to the side. "And how do you know that?"

She raised her eyebrow as she took a step back. "Because you could have screamed for that Warrior of yours twenty times over by now."

That one statement felt like a kick in the balls. The floor creaked above us and within a second Delia disappeared into black smoke. A moment later Jared opened the door and started down the stairs.

"Hey, man, you talking to yourself?"

Nervously I put my cell phone back into my pocket and answered, "Uh…yeah. Coming here was harder than I thought."

Jared nodded only half convinced, but then his head flinched and his nostrils flared. "Dude, is there a dog in here?"

Chapter Twenty-two

Jared's dog comment wasn't lost on me, not even hours later. I hid in my room like a coward, even locked the door so that no one could barge in. Tosha knocked around dinner time and I ignored her. I was a terrible person. A terrible person who was most likely turning into a werewolf.

A couple of things bothered me about the encounter with Delia. One, if Garrett's whole purpose was to take me, why didn't Delia do just that? Two, what if she was lying to me in order to get me to go to Garrett? Three, why didn't I yell for Jared the moment I saw her?

The questions were burning such holes in my brain that I finally snuck out into the courtyard and set up my targets. No one else was out, it was amazingly quiet except for the sound of arrow after arrow cutting through the air. But even after two hours nothing had been resolved in my head and I was rubbing blisters on my hands and fingers.

"I thought you might be out here," Victor said behind me.

I turned around to find him walking toward me through the grass. "No robes tonight?"

He laughed and patted his boring black shirt. "Sadly, no."

I turned back around and pulled another arrow from my quiver. "Did you need something?" I asked and then let my arrow rip. It hit the center near four others.

"Very nice shot," Victor said and came in line with me. "I was merely wanting to see how you were."

"Great," I replied sarcastically and shot another arrow, this one hitting the upper right corner. Maybe archery was also a type of lie detector. I looked over at Victor who was narrowing his eyes at me. "What am I supposed to say? My dad died, my mom is still missing, how am I supposed to feel?"

"Angry?"

"Yep," I said through my teeth as I shot another arrow. Bullseye.

"Resentful."

"Sure," I replied and shot another bullseye.

"Revengeful."

Bullseye, bullseye, bullseye, and now my quiver was empty.

"Child," he said softly and put his hand on my shoulder, "we just need some more time to find…"

"Time!" I shouted and stepped back so that his hand slid off of me. "We're out of time, Victor. My father's dead! He didn't get to see his wife before he died. My mom will never talk to her husband again, and I'm the one that has to tell her what happened. Sorry, Mom, Dad had a heart attack while he was turning into a werewolf and died, and then they cremated him so that his blood wouldn't hurt anybody else. So, remember the last time you saw him, after he got impaled by that wolf, yeah, that'll have to be your last memory."

Suddenly Victor sniffed the air and looked toward the woods, but then slowly turned his head to me. Shit!

"I'm gonna go," I said and quickly stepped away from him, but Victor wrapped his hand around my elbow and pulled me back.

"Where is it," he growled and started pulling at my shirt and moving my head to expose my neck.

"What are you doing!" I shouted, trying to back away from him and inadvertently putting my arm in front of me.

He must have gotten a whiff because he grabbed my left arm and pulled up my sleeve. His face contorted when he saw the growing wound on my forearm. "Is it from your father?"

I swallowed and nodded nervously. He hit me across the back of the head and I fell to the ground.

"You weren't to approach the bars!" he shouted over me.

I looked up over my shoulder. "He was dying! He was still human…"

"And then he wasn't. Dear god, you've been walking around here all day…"

"Well where should I be?"

"Not here!" he shouted.

"Nice," I laughed and pushed myself up from the ground.

Victor lowered his voice. "That came out wrong."

"I'm sure it didn't."

"Beckett," he said and then paused to gather himself, "you saw that your father was unable to control himself, did you think you would be any different? You are a danger to everyone inside – the humans, the vampires, the two children that are constantly running up and down the halls. You stupid, stupid boy. We have no idea how your body will react."

"What do you mean?"

"You are a hybrid, Beckett, you are half vampire. I activated you and that makes the vampire part of you more dominate. Werewolf blood is toxic to vampires, it kills our cells and doesn't allow us to regenerate. We rot slowly and painfully. We have no idea how your body is going to fight this disease."

"I didn't think about that."

"You didn't think about a lot of things."

"What will they do with me?"

He shook his head. "Child, this is beyond me. They will most likely lock you up." He waited a beat and then reiterated, "Stupid boy."

"You said that," I said and pulled my sleeve back down to cover up the wound. "Should I just leave?"

"You are as much of a risk out there as you are here."

"But then it would be my choice."

"You have little choice whatever you do. We should inform my sons of your situation."

Victor pressed his hand on my back, but I stopped and stepped out to the side. "Wait…I…I can't do this now."

"Child, they need to know…"

"I know, but…I just need one more night where I can still make choices of my own. Please."

Victor sighed and tightened his lips before replied, "Very well, but I will be at your door first thing in the morning."

"Ok."

"And you must promise to restrict yourself to your quarters."

"Ok."

"That means no interaction with Miss Cushlin. We don't need her infected as well."

"Yeah, I got it."

Victor took a step back and patted my cheek. Surprisingly there was a sadness in his eyes as he stepped away and then disappeared across the courtyard. I was alone again, and it was crushing. I put away my targets and collected my arrows, taking the time to neatly put them into my quiver.

Placing the quiver under my arm and carrying my bow, I ran inside and up the spiral staircase to my room. It was dark and undisturbed, and no sign of Tosha. I sat on the bed and stared at my father's urn wondering what the hell I was going to do. I would be locked up if I stayed. If I left, I would be completely alone with no support, no money, no clue what I would become or when. Locked up or alone. Locked up or alone. Locked up like my dad, phasing and dying in a concrete cell. No, no, no, I wouldn't do that. Alone then. But what about what Victor said about my reaction to the virus? This was maddening!

Quickly I grabbed my duffle bag I'd packed from the house today and stuffed my dirty clothes on top of them. Lastly, and carefully, I slid my father's urn inside the bag and apologized to him for the accommodations. I placed the bag on my shoulder, strung my bow across my chest, and tucked the quiver under my arm. When I opened the door, I turned toward the spiral stairs.

"Beck?" Tosha said behind me.

Seriously? With a sigh and a wave of nausea I turned around. Tosha smiled for a moment until she noticed the bag on my shoulder.

"Going somewhere?" she asked nervously, but trying to hide it.

I cleared my throat and looked at the floor. "I can't stay here anymore, it's just too hard. So…I'm gonna take off."

"Oh, ok," she replied in an eerily calm tone and walked back into her room.

I was so confused that I had to follow her. No way in hell would Tosha let me off that easy. When I peeked inside her room, she was dumping clothes into a bag she had on the bed. "What are you doing?"

"I'm coming with you."

"What? No," I said and stepped to intercept her. "Tosha, you can't."

"Oh really?" she snapped and turned from her dresser to face me. "Why not?"

"Because…because it isn't safe."

"And it's safe for you to go out by yourself?" she asked and when I didn't answer right away she turned back to her dresser and began pulling out clothes. "Unless you've forgotten, I'm the Warrior trainee, not you.

You've been shooting a bow and arrow for a week, I've been working my ass off for a year learning how to protect myself and others."

"And that's exactly why you should stay here. I can't have you lose your position here because of me."

"Uh-huh, and how are you getting out of here? Do you have cash on you? Where are you going to go? How are you going to support yourself when you get there?"

"I-I don't know!" I shouted. "I don't know anything, I don't have anything...I...I just have to go!"

Tosha stepped aggressively up to my face, her eyes blazing into mine. "Then look in my eyes and tell me you don't want me to go with you."

I clamped my jaw shut but I couldn't control my breath from sounding like a bull. I knew what I was supposed to say and do, but I couldn't find the words.

Tosha's eyes filled with tears. "Beckett, don't do this to me. I am so in love with you and it's been so long since I've felt that for anyone. You tore down my walls and forced your way in, all I'm asking is that you don't destroy me. I know you're having a hard time, anyone would, but please, please let me help you."

My arms wrapped around her as her head fell into my chest. She was weakening me with every second. I had to remember why I was leaving, but my arms were sinking further and further into her skin. With every breath she was pulling me back to her.

"I can't stay here," I whispered into her hair.

She pushed herself up from my chest and wiped her eyes. "Then we'll get out of here."

"I don't want you to get in trouble."

"Don't worry about me," she replied and stepped back to the bed.

"I can't help but worry about you, Tosha."

Even though her back was turned I could hear her sniffling. "You just need to clear your head."

I rubbed my face knowing I needed a lot more than just clearing my head. "What are you going to tell them?"

"I'm not going to tell them anything. They'll either understand or they won't."

"Do you need to find Nikki?"

"Funny," she replied sarcastically and knelt down to the floor. She reached underneath the bed and pulled out a small metal box with a lock on it. After inputting a combination, she opened the box, pulled out a wad of cash, and stuffed it into her bag.

"I'll pay you back, I promise."

"Don't be stupid," she said and ducked inside her bathroom.

Her statement was a bit loaded since all I was doing was being stupid. When Tosha came out of the bathroom a couple minutes later I could tell she'd been crying. Her face was red and blotchy, and she couldn't hide the sniffles as she put the toiletries into her bag.

"Tosha, don't do this…"

"Don't tell me what to do," she snapped and pulled her weapons bag up onto her shoulder. "Now let's go before I change my mind."

Tosha whipped by me and opened the door, gesturing for me to follow. With a sigh I turned and stepped out into the hallway. Tosha pulled on my arm when I started toward the spiral staircase.

"We'll have to go a back way," she said and started walking in the opposite direction down the hallway.

"Even though I know you're going to think I'm stupid by asking, but why a back way?"

She shook her head and I'm sure she was rolling her eyes. "Do you want everyone to see us leaving?"

"Oh."

"Yeah, oh," she said and then looked over her shoulder. "And you were going to go off by yourself?"

I didn't answer and she seemed ok with that. When we reached the end of the hallway she turned left where there was an archway to nothing but darkness. She pulled out her cell phone and switched the flashlight on which revealed a narrow set of stairs. Another damn dark stairwell and a tunnel I'm sure. I stayed close behind her until we reached the bottom of the staircase where a thick metal door stood. After unlocking the door, Tosha pushed the door open to the outside.

Once I stepped out I realized we were on the side of the manor, just around the corner from the front driveway. We crunched across the gravel and dirt to where Tosha's car was parked. The lights blinked as she unlocked the car and we ducked inside, throwing our bags into the back seat. A moment later Tosha roared the car to life and began pulling out of her parking space.

"Duck down," she ordered as she slammed on the accelerator. Knowing not to question her, I bent over as far as I could and held onto the sides of the car while Tosha sped out of the driveway.

After a big bounce and a sharp turn to the right, I knew we were free. Slowly I sat back up in my seat and heaved a sigh of relief. Tosha sniffled and wiped her cheek. I took her hand and pressed it against my lips.

"I didn't want you to leave. I know how important the program was to you."

"Let's not talk about it, ok?" she snapped.

I kissed her hand again and looked out the window. "Tell me a story?"

"What?"

"Tell me a story, like you did when I got activated. It helps take my mind off of things."

"Ok," she replied, slowing down to take another sharp curve. "What about the story of when Nikki was a spy and almost took down the Warriors?"

My eyes shot open and my head flinched. "Um, yeah. I'd really like to hear that one."

Chapter Twenty-three

After a very enlightening story about Nikki infiltrating the Warriors, kissing Cameron, and almost bringing the coven to its knees, we drove only a few hours before we started looking for a place to stay for the night. We drove on backroads in the middle of nowhere, so there wasn't much choice. Only one, in fact, and it took cash. The hourly rate option was an embarrassing bonus.

Tosha pulled into a spot right in front of our room, there was only one other car in the lot and I wondered if they'd still be here in an hour. Of course they could say the same thing about us. We grabbed our bags and brought them inside the musty-smelling motel room. Tosha flipped on the light and it didn't help the room in the slightest. The bedspread and furnishings looked like they were from the seventies, and it seemed as though they hadn't been dusted since then either. Tosha's skin was crawling with every step.

"This is gross," she mumbled.

"We can look for another place," I said and put my things on the chair in the corner.

She turned and shook her head. "No, I'm just being a pain. No one will find us here."

Tosha put her bag on the bed and rubbed the back of her neck. I came up behind her and kissed her hair. She pulled my arms around her and melted into my chest.

"Do you want to watch TV?" she asked and pushed off of me.

"No," I replied and stretched my arms above my head. "I just want to freshen up and go to bed."

"Ok," she replied and unzipped her bag.

I stepped past her and into the small bathroom. The tile walls and floor were shiny pink while the fixtures were mint green. I'm sure at one point this was in style, but now it just looked like antacid pills crushed into the walls. My face didn't look any better than it had earlier today, the circles below my eyes seemed darker and hung lower. The scratch on my arm was still red, but less itchy. I splashed some cold water on my face and dried it on a towel hanging next to the sink. When I stood back up and leaned in closer to the mirror, I blinked twice to be sure I was seeing what I thought I was. I widened my eyes and stared at the small green specs of color shining through my dark brown eyes.

"What the hell?" I whispered to myself and pulled the lower lids of my eyes down. My dad's eyes had turned yellow, maybe this was the start of things. Fuck. Would Tosha notice? Did I just tell her? What if her loyalty to the Warriors took over and she put me in a cell herself.

I splashed more water on my face and let it drip down my neck before finally drying it with the towel again. Sleep, that's what I needed. I just needed to curl up in that rickety bed out there and trace Tosha's scars until I fell asleep.

With a deep sigh, I opened the bathroom door, shut off the lights, and stepped into the bedroom. Tosha had turned off all the lights except for the light on the nightstand. She was sitting in bed with the blankets pulled up to her chest and tucked underneath her arms. Her bare shoulders stuck up out of the covers and she watched me nervously as I slowly made my way around the bed.

"Are you naked?" I asked and then cringed at how lame I was.

Thankfully she laughed a little but pulled the blankets tighter around her chest. "Is that a bad thing?"

I shook my head. "No, of course not. It's a good thing, a really good thing. Um…should I…get naked?"

What was I doing!?

"That's up to you I guess," she replied and adjusted under the covers.

After kicking off my shoes I sat down on the edge of the bed next to her. Goosebumps rose up on her arm as my fingers glided down to her forearm. She placed her hands on my cheeks and brought my face down to hers, kissing me softly on the lips. I pulled away and took her hand in mine.

"By the way, I'm in love with you too. I'm sorry I didn't say it back to you before."

Tosha forced a smile through her sudden tears. She leaned over and kissed me again, her tongue flicking inside my mouth. My hand traveled down the length of her soft back and sighed a little when I reached her scars.

"Beck," she said as she pulled away from me, "I want to be with you, and I'm scared to death about it."

"Natasha, I'm not pushing anything with us…"

"I know."

"Then let's not push it, I don't want you to be scared, Tosha."

She placed her hands on top of mine. "Do you want to be with me?"

"Of course I do," I replied quickly and squeezed her hands. "Oh my god, please don't think that, I want to do this, I do, but I don't want to push anything on you. I know this is…tough."

She bit her bottom lip and sighed before saying, "It's not just the fear of being set on fire again, but…I'm not…things aren't normal…down there."

"Tosha, I know what's there, I love your scars as much as I love you."

She crushed her lips against mine, wrapping her right hand around the back of my head and her left around my shoulders to pull me in closer. The sheet loosened and hung on the tops of her breasts. I knew I needed to stop this, it wasn't safe, but her smell, her taste, the feel of her skin as my fingers trailed down the curve of her waist was intoxicating. When I reached her scars I flattened my palm and it was over. She pulled my shirt up my chest and over my head. When our lips connected again, I pulled the sheet between us down and pressed her amazingly hot breasts into my chest. Her breath wafted in my face as she pulled away from my lips and clicked the lamp off, leaving us with only the light coming in through the curtains. Her hands went immediately to my pants, her fingers fumbling to pop the button. I rose from the bed, unzipped my pants, and pulled them down as fast as I could.

Tosha moved across the bed and pulled the blankets back. I ducked underneath and found her. There was nothing between us, her scars were everywhere, touching me, surrounding me as Tosha wrapped her leg around my hips and anchored me against her. Her pelvis started to rock gently but I was ready for her. I wanted her in the worst way, and from the way she was moaning and breathing heavy I assumed she felt the same.

In a quick move, she squeezed her leg tightly around me and whipped herself up to be sitting on top of me. I reached up and squeezed her breasts tightly and once again she began swiveling her pelvis, her thick scars created an intense and overwhelming sensation. I pushed myself up to a seated position, grabbing the back of her neck and pulling her toward me as I crushed my lips against hers.

A moment later she pulled back for air and brushed the hair out of her eyes. "Are you...are you sure?"

I smiled and gave her one soft kiss. "Tosha, I think I have the biggest erection I've ever had in my life. So yeah, I am very sure."

She lowered her head and gave a laugh. "You know how to charm a girl."

"Well, I do try." She leaned over to the nightstand and pulled something out from within the drawer. "Does this place provide condoms too?"

"Um...no need, remember?" she replied and I suddenly felt like an idiot. "But I do need...a little help. This is what I meant about it being different. It's embarrassing, but it's the only way this can work."

From the little light in the room, it took a few seconds for my eyes to decipher that she was holding a tube of something in her hand. "Is that lube?"

"Oh my god," she said and brought her hands up to her face.

"Natasha," I laughed and brought her hands down, "it's just lube. You can cover my whole body in that stuff if it means I get to have you."

"I've never used this, but Dr. Ryan said it would help. I don't know, if it's too..."

"People use it all the time, Tosha, there's nothing to be embarrassed about. Do...do you want me to do it?"

She shook her head and squeezed the tube on her fingers, and then tossed the tube on the nightstand. "No...I can. Just...take it easy on me, ok?"

I nodded and then had to brace myself at the feeling of Tosha's fingers coating my shaft with the cold jelly. She kissed me softly, almost tentatively, and I responded by wrapping my arm around her and laying her gently back down on the bed. Her body became stiff and unresponsive as I shifted between her legs, her head was even turned to the side.

I sighed and pulled away. "This was a bad idea."

She grabbed me. "No, just do it."

"Tosha, no…"

Before I could put up a fight, she grabbed me and pulled me inside of her. She gasped and I groaned loudly at the feeling of her being all around me. The grooves and ridges of her scars that caused her such pain were causing waves of pleasure to ripple through me. As I moved in and out of her it was though a dozen fingers were pressing and gliding against me.

"You ok?" I breathed into Tosha's face as my rhythm quickened.

"Mm-hmm," she replied and then began grinding her pelvis against me, pulling me in further and searching the depths within her.

A heat began to rise in my gut, a feeling I knew meant there wasn't too much time left before I was through. It wasn't my finest duration, but the sensations were overwhelming and unexpected, a bad combination if I wanted to last for a long time. My rhythm became faster, Tosha's moans became louder, and the burning in my gut began to grow into something unfamiliar. A heat spread throughout my body, beads of sweat formed on my forehead and arms. My breathing became louder, deeper, and in some ways percussive. In and out, in and out I went deeper and harder but still wanting more of her. Tosha's breathless moans changed in tone and were only released when I slammed against her. The heat in my body was raging, as was a sudden surge of rage and pain and animalistic urges. My god.

"You're hurting me," Tosha said and put her hands against my chest, but at the same moment I let out what could only be described as a roar as my entire body convulsed and released everything I had inside of her.

My arms shook with fatigue as I removed myself from between Tosha's legs and stretched out next to her. "I'm so sorry, are you ok? That was…so intense, I don't know…"

I couldn't even finish my thought because it suddenly made sense. I was stupid, so unbelievably stupid to think my infection would just somehow go away, and now here I was hurting the woman I loved in the worst way.

"Tosha, I'm sorry."

Her fingers glided across my forehead. "It's ok."

I shook my head. "No, no it's not. Did I hurt you?" She paused for a second and the delay made me want to vomit. I squeezed her into my side and pressed my forehead against the side of her face. "Natasha, please forgive me."

She lifted my head with her hands. "It's going to be uncomfortable,

Beckett, it just got…"

"Intense."

She nodded. "Yeah, really intense."

My head fell down onto her shoulder from the guilt that was radiating through me. Tosha squeezed me into her side and my fingers instantly began tracing the scars on her abdomen.

"At least you didn't burst into flames."

I lifted my head from her shoulder. "It's sad that you're trying to make this better with a statement like that."

"That's a big deal for me, Becks."

I kissed her gently. "I know. I just…didn't want to hurt you. I promised you I would never hurt you."

"I still liked it," she replied and gave me a quick kiss. "Now that the lid is off the cookie jar, maybe you won't howl like a wild animal." I froze and she gasped, putting her hand up to her mouth. "Becks, I'm sorry, I didn't mean it like that. Bad choice of words."

I shook my head and laughed nervously, hoping she couldn't see the nervous sweat reforming on my forehead. "Yeah, I know. It was crazy, right? I've uh…never made that sound before."

She kissed me one more time before pulling the blankets off of her. "I'm going to clean up."

"Ok," I replied, the pale light coming in through the windows making her scars almost glow as she walked into the bathroom.

As soon as she shut the door I scrambled to the edge of the bed and felt around for my pants. I pulled them up onto the bed and patted them down until my hand came around my cell phone. The cracked screen lit up and I pulled up Delia's number in a text.

```
You win. Even trade.
```

My foot started to shake nervously as I waited for a reply. The toilet flushed and the faucet started to run, meaning that Tosha would come out any minute. Finally, the ellipsis flashed on my screen and then one word in reply.

```
Done.
```

Chapter Twenty-four

The instructions were pretty simple – three hours, no Warriors, even exchange of me for my mom. Beyond that I didn't know what the hell was going to happen to me. Nothing good, I'm sure, but at least my mom would be free.

Tosha was sound asleep, she didn't even move when I snuck out of bed. The three-hour timeline gave me plenty of time to agonize over leaving Tosha behind. This would kill her, but I couldn't chance me killing her instead. I felt my control slip away from me when we were together. She had almost died once before because Ty couldn't control himself. I would never forgive myself if I did the same to her. She needed to be happy and with someone who wouldn't hurt her. She deserved better than me.

There was only a few more minutes before I needed to leave. I reached into my duffle bag and pulled out my father's urn, there was no reason to take him with me and I didn't want Garrett's dirty hands on my father's ashes anyway. I placed the urn on the small desk in the corner of the room, grabbed the letters I had written, and took one last look at Natasha. It took a lot of energy not to go over to her and give her one last kiss, but I couldn't risk waking her up. I looked at my watch and right on cue there was a soft knock at the door. I touched my dad's urn one last time, glanced over at Tosha, and grabbed my bag and bow.

Slowly I opened the door and quietly ducked out of the room. Victor was sitting on the hood of Tosha's car.

"Thanks for coming," I whispered.

"I was surprised to get your text," he said and pushed himself off the car. "I hope you realize how difficult it was for me to get out of the manor unnoticed."

"Do they know we're gone?"

"They do."

"Are they coming after us?"

"Not yet. Like Natasha, they believe your grief is driving your actions. If they only knew," he laughed.

"You didn't tell them?"

He shook his head. "That is your business, not mine. Now what is it I need to do?"

I sighed and adjusted my bag on my shoulder. "Just make sure the trade goes smoothly and get my mom out of there."

He gave a curt nod. "Where is the exchange happening?"

"There's a field about a half mile down the road. Tosha and I passed it on the way here. Figured that was a better spot than the motel parking lot."

"And at this hour, hopefully no one will be driving by. I assume Garrett said no Warriors?" I nodded. "And how exactly are you going to explain me being there?"

I shrugged. "I'm counting on that seeing you will throw him off a little."

Victor smirked. "Doubtful. Shall we?"

"Wait," I said and handed him my two letters. "There's a letter for my mom and one for Tosh. Can you see that they get them?"

"I will," he replied, taking the letters from my hand and tucking them inside his dark jacket.

"I'll admit I was kinda hoping for white robes," I said with a smirk.

"Terribly sorry to disappoint you, but I certainly don't wear them outside the manor," he replied flatly.

We walked to the field in silence. Things were different between us. I was no longer his grandchild. Just a kid turning into something he hated. Once the lights from the motel disappeared, I pulled out my cell phone and turned on the flashlight in order to see into the pitch darkness.

"You won't need to use that much longer," Victor said softly.

"What? The flashlight, why?"

"Soon enough your eyes will be almost as good as mine."

"Is that supposed to make me feel better?"

"I am just trying to make light of an awkward situation."

We walked silently again until we reached a narrow gravel road that cut through the field.

"This is as good of a place as any," I said and pulled my duffle bag off my shoulder. Victor sighed loudly next to me and I shined my light on him. "Am I gonna die?"

"Die at the hands of Garrett? Or due to the transformation?"

"Either, I guess."

Victor turned his face away from me and looked out into the darkness. "Considering Garrett has continually tried to obtain you, I don't think he wants you dead. I think he'll be testing your limits, but he'll see that you stay alive until you no longer give him what he wants. But the transformation, that I don't know. We've never had a hybrid be infected. I have no idea what is happening in your body or whether you'll survive."

"That's comforting," I replied sarcastically.

"If you wanted to be comforted, you should have called Cameron." He paused and turned back to me. "Why did you choose me to help you?"

"You've always helped me."

"And because you're counting on Garrett having daddy issues."

"Correct," I laughed just as headlights came around the corner a mile down the road.

Victor turned away from me and tracked the two vehicles coming our way. A moment later both vehicles turned their headlights off, but you could still hear them coming down the road.

"That must be them," Victor said. "A piece of advice, do not offer more than you already have. He will try to bait you, do not let him take your mind off what you are here to do. Make the exchange, follow his rules, and do not try to be a hero. He will kill your mother in front of you for the pleasure of it. Do you understand?"

I nodded and shifted uncomfortably. "Yeah. Thanks for being here."

"What you're doing is very brave, Beckett. I'm sorry things have come to this."

You could hear the sound of tires crunching along the gravel drive, and eventually my cell phone flashlight caught the sight of a dark SUV and another dark sedan. My knees started to shake and Victor must have sensed something and squeezed my arm.

The vehicles pulled in across from us, one parked behind the other. The driver's side door of the SUV opened first and a very large man exited and then opened the passenger door. Garrett stepped down from the SUV and couldn't take his eyes off of Victor. Maybe my shitty plan was working.

"I said no Warriors," he said.

"Technically he's retired," I replied and Garrett gave me a quick glance.

"Well, Father," he said and took a step forward, "even though you tried to have me killed, it is still good to see you. Although the years don't seem to have been kind to you."

"Hence the retirement," Victor replied. His eyes had what seemed like a mix of sadness and longing as he stared at Garrett. In some way I'm sure he still saw his sire, or his child, as he often called them. Victor was a hard ass and intimidating as hell, but every now and then you could catch the caring side of him. That's the true reason I called him.

"Hello, son," Garrett said with a smirk.

"Don't call me that."

"Then how should I address you?"

"By my name."

"Very well, Beckett Archer," he said with a smile. I hated him.

"Where's my mother?"

"In the car."

"I want to see her now."

"In time."

"I said now!" I shouted causing several large men to exit the vehicles and stand behind Garrett. I swallowed nervously before continuing, "The deal was me for my mom. If she's not here, Victor has permission to kill me on the spot."

"I wouldn't give Father that much power over your life, Beckett. From experience, he flips that switch pretty quickly."

"It was easy when it came to you," Victor said, making Garrett tighten his expression.

"But never when it came to Devin, right Father? Even though Devin deceived you more than anyone else, he still lives."

"Show the boy his mother, Garrett. This is not about you and me."

"It is about me!" he yelled and took a step forward. Victor, the badass that he was, didn't even flinch. "I escaped your assassin. I have been so close to you and your Warriors for hundreds of years and you never even knew it. And I will be the one to take you down, Father. Me, your sixth sire, your sixth son. All of this is about me."

Victor waited a beat before saying, "Bring out the boy's mother, Garrett. You have five seconds before I snap his neck and Project away."

Garrett hissed and snapped his fingers which prompted one of the big men standing in front of the sedan to open the passenger door. My mother stepped out of the car and went to run toward us when the man grabbed her by the waist. I tried to take a step forward, but Victor squeezed my shoulder to hold me in place.

"Beckett!" my mother screamed.

"It's ok, Mom."

"Yes, Abby, everything is going to be ok as long as both of you don't try and pull anything. Is that understood? You will both walk to the other side, step for step."

"What? Beckett, no," my mother cried.

"Mom, it's ok, we have to do this," I replied, my voice cracking from the nerves and emotions. I reached down into my pocket and pulled out the gold Warrior medallion. My thumb rubbed its face one last time before handing it to Victor. "Thank you, sir, for everything."

Victor nodded tensely and took the medallion from my hand. "It has been a pleasure, my boy."

"Are we done?" Garrett said impatiently.

I nodded, lifted my duffle bag back onto my shoulder, and picked up my bow from where it laid in the grass.

"One step at a time, or everyone dies," Garrett warned.

My mother took her first step through her sobs and I matched her. After six steps we were inches from each other and she reached out to me. I squeezed her hand and kissed her on the cheek.

"Keep going," Garrett warned again.

My mother grabbed my arms and buckled into my chest with loud sobs. "I can't...Becks..."

I pulled her up from my chest and squeezed her shoulders tightly. "It's ok, Mom."

"You have three seconds to keep moving," Garrett shouted.

"Mom, you have to go with Victor."

She shook her head wildly. "No, I-I can't."

"Three, two..." Garrett counted down.

"Mom, please," I said and then looked over her shoulder at Garrett. "Just let Victor take her. I promise not to pull anything."

Garrett sighed and gave a stiff nod. Victor stepped up behind my mother and pulled her away from me. She clawed the air until Victor clamped his arms around her. Slowly I turned back around and continued my way toward Garrett, trying desperately not to let the sounds of my mother's cries get to me. The last thing I wanted to do was cry in front of Garrett and his goons.

When I was only a few steps away, Garrett's guards surrounded me, stripped me of my bag and began to pat me down. Garrett took my bow out of my hand and examined it.

"It really does fill me with pride when I see you with a bow," he said as he glided his fingers over the grooves in the middle of the bow. "I'm sorry you inherited my wrist defect, but it seems that Father remembered what I used to do to my grips to compensate."

"Let's hope that's the only defect of yours I got."

Garrett raised an eyebrow and stared me down for a moment before snapping my bow in two and throwing it to the ground. "You won't be needing this. Put him in the truck."

Two of the large men behind me grabbed my arms and pushed me forward toward the SUV. My mother cried out as they pushed me into the backseat, but I couldn't bear to look at her for even a second. The large men sat on either side of me and closed the doors. Garrett sat in front while another one of his men, definitely a vamp, climbed up in the driver's seat.

"Well, Beckett, I hope you're comfortable back there," Garrett said as the driver put the SUV in gear, "we do have a few hours' drive."

I tried to shift in my seat, but the guards on either side were so big they were practically rolling my body in on itself. "I guess seatbelts are out of the question."

Garrett laughed, but the two on either side of me just growled. "I guess I should make some introductions. Beckett, on your left is Floyd. Floyd, Beckett. Beckett, Floyd. And on your right is Vincent. You might remember him, you killed his brother. Beckett, Vincent. Vincent, don't kill him."

I looked to my right just as Vincent's enormous fist came at my face.

A Tale of Tosh

Chapter Twenty-five

My insides throbbed like the beat of a techno song, but it wasn't just pain. With scar tissue the pain came with a numb, uncomfortable feeling that your brain couldn't get quite figure out how to categorize. The sheets were cool against my skin as my hand searched underneath to find the warmth from Beckett's body. Even though I was unbelievably sore, I wanted him inside me again. I didn't realize how much I missed being so close to someone. For years I had pushed the longing aside because I never dreamed anyone would be able to get past my scars. Beckett was unexpected. He surprised me at every turn. In many ways I hated that.

I stretched my arm to the opposite edge of the bed and still found no sign of him. My eyes opened in a panic, but then I heard the shower going in the bathroom behind me. My eyes started to close again but then flew open at the sound of someone clearing his throat in the bedroom.

I flipped around to the edge of the bed to try and find my weapons bag.

"Easy, now," a familiar raspy voice said.

Pulling the sheet tightly around me, I slowly sat up. "Victor?"

A dark figure stood up from the chair in the corner and stepped to the front edge of the bed. Just from his size alone I knew I was right about who it was, but why the hell was he here.

"Did they send you to come get us?" I asked.

"They who?"

"Cameron and Devin?"

"Oh no, but they are aware of your absence."

Self-consciously I pulled the comforter around me, fearing the sheet wasn't enough to hide my naked body from Victor. "So, with all due respect, sir, why are you here?"

"Beckett asked me to come."

"Nice of him to tell me," I grumbled.

"Miss Cushlin," he began and sat down on the opposite corner of the bed, "there is no easy way for me to say this, but Beckett has decided to leave."

"L-leave? I don't understand."

He sighed and pulled a folded piece of paper out of his pocket. "He left a note. I am sure it details his decision, but to summarize, Beckett became infected with the lupine virus. He decided, rightfully so, that he was a danger to those around him and that being with Garrett..."

"Shut...stop, stop!" I shouted. "Beck! Beckett," I yelled at the door. The only sound that came back was that of the shower being turned off.

"Natasha, I assure you Beckett is not in there."

"What? I-I don't..."

"He left a little while ago, Natasha. I'm sorry, he's gone."

My stomach dropped and nausea began to rise in my chest and throat. Victor extended the note to me, but I couldn't bring myself to take it.

Tears began to form in the corners of my eyes. "But...why?"

Victor shook the note, urging me to take it. "As I said, he has been infected..."

"How?"

Victor sighed again, sounding annoyed. "He was scratched by his father during a phase. Considering your current state, are you sure you didn't sustain any..." he cleared his throat uncomfortably, "...abrasions? Anything where his blood would have gotten into your bloodstream?"

I shook my head. "I...I don't think so."

Giving up on me taking the note from him, Victor placed it on the bed and rose from the mattress. "They will still want to do a full workup on you when we return, so be prepared."

Be prepared? How did one prepare for that? How did I prepare for Beckett being gone? He left. He just left me after we...after I let him...

"Miss Cushlin?"

My head shot up and I quickly wiped the tears away. Push it down, Tosh, push everything down before you make a fool out of yourself. Push it down until you can't feel anymore.

"Sorry," I replied. "Yes, I understand. When are we leaving?"

"Right away."

Someone moved around in the bathroom and it hit me. "If Beckett is gone, who's in there?"

"Beckett's mother," Victor replied softly. "That was the deal he made with Garrett."

As if on cue, the bathroom door opened and a woman stepped out of the bathroom. There was enough light shining from the bathroom that I could see it was indeed Beckett's mother, Abby. This was certainly part of a nightmare since I had just had sex with this woman's son and I was still naked under these sheets.

"Hi, Mrs. Dawes," I said, feeling my cheeks flush in embarrassment.

Abby sniffled and wiped her eyes. "Hello, dear. I take it Victor told you about Beckett?"

"Yes, ma'am," I replied and once again pushed down the emotions that were rising to the surface.

"I will give you two a moment," Victor said and stepped to the motel room's door. "But we should leave within the hour."

Both Abby and I nodded as he left the room. Abby turned off the bathroom light and sat down on the corner of the bed.

"Did Victor give you a note from Beckett? He said he had one for you too." I nodded and stared at it on the opposite side of the bed. "Well, if it's anything like mine, it won't make you feel any better. And you know…about…what he is now?" I nodded again and squeezed my arms tightly across my chest to keep everything trapped inside. "I'm just in shock, I guess."

"That's normal, considering what you've gone through," I said, my body starting to shake. "Did Garrett hurt you?"

She shook her head. "Honestly, I barely saw him."

"The Warriors will want to question you once we get back. They'll want to know everything that happened to you, everything you saw or heard."

"Yes, Victor told me. May I ask," she began and then pointed across the room to the desk against the wall, "why…why is there an urn on that desk?"

Son of a bitch.

Chapter Twenty-six

Asshole. Bastard. Coward. Douchebag. E? What insulting word started with E? Egg head? That wasn't cruel enough. Victor sat in the passenger seat next to me since apparently he didn't drive. Abby sat in the backseat of my car, crying and holding the urn with her husband's ashes. No one was talking, so in order to keep my mind occupied on the three-hour ride I had started thinking of every bad word I could describe Beckett. At first, they were random, but then I started going alphabetically.

Fuck head. Ginormous dickhead. Did that count since they were two words? Hellion. Idiot. Jerkoff.

"Miss Cushlin," Victor said, "perhaps you could reduce our speed? Mrs. Dawes wouldn't survive a crash like you and I would."

Quickly I looked down at my speedometer that showed I was going over ninety miles per hour.

"Sorry, sir."

"It is fine, child," he replied. "I know you are nervous."

"No, it's…. not that."

Victor didn't push me any further, and within an hour I was pulling through the black gate of the manor. My stomach flipped and sent a wave of nausea through me. What were they going to do to me? Could I keep my composure in front of Devin and Cameron? Doubtful.

Connor was standing on the front steps of the manor, his arms clasped behind him while he shifted his weight from leg to leg obviously waiting to rip me a new one. I helped Abby from the car and allowed her to lean her side against me in order to walk. Seeing her clutch the urn to her chest was heart wrenching. She'd lost everyone, she was alone. I knew that feeling all too well.

As we approached the steps, Connor stepped down onto the driveway.

"What the hell were you thinking," he said loudly, not caring in the slightest that I was helping a sobbing woman try to walk.

"Connor," I said, eyeing him down, "could you wait and yell at me after Mrs. Dawes is safely inside."

"I'm the least of your worries. Do you know how much trouble you're in?"

"I'm sure they'll tell me," I replied as we all stepped through the doors of the manor. "Who do they want first? Me or Abby?"

"Who?" Connor said flustered.

Victor cleared his throat and Connor immediately straightened up. Whether he was the coven leader or not, you always stood at attention when it came to Victor.

"Abigail Dawes," Victor said with a hint of annoyance and warning. "Will they be starting with her questioning? Or with Natasha's?"

"They want Tosh first, sir," Connor replied.

"Very well," Victor said and gently took Abby away from me. "I will take Mrs. Dawes to the east wing sitting room. She'll have some privacy there."

Abby clutched the urn to her chest as Victor pulled her away from me. She had no expression on her face, just absentmindedly pushing her feet down the corridor with Victor at her side.

"Cushlin," Connor snapped and took me by the arm.

I didn't fight him, it would just end up in a broken arm that I'd have to suffer through the healing for. With every step I clinched my jaw tighter and pushed emotions down to where they couldn't affect me. When we rounded the corner, Alex was already waiting for us outside the office door. My teeth started to chatter with nerves as we approached and Connor gave my arm a yank to pull it together.

Alex gave a stiff nod and lead us into the office. Cameron and Devin stood in front of their desks with Jared. Devin made a gesture and Alex closed the door. The sound of the door latching closed made it suddenly hard to breathe.

Cameron flicked his fingers to come forward and thankfully Connor released my arm. I took a staggered breath and stepped to the center of the room. Devin was stoic as usual, his arms crossed in front of his chest while

Cameron gave sympathetic, yet disappointed, eyes.

"First of all, Natasha," Cameron began, "were you harmed in any way?"

"No."

"Very well. Shall we start at the beginning then? Can you tell us why you decided to leave the manor?"

"Be..." I started and then had to press my tongue to the roof of my mouth and swallow the lump the had quickly formed in my throat. I took another breath before finally responding and saying his name out load. "Beckett...had decided to leave. I thought he was just grieving and needed some time away from where his father had just died. I knew the dangers of him going by himself which is why I insisted that I go with him."

"And after your encounters with Garrett's group, you felt you two could handle them together?" Devin asked.

"Better the two of us than him alone."

"You put him before your responsibility to the coven," Devin said.

I sighed. "I just thought it was his grief and we'd be gone a couple of days. I didn't know that he...I...didn't know."

Cameron lowered his head slightly and looked me in the eye. "So, you were not aware that he had been infected?"

I shook my head, only keeping eye contact for a moment before needing to concentrate on the carpet instead.

"Regardless," Devin said in a stern tone, "you left the manor. You turned your back on your team, your family, and your coven. That is simply not acceptable, Tosh."

"I know, sir, I'm sorry. I thought I was helping him and I would bring him back here once he got his head on straight. That's all I was doing."

"And it had nothing to do with the feelings you have for him?" Devin said and looked down his nose at me.

I clinched my jaw to keep from screaming or sobbing, my brain couldn't figure out which one. With a slow exhale, and knowing I couldn't lie to either of them, I finally replied, "Yes, I was afraid of losing him, but..."

"But you lost him anyway."

"Devin," Cameron warned.

"It's true," Devin said angrily. "Her motives were emotional, not for some kind of loyalty to us."

"That's not true," I begged, my eyes welling up with tears.

"Everyone, calm down," Cameron said. "Natasha, is your intention to return to the training program?"

"Yes," I said and swallowed the tears down.

Cameron gave Devin a look before responding, "Very well, but understand that there are consequences for your actions."

"Yes, sir."

"Two weeks with Julian," Devin said flatly.

"Yes, sir."

"Also, Natasha," Cameron continued, "your team may be just as upset that you left. You need to be mindful that you have broken their trust. That is something you will need to work out with them."

"Yes, sir," I replied, suddenly feeling my insides beginning to shake. My emotions wouldn't stay inside me for very much longer.

Connor cleared his throat behind me. "Sirs, what about any future communication with the wolf?"

My eyes shot up at Connor's snide tone and the fact that he referenced Beckett merely as a wolf.

"Thank you, Connor," Cameron replied. "Natasha, if you receive any communication from Beckett, you must report it to us immediately. It is hard for me to say this, but he is now our enemy…"

"Enemy?" I interrupted. "How can you say that? He made a deal to save his mom, you can't just label him an enemy! Beckett is a member of this…"

"Enough!" Devin shouted. "He made his choice and is with Garrett. There is no way we can trust anything he does. Beckett Dawes is an enemy of the Warriors by association. If you receive even a text message you must report it to us. Do you understand?"

"Doesn't really matter," Jared said coming to stand next to me. "We'll monitor your phone anyway."

Cameron nodded. "Thank you, Jared. Natasha, tomorrow you will report to training and afterwards you will begin your time with Julian. What you did was dangerous. Another misstep and you will find yourself outside of these walls."

"Yes, sir."

"Very well, you are dismissed."

Immediately I turned away from Cameron and walked quickly out of the office. My stomach began to churn and spasm with the emotions I had tried desperately to keep inside. I needed my room and a pillow to scream into, but I wasn't sure I was going to make it. Suddenly, hands were squeezing my arm.

"Cush, wait," Connor said and pulled me to a stop.

"For the love of god, let me go," I shouted.

He jerked, and tears started to drip from my eyes. As soon as he softened his grip I pulled my arm free and ran up the spiral staircase. By the time I got to my room I couldn't breathe, not because of the run, but because of the emotions, the goddamn emotions that I'd learned to suppress, were bubbling up and taking over.

When I burst through the door I found Nikki pacing the floor. We rarely got along, and even rarer still was I ever happy to see her, but in that moment I completely broke down and was comforted by the feeling of her arms around me. Slowly she walked me over to my bed and I collapsed face first into the mattress.

Deep, heaving sobs came out of me while my lungs burned from what I could only describe as hysterics. Nikki draped herself across my shoulders and rested her head against mine.

"They told me you left with Beckett. What happened?" she asked in my ear.

I shoved my hand in my pants pocket and pulled out Beckett's letter that I hadn't had the courage to read. Nikki rose up from my shoulders and took the letter from my hand. She read silently for a couple of minutes while I continued to cry into the mattress.

"Oh, Nat, I'm sorry."

"What does it say?"

"You didn't read it?"

I shook my head and released another loud sob. "I couldn't. Not in front of Victor."

Nikki squeezed the back of my arm. "Want me to read you the highlights? It's kinda long and sappy."

The real Nikki was always lurking in there somewhere.

"Please," I replied and pulled the pillow tightly underneath my chest and head.

"Ok," she said. "Dear Tosha, blah blah blah, it's hard to tell you this, blah blah, I was infected by my dad the night he died. I tried to deny it, I hid it from you and Victor, but now I realize that was a mistake. Tonight when we were together I know you saw it, that wasn't me." Nikki pulled the note down. "Wait, did you...have sex with him?"

A loud sob came out from deep within my stomach. I didn't need to give a real answer in order for my sister to understand.

"Oh, Nat," she said softly and rubbed my arm, but then she froze. "Oh my god, you could have been infected."

"I didn't know," I cried. "Could you finish the letter, please?"

Nikki sighed and sat back. "It was still stupid dangerous."

"Nikki, please!"

"Fine, fine. Ok, where was I," she began and pulled the letter back up in front of her. "When we were together I know you saw it, that wasn't me. When we first met, you told me I was a stupid hybrid who would get someone killed because he didn't bother to learn about his powers. I can't risk you getting hurt again. I can't repeat what Ty did to you. I need to learn how to live with what I am now.

"Please know this has nothing to do with you. I do love you, and this is killing me. It's because I love you that I have to leave. Please hate me and forget about me, and be the greatest Warrior that ever lived. I will always remember the time we had together. Always yours, Beckett."

Nikki folded the letter and tucked it under my hand. We sat on the bed quietly for several minutes and finally my breathing came to a normal rhythm.

"So, did that make you feel better?" Nikki asked. I shook my head. "Yeah, it was still a pretty shitty thing to do. Did you love him too?"

"Doesn't matter anymore," I replied and pushed myself up to a seated position. I wiped my face and asked, "Why were you waiting in here?"

She raised an eyebrow at me. "You leave in the middle of the night, you don't think they came after me?"

"I'm sorry."

She shrugged. "That's just how they are. Jared's convinced I'm keeping something from him so we had a big blow up. When they told me you were on your way back I tried to get them to let me into your meeting with Cameron and Devin, but that was a pipe dream. So I waited here. I knew you'd be coming up here eventually."

I leaned over and for the first time in over a year I hugged my sister. "I'm glad you were here."

She sniffled into my ear. "Me too. I'm sorry Beckett was an idiotic jerk."

I released her and wiped my face again. "He can't help what happened to him."

"Like hell," she replied sharply. "He got too close to his dad and he could have just as easily infected you, Nat. You need to remember that."

"I-I just don't know what to do now."

"Do? You go on, Nat. Don't let what Beckett did derail you. We weren't raised that way."

I raised both my eyebrows at her. "Nik, our mother pined over our father until she died and she could never move on enough to ever do anything substantial in her life."

"Right, and we learned not to be that way."

There was a knock at the door and a moment later Brianna stuck her head in. Just the sight of her made me start to cry all over again. She had been the closest thing I'd had to a mother besides Maddy. Brianna stepped inside the room and opened up her arms. I stumbled off the bed and ran to her. She wrapped her arms around me and even though there was no heat coming from her body, there was still a warmth in being comforted by her embrace. She petted my hair and squeezed me tightly into her chest.

"Oh honey, I'm so sorry," she said and began rubbing my back. "Did you at least get to say goodbye?"

I shook my head and began sobbing harder into her chest. Brianna walked me back to my bed and slowly lowered me down onto the mattress.

"I know what it feels like to have your heart ripped out of your chest, Tosh, I do. There's nothing any of us can do to make you feel better, but just know that you're not alone. A broken heart can heal."

"It's not just that he left me," I said and pushed up from her chest. "It's that...he didn't trust me to know what had happened. He didn't even give me a chance...I...we would have figured it out. I would have helped him...I don't...I don't care that he's...that he's a wolf. I don't care!"

I broke down once again, falling away from Brianna and letting my thick pillows catch me. Both Nikki and Brianna let me cry for several minutes uninterrupted. Honestly, I was surprised Nikki even stayed in the room since she never felt comfortable in Brianna's presence, even after all these years.

Brianna brushed away the hair that stuck to my face and looked down at me with very sympathetic eyes. "Do you want me to send up some ice cream? Onion rings? I was always partial to guacamole."

"It's ten in the morning," Nikki said in a snide tone.

Brianna tightened her lips and sighed, but collected herself and said in a calm tone, "Brownies? At least those have eggs in them."

I let out a snotty laugh and saw Nikki roll her eyes. "I want everything."

Brianna smiled and squeezed my hand. "You got it."

Nikki scooted off the bed and stepped toward the door. "I guess I'll go then."

"Oh no, Nikki," Brianna said and rose from the bed herself. "I'll have everything sent up. This is sister territory, I don't want to get in the middle of that. Tosh, honey, I'll come check on you a little later. I'll take an afternoon comfort food order if I have to. Sound ok?"

I nodded. "Thank you."

"Do you want me to call Maddy for you? Let her know what's going on?"

I nodded again. "Please. I don't think I can talk to anyone right now."

"Ok, but don't be surprised if she comes barging down your door." I smiled at the thought. "I'll gladly take you over to the house to see her if you need me to. Just let me know, ok?"

I nodded and watched her leave the room. Nikki gave me a glance and then turned to the door.

"Nik, you don't have to go."

Nikki turned around and there were tears in her eyes. Just the sight of her like that made me tear up again. She stepped over to the bed and hugged me tightly.

"I won't leave your side," she replied.

For the first time in my life it was exactly where I wanted her to be.

Chapter Twenty-seven

After eating nearly every bit of junk food the manor had to offer, I was officially bloated and had a food hangover. My eyes were red and puffy from crying and lack of sleep. I didn't bother to do anything to myself but put my hair up into a ponytail in order to prepare for training this morning. Nikki kept her word and stayed with me all day and night yesterday, not that she had anywhere else to go, but it was still nice of her and frankly something she'd never done before.

My muscles ached and were tight, my stomach sore from debilitating sobs. I bypassed breakfast, which I knew was a mistake, and went straight outside to the courtyard where the guys were already out stretching. No one addressed me, no one even looked at me. It was just as Cameron had said, they were mad and I deserved it. Since they were all giving me the cold shoulder, I chose a patch of grass a few feet away from them and began stretching my very stiff legs.

"Let's get moving," Connor shouted from the entrance of the courtyard.

The five of us jumped up from the ground and started the usual morning laps. Immediately something was wrong. My breathing was wrong, my legs were sluggish, nothing was effortless. I could outrun every one of these guys and they were passing me. After only two laps all of them were half a lap ahead of me.

"Scarecrow," Connor shouted. "Get moving or we'll be here all damn day!"

I took as deep of a breath as I could, trying to push my legs further, and yet they stayed sluggish and heavy. My lungs started to burn on the fourth lap and by then the guys were lapping me. It was humiliating. My head wasn't in the game and there was nothing I could do to get my body to respond.

When the guys finished, Connor ended my misery and didn't make me run the last lap and a half that I'd fallen behind on. He certainly wasn't happy with me and practically pulled my shoulder out of its socket dragging me over to where Roberts was standing.

The usual line up was light sparring, then a lesson on a specific technique or move, and then time with your weapon of choice. After only a few minutes of sparring with Roberts, Devin came walking down the courtyard.

"Everyone, circle up," Connor shouted.

We all immediately turned around and stood at attention.

"Good morning, everyone," Devin said curtly. "As I'm sure you have deduced, we are nearing our time to decide who will be moving on to become a Warrior. Frankly, you five still being alive is a testament to your talent and perseverance. Over the next week I will be observing you more closely. This is your final opportunity to prove that you should be one of us. So let's begin with Trevor and Tosh."

Bile jolted into my throat. I wasn't ready, my heart wasn't in it. I had never felt this way, it was terrifying and unfamiliar. I bent down and strapped my weapons belt to my waist while Roberts twirled his staff between his fingers. Together the two of us matched each other's steps into the center of our circle. Roberts gave me a nod and I did the same.

My fingers barely touched my whips before Roberts' staff was coming down on me, hitting me in the shoulder and then the face causing me to fall to the ground. I grabbed the handle of the whip on my right hip and released it in front of me. The tip of my whip snapped and wrapped around the center of Roberts' staff. He tightened his grip and jerked the staff toward his chest, dragging me forward. My right heel and left knee made drag marks in the grass. I released my left whip in the air and just as it wound its way around Roberts' wrist, I pulled hard on both whips and relieved him of his weapon.

Roberts didn't waste a moment before leaping forward and knocking me to the ground. My arm wrapped around the back of his neck and pushed his face to the ground. Roberts tightened his grip and rose from the ground, lifting me with him only a few inches from the ground before smashing me back down with all his weight. The wind was completely knocked out of me, but I still managed to elbow him in the face. When I reached back again, he blocked my hit and used my elbow as leverage to turn me on my stomach. I clawed the ground to pull out from underneath him but he had a tight grip on my arm. He twisted and raised it uncomfortably behind me.

"Tap out, Tosh," he grunted in my ear.

"No!"

He tightened his grip and twisted my arm even further. I screamed from the pain, feeling the tendons and ligaments reaching their limit.

"Tap out!"

"No," I screamed, tears welling in my eyes.

"Tosh, yield before..." Devin started to say but then a loud pop sounded and I was blinded by pain in my shoulder.

Roberts immediately released me and jumped off of my back. I rolled over and cradled my arm that hung limply from my shoulder. I hated the cries that were coming out of me, but I had absolutely no control. Devin stood over me and shook his head.

"Why didn't you yield, Natasha," he said angrily and knelt down beside me. He squeezed his hands lightly around my shoulder. "Luckily it is just a dislocation. Breathe out and count to three."

I exhaled as he instructed. "One..."

Devin flinched and popped my shoulder back into place. I let out a scream but a second later the blinding pain was gone leaving only the aching from deep inside my joint.

Devin stood from the ground. "You're done for today."

"No, just give me a minute," I grunted as I sat up from the ground and cradled my shoulder.

"You had your moment and you lost. Whether it was pride or stupidity, you let yourself get into that situation. Now get off my field."

"But sir, please..."

"Do not embarrass yourself further by begging," he growled. "From the moment you stepped into this courtyard you were not in the right frame of mind. You are lucky Trevor didn't tear you apart. Now leave before you hurt yourself or someone else. This program doesn't have room for your drama."

"But...what am I supposed..."

"I believe you are beholden to Julian. Perhaps you should start there."

Devin turned his back on me and called for Bush and Princess to pair up. While Roberts gave me an apologetic look, Connor was glaring at me. He was embarrassed for sure, especially after all the special sessions we'd had. I'd gotten out of that grip dozens of times because of our work together. I was an embarrassment. Devin was right, I didn't deserve to be on his field.

After releasing my breath, I clinched my jaw and turned toward the manor. Each step was painfully humiliating and it took all my strength not to cry. The soft grass turned into concrete as I reached the portico. I turned to the right and followed the walkway to the tall wood doors that opened into the historic Council Hall, it was the shortest route down to the dungeons.

The Council Hall door weighed at least fifty pounds, causing my healing shoulder to groan in pain as I pushed it open enough for me to slip in. My footsteps echoed loudly as I walked the length of the room to the door that led down to the dungeons.

Two tears escaped my eyes just as I wrapped my hand around the door handle. I took a step back and wiped my face taking in a few breaths to try and dissolve the redness I felt on my face. This was not how I wanted Julian or anyone downstairs to see me.

"Get your shit together," I hissed to myself and wiped my face again.

Once again, I took hold of the door handle, took a breath, and then opened yet another heavy door. Only another few minutes and there would be no reminder of my dislocated shoulder, although I'm sure the boys wouldn't let me live it down any time soon.

The stairs down to the dungeon were dark and steep, and the musty smell hinted at what would come the further I went down. I was always surprised at how well Julian and his team could stand it with their heightened since of smell, but I supposed being around similar smells for centuries you just got used to it. I waved at the camera in the corner of the receiving area, and a moment later a buzzer sounded and the door unlocked. I stepped inside and walked past the booth where a guard was watching different prisoners on the monitors.

Julian stepped around the corner with a confused look on his face. "Tosh? I didn't expect you until this evening."

"I..." I started to say and then had to clear my throat, "...Devin threw me...out of training."

Julian knitted his brows and tightened his lips at the news, obviously surprised and confused all at once. After a short sigh he flicked his fingers to follow him. "I'll start you off with the linens. Cells three, eight, and eleven can be cleared, you know where everything can be dropped off."

Suddenly he stopped and turned so quickly that I crashed into his chest.

"Sorry."

He grunted and took a step back. "Tosh, I assume I don't need to tell you, but stay away from the wolf. There will be no talking, no approaching the cell, no interaction of any kind. Is that perfectly clear?"

"Yes, sir, I understand."

"Yes, so did your boyfriend, but that didn't stop him. I don't need anyone else getting infected because they can't help themselves. Is that clear?"

I wasn't sure which part of his statement made my eyes water, the boyfriend piece or getting infected. Either way, tears came down and Julian became uncomfortable very quickly. He looked around before stepping over to a corner where a push broom was propped up against the wall.

He handed me the broom and said, "Maybe just start with some sweeping."

"Thank you," I replied, sounding pathetic as I sucked up the snot in my nose. I took the broom and headed around the corner so that Julian didn't have to look at my pitiful face any longer.

Mindlessly I pushed the broom along the long, winding corridors, ignoring the prisoners locked in the cells as best I could. The cat-calling and whistles bounced off of me easily, but it was one voice that made me stop my sweeping.

"He got infected, didn't he?"

I stood up straight, but didn't answer. The captured wolf, whose name I couldn't remember, waited a moment before clicking his tongue.

"You don't have to answer, chickie, I knew it the minute he went by my cell. It has an unforgettable smell. Funny isn't it? A virus that has a smell. It's really the combination of the virus mixing with the blood. Hey, you ok, chickie?"

I didn't give him the satisfaction of seeing me react. Instead, I sucked in the corners of my lips and bit into them until I tasted the blood in my mouth. With my broom in hand, I turned and walked quickly around the corner. Once I knew he couldn't see me anymore, I took another corner and started running until I found a cell that was empty and open.

"Fucking son of a bitch!" I screamed as I smashed the head of the broom into the stone wall. "Coward! Fucking coward!" I shouted, hitting the wall again. After that I couldn't find the words, only hemorrhaging screams from the depths of my soul as I hit the wall over, and over, and over again. When the head of the broom finally cracked and flew off, I started hitting the handle on the stone until it too splintered and cracked, leaving only a five-inch piece that flew across the cell.

All the sobs that I had forcibly kept in finally came out in massive heaves. I sat down on the hard metal bench in the cell and bent over my knees.

"Natasha?"

I looked up to find Julian standing in the door of the cell with a look of confusion and maybe even panic.

I wiped my face, but didn't apologize. "I owe you a broom."

Julian literally invoiced me for another broom to replace the one I had destroyed. Tomorrow I would need to bring him $15.35 in cash, emphasis on the thirty-five cents. I shook my head as I dragged myself up the winding staircase just thinking about having to scrounge around for change.

My legs still felt like lead. Today the two flights of stairs seemed like twenty. It felt as though I was never going to get to my bedroom. I didn't want to eat dinner with everyone, I just wanted to sleep. Maybe I'd take a sleeping pill to do so. I had barely slept in two days. When I finally reached my room I was surprised to see the door ajar, but when I pushed it open it took everything not to breakdown.

"Maddy?"

Madelyn Forebush, the kindest, most generous little old lady, turned around and gave me the loving smile I needed. Brianna was like a mother to me, but Maddy was like the grandmother who practically raised you. She'd been the only person to stay with me when I had my accident. Some of the nurses couldn't even take the sight of me, but not Maddy. She cared for me better than any doctor, and fought for me more viciously than any lawyer. Maddy got me the settlement from Ty's family. She's the one that pushed me to not give up. And she could see through me better than anyone, including Jonah.

"What are you doing here?" I asked and closed the door behind me.

Maddy pursed her lips and looked down her nose at me. "What am I doing here? What I want to know is why am I just hearing about what happened with Beckett now? And not from you, I might add."

I shrugged, sat on the corner of the bed, and purposely avoided eye contact. "He left. What else is there to say?"

Maddy sat down on the bed next to me and I could feel her laser eyes burning through the side of my face. "Natasha Grace Cushlin, never have I ever allowed you to avoid or lie to me, and I am certainly not going to allow it today."

Madelyn was the only person besides my sister who even knew my middle name, or at least dared to use it, but I still couldn't bear to look at her.

"If I talk about it, I don't know if I'll ever be able to put myself back together."

Maddy squeezed my chin between her fingers and turned my head to face her. "I've put you back together before, so consider me an expert. I'm not leaving until you talk to me. I don't care if I have to sleep here, it'll give me a night off from Ollie's snoring."

I gave a snotty laugh and then broke down immediately. My cheek rested on her shoulder while she squeezed me into her side.

"We've all loved and lost, honey," she said softly and petted my hair.

"But I didn't want it, Maddy," I cried. "I was fine until I met him and then everything went to shit."

Maddy pulled me away from her shoulder and looked at me sternly. "You were far from fine, little girl. I was with you every day after your accident and you barely open up to me. You built a wall around yourself, honey, and being with these Warriors isn't doing you any good. They practically specialize in being emotionally repressed. That's why I was so happy to see you with Beckett. You weren't fighting with yourself, you were so comfortable. It had been a long time since I'd seen that in you. I was happy to see that Beckett had torn down that wall of yours."

"He kept beating me down until I was just too tired to fight it anymore."

Maddy looked down her nose at me again. "You loved him, Natasha, and he loved you. Don't you dare minimize what you both felt."

"But it doesn't matter anymore," I snapped and stepped over to my nightstand for a tissue. "He took what he wanted and left, and now I'm this...this mess and I can't pull myself together."

"And who says you need to?"

"Devin, for one," I said and dabbed my face with the tissue.

"Oh please," she replied. "If he isn't the world's most repressed person, I don't know who is."

"But he's the boss, and I...couldn't concentrate today and Roberts dislocated my shoulder so Devin kicked me out of practice."

"Who dislocated your shoulder?"

I sat back down on the bed. "Trevor Roberts."

She nodded. "Oh yes, I forgot he was a trainee. I always wondered why you two never got together."

"Ew. Trevor? No."

"Not even to get your mind off of Beckett?"

"No!"

She shrugged. "Just thought I'd ask. There's no need to be embarrassed, honey, we've all had our rebound."

I blinked three times before I could actually speak. "I don't know how to respond to that. Beckett was a fluke, Maddy. No one wants this," I said and waved my hand in front of my stomach.

Maddy squeezed my hand. "Fine. No one wants you, is that what you want to hear? Does that make you feel better? Well I hope not, because it's, forgive my language, bullshit. Beckett saw the wonderfulness that is you, scars and everything. He made an impossible decision and it had nothing to do with you or how he felt about you. What would you have done? Wouldn't you sacrifice anything to have one more day with your mother?"

"But he didn't trust me, Maddy," I said loudly and felt the tears filling my eyes again. "I would have...we would have figured out something. I don't care that he's...he's a...oh my god I can't even say it."

I bent over and caught my head with my hands while my body shook with hurtful sobs. Maddy rubbed my back, but let me expel my sadness in silence. It wasn't until the door opened minutes later did I even sit up.

"Oh, sorry," Nikki said and closed the door behind her. "I didn't mean to interrupt."

"You're not interrupting anything," Maddy replied and stood from the bed. "I was just dropping off some kitchen sink brownies."

"Kitchen sink?" I asked and wiped my face.

Maddy smiled. "Oh you know, everything and the kitchen sink are in these brownies. It doesn't fix the heart, but for a second they make us think they will."

"Perfect, we can all gain ten pounds," Nikki said in her usual nasty tone as she put her backpack on her bed on the other side of the room.

Maddy pursed her lips and gave me a look of disapproval. It was a look I saw often when it came to Nikki. After a moment Maddy kissed my head and patted my chin.

"Remember, Tosh, he isn't the only one who loves you," she said with a warning look and then a smile. "Don't give up on everything just because of one man."

I nodded and squeezed her hand. "Thank you, Maddy."

"Anytime, little girl." Maddy tucked her purse under her arm and walked toward the door. "Always a pleasure, Miss Nikki."

Nikki didn't respond, but it didn't really matter since we all knew Maddy didn't mean it. Once we were alone, Nikki jumped off her bed and went right for the container of brownies on my dresser.

"Are you going to have one of these with me or not?"

"Why are you here? And yes, of course I'm going to eat one."

Nikki opened the lid to the plastic container, pulled out one dark, thick, chunky brownie and handed it to me. The brownie was so dense and heavy that I thought Maddy could have very well put a kitchen sink in it. The first bite was magnificent – chewy and rich, a crunch of crème cookie, and then a smooth twinge of peanut butter. It had been a while since I had such a decadent dessert, and even after just one bite I was already in sugar shock.

"You didn't answer me," I said between bites. "Why are you up here?"

"Jared and I are still in the shitter, what else is new. What is that noise?"

"Wha?" I said through another bite of the brownie, and then I heard a beep, and then another.

The sound was muffled, but close. Nikki and I both looked around the room until the next beep came and we were directed near my feet. I knelt down on the floor and looked under my bed, only seeing my overnight bag. I had used it the night I left with Beckett, and when I returned I stuffed it under the bed and didn't even bother unpacking it. Another beep sounded and it was obvious it came from the bag. I pulled it out from underneath the bed and placed it on top of the mattress.

Nikki took the bag by its straps and dumped the contents. A shirt, a pair of jeans, and a couple pairs of underwear spilled out onto the bed, and then a cell phone fell out on top of the pile.

"Is that yours?" Nikki asked.

I shook my head as I stood up from the floor. When I picked up the phone and turned it over I realized quickly whose it was by the cracked screen. "It's Beckett's."

Nikki took the phone from my hand and inspected it herself. "Why would...it was on the bottom of the bag, he must have put it there on purpose."

"Why?"

"Maybe he thought he could contact you on it," she said and turned away from me.

"But they're tracking all my devices."

"Yes," she replied and plugged Beckett's phone into my charger. "They're tracking yours, not his."

I stepped over to her and grabbed her arm. "We don't know that for sure. I can't have that in here. They told me I have to report any communication from him."

Nikki looked at me with a blank face. "Not everything the Warriors say and do is right. Sometimes you have to make decisions for yourself, Nat. Beckett put this phone in your bag for a reason. You need to decide whether you're going to find out why, or give this to Jared."

I looked at the phone and then back to her, and then back at the phone.

"Oh for fuck's sake, we're keeping the phone," she said. "How are we related? Seriously."

"What if they find out?

"Then I'll take full responsibility and tell them you didn't know." I shook my head. "Nat, they hate me already. Let them keep hating me."

"Nik..."

"Nat," she interrupted. "It's done. Damn you're exhausting sometimes."

Chapter Twenty-eight

My cereal had gone soggy from neglect on my part. Maddy's kitchen sink brownies were still in the depths of my stomach, slowly but surely killing my pancreas. Cereal was the only thing I could even think of possibly eating, but every time I would bring the spoon up to my mouth it looked and smelled revolting. It didn't help that I couldn't stop thinking about Beckett's cell phone sitting on my nightstand, just sitting there with its cracked screen and scratched up case, waiting foolishly for something to happen. I should have stopped Nikki from plugging it in, but I wanted it because it was my only connection to him which made me the biggest fool of the universe.

I groaned at how big of a loser I was being and allowed my spoon to fall back into the bowl and splash my sleeve with milk. Just as I reached for a napkin, Roberts slammed himself down in the chair next to me.

"Roberts," I said and took a napkin from the holder.

"Natasha," he replied in a scolding tone.

"I guess that's better than Scarecrow," I said and wiped my sleeve. When he didn't say anything else, I turned my head and realized he was glaring at me. "What do you want, Trevor?"

"I want the real Tosh Cushlin to come back into her body, that's what I want."

I pushed back from the table and started to stand. "I'm not talking to you about this…" Roberts took my wrist and yanked me back down into my chair. "What is your problem?"

"My problem is that you're suddenly throwing everything away."

"I am not."

"Tosh, I've known you longer than anyone else here," he said in a lower voice. "I knew you before your accident and after, and I still remember your screams as they peeled Ty off of you."

"Why are you doing this?" I asked, having to put my hand up to my face to cover my trembling lip.

"Because you fought tooth and nail to survive. Before the accident you were just a regular girl, you were nice and all, but nothing special."

"Thanks, asshole."

"But after, you planted your feet and wouldn't give in. Same with getting into this program. For months it's been you and me, top two. You know they're going to make a decision soon and you just gave up yesterday like some weak little girl."

My hand flinched, preparing to slap him, but in the next moment the very weakness he was referring to came over me like a shroud, killing any desire to attack him.

"Just leave me alone, Roberts."

He slammed his fist down on the table. "Damn it, Tosh! Get your shit together. Bring back that girl that pulled herself up from the brink of death. If I have to be paired with fucking Bush again we're going to have problems. Get it together!"

Roberts rose from his seat and left the dining room. Why did people think that by telling someone to get their shit together it would magically stop the pain that person was feeling? Fucking Beckett. The three morons started laughing and whispering behind me, I'm sure about Roberts yelling at me for all to hear. Fucking Beckett, fucking Roberts.

With a sigh, I slowly rose from the table and tried to ignore the looks from others as I walked out of the dining room. The walk to the courtyard was a blur while Roberts' voice echoed in my head to get my shit together. Get my shit together? How was that even possible when my head was working against me?

When I finally reached the courtyard the brisk morning brought me back from the thoughts swirling in my head. Roberts was already warming up, but stopped for a second to give me a challenging glance. I gave him a nod to let him think that his shitty talk with me had somehow inspired me, and then began stretching my arms and legs.

"Gather up," Connor said as he walked through the courtyard toward us. "Devin will be joining us a little later so we're going to be doing some individual weapons training until he arrives. I'll start with Scarecrow, the rest of you can work on what you learned from Devin yesterday."

The others paired up off to the side, although Roberts was less than thrilled to be working with Bush again. I pulled my non-silver coated whips from my bag and stepped into the middle of the courtyard where Connor stood waiting.

"Start off slow until you're warmed up, ok?" he said and I nodded.

We began with easy motions and blocks first – a whip to the arm, a whip to the opposite leg, slashing a weapon out of his hand. After twenty minutes or so we started in on tougher maneuvers and the more I worked, the more I started feeling like myself again, even though my muscles were already complaining.

"Looking better than yesterday, Cush," Connor teased. "Grab your knives."

"No need for that." I quickly turned around to find Devin standing behind me. "You are dismissed, Natasha."

"But sir…"

"I believe Julian is expecting you," he interrupted and gave me a challenging look.

I looked back at Connor and then to Roberts, both men urging me to do or say something, but yet again the energy and confidence just wasn't there. With a sigh, I grabbed my bag from the ground and walked across the courtyard. This time the walk seemed longer and more painful than yesterday. It was shameful and embarrassing, and yet I had no desire to do anything about it. My feet directed me through the Council Hall and down to the dungeons while my brain continued to circle through all the things I should have said or done. My days in the training program were numbered, I just knew it.

Once I stepped through the prison door only Liam was there to greet me. Liam was Julian's second in command, but he was definitely responsible for more of the dirty work than Julian was. And although he had some blood on his shirt, which probably meant he'd just tortured a vamp, he had a light-hearted smile on his face. That was Liam. Sweet, sociopathic Liam who still had his cute Irish brogue even though he was over a hundred years old.

"Hi, Liam, is Julian around?" I asked and placed my heavy pack on the desk.

"Sorry, miss, Julian is with Cameron this mornin'," he replied with his

294 ~ C.R. Quinn

thick accent and then held up a piece of paper. "But he did leave this invoice far ya for fifteen doolars and terty-five cents."

I had to smile. "It's like you're speaking another language sometimes, Liam."

"Oh now, miss, don't be tinkin' you're all high and mighty," he laughed. "I'm not the one needin' to pay fifteen doolars and terty-five cents for a broom I smashed to pieces."

I dug through my bag and pulled out the exact change I'd stuffed in the inner pocket. "Please tell Julian that I am paid in full."

He nodded, took my money, and ripped up the paper invoice. "If ya don't mind me sayin', I woulda destroyed somethin' too, miss."

"Thanks, Liam," I said and cleared my throat. "What's my punishment today?"

Liam looked around the desk and found another piece of paper that had a hand-written list on it. "It says here you need to finish sweepin' the floors, turnover cells one and fourteen, and then give cell seven a good scrub. I'll tell ya now, it's a messy one, he was a bleeder, that one."

"Thanks, Liam," I sighed and took my bag down from the desk. "Can you tell me where your lucky charms are?"

Liam laughed and shooed me away, but just as I turned away he yelled back, "Stay away from the wolf, don't even talk to 'em, eh?"

"It's getting him to not talk to me that's the trick," I replied.

My smile immediately deflated as I rounded the corner. Acting as though nothing was wrong was exhausting but necessary in order to make others feel comfortable in my presence. It also stopped me from crying in front of them. At least I could cry and sweep, or cry and wipe up blood. How morbid was my life?

With the amount of pent up energy I had from warming up with Connor, I decided to get the dirty scrubbing work done first. From the supply closet I loaded myself up with buckets, bristle brushes, sponges, and a rubber apron. Once I got to cell seven I feared I was lacking in supplies. Liam wasn't kidding, I was surprised the vamp had any blood left considering the amount that was splattered on the walls and even the ceiling. But none the less, I had to clean it up.

Since the wet sponges seemed to merely smear the blood along the stone, I was forced to use the stiff bristle hand brushes. Pushing and scrubbing, then rinsing and scrubbing again. The water in the buckets became red quickly, as did my hands. The floors were the worst since the hard, uneven stone dug into my knees and shins. The only thing beneficial about the harsh sound of the bristles on the stone was that it muffled the noise coming from the wolf's cell around the corner.

"You guys can't keep me in here," he shouted and banged on the bars. "It's gonna get bad the later it gets."

I dunked the brush into the muddy water and started scrubbing a new circle on the floor.

"You're digging your graves and everyone around here. I can't control what I do," the wolf continued to shout. "Let me out, you bloodsuckers! You don't want this."

What in the hell was he going on about? Over the next hour his shouts were never-ending. At one point he even started singing and banging on the bars like drums. The buckets of water sloshed around as I walked back to the supply closet, spilling thick, brown, bloody water onto my shoes and pants. My body ached, my clothes were damp, and I just felt gross. But my punishment wasn't over, there was still sweeping to do. The biggest question was if the broom would make it through the day. I would control myself, I would. I refused to buy Julian another broom.

After rinsing the apron and hanging it up to dry, I pulled out a standing broom and began sliding it against the floor. Sweep, sweep, smack on the ground. Sweep, sweep, smack on the ground. It was a hypnotic rhythm and a mindless activity. Sweep, sweep, smack on the ground. Sweep, sweep, smack.

"Here she is."

I looked up from my broom and saw the wolf's cell only a few feet in front of me. He was pacing back and forth in his cell, his bare chest shiny with sweat. Quickly I looked back down at the floor and began sweeping again.

"Oh come on now, aren't we friends by now?" When I didn't answer, he continued, "Suit yourself. You hanging around for the big show? These assholes don't know what they're getting into."

My curiosity got the best of me. "Big show?"

His head flinched with surprised. "Tonight's the big night, chickie. I'd think a werewolf's girlfriend…"

"I'm not anyone's girlfriend," I snapped.

He put his hands up and shook his head. "Ok, alright, whatever you say, chickie. Doesn't mean you can't still enjoy the show."

"What are you talking about?"

"The full moon, chickie," he said and started stretching and jumping around his cell. "Boy I can feel it all over. It's like an ache or an itch that runs through your whole body. You can feel the relief getting closer every minute, this burning, burning ache running through every muscle, every nerve, and then your body finally breaks out in this slow, agonizing explosion of pain and relief. It's terrifyingly amazing. You should hang around and see what your boy will go through. I wonder if he'll make it because of that whole half a vampire thing. That's been all the talk, you know. Will he? Won't he? But they don't know that's it been…

"Tosh!" Julian's voice suddenly rang behind me. "Come along."

When I turned around, Julian was standing next to me. He didn't wait another second before he was grabbing my arm and pulling me away from the wolf's cell.

"Aren't you in enough trouble?" Julian scolded as we rounded the corner. "You were warned about speaking with the wolf."

"Tonight's the full moon."

"Yes, what of it?"

"Julian, please," I said and pushed away from him. "Please let me come down here tonight. I need to see this…I need…I really need to see him phase, I need to see what's going to happen to Beckett. Please, Julian, I'll stay away from the cell, I swear, I just…. need to see it."

Julian's entire face scrunched into a scowl. "How dare you ask to view a man's most degrading moment as if it were live theatre. You being down here is not therapy, it is punishment, Tosh."

"Julian, I'm begging you…"

"Leave, Tosh," he growled. "The fact that you are even asking to do this shows you have no respect for other's pain and suffering."

"That's not true," I cried, the tears finally cresting over my lids. "I need to see what Beckett is going through."

"I will inform the sirs you are to be assigned elsewhere."

"I can watch on the monitors, no one will…"

"Don't make me take you out by force."

"Julian…"

"Get out of my sight!"

My chest felt as though it would collapse in on itself. All my protections to keep my emotions at bay had burst and everything, every possible feeling was flowing out of me at once. I ran past Julian, grabbed my bag from the supply closet, and bolted up the stairs to the Council Hall.

The rest of the way to my room was filled with avoiding eye contact with others in the hallways, almost running into one of the blood donors because I couldn't bear to look up from the ground. I let out a loud, relieved cry when I reached my room. Quickly I ducked inside, slammed the door, and immediately fell on the bed. My life was falling apart, and I wasn't doing anything to help it. It felt as though I was climbing a mountain in a mudslide, slipping and sliding and being weighted down, but continuing to search for a grip.

My back pocket began to vibrate. I reached back and pulled out my phone, pleasantly surprised by the name on the video chat. I wiped my eyes and sat up against my pillows at the head of the bed.

I pressed the accept button and said, "Hey, Jonah..." but I suddenly stopped at the sight of a precious baby girl, gurgling and making bubbles and mesmerized by the phone screen. "Oh my goodness, hi, Tilly!"

Matilda "Tilly" Thorne, daughter of Jonah and Ashlyn Thorne, was only a few months old and the cutest baby girl alive. Her hair was ice blonde, making her look bald, but she had enough to hold the adorably pink bow clipped in her hair. The bubbles between her lips made me smile and even laugh, although it was a snotty one.

"Hi Toshy," Jonah said in a high-pitched voice as he held Tilly up in front of him. "I heard you were having a hard time, so I thought I'd cheer you up."

I wiped my cheek and brushed back the stray hairs from my ponytail. "Thank you, Tilly. You're exactly what I need."

"I thought so," Jonah said in his play voice, bouncing Tilly around until she started to laugh, which in turn made me laugh. Jonah pulled Tilly back and held her cheek to cheek with him. "Damn, Tosh, you look like shit."

"Jonah!" Ashlyn shouted somewhere in the room.

"I liked you much better when you were pretending to be your daughter," I said and wiped my eyes again.

Jonah tickled Tilly until she started laughing and said in his high-pitched voice, "But you really do look like shit, Toshy. I can't lie, I don't know how to, I'm only five months old."

Just then Ashlyn came into view and pulled Tilly from Jonah's arms. She bent down and waved. "Hi, Tosh, don't listen to him or my daughter."

"It's ok, Ashlyn, they're both right, I know I look terrible."

"I'll let you two talk. Hang in there, Tosh, we love you. Say bye,

Tilly." Ashlyn took Tilly's little hand and waved it for her.

I waved back and then Jonah filled the entire screen. "You know I'm only joking, you don't look that bad."

"You're lying."

"I am," he replied. "Just now, not before. You really don't look good, Tosh."

"Who called you?"

He laughed. "Who didn't? Bri, Kyla, Maddy, even Cameron."

"Cameron called you?" I put my hand up to my eyes and began rubbing them. "Lord, kill me now."

"Oh come on, it's only because they care about you. I would have called sooner, but work's been crazy."

"So what are you supposed to do? Magically get me out of this funk I'm in? Ashlyn's the one becoming a counselor, shouldn't she be helping me instead of you?"

He shrugged. "Yeah, but I'm an expert in Tosh."

"Like hell you are."

"Oh come on," he said, "I told you you'd find someone..."

"Yes, and a lot of good that did."

"Don't minimize it, Tosh."

"Minimize!" I shouted and sat up from the bed, tears already filling my eyes. "I let this guy in, just like you told me to, and he up and leaves me, Jonah. He couldn't even bother waking me up to say goodbye, just a note saying sorry, Tosha, I'm a werewolf now, I need to be with other wolves instead of you, see ya. Believe me, I'm not minimizing how much I...loved him." I gasped for a breath. "I can't even get through the day without crying and I'm going to get kicked out of the program. And I am so stupid and weak that at this point I almost want them to do it so I can just leave here and go find Beckett. How insane is that? What the fuck is wrong with me?"

Jonah tightened his lips into his goofy lopsided smile. "There's nothing wrong with you, Tosh, those are the kind of things we all do when we get our heart broken. But you can't throw away everything you've worked for. I don't know this guy, but I doubt he'd want you to get kicked out because he hurt you. He left to protect you, not fuck with your head."

"Can we watch the language please?" Ashlyn called from another room.

Jonah looked over his shoulder. "She can't talk yet, Ash, no matter how smart you think she is."

"With the amount you swear, you need to start practicing now," she laughed.

Jonah turned back around with a guilty smile. "The only person who swears more than me is Ashlyn. There is no hope for that baby. I'm sorry, back to you."

"No," I replied and laid back down on the bed. "I'm tired of talking about it and people telling me to just get over it."

"Look, we've both had loss in our lives, you know as well as I do that you have to decide for yourself when you're ready to get over it. Only you can find that one thing that turns you around and gives you closure. Keep crying every day, Tosh, you're allowed, but don't give up everything for the douchebag who didn't have the balls to say goodbye in person."

"I think douchebag counts as a swear."

"Really? Damn, that's one I use a lot. There really is no hope for Tilly."

"Jonah!" Ashlyn shouted, running across the screen behind him holding Tilly out in front of her. "It's happening again."

"What's the matter?" I asked.

Jonah sighed and rolled his eyes. "She keeps having these explosions of poop. Why is there so much poop? She's so little," he whined.

"Jonah!" Ashlyn shouted.

"I'm sorry, I gotta help Ash…"

"Yeah, go. Thanks for calling."

"I'll call you in a couple days."

"Don't, I'm fine."

"Liar. I'll call you in a couple days."

I nodded and waved goodbye. Once the screen went dark I tossed the phone on the ground, pulled the comforter across my body, and rolled over to face the wall. The tears came quickly as thoughts of what would happen to Beckett swam through my head. I couldn't be there for him, I couldn't see his pain and try to comfort him. He was alone and with no one who loved or cared for him. And yet I hated him and wanted him to suffer and hurt as much as I did. This was torture, and I wanted to forget about this fucking day.

"Nat?"

Slowly I rolled over and stretched my eyes open, noticing how dark the room had gotten.

"Nik? What time is it?" I asked and rubbed my eyes.

"Almost seven," she said and threw her school bag on her bed. "How long have you been asleep?"

"Off and on all day," I replied and turned on the lamp next to me.

"All day? What happened?"

Slowly I pushed myself up to a sitting position and brought my knees up to my chest. "Well, first Devin kicked me out of practice and sent me back to the dungeons. I scrubbed blood off the floor and walls for two hours, and just when I thought it couldn't get any worse that stupid werewolf reminded me tonight is the full moon."

Nikki blinked a couple of times before her head flinched with recognition. "Oh, so…tonight Beckett will…"

"Phase for the first time, yeah, and hopefully live because no one is really sure what's going to happen because he's a hybrid. That wolf downstairs said he knew something but Julian caught me and started dragging me away. And then I began hysterically crying begging him to let me watch the wolf phase tonight."

"What did he say?"

I sighed and rubbed my face. "His exact words were 'get out of my sight.' So now Julian hates me, I'm an emotional mess, and all I keep thinking is if I could only see the werewolf phase that maybe…maybe I could, I don't know…get some closure? I seriously can't stop thinking about seeing this happen, it's like this pressure weighing down my chest."

Nikki licked her lips and then rubbed them tightly together, seemingly thinking about something. "So if you see this guy phase into a werewolf, you think you'll be able to move on?"

"I hope so."

"Ok then," she said and then stepped toward the door. "Come on."

"What? Where are we…"

"Just come on," she snapped. "We have to go right now if we want to do this."

Quickly I slid into my boots, not bothering to even tie them before I was following Nikki out the door.

"Where are we going?" I asked as we turned left down the hallway toward the back stairs.

"How are you so bad at this?" she hissed and looked angrily over her shoulder. "I thought they were making you into a Warrior. They're more deceitful than the devil, so how are you so bad at being covert?"

"I can be covert," I whispered as we began our dissent down the back stairs which was as dimly lit as the night Beck and I snuck out. The memory caused a painful tinge in my stomach.

The rest of the trip down the stairs remained quiet, but when we turned down to the basement level I figured we must be going to Jared's room. Even though he was almost completely sun resistant he still kept his room on the lowest level of the manor which didn't have windows. I often wondered how Nikki was able to live down here with him. But maybe it was another reason things weren't working between them, which begged the question as to why we were headed toward his room.

As we approached his bedroom door, I braced myself for the awkward and possibly volatile interaction. But Nikki just blew inside, waved me in, and shut the door quickly.

"Where's Jared?" I said with a bit of relief.

Nikki stepped over to the long table of computers and monitors as she replied, "He's working tech on a mission tonight."

"Ok, so what are we doing here?"

Nikki sat down in front of one of the computer monitors and then began quickly typing on the keyboard. "You don't live with a hacker for almost five years and not pick up a few things."

Quickly I stepped over to where she was sitting and looked over her shoulder at the monitor. "What are you doing? Is that the manor?"

"Yes," she replied and began clicking through different screens, "I just need to find the feed for the dungeon."

A few clicks later and I recognized the narrow hallway of the holding area. "That's it," I said and pointed to the screen. Nikki enlarged the screen and began clicking through the different cameras. "He's in the last row of cells, right as you turn the corner."

Nikki nodded and froze on a particular screen. "Is this it?"

I looked at the screen and saw the familiar cell, but there was no one in it. "Whe...where is he?"

"They must have taken him somewhere else. But where?"

"The board and chain chamber? Maybe they brought him in there."

Once again Nikki started clicking through screens, and finally on the fifth camera shot I told her to freeze. The camera was pointing down into the circular chamber where there was a man standing in the center with chains hanging by his neck, arms, and ankles. Nikki turned up the volume and suddenly the sound of growling and wails came through the speaker. The phasing had begun. The man's hands and arms began to flex first, his fingers tensely splayed as they began to grow in length. Next his face began to crack and elongate while the hair on his head and face became thicker, darker, and longer.

With a loud crack, the man whipped backwards and exposed his heaving chest. His fingers were now thick and tipped with sharp claws that tore his pants away from his body. He fell to his knees and caught himself with his hands while the muscles of his chest and back bulged. His cries were becoming more like howls, coming deep from within his chest and sounding more like an animal.

"What the fuck is going on?"

Both Nikki and I gasped and looked up from the monitor to find Jared standing just inside the doorway. Just then the wolf howled loudly and Jared was standing behind me in an instant looking at the monitor.

"You fucking hacked my system?" Jared yelled and pushed me out of the way to turn off the monitor.

Nikki stood up from her chair and faced him. "It can't really be considered hacking if I know all the passwords, can it?"

The two of them just stood and glared at each other. Jared took three loud breaths through his nose before finally saying, "Tosh, get out."

"Jared, this was my idea…"

Jared whipped around. "That's worse, Tosh, you're supposed to be the good one!" he yelled. "Aren't you in enough trouble as it is? Never in a million years would I expect this from you. I should report this…"

"NO," I shouted and grabbed his arm. "Please don't, I just wanted to see what Beck was going through tonight. I begged Nikki to help me. Please don't be mad."

Jared pulled my hand off his arm. "I'm way past mad. Now get out of here. Nikki and I need to have a talk."

It was the third time I'd been kicked out of somewhere today, and it wasn't getting any easier. Slowly I turned away, my feet feeling like lead as I trudged toward the door.

"I hope it was worth it," Jared growled behind me.

"Me too," I cried and shut the door.

Chapter Twenty-nine

The morning came early and I wasn't prepared. My eyes were swollen and my muscles ached from the heaving sobs I couldn't control throughout the night. Nikki never came back to our room, so either she and Jared made up, or she was dead. Obviously she wasn't dead, but she definitely could have been kicked out of the manor. Several times during the night I thought for sure the footsteps I heard coming down the hall were for me, turned in by Jared and thrown out of the manor on my ass for making a stupid plea to my sister.

Practice started in fifteen minutes and I was still lying in bed. I rubbed my face, pulled the blankets down, and placed my feet on the ground. I sat on the edge of the bed for nearly a minute just staring at the floor. The problem I was having was did I want to get up and change when I would most likely get kicked out of practice anyway? No, I didn't. I was sick of the humiliation. Devin could go screw, every one of them could.

But I was a schmuck and put weight into my feet to stand from the bed. There was no time for a shower, and I didn't really care that I probably smelled. Not that any of the boys ever smelled particularly nice, so I could let them suffer for once. As I pulled on my uniform, images of the wolf phasing flashed in my head. It's one of the reasons I didn't sleep all night, I couldn't stop seeing him phase. The amount of pain, the sound of breaking bones, and the sad, uncontrollable change from man to monster. Seeing the phase was supposed to be my turning point, but I couldn't just say it, I had to act on it. Beckett was gone, either dead or now fully entrenched in Garrett's pack. So it was time to start going back to life, my life that I had planned out so well before Mr. Asshole Dawes showed up.

Just as I sat back down on the bed to lace up my boots, Nikki walked into the room. She looked exhausted as she padded across the floor toward her bed, her hair disheveled and she was wearing the same clothes from last night.

"You ok?" I asked as she fell down on her bed.

"Uh huh," she replied face down in her pillow.

"You didn't come back, I wasn't sure what happened with you two."

"Sex, lots of sex."

"What?" I said and began making my bed. "How's that possible? He was furious. I thought he was going to throw you out."

Nikki slowly rolled onto her back, but placed her hands over her eyes. "We always had the best sex after a fight. It's probably why we fight so much."

"Um…ok. Why didn't you stay down there?"

Nikki looked up at me and shook her head. "So young, so naïve."

"What?" I replied defensively and dug around in my food drawer for an energy bar.

"Fine, baby sister, pay attention. I left for two reasons. One, I'm making his cold heart grow fonder. Two, I needed to get some fucking sleep and have him leave me alone for more than ten minutes. You know, take the toy away so that he'll want it more."

"Seriously?"

"Yeah, but it's more about getting some sleep. Close the blinds on your way out?"

I grabbed my weapons bag from the dresser and headed toward the door. "Don't you have class?"

She shook her head and pulled the comforter around her back. "Not until later. The blinds?"

Once she plunged her head underneath the pillow I knew the conversation was over.

"Thanks for last night, Nik. I'll make it up to you," I said and pushed the button for the automatic blinds.

Nikki muttered something unintelligible from underneath her pillow and I left the room. What a change the last few days had been for us, I thought as I started down the big spiral staircase while trying to eat the dry energy bar. I only wished that Nikki and I could have been this way earlier.

So many years wasted hating each other for reasons we still couldn't express, but maybe that was all behind us. I didn't want her living in my room for the rest of my life, but it was good to know there was someone else in my corner. We were all each other had and we've never taken that seriously. Maybe the situation with Beckett....

No. Nope, not going to think about him. It needed to stop and I needed to move on. He made his choice, and I'd never have the kind of closure I wanted or deserved. I stuffed the remainder of the energy bar in my mouth and headed out to the courtyard.

"Cush!" Connor called behind me.

I turned around to find him jogging toward me. "Hey, what's up?"

He slowed his pace and the two of us walked together down the corridor past the library and down the stairs that would take us outside. "Not much. How are you feeling today?"

I shrugged. "Fine. Why?"

"Just checking. After yesterday..."

"I was fine yesterday until Devin kicked me out."

Connor pulled me to a stop. "If you don't like it, then do something about it."

I scrunched my brows together and replied, "Like what? To whom? Devin? The co-leader of the coven? Sounds like a great plan, Connor."

Connor narrowed his eyes at me, a look he gave me often when I wouldn't just give in to him. "Do what you want, Cush. Just some friendly advice. But hell, what do I know? It's not like I've worked with him for almost fifty years."

Nikki's bitchiness was rubbing off on me, I thought as Connor left my side. I took a breath before stepping out onto the field. With each step a layer of dread cascaded over me. How much embarrassment and humiliation would today hold for me?

I barely put my weapons bag down before Connor shouted, "Start running, you dogs."

All five of us pushed off and began our run around the courtyard. My legs didn't feel as sluggish as the other day, so that was definitely a good sign. My lungs were open and taking in easy breaths rather than gasping for air. By the time we started our third lap around, Devin was in the courtyard consulting with Connor. But rather than panic at the sight of him, I just kept my head up and trudged through. My mind was empty, easy breaths in and out, and my muscles hadn't really started to burn.

"Hey," Roberts said behind me, "you trying to make us look bad?"

"What?" I replied and then looked back to find that I had pulled ahead of everyone with Princess pulling up the rear almost half a lap back.

"Keep it up, Scarecrow. Keep it up!"

I laughed and gave my legs a little push. Both Devin and Connor were eyeing me as I came around to start the fourth lap, but I didn't let it distract me. Nice, easy breaths, and nothing else swirling around in my head. It was just a run around the courtyard like I'd done hundreds of times, although I had never lapped anyone until now. Princess was struggling just like I had the other day. His breath was short and wheezing, his legs barely having any kick.

"Come on, Princess," I said as I came up behind him.

"Go...fuck...yourself," he said between ragged breaths.

"Wish I could," I replied. "I'd probably be in a better mood."

He gave a breathless laugh and then a cough. "Sorry."

"It's ok, we'll go in together."

Princess gave me a look before tripping and being forced to look forward.

After only a couple of minutes Roberts came up behind us. "Is this...a party?"

"Not anymore," I said making Princess cough when he tried to laugh. "Pull your gate back, Princess. That'll help."

Princess gave a nod and adjusted his gate. Apparently, the change was enough to annoy Roberts so he went on ahead to finish first, but I stayed to cheer Princess along, not that he really deserved it but I felt bad. As we approached the front of the courtyard, Connor gave the signal to bring it in.

"Thank god," Princess said breathlessly, and roughly fifteen seconds later he was able to stumble to a stop. He put his hands on his knees and bent over to catch his breath. "Thanks, Scarecrow. Not sure what's wrong with me today."

"It happens," I replied, knowing firsthand.

"Listen up," Devin said and all of us immediately stood at attention, "as part of our final decision, one or more of you will be participating in a final challenge. Some in the coven might call it a fear challenge, but whatever it is considered, it will determine if you're inducted or not."

Devin's gaze moved over to where I stood.

"Scarecrow," he said and looked at me, "I saw that you chose to help Princess with his laps. Why?"

"Um...because he needed help?" I answered tentatively.

"And you did so even though he didn't help you two days ago when you were in distress while running. Why?"

This was a trick and I couldn't figure out the angle. "I helped because I could, and it was the right thing to do."

"Interesting," Devin replied and stepped past us. "Let's get going. Thank you, Tosh, you're dismissed."

My stomach fell as the others turned to follow Devin into the center of the courtyard. Connor's eyes bugged out at me, urging me to do something.

"No."

The one word escaped my lips before I could stop it. Everyone stopped and Devin turned around very slowly.

He narrowed his eyes before saying, "What was that?"

I swallowed hard and shifted my weight evenly between my feet. "No...sir."

The group parted ways as Devin stepped between them. My heart was pounding up through my throat as he came closer and finally stopped a couple of feet in front of me.

"You're disobeying an order?"

I bit the inside of my cheek before sighing and responding, "I've fought for a year to be in this program. I had one bad day and you keep punishing me for it. I deserve to be here."

"You should remember that you are here at my discretion. Now go."

"N-no."

In one quick movement, Devin grabbed the back of my shirt and began dragging me toward the manor. I kicked my feet out front and dug my heels in, creating thick grooves in the soft grass. The change in weight distribution caused the back of my shirt to rip until Devin lost his grip and I fell to the ground. Quickly I pushed myself up and ran to my weapons bag, pulling out from within it my silver-coated whip and in the split second it took Devin to come at me again I lashed it out and caught his arm. Devin stopped and looked down at the gash on his arm that quickly started to heal.

"You dare strike the leader of your coven?"

"I won't win against you, but I will fight until I cannot kick or scream because all my bones are broken and my vocal cords are bleeding. I'm not leaving!"

Devin wiped the thin trail of blood that was left from the healed wound and then looked at me with a smile. "Welcome back, Natasha Cushlin. We've missed you."

My face fell and my grip on my whip loosened. "Wh-what?"

"All right, everyone, let's continue where we left off yesterday," Devin said as he walked back through the group.

I stood shocked, even letting my whip fall out of my hand onto the ground.

Connor gave me a one-sided smile. "I told you…"

"Don't," I interrupted.

"You should listen to me more often."

I smiled. "That's sounds painful."

"Can we get to work now?"

My body sang with relief. "Yes, please."

"You're almost there, Cush," Connor shouted as I rolled onto my back.

"My face is broken," I replied as I carefully circled my jaw around. I was being dramatic, but I had literally fallen flat on my face eleven times.

"Even if that was true, your face will heal. Now get up and let's do it again. You've got to pull back more in order to get the momentum to launch forward. You can do this, Cush, come on."

I groaned and pushed myself back up to my feet. Everything hurt – my hips, back, shoulders, even my boobs hurt and there wasn't much to them. After securing my knives back in their holder, I shook my whips to get the stress out of my arms and wrists.

With a big exhale, I circled my whips around in the air and snapped them in front of Connor. When I snapped them at him again, he grabbed an end in each hand and pulled. I tightened my grip and leaned my weight back even further, as Connor instructed, until the tension was just right. Using the momentum from Connor's pull, I flew through the air toward him, let go of my whips, and just as I pulled the knives from my back, my body met the ground face first.

"Well, you were closer this time," Connor laughed. I looked up from the ground and saw that his feet were only inches away from where I had fallen. "Ok, one more time and we'll call it a day."

Once again I stepped away from him and shook the tension out of my arms. With another big exhale, I swung my whips around and snapped them in front of Connor's face. Quickly he grabbed each end, and as he pulled forward, I leaned my weight back until I couldn't hold on for a second longer. I relaxed and allowed myself to be flung forward, grabbed my knives from my back and plunged them down. Since the knives weren't coated in silver they bounced off of Connor's chest and my body basically wrapped around him.

When I lifted my head from his shoulder, he was smiling at me. "Told ya you could do it."

"Like you said, I should listen to you more often."

He laughed and gave me a squeeze before lowering me to the ground. Practice was officially over and every muscle in my body was aching.

"You come back and somehow I still get paired up with Bush," Roberts said next to me. "How is that possible?"

I laughed and pulled my weapons bag onto my shoulder. "I would have rather worked with Bush than fall on my face over and over again. I'm sure it was Connor's messed up way of punishing me."

Together we started walking through the courtyard toward the manor, which was odd since I couldn't remember the last time Roberts had given me the time of day. It was like walking with my old friend Trevor, not the asshole Roberts who was completely focused on becoming a Warrior and stomping on anyone who got in his way.

"So what do you think of this fear challenge thing?" he asked as we stepped up into the manor's corridor.

"I don't know," I replied. "I would be ok with it if it didn't have that word fear involved. But I'm guessing if you pass, you're in, so whatever it is, it won't kill us."

"Yeah, I guess so," he replied skeptically.

"Trevor, you've got this. You know you're going to get the spot."

He shook his head. "It's so close and I'm afraid I'm going lose it. I've given up everything to be here...shit, I'm sorry. I shouldn't be saying this to you."

"Don't be sorry," I said as we started up the spiral staircase. "We used to be friends, remember? Nothing wrong with saying how you're feeling. I know I totally screwed up and I have no one to blame but myself."

"I'm hoping they'll be two spots, one for each of us."

I smiled politely. "You keep hoping that."

"I will," he said as we reached our landing.

"See you tomorrow, Roberts."

"Tomorrow's Friday, Scarecrow," he replied. "Two days away and you're already forgetting our day off?"

Friday? Holy shit, was tomorrow already Friday? This whole week had been a blur. I was barely registering hours, let alone days. Friday, wow.

When I opened the door to my room I found Nikki stretched out on her bed reading a thick hardback book that was so tall it was sitting on her stomach.

"Hey," I said and threw my bag on the bed, "how was class?"

"Fine," she replied from behind the book. "Bombed my exam, but then I went to the library."

I sat down on the edge of my bed and began unlacing my boots. "I can see that. It seriously looks like you're reading an ancient book of spells. I wasn't aware that was part of your curriculum."

"If you must know," she said nastily, although still choosing to keep the book up between us, "it's a book about folklore."

"Folklore? Seriously?"

"Well how else am I going to read up on werewolves?"

"What?" I said loudly and stood from the bed. "W-why?"

Finally Nikki was irritated enough to let the book fall down into her lap. "Because I saw a guy change into a wolf last night, it kinda piqued my interest. Is that ok with you?"

I shrugged uncomfortably and went to my dresser. As I pulled out a pair of clean yoga pants I asked, "So…anything…interesting?"

"Yes, actually," she replied and pulled the book back up.

"Like?" I asked and pulled a T-shirt out along with a pair of underwear.

"Are you sure?"

I sighed and shook my head. "No, no I'm done. That's what last night was for. I'm done," I said and walked to the bathroom. I had barely taken a step inside before my brain turned my body around and peeked around the corner. "But if you *wanted* to tell me something interesting you…"

"The penis gets bigger," she interrupted.

"Wh…sorry?"

She gave me a devilish smile. "You asked for something interesting, that was it."

"Yeah, but…"

"The book says it happens after the first phase. Actually, many features enlarge– muscles, feet, hands, and the penis."

"But how…who did the research to figure that out? And then write about it!"

We both broke out into hysterical laughter. The whole idea was preposterous, and yet something everyone would focus on. I couldn't remember the last time we had laughed like that together.

"Now shower and we'll go get dinner," she said and I ducked into the bathroom.

The hot water from the shower felt wonderful as it sank deeply into my aching muscles. It was one thing I never truly understood about my condition. I could break a bone, and it would heal within a few hours. However, I would still get headaches and lactic acid build up in my muscles. I guess I couldn't be completely invincible.

As I gave my hair a final rinse, I heard the bathroom door open.

"Nik?"

"Did you know," she began without any acknowledgement, "that in order to become the pack leader, you have to fight to the death?"

I turned off the water and pulled back the shower curtain to find my towel. "Why would anyone ever want to be pack leader, then?"

"Same reason men do everything else, more power," she replied and then looked back into the bedroom. "Someone's at the door. Want me to get it?"

"Yes, please. I think I'd give them a bit more than they were planning on," I laughed.

"But they'd get a look at those scars you hide so consciously," she said and left the bathroom.

My hand rested on my scars, my fingers resting in the grooves of what Beckett called the three fingers. It was rare that Nikki ever acknowledged my scars. It was easy to say that she didn't care, but there were times I thought it was because she denied that I was her sister when I needed her most. But all of that didn't matter anymore. What mattered was that I was starving, and I was going to have dinner with my sister for the first in decades.

I towel-dried my hair and slipped on my clean clothes, all the while trying to listen in on what was happening in the bedroom. Nikki hadn't come back, so maybe it was Jared. It broke my heart that they couldn't have any easy relationship. It was also hard not to side with Jared, I knew how big of a bitch Nikki could be.

The lingering steam wafted out of the bathroom as I opened the door. Nikki was instantly in front of me with wide, warning eyes.

"Connor is here," she said slowly and opened herself up to reveal Connor standing by the door with a plate in his hand.

"Hey, I brought you dinner," he said and held up the plate in his hand. "I thought we could hang out or something."

"Won't that be fun," Nikki said and then stepped over to her bed. "I'll leave you guys to it, then."

"What? You're leaving?"

Nikki nodded with her back to me and I could see that she was putting the big book of werewolf folklore into her school bag. "Of course I'm leaving, you don't need a third wheel."

"But where will you go," I said and grabbed her arm.

Nikki turned around and smirked. "I'll go down to Jared's. He'll be looking for me later anyway."

"I believe Jared's working another mission tonight," Connor said and placed the dinner plate onto my bed.

"That's ok," Nikki replied and pulled her school bag up over her shoulder. "I have lots of reading to do." She waggled her eyebrows at me before stepping around Connor and heading to the door. "Have fun. Don't do anything I wouldn't do." She opened the door and turned around to look at me. "Don't do anything I would either. 'Night."

Once the door shut, Connor raised his eyebrow at me. "She's a real piece of work. I don't know how you stand her."

I shrugged and stepped over to my bed. "She's my sister and we've had to go through a lot in our lives."

Connor handed me the dinner plate as I sat down at the head of the bed. "Yes, but you didn't turn into a mega bitch."

"And she was activated by a sociopath, so who knows how much of it is her and how much of that is Aidan."

Connor sat down perpendicular in the middle of the bed and pressed his back up against the wall. It was honestly a little closer than I was prepared for, but he brought me food and I didn't have to walk up and down that retched spiral staircase in order to eat.

"I forget she was activated by him," he said and unfolded my legs to drape them over his. "I was there the night we took her from that warehouse. Did I ever tell you that?"

"I don't think so," I said, trying to remember back. "Um, silverware?"

"Oh yeah," he replied and handed me a fork and knife from his back pants pocket. "Yep, I was driving that night. She was all over Cameron the whole way home."

I laughed and cut into the chicken breast on my plate. "Not surprised there. So, what are you really doing here?"

Connor flinched as I popped a piece of chicken in my mouth. "I wanted to hang out?"

I raised an eyebrow at him and bit into a piece of broccoli. After I swallowed, I replied, "You haven't wanted to hang with me in weeks unless it was to have a training session."

"Well, you've been...occupied," he replied and clicked the remote for the TV.

My stomach fluttered at Connor's dig, so I popped another piece of chicken in my mouth to cover up any reaction he might have been looking for.

"Thanks for the food."

"No problem," he replied and placed his hand on top of my leg. I stopped chewing and focused on his hand. This was trouble, and not just a hangout session. "You looked really good today, by the way."

"Thanks. It felt good today. Did they give you an idea of when they're making their decision?"

He shook his head. "Nope, just that they decided to add this extra challenge. Shouldn't be long now, though."

"Think I still have a chance?"

He looked at me and squeezed my calf. "Yeah. If they take two, then yeah."

"And if they take one it'll be Roberts?"

"Most likely," he answered and tossed the remote on the end of the bed. "Couple weeks ago I would have said it was a toss-up, but you were..."

"Occupied?"

He smirked and guided my legs off of him. "Exactly. But that's not a problem anymore, and you've come back. You just can't have something like that happen again. You can't be a Warrior one day and then be all emo the next, it just doesn't work that way, Cush."

"Great talk as always, Connor."

"But you're doing good now, all that other stuff is out of the picture and you have a good chance now."

That was it, my appetite was gone. I leaned over and placed my half-eaten plate on the nightstand, but when I rocked back into place Connor had stretched along the wall and propped himself up against my pillow.

"What are you doing?" I asked.

He raised his eyebrows and tried to look innocent. "What? We used to sit and watch movies all the time."

I tilted my head and gave him a skeptical look, because that's not all we had done. Connor was horny twenty-four-seven, and when he was in a lull he would come find me. It wasn't something I was proud of, but I was lonely too. This was the start of something, it always was, but was I cheating on Beckett?

No. Beckett left me. It's not cheating if you got dumped by a coward, and Connor was pretty good looking. Muscular, cut jaw, and a cute squint in his eyes when he smiled. He was a decent kisser, although you had to deal with the cold lips and tongue. But making out with someone who Beckett couldn't stand seemed like great revenge.

"Earth to Tosh," Connor said, making me blink and shake back into reality. "Where did you go?"

"Nowhere you want to know," I replied.

Slowly I turned my back to him and laid up against his chest. It didn't take long for him to rest his hand on top of mine, it was how things always started. After a couple of minutes, he started tracing the back of my hand with his fingertips. When I didn't stop him, he took my hand and slowly slid it between us, placing it in the crouch of his pants. I sighed as he began kneading my hand against him causing him to grow underneath. Had to give it to him though, he was very well-endowed, but he also knew it and would often make it seem as though he was giving me some kind of gift by allowing me to handle it.

Connor nuzzled into the back of my neck and pulled my wet hair to the side. I stared at the TV as he guided my hand inside his pants and adjusted his penis to be fully erect. He released a loud exhale and grazed the tips of his fangs on the thin, sensitive skin of my neck.

"Do you consent?" he said softly in my ear, nibbling the tip of my earlobe while he waited for my answer.

But what was my answer? This was trouble, I could feel it in my bones. It would purely be for revenge. Was that so bad? It didn't mean anything to Connor, it never had, so what was the harm in having a little fun.

"Yes, I consent," I said softly and within a second, Connor's fangs were sinking into my skin. I gasped and my hand reflexively tightened around Connor's penis, causing him to grunt deeply from his throat while he sucked lightly at my neck. The relaxation from the bite began to flow through my body. Biting and feeding was a tricky formula. If you fed too long, you'd put your partner to sleep. If you bit anywhere else besides the neck, the relaxation was less. However, Connor was a pro at knowing the balance between relaxing his partner enough to lessen her inhibitions, but not turning her into a ball of mush that couldn't do what he wanted.

Connor removed his fangs from my neck and licked the wounds closed. Slowly I rolled around to face him, my muscles feeling loose and humming with anticipation. Connor unzipped his pants and pulled his overwhelming manhood out, seemingly looking for me to marvel at his presentation. It took all my strength not to roll my eyes. He wrapped his hand around the back of my neck and pushed me down towards his crotch.

When I resisted, he scrunched his brows together. "What's the matter? You've done it before?"

"I know," I replied nervously. "I want more, that's all."

Connor tilted his head back and tentatively I placed my lips on his. He wasn't very responsive until I wrapped my hand around his manhood once again and began stroking him. His eyes closed in pleasure and his breath wafted against my face. After another stroke of my hand, he pressed his lips into mine and I slipped my tongue into his mouth being careful not to prick my tongue on his fangs that were still extended. His hand went to my breast, squeezing what little was there. His touch wasn't right it was rough and on the verge of painful. It wasn't anything like the tenderness that Beckett showed me.

Damn it! Fuck Beckett. Get revenge on Beckett and fuck Connor.

I pulled away from Connor and bent down to take his penis into my mouth. He moaned and entangled his fingers into my hair, something I didn't like. It was hard enough to breathe and not choke without him holding my head down. I smacked at his hand, and he loosened his grip enough for me to be able to work my magic tongue around him. He moaned and put his hand through my hair again.

I rose back up and his eyes shot open. "Don't stop," he begged.

"I told you I want more," I replied and pulled my shirt over my head. I crawled up to him, but he quickly put his hands up in front of him.

"What are you doing?"

I froze. "I-I thought it was clear."

Connor knitted his brows together and gestured at my scars. "I didn't think that meant...this."

"I can have sex, Connor."

"Seriously?"

"Yes!"

"Come on, I mean...who wants to see that."

The blood drained from my face. I was exposed and being rejected just like in my nightmares. Quickly I pushed myself off the bed and began searching for my shirt.

"Oh come on, Cush..."

"Don't!" I shouted and picked my shirt up off the floor. "Get out."

"You've got to be kidding."

"GET OUT!" I screamed and pulled my shirt over my head, securing it safely to cover my scars once again.

Connor tucked himself back into his pants and zipped them up. "This is bullshit, Tosh. I came here..."

"You came here because your usual sources dried up."

He exhaled tensely and rose from the bed. "I came to see you and have a little fun, not to see fucking melted skin. Seriously, what am I supposed to do? Whatever you can do can't really be considered sex."

"That's not true," I said, trying to fight the tears welling up in my eyes.

"What man could stay hard seeing that?"

"Beckett, that's who," I replied and felt my stomach drop. "We...he made love to me and it was wonderful."

"Yeah, and he left you, Tosh," he said in a flat, nasty tone.

My nostrils flared and I clamped my jaw down for several seconds before finally being able to say, "Just go."

"Gladly," he replied and stepped past me. "You're a piece of work, just like your fucking sister."

I didn't respond, but did flinch when he slammed the door. My knees shook and I collapsed into the floor. Deep, heaving sobs came out of me, some so hard they made me cough. I was back to being a freak. Beckett was the only person who could see past my scars and he was gone. I had put myself out there like everyone nagged me about, and I was humiliated. How was I expected to survive like this? It was hopeless. I would die alone, having been teased by finding someone who loved me for who I was, and not be disgusted by the scars that were carved into my body.

But now those scars were joined with one more, the one that was jaggedly cut into my heart. Like those on my legs and abdomen, it wouldn't heal. Feeling the deepening pain in my chest I now realized why people felt as though they would die of a broken heart. I was pathetic. For a moment I thought I was just like everyone else, for a moment I was normal, and now I was once again the hideous creature of the deep that no one wanted. Fuck Beckett. Fuck Connor. Fuck the world.

Chapter Thirty

"Nikki?" I groaned into my pillow at the sound of her phone vibrating. It had gone off several times in the last five minutes and the sun wasn't even up yet. "Nikki, answer your damn phone."

My sudden anger woke me up enough to realize and remember that Nikki never came back to the room last night. She would rather die than be without her cell phone. So what the fuck?

After a few seconds the room was calm and dark and quiet. Just as my eyes relaxed enough to close securely, the phone vibrated again.

"What the hell!" I said aloud and flung the blankets off of me. I stood from the bed and looked blankly around my room. When the vibrating sound came again, I looked to my right toward the nightstand. My phone was sitting there with a blank screen, and then it hit me.

My hand shook as I opened the nightstand's drawer and saw Beckett's phone lit up through the cracks on its face. I pulled the phone from within the drawer and unlocked it. There were several messages, all from an unknown number.

The first message read: Tosha?

The second: Tosha, u there?

Third: Please Tosha

The phone slipped out of my hand but I caught it in midair. I just stared at the screen in shock. Was it Beckett? Had he survived his first phase? Or was it really Garrett on the other side waiting to lure me away from the manor. But did he know I had Beckett's phone? How could he? Unless…

The phone vibrated again and the shock caused me to drop the phone on the ground. I stared at the phone for at least a minute before picking it up and revealing a new message: Please talk to me.

After a slow exhale, I typed: Who is this?

The ellipsis began to blink on the screen, and then: Tosha? It's Beckett! Thank god you found my phone.

My stomach flipped and I had to sit back down on the bed. My heart began to pound in my chest. This could still be a trick.

Send a pic to prove it's you.

Can't. Using a friend's phone, only have a second. I miss the wave, three fingers, and the star.

A mixture of laughter and tears came out of me, I wasn't sure what to feel. I had to stay calm and not completely give into him, and the restraint was causing me to flinch.

The ellipsis returned and then one line: I need to see you.

My heart jumped into my throat. I wanted to see him too. I wanted to punch him in the face, but also hug him. It was sick, and I couldn't explain all the feelings that were flooding over me. I was so happy he was alive, but I couldn't let go of the hatred I felt for him after what he did to me. It was confusing, let alone against the restrictions that had been placed upon me.

Please Tosha.

My jaw clinched and my leg began to bounce. My fingers hovered over the phone for several seconds before finally typing: Where?

Our motel, noon.

Our motel? Would the torture never end? I looked at the clock. It would take me three hours to get there meaning I would need to leave pretty soon.

Shit! What was I thinking?! Was I seriously considering this? There was something wrong with me. If I got caught, I would lose everything. But how could I not take this chance to see him.

Tosha, please, the Warriors r n trouble.

Oh now he was playing dirty. He knew I wouldn't be able to resist a chance to help the coven. What was I supposed to do? Ignore him? Report him to Jared? But if I did, what would they do to him? But if I got caught, I would lose everything. Was seeing Beckett one more time worth it?

Finally I typed: I'll be armed. I won't hesitate to kill you.

He replied: No tricks, baby.

Baby? *Baby*? Who the hell did he think he was calling me baby?

Angrily I stood up from the bed and headed into the shower since I would need to leave within the hour in order to get to that motel by noon.

Baby?

What a jackass, I thought as I flipped the shower on and stepped inside, not even bothering to wait for it to get warm. I was angry enough that the cold shower felt good against my hot skin.

Baby? As if nothing had happened between us, as if he hadn't thrown me away like a piece of garbage. Baby! The nerve of him.

My anger pushed me along through the rest of the morning rituals and before I knew it, I was lacing up my boots and pulling my weapons bag up onto my shoulder. As I reached for the doorknob, my chest suddenly felt heavy. One false move, one lie not covered, and I was doomed. However, despite that, my hand turned the knob and I bolted out of my room. If I didn't keep moving, I would certainly lose my nerve.

Finally I was at the bottom of the spiral staircase and heading toward the double front doors. Only a few more feet and I would be...

"Natasha?"

I froze and tightened my grip on the strap of my bag. Slowly I turned around and found Cameron standing in front of me with a quizzical look on his face.

"Good morning, sir," I said, and wondered if I could hide the fear from my face.

"Where are you off to this morning?" he asked politely.

"School," I said so loudly from nerves that it made him flinch. "Now that everything's finished, I thought I could try and talk to my professors about making up the work."

The answer flowed out of my mouth so easily I barely recognized it was me talking. Somehow the deceitfulness that usually only showed itself in Nikki was pulling me through now.

Cameron gave a slight nod as he replied, "Ah yes, I see. I am sure you will be able to make up the work, but if there is anything I can do to help with your professors, please let me know."

"Thank you, sir. I guess I'll…"

"But answer me one thing, do you often take your weapons bag to class with you?"

Damn he noticed everything, absolutely everything. I smiled nervously and answered, "Well, you never know who might be lurking in the bushes. Better to be prepared than not."

"I wish you did not have to be so prepared," he said and started to walk toward his office, "but god bless anyone who would try and jump out of those bushes at you."

His faith in me was a stab to the heart. I lied to Cameron and he had done nothing but go to bat for me. He and Brianna were the parents I wish I had, and yet here I was. It would be easy enough to stand Beckett up, give him a little of his own medicine. My left foot rocked back, but the path to the front door drew me back in. Before I changed my mind again, I stepped quickly through the tall double doors and practically ran to my car. My beautiful safe haven, my baby Merc that I paid for all by myself.

Once my weapons bag was secured in the passenger seat and my road trip soundtrack was set, I pulled out of the manor's parking area and drove through the tall black gate. I waved to the guard as I sped out of the driveway, kicking up a bit of loose gravel as I pulled out onto the road. Before speeding around the corner, I gave the manor one last look, just in case.

There wasn't much to do on a three-hour drive but jam out to music, and think. I had determined that my need to rebel was due to what I was calling the Nikki gene. Nikki always did the opposite of what she should and was never deterred by the risk of her actions. Obviously I wasn't as bad as my sister, but the fact that I lied to my coven leader and was a mile from meeting Beckett showed that the gene was pretty powerful.

The road banked to the right and the motel's sign became visible. My heart started to pound, and my hands became sweaty on the steering wheel. There was only one car parked in the motel's parking lot. Was it his? How would I know? Shit, a detail that we obviously missed. I pulled into the motel and stopped in front of the office. The same attendant from last time was sitting behind the counter. Reluctantly he looked up from his TV as I entered the office and then held his hand up.

"He's in room six," he said without looking up from his TV. "He only paid for an hour, so…"

He didn't finish his sentence, but from his tone it was obvious that this motel specialized in their hourly rates. Our overnight stay a few days ago must have been very odd for them. I got back in my car, and slowly pulled in next to the only other car in the lot which happened to be parked in front of room six.

This was it. Behind that door I would either see Beckett, or be killed, or get kidnapped, all of which seemed to be on the same nerve-wracking level. I pulled my weapons belt out of my bag and latched it around my waist. Next I attached a whip on both hips, and slid a knife into the side of my boot.

My guard went up when I stepped out of my car again, making sure to look around at all my surroundings. With a big exhale I stepped toward room six and knocked. Through the door I could hear someone shuffling around. My hand reflexively rested on the handle of the whip on my right hip. A moment later the doorknob turned, my breath caught in my throat, and the door opened.

Beckett stood in the doorway, well at least a version of him. He had gained muscle in his arms, chest and shoulders, and was wearing sunglasses. Did he think he was a movie star or something? And how did he gain that much muscle weight so quickly? Was the folklore book right?

"Uh…hi," he said nervously and scratched the back of his neck. "Wanna come in?"

"No, I drove three hours to stand out here," I replied sarcastically.

He tightened his lip and gestured inside the motel room.

"You can stay over by the door," I said as I passed him and began looking around the room for any evidence that someone else was here.

After I had cleared the bathroom he said, "I told you, no tricks."

"*Baby*," I said nastily and pulled up the blankets to check under the bed. "No tricks, *baby*, that's what you said."

"Yeah," he replied and rubbed the back of his neck again. "I realized after I sent that it was probably not a good…"

"Why am I here?" I interrupted and stood in the middle of the room, confident that we were alone.

He paused a moment, seemingly testing the waters before he replied,

"Tosha, I understand that you're upset with me."

"You don't understand anything, Beckett. Why am I here?"

He took a tentative step toward me, still wearing those stupid sunglasses. "At the risk of getting hit, I would say you're partly here because you wanted to see me. Honestly, I'm hoping it's a big reason you're here."

"Then you'd be mistaken," I replied and his shoulders fell.

"I deserve that."

"You said the Warriors were in trouble. Is that true or just a way to get me here?"

He shrugged and gave me his cute, innocent smile. "Both?"

I wanted to slap that smile right off his face. "Look, I took a risk coming here, and chose not to send the whole coven after you. If I get caught, I will get kicked out of the program. So tell me whatever it is you dragged me out here for, or get out of my way."

Beckett sighed and his shoulders fell slightly, although those fucking sunglasses stayed on his fucking face.

"Yeah, I get it, I do," he began and then leaned his back up against the wall with his arms crossed. "Garrett is coming for the coven."

"We assumed that."

"He's also recruiting wolf packs to form an army. That's actually why I'm allowed out at the moment. He thinks I'm helping recruit a pack about an hour from here, but he's bringing in packs from all over the place."

"Why is he recruiting wolves and not vamps?"

He shook his head. "It's a long story, but his numbers are growing. He only has a dozen vamps, but he's combined three packs so far and there a couple of outlier packs that are providing support. He wants an army before taking down the Warriors, and I'm pretty sure he's going right for the manor."

"Do you have proof?"

He shook his head again. "Not yet, just bits and pieces I've gathered from Floyd."

"Floyd? Who's Floyd?"

He smiled and pushed himself off the wall. "Floyd is a wolf from the original pack. Come to find out that he and a few others aren't too happy about the alignment with Garrett."

"Then why don't they just leave?"

"Can't," he replied. "You're under the will of the pack leader."

"Then how are you here?"

"I'm supposed to be helping Floyd convince this pack to help us, but he's covering for me so that I can see you."

I nodded and looked at my watch. "Well, thank you for making me drive all this way for something that could have been shared through a text."

Beckett stepped in front of me as I headed toward the door. "Tosha, please…"

"Don't," I shouted and placed my hand on my whip. "Step away from the door, Beckett, or so help me I will…"

"Tosha, please just give me a chance to explain why…"

"Oh, now you want to explain? After you already ripped out my heart you want to spit on it and shove it back in?"

"That's not what I'm trying to do, Tosha, I swear."

"Fuck you," I said and pushed him aside.

Quickly he grabbed my arm and turned me back around to face him. I countered by throwing my arms up and then thrusting my palm into his solar plexus. In an instant he barreled over and started coughing.

"I risked everything for you!" I yelled. "I gave you absolutely every part of me after you wore me down, begging me to trust you and let you in. Then you throw me away like some whore and make me drag myself back home in shame. And then you ask me to come here and you don't even have the decency to take off your fucking sunglasses? Fuck you, and fuck Garrett, and fuck Floyd, whoever the fuck he is. When you guys come for us, we will be ready and I will have no qualms about killing every single one of you."

I turned to leave and Beckett grabbed my arm once again. "Look at me."

My body froze, not wanting to give into him so quickly. When I turned around, he was fumbling to take his sunglasses off. The sight of his eyes made me flinch so hard that my arm jerked from his grip. His dark hybrid eyes were gone and replaced with an inhuman bright, glowing green.

"This is why I wore the glasses," he said, pointing to his eyes and then rubbing his chest. "They're a little…off-putting."

"Why are they…green?" I asked and placed my hand up to my mouth as the emotions started to creep up my throat.

"Interesting fact, hybrid blood plus werewolf infection equals green eyes apparently."

I cleared my throat and pointed to his newly broadened shoulders. "Is that where the uh...muscles came from?"

He nodded. "Yeah, almost overnight. Pretty painful, actually, but nothing like that first phase..."

"Stop, please," I said and had to sit down on the bed. A fit of nausea came over me, causing me to fold over my knees. Images of the prisoner transforming into a wolf flashed in my head, as well as the agonizing sounds of pain and breaking bones.

Beckett knelt down in front of me and rested his head against my knees. I didn't push him away, not even when his hand started to rub my calf. "I'm so sorry, Tosha. I never meant for any of this to happen."

Slowly I sat up, causing Beckett to lift his head from my knees and stare at me with eyes I didn't know. He was a stranger looking back at me. I placed my hands on either side of his face and immediately noticed how much warmer he was, almost as if he had a fever. With my right hand, I traced the lines on his forehead and into his hair. Carefully Beckett inched forward, his lips parting ever so slightly and keeping his bright eyes focused on me until our lips met. He was so warm, and his kiss was as soft as I remembered, but then a pain hit the bottom of my stomach and I pulled away.

Beckett's eyes flashed open. "Tosha?"

"Why didn't you trust me? We could have figured something out."

Beckett sighed and sat back on his heels. "Tosha," he began, but then rubbed his face with hands. "When Victor figured out what I was, all he kept hinting at was that without help from other wolves, I could hurt those close to me. I couldn't hurt you or my mom, or anyone else in the manor. That's why I was trying to leave..."

"I would have helped you," I cried.

He wrapped his hand around mine and squeezed it tightly. "And for a moment I thought so too, which is why I gave in and let you come with me." Beckett rose back up on his knees, cupped my cheek with his free hand, and pulled my face to be only an inch from his. "But when we were together, I felt him coming out..."

"Wha-who?"

"The wolf, Tosha, I felt him coming over me. That's when I knew I needed to leave. The thought of hurting you made me sick, and after that first phase I knew leaving was the best decision I'd made. You have no idea how out of control phasing is..."

"I saw it," I interrupted and he pulled away from me with a confused look. "I saw the wolf at the manor phase when we had the full moon."

Beckett stood up from the floor and stepped away from the bed. "His name is Adam, did you know that?"

"Uh, no, why would I know..."

"He has a wife and kid that are struggling without him. I'm guessing you didn't know that either."

I was surprised at his sudden change in tone. "Why would I know that?"

He turned around quickly. "Exactly. The Warriors take him prisoner and don't care about who he's left behind."

"He attacked us, Beckett," I said and rose from the bed. "If his family was so important to him, then maybe he shouldn't have sided with Garrett."

Beckett laughed. "They do what the pack leader wants them to do, they don't have a choice, it's engrained."

Beckett looked at his watch and shook his head. "I need to get going. Floyd can only stall for so long with the other pack."

"Come home with me."

He looked pained as he answered, "I can't."

"Why not!" I shouted.

"I'm still learning about being a wolf, and I haven't gotten enough information about Garrett's end game. I can't, I'm sorry, I can't leave yet."

Tears rose in my eyes again and my nose began to run. I understood his reasoning, I did, but it didn't change the fact that I wanted to throw my whip around him and force him to come home with me.

Beckett took a step toward me and I quickly turned my back on him in order to wipe my eyes. A moment later Beckett's very warm fingers grazed down the length of my arms causing the hairs to stand on end.

"Please understand that this isn't easy for me," he whispered in my ear.

"Sure."

"I never stopped loving you, Tosha. Thinking of you...well, it's what gets me through the day."

When I didn't respond, Beckett took a stepped around me and headed toward the door.

"No," I said and grabbed his arm. "You don't get to just leave me again, I...I have things to say to you."

He swallowed nervously and shook his head. "Tosha, I don't have..."

"When you…" I started and knew it wasn't right. "You left me and…" I started again, but my words were failing me. After a nice deep breath, I said, "What you did is unforgivable, Beckett."

"I know."

"Don't interrupt me!" I shouted and he flinched back. "You didn't even have the balls to look me in the eye and tell me you were leaving me. You broke me, Beckett, and I don't know if I'm madder at you for doing it, or myself for letting it happen. Since you left me, I've been kicked out of practice twice and got my shoulder dislocated because I couldn't stay focused. I hate you for that. I hate you for what you turned me into. I haven't cried this much since Ty died, and I swore I would never be that way again.

"And here you are, once again controlling the situation. You get me to come out here and now you're just leaving? No, I won't accept that, I'm worth more than that."

Beckett stepped forward and wrapped his arms around me tightly. "Of course you are…"

"Let go of me," I said and pushed him away.

Once again he stepped forward and wrapped his arms around. "Tosha, I love you so much."

I pushed out of his arms again. "Liar. You've been lying to me since your father died."

"Tosha, please," he begged, "everything I've done is to protect you or help my family. Did I do everything right? No. I have this creature inside me now that I can't fully control, and I could never forgive myself if I ever did anything to hurt you. Someone was going to lose, Tosha, no matter what. But you're safe and my mom is home. It's the best I could do, and I'm sorry you hate me. I deserve it, I do, but I left *because* I love you."

"Then come home with me," I cried.

He scratched his nails through his scalp. "Please don't, Tosha…I-I don't have the strength to keep saying no."

I took the two steps between us and hugged him around the waist. Instantly I could feel the difference in his musculature. The thin chest and arms I was used to were replaced with thick muscles, and as he wrapped his arms around me I was immediately surrounded by warmth.

"I am never as weak as I am when I'm with you," I cried into his chest. He squeezed me a little tighter and kissed my hair. "I hate being in love with you."

He laughed lightly and kissed my hair again. "And I love being in love with you."

"How come we can't have a happy ending?" I asked and looked up at him.

"Our story isn't near over, Tosha," he replied and brushed my hair away from my face. "Unless you want it to be."

"Of course I don't, but…how do we do this?"

Beckett shook his head. "I don't know. Seeing you today is dangerous enough, but if you can wait…"

"We'll figure it out," I interrupted.

I curled my fingers around his neck, and pulled him down to where I could kiss him once again. He moaned as I parted my lips and crushed my body against his. One of his hands reached around to my back and pulled my shirt up until his hand could sneak underneath. As he flattened his palm against my scars, he pulled away from my lips and rested his head on my shoulder.

"You have no idea how I've missed feeling these." I laughed which caused Beckett to stand up straight. "What's funny?"

"Nothing," I replied. "It's just that…"

"What?" he asked, almost worried.

"Someone told me just yesterday that no one wanted to see my scars because they were disgusting."

Beckett took a step back and his expression changed instantly. "Disgusting?"

"Well, that's what he inferred. I think he said something like no man would want to see them."

"Who!"

"Beckett? It's ok…"

"Tell me who said that to you," he growled. "Was it Roberts? Bush? Tell me, Tosha! I'll kill him."

"Beckett, calm down," I begged and put my hand on his cheek. "My god, you're burning up."

Beckett pulled my hand away from his face and stepped to the opposite side of the room. His eyes were tightly closed as he breathed deeply in and out while being hunched over his knees. I took a step toward him, but he thrust his arm out.

"No, no," he said and turned to face the wall. "I just need a minute."

"Becks, let me help you."

"Don't come near me, Tosh," he shouted and looked at me.

I gasped at how bright his eyes had become, and how his face had filled in so quickly with dark facial hair. He was phasing. Oh dear lord, he was phasing in front of me. He turned away once again and began breathing slowly in and out. I was afraid to move the slightest muscle, or even breathe.

After another minute passed, Beckett stood up straight and combed his fingers through his hair. When he turned back around, his eyes were calmer and the hair had receded from his face. He looked at me with a mixed expression of worry and fear.

"I'm sorry," he began and wiped the sweat from his forehead. "I didn't mean to yell at you."

"It's ok," I replied and began to breathe more fully. "I didn't mean to upset you."

He closed his eyes again and began breathing deeply. After several breaths he finally said, "It seems like the wolf inside me doesn't like assholes shooting their mouths off about…"

"Let's not talk about it anymore, ok?"

Beckett's eyes shot open, and they were suddenly so sad. "How could someone say that to you? Tosha, you are so beautiful, every inch of you. What I wouldn't give to lie next to you and feel those scars against me all night long. You may not think they make you beautiful, but when I see them I am amazed at what you survived. A real man doesn't see scars, he sees the strong person behind them."

I wiped the tear from my eye that escaped. "And this is why I need you, so you can say things like that to me every day."

He only gave a half smile. "Can I…can I ask how that came up? Your scars, I mean."

"No," I answered confidently. I hadn't done anything wrong. If he wanted my scars to be solely for his eyes, then he shouldn't have left me in the first place.

"Ok, I deserve that," he replied and stepped away from wall. He looked down at his watch and sighed. "I really do need to go."

"What happens now?" I asked and tucked my shirt back into place.

"I don't know. If I find another time when we can meet…I mean, is that what you want?"

"I do," I answered and my eyes burned with tears. "It's the stupidest thing I could do, but the thought of not seeing you makes…" my hand went to my chest, "I literally can't breathe when I think I won't see you again."

Beckett stepped in front of me and I was hit with a wave of heat that was radiating from his body. His warm hand cupped my cheek and he rested his hot forehead on mine. "I don't know how soon it'll be, but I'll find a way."

"Ok," I replied with a sniffle.

"I'll always text my old phone if that works. I assumed they were tracking yours."

"They are."

He nodded and stood in front of me. I tangled my fingers around his and he leaned down to kiss me. In that moment I took in every detail of his kiss – how warm his lips were, the slight scratchiness of his facial hair, his bright new eyes staring right through me and looking for acceptance. When he finally rose from my lips, he stepped away quickly.

"Can you tell my mom I'm ok?" he asked.

I nodded but kept my back to him until he closed the door behind him. What the hell did I do now? How exactly did I warn the Warriors that Garrett was coming after us, but I didn't know when or how, just that there would be a lot of werewolves with him. Devin and Cameron weren't big on generalizations. The devil was in the details, and specifically where those details came from.

But as I drove away from the no-tell motel I realized it was starting to get easier to breathe. Little by little the heaviness that had been on my chest was lifting. Beckett was alive, a little jaded and with completely different eyes, but he was still the guy that had melted me into loving him.

As my drive continued, I found myself smiling and thinking about how it felt to be in his arms again. Could we make this work? How often could I actually get away from the manor at the same time he could get away from Garrett? I was so high on the hope of seeing him again that I didn't care that the practical side of me was banging her head against the wall. This would end badly.

"Shut up," I growled to myself and hit the steering wheel. "Beckett will get us the info on Garrett's plans, and the Warriors will get to him first. The Warriors will see that Beckett helped them, and then we can be together. That's it. Done. Why am I talking to myself?"

I rolled my eyes and turned up the music, which naturally caused me to press harder on the gas. It didn't help that my engine made it so easy to go so fast, but it certainly made the long drive a little more interesting. After screeching my way through my pump-me-up playlist, my phone rang through my car. I panicked for a moment until the screen showed it was Nikki. A call from Nikki was rare and it made me nervous.

"Hey, Nik, everything…"

"Where are you?" she snapped.

"Me? Um, I'm at school."

"Really? That's the answer you're going with?"

"Um…"

"Funny thing, I'm at school too and I need a ride home. Where can I meet you?"

"Um…well…"

"Natasha, if you're going to lie, you need to be quicker than this."

"Fine, I'm not at school, what do you want?"

"Pick me up," she replied.

"What? Why?"

She sighed loudly into the phone. "Nat, I ran into Cameron before I left, he thinks you're here. I don't have my car, so I need you to pick me up. If you don't, I'm totally ratting you out. Is that what you want?"

"Ok, fine! I'm over an hour away."

"Well then I look forward to seeing you in an hour in exchange for my silence."

The line went dead, and without any real choice I'd made a deal with the devil.

Chapter Thirty-one

My sister's normal expression would be what most considered a resting bitch face, but when she was angry or pissed off, her look could kill even the strongest of men. Needless to say, as soon as I pulled into the campus parking lot her eyes were blazing a hole in my windshield. When I pulled into a parking spot, she walked right in the middle of it. She didn't even blink when I slammed on my brakes. Even though I was the one training to be a Warrior, my sister had nerves of steel. Slowly, painfully slowly, she walked around to the passenger side of the car while staring me down.

As soon as she hopped inside she flinched and said, "Who the hell have you been with?"

"Wha-what?" I answered and put the car in reverse.

"You're glowing, Nat," she said as I backed out of the space. "And believe me, that doesn't come from just driving around. It's in your best interest to tell me everything so that I can cover your lies since it's obvious you can't do this on your own. So spill."

"How about you tell me why you don't have your car?"

"It wouldn't start. I had to interrupt a meeting with Jared and Cameron to see if I could borrow Jared's car, which he said I couldn't. That's when Cameron said you were here already so as long as I could find a ride here you could bring me home. So now it's your turn to tell me what kind of trouble you were getting yourself into, and it must be good for you to lie to your precious Cameron."

It felt weird when Nikki would talk about Cameron that way,

considering all that she'd done to ruin him. With a sigh I pulled back into the parking spot and then put the car in park. "Fine, but you can't tell anyone, not even Jared."

"Oh please," she said and rolled her eyes, "anything I say to him goes right to his brothers. I promise I won't tell. So, who's the new guy?"

I shook my head. "Not a new guy. I…um…I saw Beckett."

Nikki's jaw dropped and her eyes nearly popped out of her head. "How…wha…when, no how? How…how the fuck did that happen?"

"The cell phone," I replied. "Remember? We found his cell phone in my bag?" She nodded. "Well, he texted it last night and asked me to meet him."

"And you just went?" she shouted. "What the hell were you thinking? It could have been a trap! He could have killed you, or infected you…"

"I know, I know," I interrupted. "I was prepared to protect myself, but it wasn't like that. He wanted to warn the Warriors about what Garrett's doing."

"And…have sex with you."

"No! That's not what happened."

She nodded skeptically. "Uh huh. So let me get this straight, you lied to Cameron's face, kept Beckett's communication from the Warriors, and had a private meeting with the enemy."

I suddenly felt nauseous. "Yes, basically."

Nikki flung her arms around me and squeezed me tightly. "I am so proud of you!"

"What?"

She pulled her arms away from around my neck and had a bizarre smile on her face. "Nat, you've always been the good little girl who followed all the rules, even if they're wrong. Today you broke those rules and did something for yourself for a change. So what happened?"

I shrugged. "He apologized for how he left, I yelled at him a lot, and then he told me how Garrett is planning an attack on the Warriors but he doesn't know when, which is why he's staying. He's trying to find out as much information as he can so we can be prepared. Then he asked me to get a message to his mom and let her know he's ok."

"Ok, let's go," Nikki said and buckled her seatbelt.

"What? Now?"

"Do you have other plans? If you're going to need to drum up some lies, it's best that I'm with you."

I put the car in reverse again and backed out of the space. "I'm not bad at it, I just don't do it as often as you do."

"Oh wow, look at Natty Cushlin giving some shade. 'Bout fucking time."

A half hour later we were pulling up in front of the Dawes household. I had to take a moment before getting out of the car considering the last time I was here I was technically dead for a few minutes. There was a car in the driveway, which I assumed was Mrs. Dawes'. Would she hate the sight of me?

"Are we seriously going to just sit here?" Nikki asked annoyed.

"I'm nervous to go in there."

"Why?"

I unbuckled my seatbelt and sighed as my stomach fluttered. "Because the last time I saw her I told her that her husband was dead. What if she doesn't want anything to do with me? What if the Warriors have bugged her house?"

Nikki groaned and opened her door. "I would hate to live in your head for even ten seconds. Get out of the car and knock on the door. If she slams the door, her loss. You have all the cards in this situation, so grow a pair and say hello."

She was right and I hated that. Reluctantly I stepped out of the car and made my way across the lawn with Nikki just behind me. My finger hesitated at the doorbell when I reached the door, so much so that Nikki pressed it for me. When no one answered I turned to leave.

Nikki grabbed my arm. "Nat, it's been five seconds, give the woman time to answer the damn door."

Just then the door opened. "Tosh, my goodness, what a surprise."

"Hi, Mrs. Dawes."

"Please call me Abby, dear. I think we know each other well enough for that."

I smiled at how husband had said something similar to me. "Ok...um, Abby...we'd like to...my sister and I...would like to..."

"Please forgive her," Nikki interrupted. "I'm Natasha's sister Nikki.

We understand that this might be a difficult time for you, but we were hoping you would have a few minutes to talk? If it's too inconvenient, we completely understand."

Abby shook her head. "No, please come in," she said and waved us inside.

Had we slipped into an alternate universe? I sounded like an idiot while kindness and understanding just rolled off of Nikki's tongue. It was something I had never witnessed. Had hell frozen over? Was there a way to check?

As we stepped inside the living room I was immediately taken back to the night Garrett attacked the Dawes family. Mr. Dawes was lying on the floor bleeding while Beckett was in a panic trying to help him. My eyes caught Abby staring at me.

"I can't be in this room either," she said and directed us toward the kitchen where the wall and sliding glass door had been replaced. Abby gestured toward the kitchen table where there were papers and folders strewn about. "Please forgive the mess, I'm trying to get all of Richard's things in order. I can only handle a few minutes before I'm off crying somewhere."

"Abby," Nikki said kindly, "can I make you some tea?"

I stared at my sister since her body had obviously been taken over by an alien. An alien, mind you, that had manners and compassion. Did she even know how to make tea? I was baffled.

"Oh no, dear, let me do that. You came all the way over here, the least I can do…"

Nikki shook her head. "Abby, it is no trouble at all. Why don't you and Nat go outside, enjoy the day a little and I will make us some tea."

"Oh yes! Outside, good idea," I said way too loudly. Nikki narrowed her eyes and shook her head to show her disapproval.

Abby agreed that the fresh air would be nice and we stepped out onto the deck where I hoped there were no listening devices. Abby gestured to the chairs around the large oblong table, but I shook my head and pointed to the far corner of the deck. She scrunched her brows together in confusion, but still followed me.

"Abby, I'm sorry to just drop by like this," I began and leaned against the railing.

"It's fine, Tosh, I like the company. Being in this house alone has become really difficult for me, especially at night."

"I'm sorry I haven't come over sooner."

She shook her head. "You have your own life, dear. Besides, what am I to you? I'm just the mom of the boy you liked for a few weeks."

"Loved, actually," I replied and she gave me a slight smile. I cleared my throat and lowered my voice. "Abby, I have some news."

"News? About what? Is it Beckett?" she said loudly and I pressed my index finger to my lips to keep her quiet.

"We need to keep our voices down in case the Warriors bugged your house."

She flinched. "They bugged my house?"

"I don't know for sure if they did," I corrected. "We just need to be cautious."

"But why would they do that?"

"In case Beckett or Garrett contact you, I'm guessing. But I don't know for sure."

She nodded slowly, obviously unsettled. "You said you had news?"

I nodded, leaned in closely, and whispered, "I saw Beckett today."

Abby released a loud gasp and then tears were streaming from her eyes. Her cries became so hysterical that I braced her against the deck railing. After another minute or so, Nikki came out on the deck with a cup of tea. She came to the railing, set the tea down, and placed her arm around Abby's back.

"I'm sorry," Abby cried. "I...don't know where that came from."

"Abby," Nikki began, "you have no reason to apologize. Here, have some of your tea."

Abby took several sips of the tea before placing it back down on the railing. "Thank you, you're both so sweet. So, you saw my son. How is he? How did he look?"

"He's ok, he's a lot more muscular now. He joked that it happened almost overnight."

She laughed lightly through her tears. "He always wanted to be more muscular, hopefully that makes him a little happier. Is that...it?"

"He's not any hairier, which frankly I was ready for, but his eyes changed color."

"His eyes?" Abby asked and wiped her cheeks.

"They're bright green now."

"But why?"

"Apparently that's what happens when a hybrid gets infected."

"So he's really a…a wolf?"

I nodded. "He is. He almost phased in front of me."

"What?" Nikki shouted across Abby. "You didn't tell me that."

"It wasn't a big deal, he was able to calm himself down."

"Wait, Tosh, I'm sorry," Abby said, "if you were with Beck, why didn't you bring him home?" It was a question I was hoping she wouldn't ask. "Tosh?"

"He wouldn't come with me," I replied. "He's trying to unravel Garrett's crew from the inside and get more firm information on their endgame. I'm sorry, Abby, I did try."

She nodded and patted my back. "I'm sure you did, honey, but the next time you see him, you drag him home. Tell him his mother needs him."

"I promise I will," I answered and then a thought hit me. "Abby, I know you were questioned by the Warriors, but I wonder, did Garrett ever tell you why he was so interested in having Beckett?"

"No. I only saw Garrett a handful of times and he barely spoke to me. I'm sure it was so I couldn't be pressed for information."

"You're probably right," I replied, but there had to be more to this. "How did you get involved with Garrett in the first place?"

Abby looked down at the railing. "When I met Garrett, I was the perfect target for him." She opened her eyes and looked at me. "I was young and had a father that kept me under his thumb. I was primed to rebel. Garrett knew exactly how to manipulate me. Hell, I was so mesmerized by him that I threw everything away just to be with him."

A lump formed in my throat at the harsh similarities between my relationship with Beckett and what Abby had sacrificed for Garrett. Like father like son?

"Did Garrett associate himself with werewolves back then?" Nikki asked.

Abby shrugged. "Everyone has asked me that, and honestly I really can't say. I met a few others like Garrett, vampires I mean. I remember him making a comment that I needed to be careful around them."

"Why did you leave?"

She rubbed her eyes. "We had just found out I was pregnant and he had insisted that I stay with him because being at school wasn't the best place for me anymore. I didn't realize it at the time how he was isolating me, like I said, a master manipulator. Well, I'd gone out for a doctor's appointment and when I came back I couldn't find him. He lived in this converted warehouse, and I saw that the lights were on across the way, so I went looking for him. The doors were open a little and I peeked through and saw him with a few of his friends, but there was a guy…a kid, really, he was probably the same age as I was. They were yelling at each other and then Garrett ripped that boy's throat out." She paused and held her hand at her mouth for several seconds before continuing, "I ran back to the apartment we were staying in and started to pack my things.

"Garrett came in a few minutes later and started grilling me about why I was leaving. I blurted out that I'd lost the baby and that I needed some time to myself. He just hugged me and told me that we'd try again. It was sick, he was sick. I went back to the dorm. Honestly, I was surprised he let me go, I thought he'd come after me, so I ran to Richard. I was pregnant and scared to death. I knew my father would disown me, but I was terrified what Garrett would do if he caught me. Richard saved me, and married me. He endured years of my father's hatred for him, and he'd done nothing wrong. Richard was better than all of us, and look what happened."

I wrapped my arm around Abby's shoulders as she broke down crying. "Richard would never say he got the short end of the stick. He spoke of nothing but how much he loved you and Beckett."

Abby looked up with tears still streaming from her eyes and patted my hand. "Thank you. It's just not fair. He should be here instead of me." She wiped her cheeks. "I'm sorry I'm such a blubbering mess."

"It's fine, Abby, really it is," Nikki replied comfortingly and squeezed Abby's hand. Was this what she was learning in nursing school? If it was, they were doing an amazing job.

"Abby, can I ask," I began because there was a nagging thought in my head, "that boy you saw, do you remember what he looked like?"

"What?" she asked and shook her head.

"I'm sorry, it's just something the wolf we have in custody said to me. The guy you saw Garrett kill, do you remember what he looked like?"

Abby's eyes went side to side as she searched her memory. "Light brown hair, slender and tall like Becks. I…you know, I remember thinking he looked similar to Garrett, like they could be cousins or something. I haven't thought about that until just now." Her hands went up to her face. "Oh my god, do you think…was that Garrett's son? Another son?"

I looked over at Nikki and from her expression we were both thinking the same thing – nothing surprised us when it came to what vamps would do to hybrids.

"It's possible," I said to break the uncomfortable silence.

Abby wiped her eyes again and sighed. "I just don't know what to do with all of this. It's too much…it's just too much."

"Do you want us to stay and make you dinner or something?"

She shook her head. "No, no, I'm fine. You girls have your own lives, you don't need to be hanging around an old lady like me. Thank you for giving me an update on Beck, it really gives me a sense of relief."

"Just don't tell Cameron or Devin we told you anything," Nikki said as we walked back inside. "But don't worry, Abby, we'll be back,"

Abby placed her hands on my shoulders and then pulled me in for a hug. "You take care of yourself, honey."

"I will," I replied into her shoulder.

She pulled away and looked me dead in the eye. "Tosh, Garrett is dangerous, his people are dangerous, there's no way this ends well. You need to bring Becks home."

I nodded and swallowed the lump in my throat. "I'll do everything I can."

I didn't want to promise something I couldn't keep. Thankfully Nikki pulled on my arm and lead me away from the house.

"Thanks for coming with me," I said as we crossed the front law.

"Yeah, glad I came," she replied sweetly and then, "because you're really bad at comforting people."

"Thanks, Nik, you always know what to say."

She laughed. "So, one thing," she said as we approached the car, "was the book right?"

"What?"

"You said that Beckett had gotten more muscular."

"Yeah," I replied as I opened my car door and sank down inside.

Nikki did the same and as soon as her car door was shut, she asked, "So? Did his dick get bigger?"

"Nikki!"

She shrugged. "What? I'm simply trying to confirm the accuracy of the book. So, did you check?"

"No!"

"Next time, then," she said with a smirk.

Chapter Thirty-two

The morning came and in its silence I realized how much I hated being alone. Before Beckett, I woke up every morning without issue and went on with my day. Waking up with Beckett those few times had ruined me. He had made me weak. If I closed my eyes I could remember his smooth, warm chest and the hint of a snore in his throat. Having seen him just yesterday made being without him even harder.

My legs felt like lead as I pulled them from underneath the blankets and shuffled into the bathroom to shower. Saturday training sessions were hard to get motivated for. For a year I'd woken up early and trained my ass off for this day, the last training day before the Warriors decided whether I was worthy enough to become one of them. My heart was heavy with the pressure of my fate being in their hands. What would happen if they didn't pick me? Or what if they did?

My stomach started to flip causing me to sit down in the shower. As the hot water pelted my head and back, a little voice in the back of head said, fuck it. What difference did it make what the Warriors decided?

"I've wasted a year of my life if they don't pick me," I said aloud.

Fuck them, the voice in my head replied.

It was official, I was going crazy. Sadly it ran in the family.

With a sigh, I pulled myself back up to standing and finished my shower. When I returned to my room, I laid out the standard uniform – black pants, black sports bra, black shirt. Maybe not being a Warrior would bring some color back to my wardrobe, I thought and laughed to myself. Quickly I pulled on my pants and bra, and then began threading my arms into the sleeves of my shirt. For a split second I caught a glimpse of myself in the full-length mirror standing in the corner. It wasn't often that I dared to look at myself in a mirror that showed anything below my chest. In all honesty, I couldn't remember the last time I'd actually looked at my scars.

I dropped my T-shirt to the ground and nervously turned my attention to the sight of pink scars stretching up from the waistline of my pants. What was the word that Connor had used? Melted? Disgusting melted skin.

Fuck him, the voice in my head growled.

My fingers grazed over the tip of Beckett's star scar and then across to the wave. This time it was his voice ringing in my head that if it were him, he'd show them off every day. These were my battle scars. Maybe it was time to stop hiding behind them.

"Fuck it," I said to my reflection and then turned back to my dresser. From within the top drawer I pulled out a thicker workout bra and pulled it over the one I had on. I looked like…a freak. A scary, scarred freak. Or…a survivor. A don't-fuck-with-me survivor because look at what I've fucking fought through. Yes, Natasha Grace, look at what you've gone through. Everything was cake compared to that night. Now show them just how tough you are.

Quickly I pulled my weapons bag up on my shoulder and headed toward the door. I was going to do this. I was fucking going to do this. Not for Beckett, but for me and in spite of Connor. When I put my hand on the doorknob, my stomach flipped over and the bile rose quickly in my throat. I dropped my bag on the floor and ran to the bathroom, just barely making the toilet before throwing up what little was in my stomach.

Once I caught my breath, I brushed my teeth and wiped my face.

"I'm not hiding anymore," I yelled at myself in the mirror. "There's no reason for me to be ashamed of myself and what I look like. It's done, and we're doing this." I took a step away but then looked at myself again and said, "And if I keep talking to myself like this, we'll seek medical attention. Got it?"

I nodded to myself and left the bathroom. I grabbed my phone from the dresser and plugged my earphones in my ear. With my weapons bag back on my shoulder, I jacked up the volume and began playing the soundtrack for this epic moment in my life. After taking a protein bar from the dresser, I finally opened my door and took a step out into the hallway. The music pumping through my ears was barely drowning out my nerves, and my heartbeat was pounding louder than the drums.

I swallowed the big nervous lump in my throat and closed the door behind me. I took one step, and then another, and another until my pace was on the same beat as the music. Before I knew it the spiral staircase was in front of me. This was it. The stairs would take me into the gauntlet of stares and attention I've avoided for over three years. With a breath, I opened my protein bar, shoved it in my mouth, and made my way down the stairs.

When I reached the main floor, I kept my head down and continued to eat my protein bar. The music blaring in my ears was actually a great distraction to seeing the pairs of feet suddenly stopping when I got close, someone even tripped over themselves, although I didn't have the courage to look up to see who it was. The small staircase that led to the courtyard was a welcomed sight, although it would bring an entirely new audience, but this was the point. I would show everyone I was stronger than my scars.

When I finally stepped onto the grass of the courtyard there was a perfect moment in the music pounding in my ears. As the music got faster and swelled, I lifted my head and had my own slow-mo walk across the courtyard to where the others were warming up. Nub was the first to notice and in turn he hit Princess who then hit Bush. It wasn't until Roberts turned around to see what the other three were gawking at did my heart really start pounding, especially when Roberts took a step to the side to reveal Connor.

Immediately I averted my eyes and stepped over to a patch of grass where I could warm up and pretend I didn't see everyone staring at me. Just as I dropped my weapons bag on the ground, my earbuds were yanked out of my ears. I gasped and looked up to see Connor scowling at me.

"What the hell are you doing?" he growled.

"I-I'm warming up."

"You know what I'm talking about. Are you just throwing it in my face? That's not something you want to do..."

"Connor?"

I looked over Connor's shoulder to see Devin standing a couple of feet away. Connor immediately stood at attention and turned to face Devin.

"Yes, sir?"

"Is everything ok here?" Devin asked, but his expression changed as soon as Connor stepped away from me. When Connor didn't answer immediately, Devin pressed again. "Connor?"

Connor flinched and replied, "Sorry, sir. I was talking to Scarecrow about her inappropriate attire."

"Inappropriate?" Devin questioned and looked me up and down without the slightest expression on his face. "I don't see an issue with her attire. It is similar to what the other women in the coven wear during training, as did several of the former trainees. What exactly do you feel is inappropriate?"

Connor's lips and nostrils twitched for several seconds before he finally replied, "Being the last day, I thought she should be dressed more for battle than training."

"And did you scold the other trainees for their lack of formality?"

Connor had been caught and there was no way out of this that didn't make him look like an ass. Which he was.

"No, sir."

Devin raised one eyebrow at him and then walked toward where the others were gathered. He truly was the most intimidating person I had ever met, and I liked that he was giving it to Connor at the moment.

"Let's huddle up," Connor shouted and we all congregated around Devin.

"Before we begin today," Devin began. "I'd first like to tell you how proud I am of each and every one of you for making it this far in the program. Today will be your final evaluation and we will make decisions on who will participate in a final challenge. Your performance on that challenge will determine if you will be a Warrior. That is the goal, children."

With a clap of his hands we started with the usual laps around the courtyard. Afterwards, no one even dared to speak as we started in on some basic routines. Today we were no longer friends, only competitors.

"All right," Devin began, "now we'll move on to a weapons display. Each of you will battle individually against a Warrior opponent."

The five of us quickly started looking around the courtyard to see who our opponent would be. It had to be someone who would test us beyond anything we'd experienced before. However, there were several nervous groans when Alex came through one of the archways. I don't know what the others were thinking, but all I kept concentrating on was the size of his hands and that I only came up to his waist. I would have to be a David to his Goliath.

Princess was selected to go first and then Nub, both lasting less than five minutes against Alex. While Bush prepared his daggers for his turn, Connor slithered his way behind me. He didn't say anything until Devin's attention was fully on the duel between Bush and Alex.

"You're making a fool out of yourself," he said softly.

"I hope you're messing with everyone's head and not just mine," I whispered without turning to look back at him.

"You think you're making a statement, but showing those scars exposes where you're vulnerable."

"And?" I asked challengingly and finally looking over my shoulder at him.

"And what?"

"You think they're disgusting and liked it better when I hid them from everyone," I replied and turned around to face him. "Or maybe you're just punishing me because you didn't get your dick sucked the other night."

Connor's eyes flared and then he quickly looked out over my shoulder. I followed his gaze to see that Devin was looking right at us. It was hard to tell whether his expression was one of anger or shock, but his eyes were a little wild. After only a few seconds he turned his attention back to Bush and Alex. At that moment Bush lunged at Alex who merely bent down, grabbed Bush by the ankle, and pulled him up to hang upside down like a fish. Devin allowed Bush to hang and twitch for almost fifteen seconds before finally instructing Alex to set him down.

With Bush finished, it was either me or Roberts, and I had a feeling Devin was going in order of worst to best. So I wasn't too surprised when Devin called my name.

"Scarecrow," he said firmly, "you're next."

I had almost forgotten that Connor was behind me until he leaned down to my ear and whispered, "I hope you choke."

The words rang in my ears, yet I kept my expression solid and unmovable. He was being an asshole, a guy I thought was at least my friend if not a mentor. Hell, considering how much time and effort he'd put in working with me, he had as much riding on this as I did.

After exhaling a deep breath, I attached my silver-coated whips to my belt and felt around my back to where my smaller daggers were held in place. My stomach fluttered as I took my place in front of Alex, who was roughly twenty feet away. Suddenly he came charging at me like a bull at what must have been half-speed, for him, but still faster than human speed. There was barely enough time for me to unfurl my whip from my hip, but it was important to remain patient, which was obviously harder said than done when your heart was pounding in your chest and your brain was telling your body to run.

Just when Alex was only a foot away, I snapped my whip at him which caught his wrist. Alex shouted at the pain and quickly he pulled his arm in front of him, propelling me forward until I hit the ground and rolled back onto my feet. My whip stayed wrapped around his wrist, burning through layers of his skin. While he easily dragged me forward through the courtyard's soft grass, I unfurled my second whip and began snapping it at him almost as if he were a trained lion, nicking his hand and arms with each snap. Finally my second whip caught and wrapped around his free arm. It was time for another ride.

With all my strength I leaned back, pulling my whips taught and creating massive tension, my feet making deep tracks in the grass. Alex circled both his hands in the air, wrapping the whips further around his arms and finally closing his hands around them despite the burning pain. I braced myself a moment before Alex yanked both his arms towards his body, and as Connor had instructed me time and time again, I didn't resist and instead relaxed into the motion and flew forward. Within three seconds I knew I wasn't going to make it. As the ground neared, I kicked my feet out and slid in the grass, pulling out a dagger with my right hand and slicing at Alex's ankle as I went between his legs.

The giant toppled over and reached for the ground. I took advantage and leapt onto his back, rearing my dagger up ready to plunge it down into his shoulder when Devin yelled, "Hold!"

The courtyard was amazingly quiet as I froze with my dagger in the air. Alex stood up slowly with me still hanging from his back. He reached up behind him and offered me his hand. Slowly I placed my dagger back into its holder and took Alex's massive hand. Very easily he swung me down to the ground and then held his arms out to me. Carefully I unraveled the whips from his arms, unfortunately removing a thin layer of skin which made his arms appear as though there were red snakes crawling up his forearms.

"I'm sorry," I said softly as I pulled the last silver tentacle from his arm.

He smirked. "It's the most action I've gotten all day."

"I doubt that's true," I replied and smiled up at him. "Kyla had you most of the morning."

Alex's shoulders shook with laughter. "Well done, Tosh," he said and began rubbing his forearms as they began to heal. "Dev, I need a few minutes to heal."

"Certainly," Devin replied. "Roberts, you're up. The rest of you may stay or retire. You are done for the day."

The three stooges and I exchanged glances. Was this a trick? We had all assumed this would be the longest day of our lives where our bodies would be stressed to their extremes. But after another silent moment, Princess shrugged, sighed, and turned toward the manor. Nub followed a few seconds later, leaving Bush and I to watch Roberts battle Alex.

Since I'd met Trevor Roberts, this was the first time I had ever seen him nervous. His face was pale, even a slight sheen of sweat on his forward and upper lip. To him, becoming a Warrior was everything. Then I shook with realization, why wasn't I nervous? I'd hardly been before either, only afraid that I'd be crushed by Alex more than anything else. Bush was pacing behind me with nervous energy I didn't possess. Did I even care?

Alex stepped back into view, his arms mostly healed with only a faint redness left, and announced that he was ready for the last battle. Roberts' chest rose and he held his breath for nearly ten seconds before finally releasing it and moving toward the giant.

"You got this, Roberts," I shouted and clapped my hands several times.

He looked over at me and gave me a slight nod in appreciation, and then in the next breath he cried out and flew toward Alex.

Suddenly something caught my eye and I turned my head toward the manor to find my sister standing within one of the archways. Her hand went up to her mouth when she caught sight of me. My hand went nervously to my stomach and her hand flew to her eyes while her body shook with sobs. I stepped behind Bush and walked the length of the courtyard toward her.

When I reached her, she didn't look up so I wrapped my arms around her neck. Immediately she wrapped her arms around my waist and cried into the crook of my shoulder.

"I'm s-ss-so proud of y-you," she sobbed and squeezed me even tighter.

The sound of her cries made my jaw chatter.

Nikki rose from my shoulder and wiped her face. "You truly are the bravest person I know."

My face scrunched up with emotions and I fell back into her embrace. This time she held me against her neck and shoulder while I unloaded emotions I didn't know I had. When I finally rose from her shoulder, I wiped my face and looked out into the courtyard to see Roberts being held up by his throat while he slashed away at Alex's arm. Finally Alex released him and he fell to the ground in a heap.

Devin only waited a moment before he thanked Alex for his service and then Projected away. Roberts looked bewildered and uncertain, but frankly we all were. It was just another mind fuck from the Warriors. Not a big surprise.

Nikki pulled my attention back to her. "What made you do it?"

I shrugged. "I thought it was time to show these assholes what a badass I am."

"Fuck yeah you're a badass, you're a Cushlin."

"Are you done then?"

"I think so."

"Then let's celebrate. We'll go out and get pedis, maybe go check on Abby or something. We'll even grab something to eat."

I smiled. "I'd love that, Nik."

"Well come on then, I don't have all day," she replied in the bitchy tone I was used to.

We walked arm in arm back into the manor, rounding the corner in the main foyer.

"Tosh!" Devin called. "Come with me please," he said and turned his back to me.

I gave a worried look to Nikki before peeling away from her side and following Devin past the spiral stairs and then the dining room. We were heading toward Cameron and Brianna's quarters, Victor's old suite, but why?

The door was already open as we approached. Devin led the way inside and held it open, closing it loudly behind me. Sitting on one of the couches in the sunken living area were Cameron and Brianna, both with worried expressions on their faces, but that quickly changed when they noticed my exposed abdomen. I suddenly felt incredibly insecure. Devin gestured for me to sit on the couch opposite them, which I obviously obeyed.

"Tosh," Devin began, "we'd like to talk to you about the statement you made in the courtyard earlier today."

I blinked slowly and shook my head. "Wha-what statement?"

Devin sighed and looked to Cameron who answered, "Natasha, have you ever been forced to perform..." he cleared his throat uncomfortably, "...sexual acts in return for favorable treatment?"

Oh dear lord. My cheeks flushed with embarrassment, so much so I had to put my hands against them. "Um...I not sure what..."

"Honey, you can tell us what happened. You are in a safe space," Brianna said sweetly.

Devin, however, was not as comforting. "Tosh, it is no use hiding. I heard what you said to Connor, and it is disturbing. You need to tell us everything that has happened between the two of you."

Brianna glared at him for a moment before turning back to me. "*And*, you will not be judged. Just tell us the truth."

I looked between the three of them as I swallowed the large lump in my throat. I had said such a nasty comment in anger and now I might hurt Connor's career and possibly mine.

"It's not as bad as I made it sound," I said to Devin and then looked at the Burkes. "Really, I swear. It's not like I've been raped or anything."

Brianna's shoulders relaxed and Cameron breathed a sigh of relief, although Devin narrowed his eyes at me. "You must divulge any impropriety that has occurred between you and Connor. This is not a joke, Tosh. This must be investigated."

"Investigated?" I replied in a worried tone. "There's nothing between us. Just..." I buried my face in my hands. When I lifted my head, I looked at Brianna since it seemed so much easier to talk to her than Devin or Cameron. "It started innocently enough. He was giving me extra training sessions almost every day and we really did form a friendship. Then it seemed that whenever he was between...love interests I guess...he would come to me for a...on my god, I can't believe I'm even saying this, a release I guess."

"So you have had intercourse with Connor," Cameron said flatly and his words made me want to vomit.

"No," I replied immediately. "He got all the attention."

It was the only way I could explain it. I wasn't about to say the words oral sex or blowjob to Cameron.

"Did he promise you favors in return?" Cameron asked.

I shook my head. "Never any favors, nothing like that. It's not like there were any feelings between us. We all know that Connor is a horndog, and well, I...I welcomed the company."

Cameron rubbed his chin. "Did you ever feel pressured by him?"

I shifted uncomfortably in my seat. "Um...not really." Brianna raised her eyebrows, prompting me to clarify. "No, it wasn't like that. I did it because I...because I was lonely. It's not like anyone else was knocking on my door. So I gave in, but it was my choice. The only time it got weird was the other night." Cameron shifted onto the edge of the couch and Devin sat down on the armrest next to Brianna. "He started...nudging me to do things, and I was...I've been so confused and hurt since Beckett left and Connor did take advantage of that. He's no angel. I gave in, but I decided I wanted more. It was out of spite for Beckett. But...but Connor told me that my body was too disgusting for him, we fought, and I kicked him out of my room. Connor was being an asshole to me today, so I made the comment. I'm sorry."

Devin narrowed his eyes. "And all this time you had no thoughts about how you were behaving with your superior?"

"It never meant anything," I replied and wiped a few beads of sweat off my forehead. "The first time it happened we were friends and you hadn't assigned him to the program. I guess...I don't know. I'm sorry, I see now that it was wrong."

"Tosh, honey," Brianna began, "this isn't your fault."

"Not completely, that is," Devin mumbled and Brianna glared at him again.

At the same moment the door to the room burst open and the Burke twins came running inside.

"Ada! Mama!" they squealed. "We beat Auntie Ky!"

A moment later Kyla, no doubt the most beautiful woman in the coven with her incredibly long red hair, walked casually inside the room with an irritated look on her face.

"Your children are exhausting," she said to Cameron and Brianna who both agreed without an ounce of sympathy. "Are you ok with them now? I'd like to go and tend to my husband's wounds."

We all knew what she meant, except the twins, who suddenly stopped their dancing and looked at their aunt.

"Uncle Awex is hurt?" Olivia asked with wide eyes.

"Only a little," Kyla replied. "I hear Tosh gave him a challenge today."

I shook my head and turned back in my seat. "Hardly."

"Uncle Awex has to run to find his money?" Jack-Jack asked.

"No, baby," Brianna replied and pointed up to a desk in the far corner of the room. "Why don't the two of you draw something while Mama and Ada talk to Tosh." Olivia squealed with excitement and ran to the desk while Jack-Jack shrugged and dragged his feet. "Thanks, Ky. Have fun *tending* to Alex."

"Always do," she laughed and left the room.

Once the twins were settled, all eyes came back to me. "I will speak with Connor," Devin said as he rose from the couch. "It goes without saying, Natasha, that in the future, sexual acts with superiors should be avoided. But in no way should Connor have been involved with you or nudged you to do anything. If you feel any kind of retaliation from him, you will tell us."

"Yes, sir," I replied. I wanted to die. Devin left the room and I stood from the couch, but Cameron gestured for me to sit back down. "Is there something else?"

"There is," he replied and my stomach sank. "I hear you visited with Abigail Dawes yesterday."

My eyes widened. "Yes, I-I hope that was ok."

He nodded. "Of course, I am very happy that you did. She has suffered a great loss, and I believe she trusts you much more than any of us."

"How did you find out?"

Cameron gave a smirk. "Being a coven leader has its perks."

Brianna rolled her eyes. "He talked to her this morning," she said to me and then tilted her head at her husband. "Don't make it sound like you're the mighty and powerful Oz or something."

Their banter always made me smile, especially in the way Brianna could always cut through her husband at the same time of having an obvious undying love for him. Life goals.

"Fine," Cameron said and slowly looked back to me, "I spoke with Mrs. Dawes this morning and she mentioned that you and Nikki had stopped by."

I nodded. "Yes. Nikki was surprisingly helpful."

"Very nice. In your time with her, did she say or remember anything useful?"

My mouth became instantly dry. It was impossible for me to stop my heart from racing and giving me away. "Useful how?"

Cameron pushed back and put his arm around Brianna's shoulders. "Mrs. Dawes has been reluctant to divulge much of anything to us."

"She's grieving, Cam," Brianna said. "How would you be if I died and someone was pestering you with questions."

"I fully understand the circumstances," Cameron replied defensively. "Which is why I am hoping perhaps she might have divulged something to Natasha in hopes that she trusts her more than the rest of us."

"Well, actually she did," I said, being careful to monitor all the words that came out of my mouth.

"Enlighten us," Cameron said.

"I don't exactly remember how the topic got started, but I had asked her if she remembered her time with Garrett when she was in college, trying to see if there were any similarities to what he was doing then to now."

"And?" Cameron pressed, removing his arm from around Brianna's shoulders and leaning forward.

"I had her think back to the people Garrett associated himself with back then, and she remembered there was a young man there she thought he looked similar to Garrett."

"Interesting that she did not tell us any of this."

"She even said that until that moment she had never thought about it again because she saw Garrett kill him, and then she fled."

"Yes, she did tell us she fled because Garrett killed someone. What conclusion have you come to with this new information?"

My stomach flipped a little with the fact that Cameron was asking my opinion. I'm sure he had a theory of his own already. "My thought is that this other guy was Garrett's son. Garrett was adamant that no one hurt Beckett, he needed him. Maybe he specifically needs a son to…I don't know. That's what I can't get my head around."

Cameron nodded. "Interesting theory, if that young man was indeed another son of Garrett's."

Brianna shivered. "I hope to God he's not another Aidan Pierce."

"But how do the werewolves fit into all of this?" Cameron asked.

At the mention of the word I was reminded of Beckett's warning. The tricky part was how did I add it in the conversation without Cameron asking too many questions.

"Sir," I began in a very serious tone, "are the Warriors preparing for battle against Garrett?"

Cameron tilted his head curiously. "Do you believe that Garrett has come to challenge us."

352 ~ C.R. Quinn

"Yes, but with help from the wolves. I believe we should be prepared."
Cameron smiled. "We?"

I blushed and looked down at my hands. "The Warriors, sir. I'm sorry, I didn't mean to assume..."

"Natasha," he laughed, "I am happy to see your strategic and critical mind at work. But have no fear, we are thinking along the same lines. We are still sending scouts trying to find Garrett, but we are also preparing ourselves for a direct attack."

Brianna looked over to where the kids were lying on the floor drawing.

"They will be fine, love," Cameron said and squeezed his wife's hand. "We are in a fortress to begin with, but we will find Garrett before he comes to us." Cameron looked over at me again. "Natasha, although my wife informs me this might be too personal of a question, I would like to know how you are doing?"

"Sir?"

Brianna gave him a warning glance, but he continued, "I know that Beckett's departure was difficult for you." My stomach sank. "You had a rough couple of days this week at practice, but you seem to have recovered."

I shifted uncomfortably in my seat, crossing my arms in front of my bare stomach. "I'm ok," I said with a hint of truth. "I'm embarrassed at how my performance was affected."

"It happens," Brianna said, coming to my defense. "Between Beckett leaving and this incident with Connor, we're very concerned about you."

I sighed and nodded, feeling as though I was sitting across from the parents I never had, making the lies even harder to bear. "I'm dealing with it."

"That is good to hear," Cameron said with a delighted smile. The sight of it made me feel like shit.

"Toshy!" Jack-Jack shouted and ran to my side. "Here's your picture."

Jack-Jack handed me a crayon drawing of what I assumed was the manor against a bright sun and tall green grass. "Thanks, Jack-Jack, I love it."

He gave me a hug and darted off toward the tall doors that led to the lanai overlooking the gardens. "Mama, can I go outside now?"

"Please do," Brianna said enthusiastically. "Run around until you drop."

I laughed just as Livy placed her drawing on top of her brother's. My smile left my face slowly as I took in what I thought the picture was showing.

"Livy, who's this?" I said pointing to the far left of the picture where a small figure dressed in black stood with straight, dark hair.

"That's you, Toshy," Livy replied and then pointed to the figure next to me. "And that's Beckett. I drew him as a wolf because that's how I saw him."

Both her parent's eyes shot up and looked between me and their daughter. Brianna rose from the couch quickly and stood over my shoulder. Gently she ran her fingers through her daughter's soft curls, trying not to startle her, I assumed.

"Baby girl, when did you see Beckett as a wolf?"

Livy looked up over her shoulder at her mother with her big black eyes. "In my dweam wast night."

Brianna looked across to Cameron who stood slowly from the couch. "Monkey, why did you not tell us about this dream?"

She shrugged. "You didn't ask me about my dweams."

"Who are all these people here, Livy," Brianna asked, moving her index finger around the center of the picture where there was a mix of humans and wolves.

Livy looked down at the page. "The udder wolves, Mama. There are wots and wots of dem. Can I go pway with Jack-Jack now?"

Brianna sighed and nodded, and little Livy ran out the doors to find her brother. My heart was racing, not only for the fact that it seemed that Livy had had a dream about a battle, but that she drew me next to Beckett. What did that mean? Would Cameron suspect that I had been in contact? Would they ask me about why I was drawn standing next to him?

"Natasha?"

"What!" I shouted and startled both Cameron and Brianna. "Sorry."

Cameron eyed me before extending his hand. "I asked if I could have the drawing. Would that be all right?"

"Oh, yes, sorry," I replied, rose from the couch, and handed him Livy's drawing. "I didn't know that Livy was still having prophetic dreams."

"Neither did we," Brianna replied. "Cam, what do we do?"

Cameron reluctantly drew his eyes away from the drawing. "I should speak with Devin, possibly Father. I do not want us to evacuate the children and cause a panic. This drawing shows no sign of the manor. I do believe the children are safe, my love, however, it is obvious that we should be prepared. Natasha, thank you."

"For what?"

He smiled. "If you had not been here, Olivia most likely would not have drawn this. Thank you, you are certainly dismissed."

"Thank you, sir," I said and practically leapt from the couch.

When I came into the hallway, Nikki was anxiously waiting. "Good?"

I nodded, grabbed her wrist, and pulled her down the main corridor. "We need to get out of here before I burst."

Chapter Thirty-three

I'd only had one other pedicure in my life, so the attendant was not thrilled with what she had to work with. Pedicures turned into lunch which turned into shopping until almost dinnertime. During our sisterly time together, Nikki and I gabbed about my night with Connor, my slip of the tongue that caused the uncomfortable sit-down, and then finally how Livy had drawn our fears out with paper and crayons. It was the most time we'd ever spent together. When we returned to the manor Nikki received a text that stopped her in her tracks.

"You ok?" I asked.

"Um, yeah. I need to…" she paused and looked around her, "…can I borrow your car? Mine still isn't fixed and there's…uh…something at school I need to take care of."

"I'll take you over there. It's not like I'm doing anything."

"No, it's just a problem with a project I'm working on," she replied and ripped the keys from my hand. "I'll catch up with you later." She turned to walk away but then turned back around and hugged me tightly. "I love you, Nat."

Without another word, my sister stepped away and basically stole my car. I sighed and stepped through the manor door, and then immediately caught my breath.

"J-jonah?"

Jonah Thorne, Head of Operations at Facility East, previous crush, and my dear friend, was standing in the foyer of the manor as if he hadn't literally just flown across the country.

"Tosh!" he shouted and opened his arms.

Even though he was a married man I still ran to him and gave him a big hug. "What are you doing here?"

"Glorified delivery boy," he replied.

"What?"

"I brought a possible new recruit for the Warriors."

"Oh," I replied. "And you decided to trek all the way out here?"

He shrugged. "Maybe I wanted to see how you were doing."

I narrowed my eyes. "Or maybe you wanted out of the land of poop and baby vomit."

He widened his eyes as he nodded. "There is so much of it."

"As you've said."

"Want to grab dinner?"

"Um...well," I began, but then Jonah placed his hand on my back and pushed me toward the dining hall.

"Come on, I'm delirious with lack of sleep and jet lag. Humor an old man."

"You're only a couple years older than me."

"I feel like I have one foot in the grave," he laughed. "I cannot wait to sleep for a whole night in peace and quiet."

"And let Ashlyn suffer in your place."

He smiled. "Honestly she was practically kicking me out the door. My mom said she'd drop by. I think Ashlyn likes her more than me anyway."

We laughed as we turned into the dining hall. I'd only eaten a few hours ago so I didn't put much on my plate. Jonah, however, piled on two layers and carried one roll in his hand and another in his mouth. I shook my head and led him to a table in the far corner. We had just put our plates down when Jonah pulled his cell phone out of his pocket and checked a text.

After taking a bite from his roll, he said, "Let's eat outside."

"What?"

"Yeah, out on that terrace thing. It's too noisy in here," he said and put his phone back into his pocket.

"Um, ok."

"Can we go through that secret passageway thing again too?"

I paused and rolled my eyes before I gave in and picked up my plate. We walked the length of the dining room and made our way into the kitchen. Jonah smiled like a kid when I opened the secret passageway, which was actually a servant's hallway that led into the ballroom. The opposite door was left slightly open allowing a sliver of light to spill into the passageway to illuminate our way. The ballroom was flooded with wide rays of late afternoon sun coming through the wall of windows and tall glass doors. The bright glow of the sun seemed to set the gilded room ablaze as it glimmered off the golden walls and accents, it was almost too bright to look at comfortably.

We crossed the room and made our way outside onto the wide terrace overlooking the gardens and the giant fountain in the middle of the grounds. Jonah sat down on the step of the first landing and I sat alongside him.

"I'm surprised you want to sit here."

"Why?" he asked and shoved the remainder of his first roll in his mouth. He was a creature sometimes.

"Remember what happened the last time we were both sitting on these steps?" A hint of recollection came across his face. "Worst, most awkward moment of my life. Did you ever tell Ashlyn about that?"

"Are you kidding? From the time we rescued her she's been a bag of hormones, a beautiful bag of hormones of course, and then that changed into post-partum and lack of sleep. So I figured it was best not to tell her."

"But you guys are happy, right?"

"Oh yeah," he answered. "I don't mean to make it sound like we're miserable. It's just the lack of sleep and the stress of a baby. No, we're great, and Tilly is great. It's amazing how much I love that pooping machine. But how are you? You look better than when we video-chatted."

"I think I'm over the hump."

"You really liked this guy, huh?"

I concentrated on my plate as I answered, "I love him." From the side of my eye I saw Jonah flinch. "What? You didn't think it was possible? It's not like my scars prevent me from loving someone."

"Yeah, but that chip on your shoulder sure does," he replied.

"It's not as big as it used to be."

"Probably because of this guy."

"Beckett, his name is Beckett."

"He chipped away at you?"

I nodded. "Maybe a little too much."

"What do you mean?"

I shrugged. "I don't know, I just feel...different. I don't seem to care as much about certain things as I used to."

"Example please."

I looked at him and then pointed over my shoulder at the ballroom behind us. "Take that room back there. Before, I would have stood in the middle of it and imagined my Warrior initiation ceremony. Today I just walked through it to get out here. And then today..." I paused and gave a pleading look, "...please don't say anything to anyone about this."

"You have my confidence, I swear."

I sighed and felt my eyes twinge with tears. "I don't know if I want this anymore." Jonah's face froze. "I know, it's shocking to me too."

"I just never thought I'd hear that from you."

I shook my head and wiped a tear that was about to leak from my eye. "Me either. Today, my stomach should have been in my throat, especially when Alex came walking into the courtyard, but I just...I just did what I was supposed to and fought him. And I did it well, Jonah, better than anyone else, but when I was done, I had no feelings one way or the other about it. I don't have that burning in the pit of my stomach like I used to. And now when I should be a ball of nerves, I went for a pedicure with my sister and now I'm sitting here with your sorry ass. I don't know what's wrong with me."

Jonah twisted his lips and then answered, "Maybe it's that guy."

"Beckett?"

"Sure," he answered snidely. "You could say his name was Duncan and I'd agree with you. My brain is mush right now."

"That's great," I replied and moved the food around on my plate with my fork. "I'm glad I'm looking to you for advice."

Jonah laughed as he stabbed a bunch of green beans onto his fork. "I never promised I'd be giving advice. You're lucky my eyes are even open."

"You're the one who insisted we come out here. Go to bed then," I said nastily and got up from the hard step.

Jonah squeezed my leg. "Sit down, Tosh, come on. I know this is serious." Reluctantly I sat back down on the concrete step and put my plate next to me. "I'm not lying when I say my brain is mush, that's an absolute truth, so I can't give you anything profound, and I certainly don't understand all that's happened in the last couple of weeks. What I can say is that maybe the reasons you joined the program don't matter as much to you now. You've had a year to grow into a different person, and you met someone. The right person can change your life forever. This Pickett guy…"

"Beckett."

"Whatever. He changed you, which might be a good thing, and please don't take offense to this, but you don't have a lot of…experience."

"That's a kind way of putting it."

"I'm just being honest, Tosh. I'm just worried that you might be throwing away everything you've worked your ass off for because of this guy. Don't be taken down because of decisions he made for his best interest."

"It wasn't as simple as that," I replied defensively.

"Fine, let's say it wasn't. You're a big girl and you can live your life the way you please. I just don't want you to sit around pining for him to come back, when that probably won't happen."

My will gave way and I let the tears fall. I didn't care about losing it in front of Jonah.

He leaned in and rested his shoulder against mine. "I didn't mean to make you cry."

"It's ok," I replied and wiped my face. "You're just being honest."

"Don't be too impressed, I've given a similar speech to Katie at least a dozen times."

"Did it help her?"

"Probably not as much as I hoped it would."

I laughed, but then reality sunk in. "You're right, though, I can't just sit and wait for something that might never happen."

"Could you text that to Ashlyn for me?"

"Text what?"

"That I was right about something. I need to prove to her that it does happen sometimes."

I laughed, and for the next hour we gabbed about everything from his sister's rollercoaster life, his mother's new boyfriend whom he liked very much, and finally how he and Ashlyn were getting along better now that the baby was sleeping through the night. By the time we were out of topics, the sun had set behind the trees causing dark shadows to be cast on the grounds below.

"I need to get some sleep," Jonah said and rose from the concrete step.

I didn't argue since my butt was officially cold, numb, and flat. "How long are you staying?"

"Leaving in the morning," he replied, stretched his back, and then twisted it hard enough to make a loud crack. "I feel like I'm ninety years old."

"You kinda look it too," I laughed and we headed back into the manor.

"Thanks for having dinner with me."

"It's the least I could do," I answered and opened the door to the ballroom. Jonah took the door from me and I ducked inside. With the sun behind the trees, the beautiful gold room had lost its glow and shimmer. "Thanks for being honest with me."

Jonah wrapped his arms around my shoulders and hugged me tightly into his chest. "I'm proud of you, Tosh."

When he released me, I looked up at him. "For what?"

"For opening yourself up. You used to be convinced that you would be alone for the rest of your life."

"I'm still alone," I replied snidely.

"But you let yourself be loved," he said in a soft voice. "You've come a long way since last year."

I nodded and swallowed the lump in my throat. "Thanks. I miss having you here in person. You're a really good friend."

He gave an awkward smile. "Just uh…remember you said that."

Before I could ask him what he meant he disappeared through the secret passageway. I gave the empty ballroom one last look. There was no excitement or awe of being in the room. No fascinations of Devin or Cameron pinning that gold circle on me. It was just a room. I wasn't sure how to process the lack of feelings I had so I made my way through the main door and headed to my room. The manor was oddly quiet, and I only passed two other people from the ballroom to my floor. When I reached my door, Princess came out of his room further down the hall with two large bags hanging from his shoulders.

"Going somewhere?" I asked as he approached.

"I'm leaving," he replied in a low voice.

"Are they giving notices already?"

He shook his head. "I don't think so."

"Then wh…"

"It's inevitable," he interrupted. "My performance has been crap the last few days, my heart just isn't in it anymore. It's obvious who they want so why should I bother staying. Honestly, I wish it had been you."

"Wh-what are you talking about?"

"They took Roberts out about an hour ago. He was bound and gagged, it was obvious they were taking him on that fear challenge thing. You didn't know?"

"No…I was having dinner with a friend."

My cheeks felt flush, causing me to lean up against my door.

"I'm sorry, Tosh," he said and adjusted the bags on his shoulders. "Like I said, I was really rooting for you to get the spot. Roberts can be an asshole sometimes, but not you, no matter how often we were jerks to you. In my worst moment, you were there to pull me to the finish. I'll never forget that."

"I'll see you around then, Princess."

He smiled. "It's just Walter. Good luck, Tosh."

Walter, formerly Princess, patted my shoulder before stepping past me. My brain was on overload and I was flooded with conflicting emotions. At first, the fact that Roberts had been chosen for the challenge made my heart sink, but then a moment later it was as though a weight had been lifted off my chest. I was…relieved? How was that possible? I should be crumbling into a ball because my dreams of becoming a Warrior have been crushed, a year of my life painfully wasted, but instead a smile stretched across my face. I opened the door to my room and stepped inside. Someone grabbed my arms and pulled them behind me, and then placed a thick canvas bag over my head.

"Scream and you're dead," was all that he said.

Chapter Thirty-four

With my wrists and ankles bound with zip ties, I was carried out of my room, down the back stairwell, and then across the gravel driveway. Next there was the sound of a van door sliding opening and I was thrown inside. A utility van maybe. One that had no carpet on the floor and plenty of open room. The van spun around, causing me to roll and hit the exposed metal sides of the interior. I never came into contact with any other passengers as I rolled uncontrollably around the back of the van.

After what seemed like twenty minutes the van slowed and bobbled around on an unpaved surface. When we came to a full stop, the side door slid open. Someone grabbed me by my bound ankles, dragged me out of the van and onto their shoulder. After being carried for a few seconds I was put down on my feet, the ties around my wrists and ankles were snapped free and whatever had previously secured the canvas bag around my neck was removed. I waited a moment before tentatively touching the bag's edges with my fingers, waiting for someone to smack them. When that didn't occur, I quickly pulled the bag from my head and threw it to the ground.

Quickly I turned around to take in my surroundings. I was on an athletic field, soccer maybe, with a set of bleachers up ahead on the right, but nothing much else around. Behind me sat the van several feet away abandoned with the doors left open. It was Julian's van, I'd know it anywhere. It was white, otherwise non-descript, and had odd dents from past prisoner transports. So at least one question was answered, this wasn't Garrett. Was this truly my fear challenge? Had I'd been selected in addition to Roberts? I had no weapons, and I was only wearing jeans and a loose sweater, not necessarily appropriate battle gear.

Knowing there was a slim chance, I stepped back to the van to see if perhaps I'd been left a weapon, truly praying that I'd see one of my whips or even a dagger. When my search of the van produced nothing, I opened the passenger door and bent down to check if there was anything under the seat. Nothing. Damn it. When I stood back up, something caught my attention in the side mirror. There was a soft light shining in the distance. When I turned around to see the source, I found a young woman slowly walking toward me. She was holding her right hand out in front of her, and rising from the center of her palm was a flame. A Firestarter.

As she drew nearer, I crumbled backward into the corner of the door and fell to the ground. The Firestarter opened her left hand and drew the flame from her right hand creating an arc of fire between them that was so bright it illuminated her young face. She tilted her palms down and sent her streams of fire into the ground. My heels dug and slipped in the grass while the door hinge kept rocking me forward as the flames ate their way toward me.

My legs slid out from under me and I crawled behind the van's door just as the Firestarter directed her streams of fire at me. Within seconds the entire van was on fire. I looked wildly around trying to find anything I could use for shelter. The bleachers looked like the only option, and that was a terrible one. I jerked my hands away from the blazing hot door and knew there wasn't much time. Tears filled my eyes as fear sank my feet further into the ground. I couldn't move, let alone run across the field completely exposed.

"Come on!" I shouted to myself as thick black smoke began rising from the van.

With a loud scream, I jumped out from behind the van and ran toward the bleachers. The Firestarter caught sight of me and her flames were quickly chasing after me. Just when the bleachers were a few feet away, the van exploded behind me, the impact throwing me forward into one of the bleacher's metal beams. My head pounded and sent a shockwave through my body. Blood trickled down my forehead and right cheek. As I wiped the blood out of my eye I saw that the Firestarter had also been knocked back by the explosion, but she was rolling over onto her side when she caught sight of me again. I stumbled into the network of the bleacher's support beams, my sight and balance definitely hindered by the head injury, although I could feel the skin stretching and stitching back together.

Moments later I was in the center of the bleacher's underbelly, hiding behind a tall beam and trying to catch my breath. The Firestarter had returned to her feet and was walking toward the bleachers with glowing hands. What was the end game here? If this was a fear challenge, then they had won because I was terrified. If it looked like I'd die would they call a timeout or something?

The bleachers squeaked a moment before bright orange flames surrounded me. The back of my sweater caught fire, sending me to the ground in a panic. Quickly I rolled in the loose dirt until the flames were extinguished. My back was screaming in pain while images of Ty surrounding me in flames flashed in my head. Not again. I couldn't have this happen to me again. I was a sitting duck under here, but I didn't know where else to go. Not again, not again.

"Get up!" I shouted to myself.

My arms shook as I gritted my teeth and crawled along the ground, trying to get out the other side of the bleachers. Not that I knew what I would do once I stepped out there since I'd be completely exposed. The Firestarter caught sight of my movement and directed her flames between two of the benches. The fire was too high to hit me and actually illuminated the area, and that's when I saw it. Sitting at the opposite end of the bleachers sat my weapons bag. My beautiful weapons bag full of instruments of pain that would make this Firestarter wish she'd never let a flame leave her hand. The trick was how I would get to the weapons without catching on fire again.

The Firestarter had changed her tactic and began shooting short bursts of fire between the benches, each time going through a lower rung. When she was finally low enough to kneel on the ground, my weapons bag was within my reach. A ball of fire hit me in the left arm just as I leapt for the weapons bag. Once again I dropped to the ground and rolled the flames out from my arm. Quickly I wrapped my hand around one of the whips inside the bag. Just as the Firestarter reared her left hand back, I snapped my whip forward causing her to scream as it wrapped around her wrist. In the next second I grasped the whip with my left hand and pulled back roughly. The Firestarter fell to the ground and immediately I jumped on her back, wrapped one arm in front of her neck and the other around her head. She placed her hot hands on my forearm around her neck as I began to squeeze the air out of her. Wisps of smoke began to rise from my arm as her glowing hands burned through my sweater and began melting my skin. My body jerked as the pain and panic grew, but only a few seconds more and she would be unconscious. Just a few more seconds, for the love of God just a few more seconds.

Slowly but surely the heat underneath her hands became less and less until she no longer struggled underneath me.

"Tosh!" someone yelled. "Tosh, let her go!"

The person yelling flipped me over, took the Firestarter from my arms, and laid her on her side next to me. When he returned, I saw that it was Jared, flailing and yelling other words to me, but I couldn't comprehend what he was saying. My brain overloaded and started firing everything at once. My skin was melting, my clothes were on fire, it was all around me.

"Put it out! Put it out!" I screamed and tried slapping my arms and legs.

"You're not burning, Tosh," he yelled when he finally caught my arms and held them up in front of me. "Look! You're not burning."

My eyes finally focused and I could see that there were just holes where the Firestarter's heat had burned through my sweater revealing red welts where my skin was starting to heal.

"You're healing, Tosh, I promise," he continued to say. "You're ok." Jared stood up and forcefully lifted me from the ground by my arms. "Can someone help the unconscious girl?"

I looked out in the direction he had shouted and saw that the field parking lot suddenly had several cars and SUVs. A group of men all dressed in white were attending to Julian's van by extinguishing the flames and breaking it down into pieces. Jared pulled me into his side as two other men in white ran to the Firestarter's side.

"Are…are those Cleaners?" I asked while stumbling along the field.

"Yep. They've been on-call for you and Roberts tonight."

"But…Julian's…van…"

"He wanted a new one anyway," he replied and dragged me alongside him.

My head was spinning as more and more realization was hitting me how much of my torture had been planned. I looked back at the Firestarter who was still on the ground but now being attended to by two Cleaners. "Who was that girl?"

"A hybrid from Facility East," Jared replied casually and I looked up at him completely flabbergasted. "What?"

"That's why Jonah's here. He brought her, didn't he?"

Jared nodded. "And he and Diana are probably not going to be too happy that you put her in a sleeper hold," he replied and then squeezed me into his side. "Hey, they all knew the risks and still agreed to it, so don't worry too much, ok? Nikki's in the Jeep. She's been ready to kill us all since we got here."

I looked to where Jared was pointing and saw Nikki pacing in front of his Jeep. Tears fell over my eyelids the minute we made eye contact. My knees buckled a little before breaking free from Jared's side and running to my sister. In all my life I had never heard my sister cry so hard. She was practically shaking as she squeezed me uncomfortably into her chest.

"These people are sick," she cried and rose up to look at me. "I can't believe..." she paused and wiped the tears from her face, "...they're just fucking sick." Nikki looked over my shoulder and yelled, "Can I take her home now?"

Jared came up beside me. "Yeah, the Cleaners can handle things here."

"What happens now?" I asked and climbed up into the backseat of Jared's Jeep.

"You have to meet with Cameron and Dev. They've been watching everything from the manor."

My stomach sank even though the adrenaline was still pumping through me. Jared closed his door and started the car. Nikki climbed up in the backseat beside me and pulled me into her side. I couldn't tell who needed who more in that moment. My worst nightmare had come true and I came out the other side. Nikki held me tightly as I choked on the sobs that came out from deep within me. The trip back to the manor took roughly twenty minutes and only when we were a few minutes out did Nikki pull me up and instruct that I "pull my shit together."

I sat up in my seat and wiped my eyes. Jared rolled down the windows in the back and the cool breeze helped pull the redness from my face. Nikki squeezed my hand tightly when we pulled through the manor's gates. I knew she was struggling with the possibility of me becoming a Warrior, and for the first time she wasn't alone. My stomach was churning and doing backflips about what might happen next.

A few minutes later Jared escorted me through the manor doors and toward Cameron and Devin's shared office. When we turned the corner, Roberts was sitting on the bench on the other side of the office's door. His face was covered in dirt, a cut across his cheek, and his clothes were dirty and torn. He smiled when he saw me, his bright white teeth in severe contrast to his dirty face.

"You too?" he asked as I sat down. "I was hoping. They put me in a cave-in and attacked me. You?"

I put my hand through one of the holes in the arm of my sweater. "Firestarter."

His face fell. "You're shitting me."

"I wish, but hey, I put her in a sleeper hold by the end of it."

His laugh died in his throat and he sighed. "Good for you, Tosh. No one will be calling you Scarecrow anymore. Ty would be proud."

I flinched at Ty's name thinking how I wouldn't have even had a fear challenge if it weren't for him. In some ways he was the reason I was here.

"Cave-in?" I asked, thinking my challenge was a lot more difficult than his.

He nodded. "Got trapped in a collapsed mine when I was young. Haven't been able to go into dark, closed spaces like that since. Caves are the worst, practically had a panic attack in there, but like you I got through it."

"Now we wait," I sighed but a moment later the office door opened and Devin stepped out.

"Trevor, please come inside," Devin said and gestured into the office.

Roberts stood up nervously and wiped his hands on his pants. He paused and looked down at me.

"Good luck," I said and he nodded. It was the first time I'd ever seen Roberts less than a thousand percent confident.

When the door shut behind them my body collapsed over my knees. I didn't know what to do with myself. Muscles were twitching and flinching, flashes of the Firestarter's flames looping in my brain, so much so I jerked off the bench and began pacing.

What would they say to me? What would I say back? What about Beckett? Should I tell them? Would it matter since I had no idea if I'd ever see him again? Why was my life so full of questions and not one real answer to be found?

Only five minutes passed before the office door opened and Roberts stepped out with a big smile on his face.

"Well?" I asked.

"I'm in," he said breathlessly. "I...I can't believe it."

"Why not? You're the best we have," I replied.

In an odd moment, he opened his arms and hugged me. That had never been us, but I assumed he was just as much of a mess of emotions as I was.

"I'm crossing my fingers for you," he said in my ear.

I patted him on the back and he shuffled down the hall in exhaustion.

"Natasha?" Cameron asked from the office doorway and snapped me to attention. "Please come inside."

I sighed loudly through my mouth and stepped into the office. Devin was leaning against his desk with his arms crossed while Cameron came to stand next to him.

"Natasha," Cameron began, "to say that the last few weeks have been a rollercoaster would be an understatement."

"Yes, sir," I answered and wrung my hands in front of me.

Devin rose from his desk, but kept his arms crossed in front of him as he said, "Tosh, if we had to make this decision two months ago, there would be no question that you would be a Warrior. But this week alone you have shown how susceptible you are to outside influences."

I was going to vomit right here on their priceless area rug. "Yes, sir," I replied with threatening tears.

"You shut down for three days which is something we cannot tolerate," Devin continued in a harsh tone. "Our enemies do not care that your heart is broken. As a Warrior you must persevere and put whatever problems you have to the side. It is not easy, but it is necessary in order to be successful."

"Yes, sir," I said and looked up at the ceiling, allowing the tears to fall down my cheeks. "I understand."

"That said," Cameron began, "we both agree that your performance today speaks for itself. I also believe that you have learned a significant life lesson, and found a new strength within you."

"I did?" I asked stupidly and both of them laughed.

"Natasha, in the last two days you have made a complete turnaround and outperformed your colleagues. Therefore," Cameron said and stepped forward, "we would like to ask you to be a part of our family permanently." My jaw dropped. "Welcome to the coven, Natasha."

My hands instantly covered my face as tears drained down my cheek. "Th-thank you."

Cameron wrapped his arms around me. "We are happy beyond words, Natasha."

I nodded and took a step back to see Devin. "Thank you, sir, for all your training."

He smiled. "You were very easy to teach, Tosh. Now we must discuss a very important, and somewhat complicated subject."

"What's that?"

Cameron turned his back and walked back to stand next to Devin. "Natasha, what we tell you now is extremely confidential and cannot be discussed with your friends, family, or even other coven members. Is that understood?"

"Ye-yes, sir," I replied nervously.

"Natasha, as you are well aware, Brianna is the first vampire in history without a sensitivity to sunlight. That is because, we believe, she was Turned by three vampires – Victor, Eris, and myself." My eyes widened at the information. "You and Trevor will be the first to truly test out our hypothesis. Therefore, if you are comfortable enough, we would like to Turn you with a combination of me, Devin, and a Warrior of your choosing."

I blinked several times before finally responding, "Um, ok, I…um…when? When would you Turn me?"

"That is also up to you," Devin answered. "We can Turn you before you're inducted, or if you choose to wait, we can induct you as a hybrid. I know my brother would prefer to wait until your studies are complete, but it is your choice."

This was real. Everything was finally in front of me and all I could think about was if they Turned me, Beckett and I could never be together. His blood would be poison to me. I must have had a panicked look on my face since Cameron said, "It is not something you need to decide on tonight, Natasha."

"What is Roberts doing?" I asked.

"He is being Turned before his induction," Devin replied. "But that doesn't have to be your decision as well. As you have shown us several times, you do things your own way and in your own time."

I laughed uncomfortably and way too loudly. "I-I need to think about it."

Cameron nodded. "Yes, it is the biggest decision of your life. It should not be taken lightly."

"Yes, sir. Thank you, sir."

Devin smiled, which didn't happen often. "Congratulations, Tosh.

Now go and celebrate, or fall into your bed, both are acceptable tonight."

I nodded and backed out of the room. When I closed the door and turned around I found the faces of Brianna, Jared, Alex and Kyla, and even my sister looking at me expectantly.

"Well?" Brianna asked nervously.

"They must be crazy because they're letting me in."

Cheers rang out in the stone hallway as the family crushed me with their congratulatory hugs. Even though I knew Nikki wasn't all that thrilled about me becoming a Warrior, she still put on a happy face and cheered with the others.

"Let's celebrate," Jared said loudly. "Let's watch Tosh get trashed."

I laughed nervously along with everyone else. "Thanks, everyone, really, I mean it, but I can barely feel my legs. I really need to crash."

"Ah, come on, really?" Jared whined.

"Leave her alone, Jer," Brianna chided and then rested her hand on my shoulder. "Go get some sleep, honey, we'll celebrate tomorrow."

"I'll take you up," Nikki said and put her arm around my waist.

"Thanks, Nik," I replied and settled into her side. "Goodnight, everyone, and thanks again."

The family bid us goodnight as Nik helped me down the hall. By the time we got to the grand spiral staircase I started to worry if my legs would even be able to go up so many stairs. All my energy was draining out of me.

"Nik? Will you help me?"

"I'm practically carrying your ass up these stairs as it is."

"No, not that. I might need you to cover for me tomorrow."

"Uh-huh. You going where I think you're going?"

I nodded. "I've got to see him."

She raised her eyebrows at me. "You realize you're basically spitting in their faces minutes after they asked you to be in the coven. Not judging here, just making you are aware."

"Will you cover for me?"

She laughed. "I will always cover for you when you rebel against the machine. You're finally acting like a Cushlin."

Chapter Thirty-five

Getting ahold of Beckett was actually pretty easy since when I got back to my room there were nearly twenty texts on his phone that I'd stuffed in my nightstand drawer. He'd had a horrible feeling that I was in trouble. I wasn't sure how he'd know, but I knew there was no way he would have imagined what I had been through. Thankfully he was pretty sure he could get away and meet at our usual motel.

The adrenaline fatigue helped me sleep through the night, allowing my body and mind to fully heal. When I woke, I literally bounced out of the bed and ran into the shower. By the time I returned to the bedroom, Nikki was sitting up in bed, although she wasn't too happy about it.

"So where are you going if anyone asks?" she yawned.

"I'm just going for a drive to clear my head," I replied and pulled my weapons bag up on my shoulder. "It's not too far from the truth. I have to figure out what I'm going to do."

"Well, don't forget to have a little…fun."

"Nik…"

"All I'm saying is that if you get caught, at least you got your kicks."

I paused and stared at her, debating whether or not I should admit I had already planned for the possibility, but on second thought I decided it was best to keep it to myself.

"I'll be back this afternoon," I said and headed to the door.

"Nat," Nikki said in a worried tone, "be careful, ok?"

I nodded and opened the door. "I will. See ya later."

She waved goodbye and fell back into bed. I closed the door and my feet propelled me down the hall to the spiral staircase. My heart was beating against my ribs at the notion that I would be seeing Beckett in a few hours. Together we would figure out what to do. Realistically this was probably the last time we would see each other. But in my heart there wasn't a version of this story where we weren't together. We hadn't gone through all of this only to live our lives wondering how things might have been.

When I reached the bottom of the staircase, I turned to walk toward the front door when someone called my name from behind. I stopped and turned around to find Jonah walking quickly to catch up to me, although the girl who was with him lingered behind. Even with her head tilted down to the ground I recognized her as the Firestarter from last night.

"Hey, I was hoping I would catch you before we had to leave," Jonah said and then awkwardly looked down at the floor. "How mad at me are you?"

"I'm not," I replied. "Afterwards I realized why you said what you did."

Jonah put his hands in the pockets of his jeans and shifted his weight back and forth. "Can't say it was the highlight of my job, but I knew you could do it. That's why I was hoping we'd run into you. I'd like to introduce you to Lyla."

"Technically we've met," I replied flatly.

Jonah narrowed his eyes at me and then gestured to the Firestarter. "Tosh Cushlin, meet Lyla Firino."

My breath caught. "F-firino?"

She nodded. "Yes. I'm...Ty was my cousin." My eyes immediately began to water and I took a step back. Lyla took a step forward and gave me a pleading look. "When Jonah asked if I would come out here, I jumped at the chance."

"To hurt me?"

Lyla's face fell. "What? No, no to help you."

"You call setting me on fire helping me?"

Jonah squeezed my arm. "Listen to what she has to say, Tosh."

Lyla looked down at her hands. "They said this was to help you become a Warrior, that's why I did it." She looked back up at me with tears in her eyes. "My family and I have always felt terrible about what happened to you. You were the victim of Ty's recklessness, and...and I just wanted you to know...that I'm sorry for the pain my cousin caused you. I hope that you won't be fearful of us in the future."

Lyla extended her hand, but I didn't take it. Jonah nudged me with his shoulder and then urged me with his eyes. Even though I'd won against her last night, my hand still shook as I reached across and took her hand. Her palm was warm which alone made me uneasy.

"Have a safe flight home," I said and pulled my hand out of hers.

"Where are you off to?" Jonah asked.

I froze for a moment and then replied, "Just taking a drive. I need to clear my head. Lots to think about, you know?"

He nodded and hugged me tightly. "You're sure you're ok?"

"Yeah, just need to figure out some things."

I stepped out of his hold, thanked him, and waved goodbye. Jonah saw through me better than anyone, probably because he'd had a lot of practice with his sister. If I stayed a second longer he would know something was up. For all I knew he already did, and I wasn't entirely sure he would keep that to himself.

Once out the door, I walked quickly to my car, plugged in my phone and set the playlist for the long drive. It should have concerned me that I had no qualms about lying and betraying my coven. But the bad Cushlin side of me was flaring up and just didn't give a shit.

When I pulled up to the small motel there were no other cars in the parking lot. I parked in front of the office and found the same miserable man behind the desk staring blankly at his TV. He barely peeled his eyes away in order to help me.

"Is room six available?"

He raised his eyes to me, his lids only open halfway in a stark expression. "Does it look like there's anyone here?"

"Um, no. So…"

"How long?"

"Oh, um, an hour I guess," I replied and dug in my pocket for the cash.

"Big spender," the man said sarcastically.

"Two then."

He gave a slight laugh as he took the money from my hand and handed me an old-fashioned motel key with the plastic tag attached to it. I pulled into a spot several doors down from room six, and just as I turned to close the motel room door I saw another car pull into the parking lot. My stomach flipped and a smile stretched across my face.

Quickly I ran to the mirror on the wall and futzed with my hair and clothes. A minute later there was a knock at the door and I nearly jumped with excitement. After one last big breath, I stepped over to the door and looked through the peephole to find Beckett fidgeting with his sunglasses.

When he reached back to knock again, I opened the door and lost my breath at the sight of him. He gave me a smile and stepped inside. I closed the door behind him and as soon as I turned around his hands were cupping my cheeks. I gasped at their warmth and further still at how warm his lips were. His tongue found mine and we began exploring each other's mouths. After only a couple of minutes Beckett pulled away from my lips but kept his hands on my face and hovered over me.

"Are you ok?" he said breathlessly.

I nodded. "Are you?"

"I was so worried about you."

"Becks, are you in control?"

He blinked and lifted his face away. "What? Control, like am I going to phase?" I nodded nervously. "Uh, I-I don't believe so. Why?"

Quickly I wrapped my arms around his neck and jumped to pull my legs around his waist. I kissed him softly and his hands rested in the small of my back.

"Tosha," he said and tilted his head back to look at me, "I don't know if I…I don't know what will happen, it's not something I've tested yet."

I raised my eyebrows. "I hope not," I said sternly.

He smiled for a moment, but then rested his forehead against mine. "I could never forgive myself if I hurt you."

"We'll stop if you feel like you're losing control," I said and flicked his earlobe with the tip of my tongue, then sucked it into my mouth. He moaned and tightened his arms around me. "I came prepared."

Beckett's eyes flared and a devious smile stretched across his face. "Have I told you how much I love you?"

My stomach fluttered at his words. It had been so long since I had been loved, and now the thought was energizing my body. "Why don't you show me," I said seductively and squeezed my legs around his waist.

Beckett held onto my legs and laid me down on the bed, placing his weight on top of me. His lips traveled down my neck and then across my collarbone, finally making a trail down the center of my chest. I grabbed the ends of my shirt and Beckett lifted himself up so that I could pull it over my head. He hovered above me and looked down upon my abdomen. His hands slid up my scars and he kissed them. I released a high-pitched sigh as he reached up and squeezed my breasts.

"My bag," I said softly and pointed to the nightstand.

Beckett stood from the bed, grabbed the bag and fished around inside. First, he pulled out a small dagger and raised one of his eyebrows. I smiled coyly and removed my bra. Beckett put his hand back inside my bag and pulled out one of my whips that I had tightly coiled.

"Was this what you meant by being prepared?"

I unbuttoned my pants and pulled them down below my hips. "I prepared for every possible scenario." On the third try, he pulled the small tub of gel and handed it to me. "Thank you, now drop your pants."

He laughed and unbuttoned his jeans. "Do you ever get tired of bossing me around?

"No," I laughed.

He smiled and lifted his shirt over his head. I gasped at how muscular he had gotten. His pecs were rounded and firm, a chiseled trail down the center of his abdomen then cutting into six soft compartments. Beckett placed his hand self-consciously over his stomach. I sat up on the bed and pulled his hand away. Like he had done with me, I kissed his abdomen several times and felt his muscles relax under my lips.

Gingerly I unzipped his pants, feeling the bulge underneath and freeing him from the confinement. I looked up from under my lashes as I took him into my mouth, watching as his face melted into pleasure while his breathing increased. Beckett wrapped a hand around the back of my head and pulled me away from him. Within seconds shoes were flying, pants and underwear were stripped, and finally hot naked bodies were colliding.

Beckett laid between my legs, slowly gliding in and out of me. As it was before, the feeling itself was numb, but there was memory of the true feeling in the back of my mind. Really the most pleasure came out of his chest pressing against me, the sweat building between us due to the heat he was generating. He was being incredibly gentle, and going slow in order to caress my breasts and the sides of my hips, but I wanted more of him. I tightened my legs around his waist and rocked to the side, rolling him on his back. Beckett's eyes were wide with surprise, but then melted once again as I glided my pelvis back and forth. His fingers dug into my hips and legs, somewhat clawing at the thick scars. I took his hands and moved them to my breasts. Easily he took over and squeezed them tightly as I rubbed against him harder and faster until his body started to tense and fierce breaths came from within him. But it wasn't just the feeling of him touching me, it was how he as looking at me. I felt beautiful and free to share myself with him.

In a swift move he wrapped his arm around my waist and flipped me on my back again, pulling my left leg up and crooking it through his elbow as he pounded against me and finally released all of himself inside. His body collapsed on top of me, although he was breathing heavily in my ear. My hands went to his back, but he shook his head.

"Don't...just...give me a second," he panted.

I froze and held my breath. My bottom lip began to tremble at the scarily familiar position of having a loaded weapon between my legs.

Slowly Beckett came back to me, first caressing my cheek with his fingertips, and then with a kiss on the side of my neck. When he finally pressed up on his elbow I noticed his green eyes were a little brighter than before. I brushed the hair away from his sticky forehead and his face melted into my palm.

"Are you ok?" I asked softly.

He nodded and rolled off of me, but pulled me over to rest on his chest. I curled into his side and wrapped my leg over his hips. Mindlessly he began tracing my scars with his fingers, finding his favorites of course, and seeming to concentrate on the one he called three fingers. We laid there for nearly ten minutes in silence, our breathing the only sound between us. The heat from his body began to lessen, still not to a normal level but not feverish like it had been earlier.

"Becks?"

"Hmmm?" he replied lazily. I looked up to find that his eyes were closed and he had the most peaceful expression on his face. I hated to break it.

"We need to talk." It was the worst thing a girl could say to her boyfriend.

Beckett opened his eyes but concentrated on the ceiling. "I know. Things are getting complicated."

"More than you know," I said and sat up on my elbow.

"Does this have to do with last night?"

I nodded. "How did you know I was in trouble?"

He rubbed his face with his hand. "That's part of the complication."

"I don't understand."

"We're connected, Tosha," he said, his tone almost sounding frustrated. "I talked to Floyd about it, he says that when wolves find a strong mate, their souls are connected." I raised a skeptical eyebrow at him. "Hey, it sounded like a lot of hippie-dippie bullshit to me, but I was literally having a raging panic attack until about an hour before you contacted me."

"Why is it complicated?"

Beckett rubbed his face and then rose to a sitting position on the side of the bed, his head drooping down into his chest. "Because, if Floyd is right, they could be getting information about you I don't want them to know."

"How's that?"

"It's complicated," he replied and rose from the bed.

"Then uncomplicate it."

He reached down to the floor and began pulling his pants back on. "I-I can't, Tosha. There are things we just can't discuss. It's safer that way." When he finally turned around, the strain and worry on his face was evidence he wasn't lying to me. He really thought that whatever it was, it was safer not to tell me. "So, what happened last night? Were you in trouble?"

"It's complicated," I replied snidely and rolled to the other side of the bed to gather my clothes.

"Don't do that," he said sharply.

"Why not? Like you said, we shouldn't be talking about each other's business." I slid on my underwear and pants so fast they gave me rugburn. "I'm just the whore you meet in a seedy motel every couple of days."

"You asked *me* to meet you," he replied and stepped to the far corner of the room. "You think this is easy for me? Every second I'm away from you, it kills me. Being with you now and knowing I have to leave you, kills me. I-I thought I could do this, but now...I don't know what's worse. I'm dying inside, Tosha, and fucking Garrett is pulling my strings. If I don't do exactly what he says, you or my mom are dead, but if I do what he's forcing me to do I'll be dead anyway. So..."

"What?" I interrupted. It sounded more like a cry than a word.

Beckett looked up at me and swallowed. "I shouldn't have said that."

"Well, you did. What is he forcing you to do?" I asked and pulled my shirt over my head.

"Tell me what happened last night."

I sighed knowing I would be putting more stress on the situation. "They made me a Warrior last night." His eyes widened, and a sliver of a smile formed across his lips until some of the realization hit. "They put me through a challenge, and I won. The challenge is what you felt last night, I'm guessing."

"What was the challenge?"

I sat down on the edge of the bed. "I battled a Firestarter," I replied and looked over at him. "Ty's cousin, actually. There were a couple of moments I thought for sure I was going to die, but somehow, I pushed through. They're inducting me and Roberts."

"Tosha," Beckett began softly, "this is what you wanted."

"I know," I replied, feeling the tears stinging my eyes.

"Then why are you crying?"

I looked up at the ceiling. "Because if they Turn me, we can never be together. Vamps and werewolves, sworn enemies for all time, and your blood would be toxic to me. The Warriors are hunting Garrett and you've lost their protection because you defected. Shall I go on?"

"Tosha, if I'm the only thing holding back your happiness, then forget about me."

I stood from the bed. "How can you say that? I *tried* to do that, and you pulled me back. It's not that easy for me to just forget you. I don't want...anything...without you. You have to be there, next to me, it's just how it has to be, Becks."

Beckett leaned back against the desk, folding over slightly at the waist and white-knuckling the edges. "Tosha," he said and then paused. "Tosha, he's forcing me to challenge the pack leader." The blood ran from my face. "It's a battle to the death. There's no way I'll win, although Garrett is determined."

"Then don't do it!"

"I don't have a choice, Tosha!" he shouted. "It's either I do it, or he goes after my mom, or you, or anyone else he can find to torture me with."

"You...can't!" I cried and ran to his chest, squeezing him tightly around the waist.

"Don't make this harder on me," he said, his voice cracking slightly.

I looked up at him and placed my hands on his face, pulling him down to my eye level. "Come. Home."

Beckett shook his head. "They'll kill my mom."

"We'll protect her."

"They'll come after you."

"And we'll be ready for them," I replied and shook him slightly. "Come home, Beckett, come back to the manor."

He pulled my hands away from his face. "I'm an enemy of the Warriors, Tosha, they won't just let me walk into the place."

"I'll prepare them." I sat down on the bed and began lacing up my boots. "I'll tell them you're coming with intel about Garrett, but you and your mom need protection. They'll do this, Beckett, they do this all the time."

"They'll lock me up," he said flatly and I gave him a stern look.

"It's better than being killed."

Beckett was silent for a few moments, tapping his fingers on the desk while he debated the situation in his head. With a sigh, he pushed himself off the desk and replied. "Fine."

I jumped from the bed and slammed my lips against his. Just as Beckett's hands went underneath the back of my shirt, there was a knock at the door. We both jolted away from each other at the sound and then froze.

"Dawes!" someone shouted and banged on the door. "We know you're in there."

Beckett looked at me and put his index finger up to his lips. Next, he began grabbing the remainder of my things and pushed them into my arms before pointing to the closet. I widened my eyes in an are-you-effing-kidding-me look. His response was to push me into the closet and pull the split door closed.

I stopped the closet door with my hand and whispered. "Let me help you."

His jaw twitched as his face contorted with conflict, and then he shook his head. Tears instantly formed in my eyes as he gave me a hard kiss on the lips, and then closed the closet door. The next thing I heard was the shower being turned on and the bathroom door close. Through the hinge of the closet door I could see him cross back to the front of the room.

"Yeah, I'm comin'," he shouted at the door before shrugging into his T-shirt. He raked his hands through his hair before exhaling a resolved sigh. When he opened the door there were three men crowding the doorway. "Hey, guys, Stevenson, guess you caught me."

The first man pushed his way inside while the other two stayed in the doorway.

"Where is she?" the first man said as he walked slowly to the end of the bed. His skin was pale and his eyes dark and dead. Definitely a vamp, and from the lack of musculature, I assumed the others were as well.

"She's in the shower," Beckett said and pointed behind him. "Look, we don't need to involve her. You came for me, here I am, take me back. I wasn't running away or anything."

"Then what were you doing?"

"Getting laid," Beckett laughed and I wanted to punch him in the face.

The vamp seemed skeptical. "You came all the way out here to get your dick wet?"

Beckett shrugged. "Hey, Garrett told me to make nice with the nearby pack, so I did. We just both wanted to have some privacy for a few hours."

"So you're over that other girl?"

"What girl?" he asked and began lacing up his shoes.

"You know what girl," the vamp replied. "The one with the Warriors."

Beckett shook his head and stood up from the bed. "Her? Please, there was never anything there." My jaw clenched and it was evident Beckett was purposely keeping his back to me. "So, you want me to follow you out…"

"Not so fast," the vamp said and pressed his hand against Beckett's chest. "Garrett wants us to bring you in personally."

Beckett put his hands up and stepped back. "Come on, man, there's no need for that. I'm coming back…"

The vamp stepped forward and grabbed Beckett's arm firmly. "You've got a date with Vincent tonight."

Beckett flinched back, but the vamp grabbed his shoulders and threw him into the desk face first. The other two vamps stepped inside to subdue Beckett and bring him to a standing position with his arms behind his back. A low growl came out of Beckett's heaving chest as the vamps tripped over themselves and the furniture to get him out the door.

"If you phase, I swear I'll snap your neck," the main vamp said before putting his knee in Beckett's back.

A soft whine escaped my lips, and the main vamp froze for a moment. I held my breath, wishing I could stop my heartbeat as well. The main vamp shouted an order and all of then spilled out of the motel room. Once the door closed, I fell into the floor of the empty closet. In a loud burst of emotion, tears and wails came out of me as I gasped for air. Everything had gone to shit in a matter of minutes. One moment Beckett was coming home, and the next he was being dragged out of here. Was Vincent the pack leader? Were they taking him to battle the pack leader now? He would die. There was no way he would survive a challenge like that. But what could I do?

"You're a fucking Warrior, Natasha," I yelled at myself.

With a deep exhale, I slid open the closet door, finished putting myself together, and shut the shower off in the bathroom. Within two minutes I was revving my car to life and pulling it up in front of the motel office. The man behind the desk looked up as I ran inside.

"The men who were just here, which way did they turn out of the parking lot?"

He shook his head. "Can't say."

I grabbed his ear and pulled him roughly toward me. "Tell me! Or this gets much worse."

"Right," he screamed. "They turned right!"

I released him and jumped back into my car. The tires squealed on the pavement before catching and propelling me forward. I whipped the steering wheel to the right and put the pedal down to the floor. The Mercedes engine roared and stretched out as we peeled down the old highway. Within minutes I was coming up upon two cars as they curved around a bend, one of which looked similar to what Beckett had been driving. My hands squeezed the steering wheel tightly and prayed that my tires would hold the road.

Just as I made it around the bend, I slammed on my brakes to avoid a car that was sitting lengthwise in the middle of the road, within it, Beckett was banging on the window. I pulled the steering wheel as hard as I could to the right and caused the car to flip and dive through a thin wooded area. My head hit the rearview mirror as the car rolled down an embankment, glass and debris swirling around me, finally landing upside down and rocking to a stop.

Blood dripped from my head down onto the roof of the car. I knew it wasn't over, they would come after me. My weapons bag had been on my passenger seat and was now resting on the roof of the car near the window. I stretched my arm out and my fingertips could only brush the side of the bag. The seatbelt wouldn't release, no matter how hard I pressed the button. Behind me I could hear the sound of someone coming down through the woods. Blood was draining into my eyes as I stretched to reach my weapons bag, but barely able to touch the strap.

A branch broke on the other side of my car, and a second later there were hands grasping the driver's side door. As if it were a feather, the car was flipped right side up. The blood from my head wound dripped down my cheek although I could feel it starting to heal.

"Your boyfriend is a bad liar," the vamp said, and I recognized him as the main guy from the motel room.

My weapons bag had fallen back down on the passenger seat. Just as the vamp ripped the door from its hinges, my fingers caught the hilt of a dagger.

"Well let's get this over with," he said and reached inside the car.

Just as his hand pulled on my arm, I used the force to pull the dagger from the weapons bag and plunge it into his lower chest, unfortunately missing his heart. He screamed and stumbled back, giving me just enough time to grab the strap of my weapons bag before he grabbed me around my waist and threw me from the car. My back and head slammed against a thick tree and I fell forward to the ground. It took several seconds for the sharp, radiating pain to register. When I pushed myself up to my knees I realized a large splinter of wood had pierced through the palm of my left hand.

The vamp stared in disbelief as I pulled it from my hand. "Slut from the pack my ass," he said and then pulled the knife from his chest. "You're from the coven, aren't you?"

Cradling my left hand to my chest, I pulled myself back with my right hand and felt the canvas material of my weapons bag. I just needed another minute or two to heal enough where I could use my left hand.

"Who's Vincent?" I asked, reaching behind me in order to feel around inside my bag.

"You were in the closet, weren't you?" he said and threw the knife down on the ground. "The thing about showers, the water makes a distinct noise when it hits a body. It was a nice touch though."

"Who's Vincent!" I shouted and found the handle of my whip.

The vamp stepped forward. "He's the pack leader. Garrett needs Beckett to be the pack leader and the only way that happens is killing Vincent through a pack lead challenge. Not that Beckett has a chance, he's still a pup."

"Why? Why does Garrett need Beck to be pack leader?"

He shook his head and clicked his tongue. "Oh there's no time for that. I need to get back in time to see Vincent rip Beckett to shreds. I can't stand the wolves, but I do like the way they battle."

I grasped the handle of my whip and threw it out in front of me. The whip's end snapped and wrapped around the vamp's neck. He hissed and grabbed at his neck, his fingers burning from the silver coating. With a grunt, I pushed off the ground and leapt to the other side of him. The vamp fell backwards and wriggled as I dragged him toward the car, threaded the handle of my whip through the steering wheel, and pulled the whip until the vamp's body was pressed into the corner of the car.

The silver whip was burning through his neck, but certainly not fast enough. He fought forward and I lost a little ground. I slammed my leg into the side of the car for leverage and pulled the whip back, craning his neck back again. While he pulled at the whip with one hand, the vamp reached over and clawed at my leg. I lurched forward and lost several inches of slack. With a loud cry, I wrapped the whip around my wrist and pressed back against the car until I was almost parallel to the ground. I needed another weapon. I needed my dagger.

My bleeding leg protested as I pressed into the car once again and looked over my shoulder. The dagger was a foot away on the ground. I could reach it with one hand, but that would mean losing the leverage I already had. The vamp clawed at my leg once again, this time taking a large chunk of skin and muscle out of my calf. The pain caused me to instantly let go of the whip, causing both of us to fall to the ground.

Quickly I reached for the dagger and when I rolled over the vamp was leaping in my direction. With a swipe of the dagger I slashed directly across his throat. His trajectory continued forward and he toppled on top of me. Thick blood began slowly leaking from his throat while he gagged and choked over me. With some effort, I pushed the vamp off of me and rolled on top of him. I grabbed his hair with one hand and stretched his head up, and then slashed, slashed, slashed and slashed at his neck until his head came free from his body.

I dropped the severed head to the ground, rolled off to the side onto my back, and cried. It was a combination of pain, disgust at what I'd done, and fear of what would happen to Beckett. This was the worst-case scenario, the end of everything in my life. Once I caught my breath, I sat up from the ground and unwound my whip from the vamp's nub of a neck. There was still a large hole in my calf so I crawled painfully to the car and pulled my cell phone from within the center consol.

I slid back down to the ground and dialed the phone with a shaking hand.

"Hey," Nikki said on the other line, "you on your way back?" I broke down at the sound of her voice. "Nat? What's wrong? Are you in trouble?"

"Ohmygod, Nik, you have no idea how much trouble I'm in."

Chapter Thirty-six

After roughly two hours of laying in an abandoned field twitching, crying, and groaning in pain from my calf growing back, two white vans broke through the wood line. Anyone would have recognized them as the Cleaners, even before they piled out of the vans in their crisp white uniforms. I never understood why they would wear white when they had to deal with so much blood and grime. Seriously, how did they keep their clothes so white?

After hanging up with Nikki I didn't know what to expect. She said she'd get me help, and that was the last I'd heard. I seriously doubted that Nikki had called the Cleaners on her own, only a Warrior could have done that, which meant this had blown up within seconds of my phone call. When Jared's Jeep plowed through the woods, I gave a slight sigh of relief that at least it wasn't Devin. Jared jumped out of his Jeep and spoke with one of the Cleaners before walking over to me. His jaw was firmly set as he stood above me.

"Can you walk?" he asked flatly.

I shook my head and showed him my calf that was still only half healed. "I'll need a little help."

He bent down and grabbed my elbow, pulling me up to a standing position. I flinched and drew air through my teeth as soon as I put weight on my leg. Jared sighed, lifted me in his arms, and carried me to his Jeep.

"I can walk, I just need help."

"I don't have the patience for that," he replied without looking at me. He opened the passenger door and set me down on the seat. When he went to close the door, I stopped it with my hand.

"They're going to kill him, Jared."

Jared's face didn't show even the slightest bit of emotion. "That's not my problem."

"You were Beckett's mentor! Don't you care?"

"He made his choice, Tosh," he replied angrily.

"We could still track him, Jared, please…"

"Track him?" he shouted. "You have got some fucking balls asking me to do anything. Look at this, Tosh," he said and pointed to my car that was in pieces. "You could have died and we would have no idea what happened or where you were. You're such an…a fucking idiot!"

My arm barely made it inside before Jared slammed the door. Within the next second he was hopping up in the driver's seat and starting the engine.

"Where's Nikki?" I asked as we bounced through the rough terrain toward the road.

"Your sister is being interrogated, I'm sure within an inch of her life." He jerked his head and narrowed his eyes at me. "They brought in Julian, Tosh. The last time he questioned her they used non-human protocols. Who knows what the fuck they'll do to her now. Did you ever think of that? During all of this, did you ever think about those around you? They're bringing in Maddy, too."

I gasped. "But she didn't know anything…"

"You think they care!"

"I'm sorry," I cried into my hands, causing the tears, dirt, and blood to mix into a reddish mud. "I didn't mean for anyone to get in trouble. I just…"

"Needed to get laid?"

"No!" I shouted and rubbed my hands on my pants. "It wasn't like that."

"Oh, so you just decided to betray your coven. The same coven that you've wanted to become a part of for over a year and who has spent endless time and money training you, and made you a part of our family. I'd rather it be because you just wanted to get laid, that makes it less shitty, I think."

"I couldn't abandon him."

"But you could abandon us? Do you know how long it took my family to accept and trust your sister? Well, that's all gone. We're done, totally done. I hope all of this was worth it for you two because after today I don't know what you'll have left besides each other."

At the speed Jared was going, the motel came quickly on our left and I broke down. Jared didn't even flinch at my loud hysterics. There would be no sympathy found when he dragged me back into the manor. To them I would be a traitor, and I would crumble in front of them.

Jared drove so fast and swerved around traffic so much I almost vomited in his Jeep. It could have also been the feeling of eminent doom that awaited me. The roads that curved up into the hills of the city had always been welcoming, but today they were taking me to pain and confrontation. The tall black gates suddenly made it seem as though I was going into a prison. The gate guards even stared at me in judgement as we went past.

The Jeep was hardly parked before Jared was opening the passenger door and pulling me out by my arm.

"I can walk in on my own," I said, trying to pull my arm out of his grip, but failing.

"Actually, you can't," he growled as we stepped up the wide front steps. "You're lucky Julian's guards aren't out here to escort you in."

My breath caught in my throat. I knew I was in trouble, but not Julian level trouble. When we walked through the front doors people literally stopped in their tracks and gawked at me. Initially I was amazed that everyone knew what I had done, but then I realized that I was dirty and covered in blood.

When we turned the corner to reach the sirs' office, Nikki stood up quickly from the bench that sat in the hallway. Her face instantly went from concern to anger.

"For fuck's sake, you couldn't give her a napkin to wipe her face?" she snapped and glared at Jared.

"I was hoping it would garner some sympathy," he replied flatly and Nikki rolled her eyes. "Was your questioning...ok?"

"Like you care."

Jared's nostrils flared. "You're right, I don't. Where's Maddy?"

"She's still in there with them. Can I have a moment alone with my sister, please?"

Jared released my arm and headed toward the office door.

Nikki hugged me tightly and whispered in my ear, "I'm so sorry. I couldn't help you without telling him."

I pushed out of her arms. "Please tell me they didn't hurt you."

She shook her head. "No, nothing like the last time Julian questioned me. It was intense though, they're not going to go easy on you."

"I'm sorry I dragged you into this," I said and caught the tear before it dripped down my face. "They're going to kill him, Nik."

"What?!"

I nodded feverishly and wiped another tear. "They're forcing him into a battle with the pack leader."

Nikki's eyes flashed. "That's…to the death."

"I know!" I sobbed and she hugged me tightly once again.

"Tosh!" Jared shouted and waved me down the hall.

"Don't let them bully you, Nat," Nikki said firmly and squeezed my shoulders. "You made a mistake, and hell knows they've made plenty of them too."

I bit my bottom lip and nodded. The office door opened and I held my breath for a moment until Maddy came out from within. Jared stepped toward her, but she put her hand up to his face and walked past him. When she caught sight of me, she gasped and then gave Jared a dirty look.

"You couldn't let her clean her face?" she said causing Jared to tighten his jaw and look up at the ceiling in frustration.

"I'm so sorry, Maddy, I didn't mean for you…"

"Believe me, honey, they are more afraid of me than I am of them," she said firmly even though her soft, wrinkled hand on my cheek was incredibly gentle. "Tell me what you need."

"I don't even know," I cried.

She patted my cheek one last time. "Well, when you do, you tell me."

"Tosh," Jared called and waved me forward.

Maddy hugged me and whispered, "Tell them why you really did it, honey." When she released me, I gave her a questioning look. "Be honest with yourself, it'll go a long way."

I nodded, even though I wasn't completely sure what she was referring to. My heart pounded out of my chest as I walked to the office door. Jared fell in line behind me and closed the door once we stepped inside. Devin stood in front of his desk with his arms crossed tightly in front of his chest. Brianna was speaking with someone hiding behind the tall sides of an armchair. Only the legs of the person could be seen, and considering the tight fit of the pants, I assumed it was Cameron. Why was he hiding in the chair? Why wasn't he staring me down in disappointment and disgrace like Devin was doing? After another moment Brianna threw her arms up and stepped away from the chair.

The sound of Devin clearing his throat made me jump and face him. He raised an eyebrow at me and eyed me up and down. "Do you require any medical attention?" I shook my head. "Very well, we can get right down to it. You have been in contact with Beckett?"

"Y-yes, sir."

"How?"

"He snuck his cell phone into my bag. But…but I didn't find it right away."

"How long was it before he contacted you?"

"Um," I began and wiped my nose on my ragged sleeve, "about a week."

Devin raised another eyebrow and looked down his nose at me. "And the day you were brought back from the motel, were you told to tell us if Beckett contacted you?" Tears welled up in my eyes at the question and my jaw began to rattle. "Natasha?"

"Ye-yes."

"Did you understand that order?"

A tear dripped from my eye and down my cheek. "Yes."

"And you disobeyed that direct order?"

"Yes," I cried and covered my face with my hands.

Devin sighed loudly. When I finally pulled myself together, he continued, "Why did Beckett contact you?"

I swallowed hard and answered, "He said he wanted to see me, to apologize for leaving the way he did."

"And when was this?"

"A couple of days ago. Friday."

Suddenly Cameron stood up from his chair and looked at me with flaming eyes. "I saw you on Friday. You said you were going back to school. You lied to my face!"

"I'm sorry," I cried. "I just went to say goodbye to him. I needed closure and that's all I planned on doing."

"It is obvious you did more than that," he growled and sat back down in his chair.

I looked back at Brianna who simply shrugged and shook her head.

"I just wanted to see him. I didn't think it would hurt anyone, and I thought it would just be the one time."

"Oh, but it wasn't, was it? Was Mrs. Dawes also being contacted?"

"No, I-I told her..."

"When did he contact you again?" Devin interrupted.

"Late last night."

"And how is he able to contact you without Garrett knowing?"

"He was using a friend's phone."

"A friend?"

I nodded. "Floyd, I think he said."

"And what else did he say?"

"He said they were coming after us."

Cameron jumped up from his chair again.

"For crying out loud, Cam," Brianna said loudly, "either sulk in your chair or join the damn conversation."

"I guess I will join the damn conversation then," he yelled back and in an instant was next to Devin. "You sat in my quarters with my wife and children, and gave us this warning. All this time I thought it was your concern, or even perhaps your developing skills as a Warrior, but all the while you were merely sharpening your deception skills instead."

"I'm sorr..."

"Did it never occur to you that we could trace any calls that came in and locate Garrett and help Beckett in return?"

"N-no. I didn't think..."

"Precisely," Devin interrupted, "you didn't think! We just don't understand, Tosh. You were the first to apply to the program, you worked harder than anyone else, why would you throw this all away?"

"I-I don't..."

"I want an answer!" Devin shouted.

"I had options!" I yelled in response, Maddy's words suddenly ringing true in my head.

"What?" Cameron asked.

Tears streamed down my face as I replied, "After my accident I thought my life was over. My parents were gone, my sister abandoned me, no man would ever love me, and I would never be able to have a family.

What the hell was left to live for? And then when Aidan and Elaina were attacking hybrids, I wanted to help, I wanted to be a Warrior. If I was to be alone, at least I would be helping people. And when the announcement came about the trainee program I was resolved in my decision. I kept my head down and buried my feelings and I was fine...un...until I met Beckett. I wasn't prepared for him, I-I didn't know what to do. He..." I placed my hand over the scars on my stomach and began to sob, "...he made me believe...there was more, that someone could actually love me, all of me. I was ready to sacrifice anything to be with him."

"Well you have succeeded in that then," Devin said. "Effective immediately your status as a prospective Warrior has been revoked."

"No, no please..."

"You are to be out of the manor by the end of the day," he continued over me. "And because of your actions, as well as Mrs. Dawes, her protections and surveillance will be revoked."

"No! Please don't kick me out, please! This is all I have."

"Perhaps you should look for other *options*," Devin growled.

"I'm begging you," I sobbed. "We have to help Beckett, they're going to kill him! We need to send a team, I have to go after him."

Devin rounded on me in an instant. "You dare to tell me what we should do? You made us look like fools, Natasha! You made your choice, as did Beckett, and the two of you can live with those consequences."

My knees buckled under me as Devin turned his back to me. Brianna caught me before I hit the floor and helped me toward the door.

"I've gotcha, honey," she said in my ear.

"I...can't...breathe."

Brianna secured her arm around my waist and took on all my weight. My feet were barely touching the floor as we stepped out into the hallway. Nikki jumped up from the bench and caught my shoulders as I fell into her arms. The office door slammed loudly causing us all to flinch.

"What happened?" Nikki asked.

"I'm out," I cried. "I...ha-have to...leave."

"Come on, honey," Brianna said and pulled me back to a standing position, "let's get you out of the hallway."

Once again she took my weight and pulled me along the hallway with Nikki following alongside. People were stopping and staring at us as we made our way to the spiral staircase. I just wanted to die. I was a complete spectacle for all to see, it was a nightmare come true.

"Nat, try to walk," Nikki said annoyed, but also trying to keep me upright.

"What am I…what do I do…now?"

"You put one foot in front of the other," she replied harshly. "Literally, Nat, come on." Suddenly Nikki whipped her head at someone coming toward us in the corridor. "What are you looking at!"

"Tosh, honey, let me carry you up the stairs."

"No," I replied, shaking violently. "I'm not a victim."

"Then stop acting like one and pick up your damn feet," Nikki commanded. Even Brianna squawk at her tone, but it was the slap in the face I needed.

We made our way up the spiral staircase, and standing at the top of our landing was Roberts.

"Tosh, tell me it isn't true," he said as we approached.

"Not now, Trevor," Nikki said, pushing him out of the way so that Brianna and I could pass.

"So it's true? You're out?" I stopped at his words and slowly turned around. "What did you do?"

My chest heaved as I tried to catch my breath. "I loved someone more than the coven."

Roberts knitted his brows in confusion, which I was semi-thankful for. It meant that what I'd done hadn't completely spread through the coven. Nikki wrapped her arm around my waist and pushed me toward my bedroom. Brianna opened the door and gasped. In the middle of my room was a stack of collapsed boxes. The sheets and comforters had been stripped from both beds along with the pillows.

"Those jerks didn't waste any time," Brianna groaned.

"Oh my god," I cried and collapsed down on the bare mattress, "where am I going to go now?"

Brianna squeezed my shoulder. "Tosh, you are not without resources, honey. I'll call Renee, she'll get you into the Facility right away."

"Do you…" Nikki began tentatively, "…do you think she could get me in too? I know I don't have the best reputation over there."

Brianna nodded and gave Nikki a rare smile. "Sure, I will call her right now."

Brianna stepped out into the hallway and closed the door behind her. Nikki sat down next to me and once again I broke down on her shoulder.

"He's going to die, Nik."

She hugged my shoulder into her chest and rested her cheek on the top of my head. "You don't know that, Nat."

"There's no way he'll survive, Nik, and no one else seems to care."

"Maybe he'll win."

I rose up from her chest, wiping my nose on my ripped sleeve. "Since when are you an optimist?"

"Maybe I'm learning from my baby sister," she replied and wiped my cheek. "What would you think if…since we're both starting over, if we go to the Facility and get on our feet, and then…maybe we could get an apartment together? Really be sisters and help each other through this. What…uh…what do you think?"

"What about Jared?"

She snickered. "We've been circling the drain for over a year now, it's just not working anymore. We're either fighting or having wild make-up sex. And when that gets stale, we fight again. We've been too lazy to really do anything about it, but today was the last straw for him. Not that I blame him, I just didn't want to be the one to end it. So? Do you want to live together or not? If not, just tell me, I can take it. I've been on my own before, I'll survive, I always do…

I threw my arms around her. "I love you, too, Nik. We're all we have left."

Nikki hugged me like she never had before. I missed this hug, I missed the love of my big sister, and she was the only one I could count on from now on. The only thing that broke us apart was Brianna coming back into the room.

"Renee said she can have rooms ready for you two tonight," Brianna said and moved the stack of boxes to stand up against the dresser. "And she also says that the boys are being jerks. Do you want me to take you over to Maddy's first? She was worried about you when she left."

I shook my head. "I need to go to Abby's first. She needs to know what happened today."

"I'll go with you," Nikki said and rose from the bed. "Get cleaned up, I'll go get my stuff from Jared's room, and come back to help you."

Brianna took Nikki's place on the bed beside me. "Tosh, honey, this doesn't change anything between us. Whatever help you need, I am here for you."

"I'm not sure Cameron would like that."

Brianna rolled her eyes. "Honey, when it comes to you, it is so much more than you going off and meeting Beckett. To him, you're not just a trainee, you're more like another daughter."

"I-I am?"

She squeezed my hand and wrapped her opposite arm around me. "I think he's madder at the fact that you could have gotten yourself killed today than he is that you met a declared enemy. He feels betrayed, Tosh, and when men get their feelings hurt, they are worse than ten million PMSing women." I gave a snotty laugh at her analogy. "He'll come around, Tosh, I know he will. And god help Livy. I'll be surprised if he lets her leave the house once she hits puberty. Fathers and daughters, it can be a complicated dynamic."

I nodded. "I would have liked a father like Cameron. I think the worst part was seeing his face today, the disappointment and anger in his face."

"He'll come around, honey."

"But it'll be too late," I said and started to cry again. "Beckett will be dead and I did nothing to help him."

"Don't give up on him now. You find yourself doing the most extraordinary things when you think you have no other options."

I melted into Brianna's shoulder and closed my eyes at the feeling of her fingers tracing my forehead. She was such a mom, knowing exactly how to soothe a traumatized child. And she wasn't placating me with her advice. If anyone knew how to fight through the worst of circumstances, it was Brianna. But could I be as strong as her?

"And you're forgetting one important thing," she said and tilted my chin up.

"What's that?"

"Livy's drawing, the one she drew yesterday."

"What about it?" I asked, trying to think through the fog of the last twenty-four hours.

"In the picture, Beckett was alive," she replied and a flood of relief came over me. "And you were together, remember?"

"D-do you think it's true?"

She shrugged. "It's possible. Isn't it better to have a little hope?" I nodded and fell back into her shoulder. "Of course, it would also mean we're going to war with a pack of werewolves. But again, she's five, so who knows."

Chapter Thirty-seven

With my car destroyed, Nikki and I were forced to load our things into hers which we practically had to roll out of the driveway in order to get it started. After dropping our things off at the Facility, we drove to Abby's and shared what we knew. Through tears I told her that I couldn't save her son and that he was most likely fighting a battle to the death, and no one was going to help him. From that point on we hit Abby's liquor cabinet pretty hard. If I was drunk, then Nikki was over the moon wasted.

"Did you see..." Nikki slurred and splashed some of her drink on the floor of the deck, "...did you...see Lana look..." hiccup "...at me when we walked in? Such a bitch."

"You did throw furniture at the guards the last time you were there," I replied and put my glass on the outdoor table.

"Five years ago," she said in a raised voice. "You see," hiccup, "that's the problem," burp, "with vamps. They always hold a grudge."

"You need some water."

"You need water," she slurred and sat up for only a moment before she leaned over her knees. "Maybe I do need some water."

"There are some water bottles in the fridge," Abby replied from her seat near the sliding glass door. "The bathroom is to the right of the living room if you need it."

Nikki groaned and rose slowly from her chair.

"Do you want help?" I asked.

"I'm good," she replied and took a wobbly step forward. "Lana's still a bitch. Did you..." hiccup "see the way she looked at me?"

"Yes, Nik. She's a bitch."

"I know, right?" After a few stumbles, Nikki finally reached the sliding glass door and went inside.

"I'm sorry, Abby, I'll call a cab once Nikki feels a little better."

"Don't apologize, Tosh," Abby replied. "We've all had a terrible blow today. I honestly can't believe you're sitting here after that accident."

A shiver went through my body at the thought of the car flipping over and over again. "Well, it wasn't the first time, but I hope it's the last."

"You two girls should just stay here tonight. I have plenty of room, and…and I wouldn't mind the company."

Tears began to well in my eyes again at the feeling of helplessness. "I'm sorry, Abby, I'm so sorry…"

"Tosh," she said firmly, "none of this is your fault. You did what you could, honey. You can't torture yourself like this."

"There's nothing worse than feeling helpless."

She nodded and rose from her chair. "I'm getting more wine. Do you need anything?" I shook my head. "I'll check on your sister, too."

"You don't need to do that."

"I want to," she replied.

Abby slid open the glass door and stepped inside. Tears welled up in my eyes again as I thought about all she had been through in just a couple of weeks. At least I had Nikki, but Abby had no one. It wasn't fair. When would any of us get a break in this life? What had we done to deserve this?

A breeze came over my face and rustled the leaves in the trees at the far end of the yard. A loud snap came from the same direction which caused me to turn in my chair. The yard itself was covered in shadow from the trees, with only a slight amount of light coming from the moon and city lights. Just then a deer darted out of the woods and ran into the neighbor's backyard. Something nagged at me to keep looking at the woods, almost as though my eyes were seeing something my brain was unable to process. The hairs on my arms stood on end. Was there someone there?

I rose from my chair, although my legs were weak from the alcohol. Holding the railing tightly, I went down each step slowly but froze when a person stepped out from the edge of the woods. Once he was further in the yard, the silvery moon reflected off of something in his hand. From the curving lines and length, it appeared to be a bow.

"Beck?" I said breathlessly.

He put his index finger up to his lips, gesturing for me to be quiet, and then waved me toward him. He'd survived and come home.

"Beckett, but how," I said as I stepped onto the grass. Beckett waved me forward again and clumsily I ran to him, but slid to a stop when he raised his bow. I heard the sound of the arrow cutting through the air before it sank into my stomach. "Beck…" another hit, this time in my lower abdomen and knocking me down to my knees. In the blink of an eye my head was wrenched back by the hair and Garrett was glaring down at me.

"I come for Abby and get you as well," he said in a delighted tone. "Do you have any idea the trouble you caused me? I have no other sons of age, only stupid girls like you. Girls can't be pack leaders. Do you see the problem?"

I screamed and fell onto my back as he yanked the arrow out of my stomach. "The burs on the shaft," he said with a smile, "they add a little drag but they provide such destruction to your insides."

Garrett licked the shaft of the arrow and then licked his lips clean. "So sweet and warm, but don't worry, I won't drain you. I'd rather watch you suffer."

"Nik!" I screamed before he planted his hand over my mouth.

"You have," Garrett began and removed the second arrow from my lower abdomen, "messed with me," he said plunging it in and out again, "for the last time." He lifted my shirt and looked curiously at my abdomen. "So it is true," he said. "You're a real-life Achilles, aren't you? Shall we test it for sure?"

I screamed into Garrett's hand as he thrust the arrow into my scarred body again and again. Suddenly a gunshot rang out and hit Garrett in the neck. His blood splattered on my face before he fell back and out of my view. Another shot sounded, but I couldn't move. My body was at war with itself. Every nerve was firing causing my body to shake and flinch uncontrollably.

Nikki's face came into view above me, her tears dripping down onto my face. "Abby bring me a knife and some towels!"

"I don't," I coughed, "I don't…feel it."

"The pain?" Nikki answered.

"The healing," I groaned, and then seeing her eyes dart from my wounds back up to me I could tell she knew what I was talking about. The stretching and pulling that came whenever we would heal, it was absent. It usually came within seconds of being injured, and yet I felt nothing.

"Jared!" she yelled toward the woods.

"Jer?"

"Stay still, Nat," she commanded and then Abby was at her side. "Abby, I'm going to drain some of my blood on her, and then I need you to put pressure on the wounds with the towel. Ok?"

Abby nodded and came around to the other side of me. Nikki's face flinched as she cut down the length of her forearm. It was a dangerous cut even for her, but she quickly flipped her arm over and squeezed a good amount of blood onto my stomach. Abby wadded up a small towel and pressed it on my stomach. The pain was nauseating and brought tears to my eyes. Nikki wrapped another towel tightly around her arm and shouted at the woods again. "Jared, we need you now! Nat, I said be still," she snapped. "Abby, lift the towel for a second."

"Anything?" I said through clenched teeth as she guided Abby's hands to press down once again.

"No," she said with a shaking voice and looked down at me. "The worst wounds are in your scars, but nothing around them is healing either. We've got to get you to the Facility."

"Is she healed enough to move her?"

I lifted my head slightly to see Jared running toward us, although I still had no idea how he got here.

"She's not healing at all!" Nikki shouted at him. "She's losing a lot of blood, bring the Jeep out here so we don't have to carry her that far."

Jared didn't wait a second before disappearing.

"How did...Jared get here?"

Nikki unwrapped the towel from around her arm which was still seeping blood and licked it closed. "I guess he was surveilling us. We came out of the house when we heard the gunshot. He must have heard you, or saw something...oh my god, Nat, I'm so sorry. I should have been out here with you."

I squeezed her hand as tightly as I could, but our hands were slick with blood and I was getting weak. "I thought it...was Beckett. But...Garrett."

"Did he say anything about Beckett?" Abby asked and accidently lessened the pressure on my abdomen which cause Nikki to snap at her.

Jared's Jeep came roaring up beside us. My body shook as he lifted me from the ground, and I couldn't help but scream from the searing pain.

"I know, I know it hurts," he said softly in my ear. "We're gonna getcha all patched up, ok?"

I nodded nervously and began to cry. It was the pain, where the wounds were, the fact I wasn't healing, was Beckett already dead, would Garrett come after me and Abby again. Nikki climbed up in the backseat and put pressure on my abdomen again while Abby secured herself in the front seat.

The streetlights streaked across the windows above me as Jared squealed down the street. They were almost hypnotic and made my eyes heavy. Just as they would begin to close, Nikki would shake me and yell at me to stay awake. Each time I would open my eyes again, the streetlights would pass by even faster.

"Almost there," Nikki said and squeezed my hand. I knew she was right when the streetlights disappeared and the shadows of trees began to surround us. My eyelids were getting heavier and heavier with each shallow breath. I was cold and really tired. So, so tired. Maybe I could just close my eyes for a few minutes…

My eyes flew open with the feeling of my cheek being slapped. I gasped and found Nikki looking wildly at me. "Don't you dare close your eyes," she screamed.

"Hang on!" Jared shouted from the front seat before he turned the wheel sharply to the left. The tires squealed and Nikki braced herself against me to hold me in place as we turned into the hidden drive of Facility West. They must have waved us through the gate since Jared roared the engine and curved up the hill. The surrounding lights from the Facility's campus began to bleed into the windows. With help so close, maybe I could close my eyes now. They were so heavy…

"Come on, Tosh," a man said in the distance, "come back to us."

I stretched my eyes open one at a time. We weren't in the Jeep any longer. The bright fluorescent lights burned my eyes. When they finally adjusted, I realized Dr. Ryan was hovering over me.

"She's back," he said to others in the room. "Tosh, it's Dr. Ryan, can you understand me?"

I nodded. "I'm cold."

"You're in shock. We need to start an IV, ok?"

"Not…healing."

"It could be because you've lost a lot of blood…"

"My blood didn't work on her either," Nikki said from somewhere in the room.

Dr. Ryan looked over his shoulder, "Could it be because the injuries are so severe? Or maybe…the location?"

Nikki didn't answer, but it made sense. I'd been stabbed multiple times in my scars, the one place I couldn't heal. Now that curse was spreading like a virus through my body. A nurse stretched out my arm and began prepping it for the IV while Dr. Ryan shouted out medical nonsense to others.

"Nikki, can you give blood?" Dr. Ryan asked as another nurse began cutting my shirt off.

"Yeah, sure I can."

"Good, we'll keep trying it. Maybe she just needs a jumpstart," he replied and began painfully examining the wounds.

Nikki came to stand at the end of the table and squeezed my feet. "Nat, I'll be right back, ok? Don't go into any white lights or anything."

I nodded with a smirk before she turned and left the room. The drugs were starting to kick in like a weighted blanket and it was a welcome relief. Just then, the door Nikki had gone through burst open and Devin came inside.

"Not a good time, Dev," Dr. Ryan said, but Devin ignored him and came to my side. There were two of him, thanks to the drugs, but I was pretty sure he was there.

"Abby?" I whispered.

"Protected," he replied. "It was Garrett? You're sure?"

"I thought…it was…Beckett at first."

"Devin, we can do this later," Dr. Ryan growled.

"No, John, we can't," Devin snapped and then brought his attention back to me. "Tell me what he said."

I gritted my teeth as John probed my wounds. "He came…for Abby."

"What else?"

"I…was a bonus," I said and breathed heavily with relief before John went to another area of my stomach. "No more…sons of age."

"That's what he said? Sons of age?" I blinked my eyes slowly, it was as much of a nod as I could give. "Why does he need a son? What is he doing!" Devin shouted and slammed his fist down on the table.

"Devin, out!" Dr. Ryan shouted.

Before Devin could reply, alarms began to sound with lights flashing, and people screaming in the distance. Devin raced to the door but he was met with Jared opening it at the same time.

"We've got a problem," Jared said before a loud roar sounded and the two of them disappeared out the door.

Another roar sounded, and in a way, it seemed to call to me. It was for me, the sound calling my name in a primal way.

"Beckett," I said softly and tried to sit up. A nurse pulled at my shoulders, but I pushed her away. "Beck," I said again, this time rolling to my side and pulling at my IV.

"Tosh, stay still," Dr. Ryan commanded, but I didn't care. I could hear Beckett calling to me, it hit me deep within my soul. "Don't make me restrain you, Tosh."

"Beckett," I said a little louder, and this time the door opened with Devin and Jared backing their way inside with their hands up defensively.

"Easy, boy," Devin said firmly and pushed his hands out in front of him.

"Dear god in heaven," Dr. Ryan said and stepped away from the table.

Another roar sounded which made Jared jumped backwards further inside the room, and that's when I saw him. A wolf standing on his hind legs ducked through the doorway. His fur was dark brown with an ombre of lighter brown stretching out from his chest that was caked with dried blood while new bright red blood dripped from three large gashes that began at his shoulder and ended well into his abdomen. The wolf's eyes were bright green and I would know them anywhere.

"Becks," I called and stretched out my arm.

"No," Dr. Ryan shouted, "no, no, no! He can't be in here."

Jared looked over his shoulder and replied, "I'm not sure he's giving us much of a choice, doc."

Finally, Jared stepped aside and allowed Beckett to come to my side. He looked down at me with those bright green eyes and I could see the pain in them. His breath was heavy and wet sounding through his soft whimper.

"You're...alive," I said as another rush of drugs flowed through my body.

Beckett took another step forward and placed his paw on my forearm. He released another whimper before his eyes rolled up in the back of his head and he collapsed to the ground. I screamed at the sudden pain in my arm and looked down to see a scratch where Beckett's claw must have sunken into.

"Oh shit," Dr. Ryan said under his breath.

"What the hell do we do now?" Jared shouted.

Dr. Ryan stepped away from the table and held his hands up in a commanding way. "Ok, this has just gone to shit and we have a hazardous situation on our hands."

"Beck," I said through the drugs.

"Yes, Tosh, Beck is here. Well, I guess we're all assuming it's him. Jesus, his blood is all over my floor. Devin, can you and Jared get him up on a table?"

"What? No," Devin replied quickly. "His blood is toxic to us."

"Then put some hazmat suits on and get him on a table! None of us are strong enough to do it."

"I would watch your tone, doctor," Devin growled.

"This is my medical wing, not yours, Dev. Now move him to a table so I can help Tosh."

"She has to be quarantined."

"Everyone is getting quarantined," Dr. Ryan shouted.

"Everyone? You can't let him stay here."

"Why not?"

"He's a werewolf!"

"He was a hybrid first, and if anyone has an issue with that, they can fight me on it once I'm done saving everyone's life which I can't do until everyone else gets out and lets me do my job!"

The room was quiet for several seconds before Jared broke the silence with, "Dr. John, growing some balls."

"Put on the goddamn hazmat suits, I've got to help Tosh before she bleeds to death."

"Please help Beck," I slurred as the drugs started to kick in and make everything around me fuzzy.

"I'll see you on the flip side," Dr. Ryan said over me.

"Help Beckett," I said before my head flopped to my shoulder.

"Yes, yes, Tosh, everyone's getting saved today."

A Story of Beck & Tosh

Chapter Thirty-eight

Beckett

I wondered if there was an area of my body that didn't hurt. With every breath my chest resisted and sent shooting pains all the way down to my stomach, which caused me to take shallower breaths which eventually made me feel as though I was hyperventilating. Finally, I gave up and took in a solid breath which only resulted in a coughing fit. My eyes shot open with the piercing pain that radiated through my body and there were grunting sounds I'd never heard myself make.

When the acute pain subsided and only a dull, restrictive pain remained, I finally took in my surroundings. The bright florescent lights shined off the white, sterile walls and stung my eyes. I'd made it to Facility West, that much I remembered, but everything after I crashed through the glass doors was a little hazy. Considering I was lying in what looked like a medical bed, it seemed that I hadn't been thrown into a cell, at least for now.

A large piece of gauze was taped over my chest and stomach, although the tape was already starting to peel at the edges. It was probably my higher body temp at work. Cautiously I felt down to my hips to find I was wearing some kind of loose-fitting pants, which made me happy. Being a werewolf meant you were often naked. Either you phased while dressed and ripped all your clothes, or you phased back into human form in one place and your clothes were in another. I hadn't gotten comfortable with being so exposed. Other wolves didn't seem to mind, but I'd had my fill of seeing men walking around with their dicks swinging free.

Someone coughed which made me jerk, and then groan in resulting pain. With my new body, I generally healed pretty quickly, not Tosh fast, but much faster than I used to as a human. But the three gashes that stretched across my chest and abdomen were deep, so it wasn't that surprising they weren't fully healed yet.

Carefully I turned my head to my right and found another medical bed parallel to my mine several feet away. My chest fell at the sight of Tosha lying there with tubes and wires connecting to various machines. She looked pale and weak, which begged the question – why? Why wasn't she healing?

I groaned painfully as I sat up in the bed and swung my legs off the side. "Tosha? You awake?"

"What are you doing?" Tosha said in a soft, raspy voice.

"I'm waiting for the pain to die down before I come over there."

"No," she whined. "Stay…there. You're hurt."

"There's nothing that can stop me from coming over there," I replied and painfully pushed off the edge of the bed.

My wounds screamed and stretched in new ways as I shuffled across the floor toward her bed. I had to smile when the heart monitor began to beep faster as I approached.

Her face looked pained as I reached down and touched her cheek. She took my hand and pressed it into the side of her face while tears streamed from her eyes. "I thought you were dead," she cried.

Painfully I leaned over the railing and pressed my forehead against hers. "When I saw you crash down that embankment…I thought…" I cleared my throat of the emotions coming from remembering the moment. "But when Stevenson didn't come back...I knew you were ok. But now…" Painfully I rose up from the bed, stretching my wounds once again from a different angle. "What happened? Why aren't you healing?"

A door opened behind us, making me turn and see Dr. Ryan coming through the door in what looked like a hazmat suit without the hood covering his head. It must have been the expression on my face that made him look down at himself. "Forgive the outfit, it's just a precaution."

"So that I don't infect you?"

He looked guilty and gestured to my bed. "Can I convince you to sit while we talk for a bit?"

I nodded and he brought the chair over to me. He extended his latex-gloved hands to help me sit down. I was a walking disease.

"Now that you're awake, we don't have much time before the Warriors come barging in here, so let me get right to it," he began. "Beckett, as I'm sure you're aware, you have three large lacerations across your chest and abdomen. I nearly broke my back stitching you back up, but you seem to be healing nicely. Based on some other healed injuries, I'm guessing your new…um…situation, allows you to heal faster?" I nodded. "Then there you have it. Based on your rate of healing, I would say you'll be completely healed within the next day or so. That said, here's the uncomfortable part of the conversation."

I shifted uncomfortably in my chair. Tosha reached through an opening in the bed railing and I gently took her hand for support. "Ok, shoot."

Dr. Ryan sighed before saying, "Beckett, you came onto Facility grounds, destroyed the glass entryway, bled down the entire length of the atrium, and took two doors off their hinges in the medical wing. You put a lot of people in danger, Beckett, and we're basically having to do a toxic cleanup on the entire main floor of the building."

"I-I'm sorry. I couldn't control…"

Dr. Ryan held his hands up. "We all know why you did it, Beckett, but Lana doesn't want you here. I fought on your behalf because at your core, you're a hybrid first, and it's our duty to help you. But as soon as you've healed, Lana wants you out and the Warriors are chomping at the bit to get ahold of you. So as long as you're under my care, you're safe, but once you've healed, I can't help you. You understand, don't you?"

I nodded. "I do. Thanks, doc."

"There's only one caveat," he said and crossed his arms. "Lana is looking for any excuse to get you out of here. If you phase or have any kind of outburst that puts any of us in danger, believe me, she will take drastic measures to remove you. I'm sorry to say it, Beckett, but you do pose a threat to us, which is why you will only see me for your care. I can't expose my staff to this. I hope you understand."

There wasn't much of a choice. Again, I was a walking disease. "Sure, doc. Believe me, I know how toxic my blood is."

Dr. Ryan gave a nervous smile. "Good. I expect the Warriors to be bursting in at any moment, so let's move to Tosh before we're interrupted." I squeezed Tosh's hand and kissed her knuckles before Dr. Ryan continued. "Tosh, as we saw when you came in, you're not healing, which obviously concerns us. My guess is that your injuries are so severe, and possibly because they are in your scarred area, your body has gone into shock."

"He hurt you where your scars are?" I asked and she nodded. I rested my elbow on my knees and caught my head in my hand. I didn't care how much it hurt. "Oh my god, Tosha, I'm sorry. I'm so, so sorry."

She squeezed my hand. "It's not your fault, Becks."

"It is," I replied. "All of this is my fault." I looked back up at Dr. Ryan. "But she's getting better. She's not healing like normal, but she's still going to be ok. Right?"

Whenever it took a doctor more than three seconds to answer, you knew it wasn't good. "We're doing everything we can. It's just that...I'm sorry, Tosh, you're not responding to anything we're giving you. I'm concerned about your organ function at the moment. We're doing everything we can."

"It's ok, Dr. Ryan, I believe you," she replied in a weak, yet hopeful voice.

"In all honesty, I don't think it helped having a werewolf barge into the room while your wounds were fully exposed, and then scratch you on the arm."

"The what?" I asked and shot her a look. "What scratch?" I looked back to Dr. Ryan who then pointed to Tosha's right arm that had a bandage taped to her skin. "I? I did that? I scratched her?"

"Right before you collapsed," Dr. Ryan answered.

"Oh my god," I groaned and my head found my hand once again. "Tosha...oh my god. I-I can't believe..."

She squeezed my hand. "Beck, it's ok."

"No! It's not ok," I said and stood up from my chair too quickly and flinched from the pain. "What have I done," I groaned.

"We've tested your blood, Tosh," Dr. Ryan interrupted, "we found the lupine virus, at least that's what we're assuming. It's the same virus we saw in Beckett's father. I'm sorry."

Tears stung my eyes and I gritted my teeth. Garrett had destroyed her outside, and I had destroyed her inside. I wanted to hit myself in the chest to inflict the most amount of pain possible to overshadow the pain in my heart.

"We'll be watching your vitals closely and treating you as best we can. Just try and get some rest, which is easier said than done. But, Beckett, if you could refrain from infecting her further?"

"Why would I…"

"Your wounds, Beckett," he corrected. "They can still leak blood and fluid. Just be careful, that's all I'm saying."

I nodded. "Yeah, doc, sorry. I'll be careful."

Dr. Ryan gave an apologetic look. "Just keep fighting, both of you. I'll keep the Warriors at bay as long as I can, but I know it won't be much longer."

Dr. Ryan turned on his heels and left the room, and it seemed as though he took all the air with him. Tosha squeezed my hand and it turned me back to her. At first glance, she wasn't the Tosha I knew. She was pale and frail-looking. Tosha was strong, the strongest person I knew, and I'd made her this way.

"I'm so sorry," I said with a break in my voice.

She squeezed my hand. "You have to stop, Becks," she said weakly, and then suddenly tears began rolling down her cheeks. "I can't believe you're here. What happened? What happened after they took you?"

"First things first," I replied, feeling the wanting urge to be close to her. I looked at the wide mechanical railing and saw a small lever. With a gentle push, the railing clicked with a release and lowered down to the side. As if on a spring, I lunged forward and kissed her with nothing coming between us. They weren't kisses of passion, but those of fear and relief. Our tears mixed together while our hands searched each other's faces. I wondered if I could crawl into the bed next to her. I needed to hold her, cradle her, anything to make her feel better and heal my soul.

"Get away from her!" someone shouted behind us.

Abruptly I pulled away from Tosha's lips, and turned to find Connor standing just inside the room. His face was fierce, and his fists clenched, fangs out. My ears perked up and a shiver went down my spine.

"Haven't you done enough?" Connor shouted.

"Oh you want to go?" I challenged and then he was a blur until his hands were around my neck and shoulders.

We pushed against each either, and I could feel my wounds ripping open while Tosha screamed at us to stop. The wave of my pores opening rushed over me and I could see my skin darkening. I could crush him, I could rip his throat out, or maybe just bleed on him. I wanted to rip this bastard's head off if I could only…

Suddenly Connor was flying backward and landed on the floor. I didn't ask why or how, simply stepped forward to follow after him when a set of hands grabbed me by my throat and held me against the wall. It was Victor, and his fangs were fully extended. He was too short to stretch me off my feet, but his grip was pushing me painfully through the wall. Literally. I could literally feel the wall bending and cracking around me.

"Calm yourself," he growled. "Or you will be put down." Victor squeezed my neck again and banged my head against the wall. "Do not give them a reason, Beckett," Victor said in another low growl, and I realized in a way he was really trying to help me. I gave a nod as best I could and he lessened his grip only slightly, allowing me to breathe and start to calm my body. On the other side of the room Devin was holding Connor down on the ground until two guards came in through the doors with Dr. Ryan right behind them.

As if Connor weighed nothing, Devin rose from the floor holding Connor by his throat. "Take him," he shouted to the guards who quickly took him by the shoulders and dragged him from the room.

"What the hell happened in here!" Dr. Ryan shouted. "I literally left the room five minutes ago."

Suddenly Victor jolted away from me, causing me to fall down to the ground.

"John, you're needed here," Victor said. I looked down at the large gauze pad on my chest and noticed the bright red spots spreading and staining the clean white cloth.

Painfully I pushed myself up from the floor. Dr. Ryan glared at me and pointed to my bed. Once I sat down, he slid over a tray with a few different instruments. Next he pulled on a pair of safety glasses and secured a surgical mask over his mouth.

"Sorry," I mumbled as he began to pull the tape away.

He shook his head. "It's your funeral, not mine. Next time, give a little thought to the sobbing girl over there before you decide to have a Battle Royale in front of her."

I looked over Dr. Ryan's shoulder to where Victor and Devin stood over Tosha's bed. Through the small space between them I could see her wiping her eyes. Damn it, I was a douche.

Victor turned away from Tosha's bed and raised an eyebrow at me. "Have you calmed yourself?"

I nodded and looked down at the floor. Dr. Ryan peeled away the gauze pad from my chest, leaving the one on my abdomen, and exposing

410 ~ C.R. Quinn

the three large gashes starting from my left shoulder and cutting diagonally down. Tosha gasped and I caught her eye from around Devin's side. In this moment I finally understood how exposed she felt when showing her scars.

"Good news is," Dr. Ryan began, but paused as he dabbed a folded cloth on one of the gashes, "you didn't pop any stitches. It was just a lot of seepage. I'll get another pad. Please tell me I can trust you to stay on this bed and not stretch them again?"

"We will see to it," Devin said firmly and then narrowed his eyes at me. Devin didn't like me before, and I certainly hadn't won any bonus points since I left.

"Be back in a sec," Dr. Ryan said and left the room.

"Let's get to it, shall we?" Devin said and stood roughly three feet from the foot of my bed. "Where's Garrett?"

I shrugged. "I dunno." Devin's jaw flinched as his lips tightened into a thin line. Tosha, through her pain, was still able to glare at me. "Sorry, what I mean is, since I escaped, I'm sure he's packed up and left where I was held."

"Where would he go?"

I shrugged again. I was asking for a beat down. "I was only ever at the one place. I wasn't privy to his other safe houses."

Devin sighed in annoyance. "What's his plan?"

"To attack the Warriors."

"We know that," he said and narrowed his eyes. "When, where, how, what are the details."

"I would like to see my mother."

"The plans, Beckett."

"I want to see my mom."

"Beck," Tosha pleaded from her bed, "what are you doing?"

"I'm sorry," I replied softly to her and then looked back at Devin. "You want information, I want to see my mother. It's that simple."

"We do not have time for this!" Devin shouted. "Garrett could be making his way to us now."

"I doubt that," I answered.

"And why is that?"

"Once I see my mom…"

"Enough!" Devin shouted over me. "How did you know Tosh was here? Of all places, how did you know she was brought here?"

I shook my head. "Bring my mother here…"

"You would sacrifice the lives of hundreds of hybrids that live here, and possibly even the life of your girlfriend just so you can see your mother?"

"I'm not sure why this is such a big deal. Bring my mom here, and I'll tell you what I know. When I'm done, throw me out on the street, put me in one of your cells, I don't care. I'll tell you everything, but after I see my mom. I won't budge on this."

Devin's lips disappeared inside his mouth while his nostrils flared and his chest heaved like a bull. Finally, after a minute he sighed and let his arms fall loosely down at his side. "Very well. Since it is neither safe to transport your mother at the moment, nor be around you with your wounds, you won't be seeing her until you are fully healed. Since you are refusing to cooperate, you will be treated like any other prisoner of the Warriors."

"What does that mean?"

"It means you will be tried for your crimes."

"My-my crimes?"

"In addition to you being a traitor, you've also trespassed on Facility property, destroyed the front of the building, and endangered everyone here. So yes, your crimes. You'll be tried in front of the Elite Council, possibly the entire coven. Let everyone hear your reasoning for your actions. No backroom deals now, Beckett. Enjoy the bed you've made for yourself."

After taking two steps toward the door, Devin completely disappeared in a cloud of smoke. Victor sighed and stepped in front of me.

"You won't change my mind, sir."

He shook his head. "And I don't mean to. Your stubbornness and your convictions prove you are absolutely my grandchild." He patted me on the shoulder. "I am glad you survived your injuries, and my sire for that matter."

"Why are you here?"

Victor knitted his brows. "Pardon?"

"Why did you come here with Connor?"

He looked confused as he answered, "I came to see you, of course. Why wouldn't I be here?"

"And Connor?"

Victor shifted his gaze to Tosha. "He stated to me he wanted to see you and apologize for what happened between the two of you. I am sorry it escalated as it did."

"What happened?" I asked.

"Nothing you need to worry about," she replied, which meant I really did need to worry about it.

Victor shifted uncomfortably. "Well, I will leave you two. Miss Cushlin, keep fighting, my dear." He patted my shoulder again. "Please do keep the wolf inside you, for all our sakes."

I nodded and he quickly left the room. Tosha shifted painfully in her bed. There was still an ache in my chest to lie next to her, but it wasn't possible. Then an idea struck me.

Quickly I released the brake on my bed and steered it over to Tosha's bed until they were aligned. Next I folded the inside rail of the bed down. It was as close to a full-size bed as we were going to get.

"What are you doing?" she asked.

"I need to be next to you, unless you don't want..."

"No, I do, I really do."

Slowly I climbed up into my bed and laid out alongside Tosha. My fingers interlaced with hers and her head fell on my shoulder. "What happened between you and Connor?"

"Nothing," she replied and rubbed her face. Why was she lying to me? "I feel like garbage."

"Are you mad at me?"

She sighed and avoided me by looking up at the ceiling. "I...I just don't understand, Beck. Why won't you help them?"

"Tosha, the minute I give up what I know, I lose all bargaining power. They'll lock me up in a cell and I'll never see my mother again. I know they're your people, but..."

"They were your people too, remember?" she snapped and then flinched from the pain. I squeezed her hand and folded it gently into my chest. "They're not my coven anymore"

"What? Wait, what do you mean?"

Tosha turned her head and the tears were already coming down her cheeks. "They kicked me out."

"What! Why?"

"I broke the rules, Beck, I broke all the rules. After the accident, I knew there was no way they would let me stay."

"Bastards," I growled.

"No, it was completely my fault, I kept choosing you over them."

"Still, it's shitty. I'll talk to them, tell them I forced you to come..."

"Becks, I came to you because I wanted to. I have to take responsibility for what I did. It's just…" she broke down and placed her hand over her face. When she was finally able to pull herself together, she continued, "I don't know what the hell I'm going to do now, and everyone is mad at me, especially Cameron, he just hates me. I think I'm more upset about that than anything else."

"Then screw him."

She shook her head. "No, he has every right to be mad. I just didn't realize how much…how much he reminded me of having a dad. He's really been like a father to me and I lied to his face. He could barely look at me when they brought me back."

Awkwardly I tried putting my arm around her as she broke down again, but instead I succeeded in pulling at my stitches and knocking her in the head. At least it made her laugh a little and slow down her tears.

She adjusted painfully in her bed. "I'm really not used to being in this amount of pain for this long."

"Want me to call Dr. Ryan? Get you some more pain meds?"

She shook her head. "No, I just want to sleep."

"Ok," I replied and began tracing my fingers over her brows. "But you need to promise me you'll wake up."

Tosha stretched her eyes open and glared at me. "Well aren't you the optimist."

I smiled for a brief moment, making her think that I was kidding, but then it left my face. "No seriously, I'm going to need that promise."

Chapter Thirty-nine

Tosh

"Tosh?" someone said. That was me, right? That was my name. I was Tosh. At least I was pretty sure. Even through sleep I could feel the nauseating pain that was no longer just radiating from my stomach. My body was on fire, yet I was shivering, and every shiver sent another wave of pain along the already frenzied nerves.

"Tosh, can you hear me?" the same person said and this time a freezing cold hand was placed on my forehead causing my eyes to shoot open. Leaning over me was Dr. Ryan with Beckett looking over his shoulder. "Can you hear me, Tosh?"

His words were registering, although I couldn't remember how to speak. My eyes fluttered closed, I was so tired and it hurt so bad, and why was that beeping so loud? It was high-pitched and loud. Someone should turn it off.

"Natasha, I need you to stay awake," Dr. Ryan shouted and shook me.

I stretched my eyes open again. "What's...that...beeping."

"That's you," he replied. "Your vitals are crashing, Tosh. Despite all the meds we've been giving you, your body has gone septic."

"Wh-what does...that mean?"

"It means your organs are shutting down," Dr. Ryan said with an eerily calm voice.

"I'm dying? But...I'm a healer."

"Your body isn't fighting anymore. We think the trauma to your scarred area, and then being infected with the lupin virus, just overwhelmed your healing ability. Medically I don't know what else I can do."

"I don't want to die," I cried. "Not like this…"

"There is one last option," Dr. Ryan interrupted with knitted brows.

"Anything."

Dr. Ryan sighed and gave me a sympathetic smile. "We can try giving you vamp blood. It's the only thing we haven't tried."

I shook my head. "No, no, I…I'm not activated. No…"

"Tosha," Beckett said and nudged Dr. Ryan aside, "please, you have to try this."

"You…know…I can't."

Beckett squeezed my hand tightly and brought his face down to mine. "Natasha, I know you, I know who you are. You are nothing like Nikki. Do you understand? Nikki is a miserable human being because of the choices she made, not because she was activated? You are the most incredible person I know and no amount of vampire blood will turn you into what she's become. Please, Tosha, you have to do this."

Tears burned my eyes as they crested my lids. My teeth were chattering with fear and fever. I wanted the pain to stop. I wanted to have a life with Beckett. But in order to have that, I had to do the one thing I feared more than fire. "But…who?"

Beckett's face relaxed a little in relief before he rose up and looked to his left. I followed his gaze and immediately broke down in a loud sob when I saw Cameron standing at the end of the bed.

"Apparently I am the most generic vampire of those around you," he said with a slight smile.

"But…but you…hate me," I cried.

His face fell as he rested his hands on his hips. "Natasha, I am sorry for my reaction the other day. Brianna has helped me realize that I overreacted and the reason I did was because…" He cleared his throat and placed his hands down on the footboard of the bed. "Natasha, I was disappointed and angry, and I reacted badly. I would never want you to feel as though I had any hatred for you. Natasha, you are a part of our family whether you are a Warrior or not."

"I'm…scared."

"Impossible," Cameron replied. "Natasha Cushlin literally walked through fire and survived. She can drink a little blood."

"What if…it changes me."

"You are too strong a person to let anything change who you truly are."

One of the monitors began beeping causing Dr. Ryan to come around to the other side of the bed. "If we're going to do this, we need to do it now."

"Tosh, please do this," Cameron said and my breath caught in my throat. Never had he called me anything but my proper name.

"Ok," I cried.

Beckett kissed my hand. "It's going to be ok, Tosha."

"I…love you."

He leaned down and pressed his lips softly on mine. "Love you more."

As he stepped back, Cameron took his place at the side of my bed and rolled up the sleeve of his shirt. "Are you familiar with how we do this?" I shook my head. "I will bite into my wrist and you will need to drink from the puncture wounds immediately or else they will close."

I nodded and assumed the one-sided smile from Cameron was because he could hear my teeth chattering. With a soft click, Cameron's fangs extended and he sank them into his wrist. A small amount of dark, thick blood seeped from one of the puncture wounds as he lifted his wrist to my mouth. My body tensed and I closed my eyes as I swallowed a small amount of blood.

"You must take more," Cameron said and petted my forehead gently.

I did as he asked and allowed the sweet-tasting blood to trickle down my throat. When he felt I had taken enough, Cameron petted my hair again and pulled his wrist away from my mouth. Beckett immediately stepped back up to the side of the bed and looked down at me with his most worried face.

"I'm ok," I reassured him and patted his hand.

"I'll believe it when you jump out of this bed," he said and then looked up at Dr. Ryan who was studying the monitor. "How's she doing, doc?"

"It's too early to tell," Dr. Ryan replied and stepped around the bed.

"Beckett, a word?" Cameron asked.

Beckett sighed. "Not to be disrespectful, sir, but if it's about seeing my mom, I'm not going to budge."

"Humor me," Cameron said with a raised eyebrow, and Beckett reluctantly stepped away from the bed.

Dr. Ryan gave me a smile and pulled the blankets down to my legs. "I want to check your wounds, if that's ok."

"Sure," I replied. "Is it hot in here?"

"Maybe the blood has made you flush," he said and carefully pulled the dressing off my abdomen.

"It just feels…really hot…all of a sudden."

I could feel the sweat beading on my forehead, but it wasn't just my cheeks that felt flush.

"I'm hot, really hot."

Dr. Ryan secured the dressing back onto my abdomen and then looked between me and the monitor. "Your temperature is about the same."

I shook my head as a fiery heat rushed through my body. "No, something's wrong."

Beckett was suddenly squeezing my hand. "Tosha, what's the matter?"

"I'm…burning."

"Where?"

"All over!" I shouted and pushed everyone away. My abdomen was on fire, I knew that feeling. I was burning. Painful, frenzied burning that was spreading over my entire body. Why wasn't anyone doing anything?!

"Tosh, calm down," Dr. Ryan said and tried pushing my shoulders down.

"Help me!" I screamed and tried patting down my burning skin.

"Tosha!" Beckett shouted and held my wrists together. "You're not on fire. You're not burning."

There was fire all around me, a bright yellow and orange ball of fire on top of me.

"Get him off of me," I screamed. "He's killing me! Ty you're killing me."

"Natasha, look at me," Beckett said sternly. "There's no one here. Ty isn't here!"

Another wave of burning pain rushed over me and all I could see was red. My skin was melting and pain radiated from within me. Ty was weighing me down, his internal fire encompassing every inch of me, and no one could hear me. No one was coming. Ty was dying and I was being burned layer by layer.

"Hold her down," someone shouted right before there was a sharp pain in my arm.

"Just let me die this time."

What was that noise? My eyes were still heavy enough to stay closed, but my brain had started to stir because of the loud sound of a bear growling. Since I was pretty sure the Facility hadn't placed me in a zoo, I had no idea what was happening or where I was.

Keeping my eyes closed, I let my brain begin to take stock of my body. I didn't have the burning, radiating pain anymore, although the left side of my body was very warm and moist with sweat. It also happened to be the same side the growling was coming from.

The pain still hadn't resurfaced, which was a good sign. Slowly I stretched my eyelids open, but had to squint from the harsh florescent lighting above me. The loud growling in my left ear made me turn my head, and I was happy to find Beckett squeezed up next to me in the hospital bed. No wonder I was so hot. The heat from his body had even worn away the medical tape holding the dressing to his chest, causing the thick pad to peel away and expose the tops of three red scars. Curiosity got the best me and my fingers grazed one of the wounds. Beckett's hand snapped up and grabbed my wrist. His eyes flew open like a madman's and his nostrils flared.

"I'm sorry," I said.

His eyes finally focused and looked down at me. "Oh thank god," he said relieved and released my wrist. Gently he cupped my cheek with his hand, his face creased with concern. "How do you feel?"

Quickly I took another survey of my body and replied, "I think I'm ok."

"You scared the shit out of me, out of all of us."

"I don't know what happened. It felt like I was burning again. I was right back to that night, everything felt the same and I couldn't get away."

"That's what I thought. You kept shouting out for Ty."

My face fell. "I'm sorry. I don't remember that, I just remember the pain and the heat. I seriously felt Ty's weight on top of me, but then it all went dark."

He nodded. "The doc knocked you out. When your vitals started to level out, we figured you were out of the woods."

"I would have rather had the death flu like you did when you got activated."

He gave a curt laugh. "Me too."

Gently I touched his brow and pulled him down to my lips. He was more reserved this time, hardly even opening his mouth to me. I went to move closer, but the tape from his dressing stuck to my neck, making me pull away. Beckett laughed lightly, pulled the tape away from my neck, but then rolled off the bed completely.

"This is a bit pointless," he said and walked toward the bathroom at the other end of the room.

From my bed I could see him looking at himself in the mirror as he slowly peeled the entire dressing from his chest and stomach. He sighed loudly, his hand hovering over one of his new scars. I think I even saw him snarl. With another sigh he turned away from the mirror and stepped back into the room. It was the first time I'd had a full view of the three scars tearing across his body. The claw marks were bright red and painful looking, and he must have seen the tears in my eyes since he put a self-conscious hand on his chest.

"Will you still love me now that I have these scars?"

I snickered. "Honestly, I don't think I could handle looking at them every day. So sorry we have to break up over something silly like a few scars," I said sarcastically.

He smiled and sat on the edge of the bed. "I see. You want to be the only one with the scars, huh?"

"You know it," I replied. "Do you think they'll heal completely?"

He shrugged and looked away. "Don't know. They're much worse than anything else they did to me."

"What did they do to you?"

He sighed. "Don't worry about it."

I reached up and gently touched one of the scars. "They look just like your dad's."

"Same wolf," he replied. "It's Vincent's signature."

"We'll make him pay for that."

"*We*," he replied with a raised brow.

"I have a little fight left in me."

He laughed and squeezed my leg. "Probably more than any of us, baby."

The door opened and Dr. Ryan stepped inside in his white suit that made him look as though he was cleaning up toxic waste. "Morning. Tosh, I'm very happy to see you awake. You look so much better already." He looked over at Beckett and his shoulders dropped. "Beckett, I don't think I've been so disappointed to see someone heal so quickly."

Beckett stood from the bed and put a protective hand on his chest. "It's ok, I knew it would be happening sooner rather than later."

"I'll have to let the Warriors know. If I don't, Lana certainly will."

"Do whatcha gotta do, doc. I'm ready for it."

Dr. Ryan lowered his eyes and nodded sadly. "Well, let's take a look at you then, Miss Tosh."

"Sorry about yesterday."

He shrugged. "Brianna went into a coma. Beckett here had the flu from hell. You decided to reenact the worst day of your life. But the drugs seem to have calmed your body down enough to recover pretty quickly. Most people suffer a couple of days after activation."

"I don't think I could burn for two days."

After doing the normal checks like blood pressure, pulse, and temperature he said, "Everything is normal, that's good news. Now let's take a look at your abdomen and see how those wounds are healing."

I nodded and pulled the blanket down. Dr. Ryan lifted up my gown and removed the tape from the dressing. When he pulled the dressing down, he flinched.

"What?" I asked, unable to see over my gown.

Beckett came to stand at the foot of the bed. "Doc, what's the matter?"

"Um...well," he began and then pulled the dressing down again.

Beckett's face went pale as his jaw dropped.

"Will someone please tell me what's going on?"

Dr. Ryan removed the dressing altogether. "Look for yourself."

"Huh?"

Nerves fluttered in my stomach. I braced myself for the pain of sitting up, but as I clinched my ab muscles the absence of pain made me gasp. Quickly I sat up and pulled the gown up to my chest. Not only were there no scars from Garrett's arrows, there were no scars at all. Nothing. Where there should have been thick swirls of red and white melted skin, there was new, fresh, pink skin. I pulled the blanket further down exposing beautiful smooth legs and everything in between.

"Son of a bitch!" I shouted and jammed my fist into my stomach. "That! Was! It!" I screamed and continued to hit myself. "Was that it? Was that all I had to fucking do!"

Beckett grabbed my wrists. "Natasha, stop!"

Deep, guttural sobs came out of me as my head fell into his chest. "I could...have fixed this...all this time."

"Tosha, you couldn't have known."

"Something so simple," I replied and Beckett wiped my cheeks with his thumb. "I'm so stupid."

"Stop, you had your reasons."

"Um...not to interrupt," Dr. Ryan began, "but I think we should do a full exam."

"I thought you already did..."

"An internal exam," he interrupted. "We'll need to do an ultrasound, gynecological exam, a full blood workup."

"A gyno exam? Really?"

He smiled. "Can't say I've ever had a patient look forward to one of them."

I smiled up at Beckett. "This could change everything." He smiled and traced the side of his finger down my cheek. He had a look of deep understanding of the possibilities. Then something hit me. I looked down at my right forearm that had a bandage covering the scratch from Beckett's claw. Quickly I ripped the bandage from my arm and once again the scar had healed. I looked back at Beckett and then to Dr. Ryan. "Let's do the blood work first."

Chapter Forty

Beckett

While I sat on my bed alone, waiting for Tosha to return, I strangely felt as though I was back in the old days in the hospital waiting room while my wife delivered her baby. It was odd to me that I was associating Tosha with being my wife and having my child. A few weeks ago neither would have been possible, but today she was practically beaming as Dr. Ryan walked her out of the room for her exam. I was ecstatic that she had healed, I really was, but there was also a part of me that missed seeing those scars. It was weird how they made me feel, the connection I felt with Tosha whenever I touched them. I would miss them as much as I would miss her.

The slashes covering my chest and abdomen had sealed themselves, leaving only scars behind. Honestly, I was surprised the Warriors hadn't dragged me out yet. I was having difficulty preparing myself for a life in a dungeon. What was even harder, was imaging a life without Tosha. Even if by some miracle the Warriors didn't throw me in prison, there was no way I could subject Tosha to a life with a wolf. She deserved more, especially now.

I shot up from my bed when the door to the room opened. Tosha shuffled inside in her hospital gown and socks and a smile that touched her ears. You would never have known that she was close to death twelve hours earlier.

"How do you feel?" she asked and I scrunched my face in confusion.

"Um...fine. Why?"

She responded by leaping forward, knocking me back flat on the bed, and kissing me with such fury that it was hard to breathe. When I finally caught my bearings, and my breath, I pushed us both up to a seated position. "Ok, ok, I'm guessing you have good news?"

"I don't even know where to start."

"Let's start with the obvious. Scars?"

"Not one!" she cheered. "New...everything! Ovaries, cervix, an actual vagina. Dr. Ryan said we'll keep monitoring to see if I ovulate. Oh my god, I'll have a period. Can't say I've missed that, but it means...if everything works like it should, I...could..." She paused and tears formed in her eyes.

"Babies," I answered for her.

She hugged me tightly around the neck. "No lupine virus either," she whispered in my ear.

Quickly I pulled her away to look her in the eye. "You're sure? They-they're sure?"

She nodded with glassy eyes and I crushed her into my chest. The relief I felt was overwhelming. Had I been holding my breath for the last hour? It surely felt like it. Tosha snaked her way out of my hold and kissed me once again. She had been released from her shackles. There was a strange new energy vibrating from within her. The hint of sadness that was always behind her smile was gone.

When she finally pulled her lips away from mine, there was excitement in her voice as she said, "You know what this means, right?"

"Uh...not really."

Normally I would have received an eye roll or an annoyed glared, but her joy beamed out of her when she answered, "It means I can fight against the virus. So, if there's ever an accident, or even a scratch, I won't be infected." I didn't share her excitement, and that seemed to irritate her. "This is good news, Beck, I thought you'd be a little happier about it."

"Tosha, the fact that you're lupine free...I...I can't even tell you how relieved I am. But there's not going to be another chance for you to become infected."

Her face fell slightly. "W-what do you mean?"

"Tosha, what do you think is going to happen once I get out of here? I'm either in a cell or they'll find a way to dispose of me."

424 ~ C.R. Quinn

She stiffened and sat back on the edge of the bed. "You're being ridiculous. No one is going to *dispose* of you, Beckett."

"And you're not being realistic, Natasha," I replied and her eyes flared. "The Warriors aren't saints. Werewolves and vampires hate each other, it's engrained in their DNA. There's no scenario where they just let me go and I live my life. There's no us being together. There's no little house in the country where we get to raise our family and have enough open space where I won't be a threat every time there's a full moon. There won't be T-ball, or karate, or cookouts with the neighbors while all the kids run around the yard. None of that is possible."

"Really?" she said with a raised brow. "Being impossible and all, it sure seems as though you've spent a lot of time thinking about it."

"This is your fresh start, Tosha. You need to take it and run." Tosha jumped off the bed and began pacing in front of it. "You know I'm right."

"I know you're an idiot," she shouted and pointed her finger at me. She came over to the side of the bed and hit me in the chest. "You're an idiot, Beckett Dawes, a complete moron! I have given up the coven that has been my family, my vocation, my future, for you! I threw away a year of grueling, agonizing training, for you, asshole. And you think you can just sit there and tell me that things with us just aren't possible? No way. If you don't want to be with me anymore, it better be because you don't love me, and not some other bullshit excuse about protecting me. So say it, say you don't love me. Say it to my face and I'll leave you to rot. Go on, say it. Say it!"

"I do love you, Tosha."

"Then what's the problem!"

"I can't be like Ty!" I shouted back.

"What?" she whispered as if I'd taken the breath out of her.

"Wanting to protect you isn't bullshit, not to me. Ty destroyed you! You're…" I jumped off the bed in frustration, "you were screaming his name and reliving what he did to you. I cannot, *cannot*, be the guy that does that to you again."

"Because you love me."

"Of course I love you, that's not the issue."

"That is absolutely the issue," she replied and stepped forward to be only a few inches away. "You love me, I love you, it's that simple. You're a wolf, that's a little more challenging, but I'm a Healer and we've now proven that I'll heal from anything that might happen. I don't see the issue here, Becks." She took a final step and wrapped her arms around my back, nestling the side of her face against my chest. "There's no reason we can't have that little house in the country someday."

I licked my lips and counted to three before I answered, "They're not going to let me go, Tosha."

She looked up. "You don't know that."

"I have a pretty good idea."

"But you're wrong a lot."

I half-smiled and then kissed her gently, but my face fell looking into her eyes and worrying that I'd never be able to get lost in them again. She opened her mouth to say something, but was interrupted by someone coming through the door.

Immediately Tosha was brought to tears when she saw Nikki come into the room. Nikki dropped the bags she was holding and welcomed her weeping sister into her arms. I felt as though I was intruding on their private moment, although I was surprised it was happening in the first place. Something had obviously changed for the better after I left.

"Let me see, let me see," Nikki said and pulled out of their embrace.

Tosha stepped back and pulled up her gown enough for Nikki to see the absence of scars on her legs. Nikki teared up again and even slid her fingertips down Tosha's thigh.

"That tickles," Tosha giggled.

"Not that you couldn't show your old self off, but I thought you'd like to show off your new skin," she said and handed Tosha one of the bags.

Tosha reached in and pulled out a small white top. "It's a crop top, Nik."

"No shit, Nat. How else are you going to freak everyone out? What are you worried about, you went to training in less than that only a few days ago. Trust me, it'll be good to throw this in you-know-who's face."

"Who?" I asked and stepped forward. "Who, you-know-who?"

Nikki quickly changed the subject and threw me the other bag she had dropped on the floor. "Brought some clothes for you too."

"What's happening? I don't understand…"

"Yeah, so here's the deal," Nikki interrupted. "Warriors are outside to take you in, Beckett. They've convened the Elite Council..."

"What's that? The Elite Council?"

Nikki raised her eyebrow. "If you'd shut up long enough, I could tell you.

"S-sorry."

"The Elite Council is made up of high-ranking Warriors. They'll question you and then decide what to do with you."

Tosha gave me a worried look, but I shook it off. "I told them I wouldn't talk until I saw my mom."

Nikki nodded. "Abby has been at the manor since Garrett attacked Nat. I saw her this morning, she's fine and waiting to see you. You got balls, Beckett Dawes, I have to give you that. They don't negotiate with anyone."

"Ok. But if they do a bait and switch thing…"

"Yeah, yeah, wolf boy, we all get it. Calm down."

"Wolf boy?"

"I could think of something worse if you want," she challenged and I shook my head. "Ok, you guys need to get dressed and knock on the door when you're ready, then we'll be off."

"Thanks, Nik," Tosha said and put her bag of clothes on the bed.

"They want to see you too, Nat." Tosha's eyes grew large, but Nikki gave a sly smile and then turned toward the door. "Just go in there and tell them to suck it."

Tosha laughed as the door closed behind her sister.

"Who was she talking about?" I asked and dumped the contents of my bag on the bed.

"The Elite Council. I'm sure they just want to talk about when Garrett…"

"No, the 'you-know-who' part. Who was she talking about?"

"The guy who told me my scars were disgusting."

"And his name would be?"

Tosha looked up and shook her head. "It doesn't matter."

"It matters to me."

"Why, so you can rip his head off or something?"

"Well…yeah."

"I can fight my own battles, Beck. Did it before I met you, and I can do…"

"I know you can, but…"

"But nothing. Now get dressed before they barge in."

Knowing the look on her face, she was done with this conversation. As I shrugged into the T-shirt they'd given me, I couldn't help but steal glances at Tosha and her new body. The absence of scars once again made me happy, yet depressed. Tosha caught me looking and quickly slid the thin plaid shirt over the crop top Nikki had brought her.

"You ready?" she asked and pulled her hair out from inside her shirt.

"No," I replied and stepped over to her. I kissed her softly, just enough that wouldn't lead to more, but had the hint of how much I loved her. "I'm sorry. I don't want us to leave here being upset with each other."

"Me either," she replied, but her tense expression didn't relax. "There's a lot we need to talk about."

"I do love you, Tosha."

"I know. It's why you're acting like an ass," she said sounding very much like her sister. "Ready now?"

I nodded and then knelt down to lace up my sneakers. Tosha crossed the room and banged on the door. A moment later Victor and Jared came into the room.

"Hey, man," Jared waved from across the room, and then flinched. "Nice eyes."

I gave him an awkward nod. "Thanks. How's this working?"

"Well, we have Warriors outside waiting to escort you from the building. We're going to take a back entrance to lessen your exposure."

"I'm not planning on attacking anyone."

Victor narrowed his eyes. "It is for your own protection, child. The security outside your room has not only been to keep you in here, but to keep any rogue vampires out. The fact that you are here is very upsetting to many people."

"Nice," I replied sarcastically. "And I'm supposed to trust that these other Warriors won't try and take me out along the way?"

"The Warriors have strict orders, and they certainly won't disobey them while I am here," Victor replied.

"And they'd have to go through Alex," Jared said with a smirk. "Don't worry, Beckett, no one will mess with you with us around."

"Forgive me if I don't share your confidence," I responded and looked nervously at Tosha. She squeezed my hand and gave me a soft kiss. I sighed and couldn't think of anything to say that would make this moment any easier.

She released my hand and gave me a nod. "It's going to be fine."

When we stepped forward together, Victor put his hands up. "Beckett, we will need to take you separately. Miss Cushlin, you will go in the second car with your sister."

I exhaled loudly and then had to count to ten slowly in my head. My nerves were starting to fire causing the heat to rise in my body and tiny beads of sweat appeared on my arm.

"Uh…Beck, you ok?" Jared asked nervously.

I nodded. "Sorry, just give me a second."

"Child, if you cannot control…"

"You're about to walk me to a prison cell," I snapped and planted my feet to steady myself. "You're separating me from the one person I trust, and you tell me there are vamps that might want to kill me. That's gonna churn things up a little, ok? I just need a few more seconds."

Once I reached twenty-five, the heat began to retreat. When I opened my eyes, Victor and Jared were up against the wall. It was almost humorous. Almost. Only Tosha stood her ground and she was giving me an encouraging look.

"Better?" she asked.

"Yeah, let's get this over with."

Victor opened the door and gestured for me to leave first. As soon as I stepped out of the room, Alex was waiting. Even though his size would make even the toughest man cry, he gave me a smile.

"Beckett it is good to see you again," he said and stepped to the side, exposing several other guards that had been hiding behind him.

"You're probably alone in that feeling."

"You have more friends than you think," he replied. "Now, for everyone's safety, we're going to surround you and escort you to the cars outside. Everybody ready?"

I looked around and found Tosha back near the door. She gave me the same prompting and encouraging look she had a few moments ago. In her head she was probably shouting at me to get moving. I sighed nervously as the Warrior guards circled around me, and I hated to admit that their sicky-sweet smell was overwhelming. Considering they were taking me into a mansion full of vamps, I would need to figure out how not to gag.

Victor patted me on the shoulder. "You will be fine, child."

Without turning to face him, I gave a nervous nod and the circle of guards began to move. Once out of the medical wing the group ducked into a stairwell that led us into the basement, and eventually outside where several large SUV's sat idle. Alex directed me forward toward the center SUV with Jared, Victor, and one other guard following behind.

Alex opened the passenger door and said, "It's probably best you lay down in the back. Just in case Garrett has surveillance near the manor."

"Can you make Jared promise not to make any jokes about the dog being in the back?" I said as I climbed back into the third row.

"Damn it, man, you beat me to it," Jared laughed.

He and the guard I didn't know filled the middle row while Alex settled into the driver's seat and Victor on the passenger side. My stomach flipped as the SUV lurched forward. It was hard to keep the bad thoughts of what might happen to me out of my head. I tried thinking about seeing my mom, Tosha's new scar-free body, but the image of me sitting in my dad's old prison cell continued to take over.

"So, Beck, if you're really good, you'll get some extra belly rubs when we get home," Jared said.

"Nice," I replied and laid down.

"Jared," Victor growled from the front seat, "you are to refrain from those kinds of remarks."

"Come on, Dad," he whined, "I've been working on them all morning."

"Yet again you put your energies in the wrong place, child."

"I disagree. Listen to this one…"

"No, I will not. Let us concentrate on getting to the manor safely."

The SUV became very quiet as Alex steered us down one windy road after another. My stomach was starting to flip for another reason now.

After a few minutes, without turning around, Jared said, "Beck, I'm curious."

"*Jared*," Victor warned from the front seat, but that didn't stop Jared from continuing.

"Are you allowed up on the bed at night?"

"Why don't you ask your mom," I replied and the SUV erupted into laugher, and for a moment my brain shut off. "What else you got, Jer?"

The remainder of the ride to the manor was full of insults and laughter. Even Victor cracked a smile at one point. But the mood changed quickly when we approached the manor's black gate. When the SUV finally stopped and Alex gave the all-clear, I sat up in the backseat to find that we were at the same back entrance Victor, Jared, and I snuck out of the night of our field trip.

"Have no fear, child," Victor said, "we are taking you up through the tunnels to the library where your mother awaits."

With a loud sigh, I climbed out from the very back of the SUV and stepped down next to Victor. The other SUVs circled around us and within a minute I was once again surrounded by Warriors. With Tosha and Nikki bringing up the rear, our large group entered the manor and made our way through the narrow tunnels. It was funny how much of my eyesight had improved and I no longer needed the aid of a cell phone flashlight to see my way through the darkness of the tunnel.

Victor directed us up a steep set of stairs and the nerves in my stomach started to churn. I was pretty sure that at the top of these stairs would be the vaults, and then the secret door into the library where my mother waited. How would she react to me? Would she see a difference? Would she be scared of me?

Shortly after we passed the vaults on our right, Victor typed in a code on the keypad, causing the wall to swing open and flood the dark tunnel with an uncomfortable light. After my eyes focused, I could see the walls of books just ahead, and then heard the squeals of children. Victor waved the guards away and allowed me to enter the library alone. My mother stood up from the couch she was sitting on when she saw me, and her audible gasp made me freeze.

"Beckett!" Olivia shouted from a corner in the room and came running toward me, but she quickly changed course. "Toshy!" she squealed, and both she and her brother ran to the real person they wanted to see.

When I looked back at my mother, she was holding her arms out to me with teary eyes and I quickly went to her. My mother wrapped her arm around me and I was suddenly surrounded in the comfort and safety I'd felt for as long as I could remember.

"Hi, Mom," I cried into her shoulder.

She released me and brought my face up from her shoulder and held it in between her hands. "Becks, I…you look…"

"I know," I replied and pulled her hands away from my face.

"So…you're…a…"

"Yeah. I'm not used to saying it out loud either," I finished for her. "I'm so sorry, Mom. I'm sorry about Dad. I'm sorry I couldn't tell you like I wanted to. I'm sorry…"

"Becks, honey," she interrupted and once again cupped her hands on my cheeks, "I'm sorry. If only I had told you the truth about Garrett, maybe…maybe you would have…I don't know. I just don't know…"

"Mom, please…"

"Beckett, your dad, Richard I mean, he loved you so much. There was never a day he didn't think of you as his own. I left Garrett because I realized he was a monster, he was never your father, never…"

"I know, Mom," I interrupted and pulled her hands down from my face again. "I talked with Dad before he…died. He told me everything. I don't blame you, either of you." I wiped my eyes quickly. "Dad really loved you, Mom. His last thoughts were of you."

I caught my mother as she broke down, and I hoped I was able to give her the comfort she'd always given me.

Alex came through the library door and my heart sank. "I'm sorry, Beckett, it's time."

"Already?"

He nodded. "I'm sorry, everyone is convened and waiting."

My mother lifted her head from my chest, worry sinking into her face. "W-what's going to happen now? Where are they taking you?"

"I'm not really sure, Mom."

She squeezed my face tightly between her hands. "Do NOT protect that man, Becks. Do whatever they ask of you, do you hear me? I cannot, *cannot*, lose your father and then lose you. Do you understand me? Tell them everything they want to know, I don't care how…"

"Mom," I said calmly, "I don't have a lot of control over this."

"You have more than you think," she whispered and bore her eyes into mine.

I hugged her tightly for only a brief moment and when I turned away from her I was surprised to find Nikki at my side. She placed a gentle hand on my arm and said, "I'll be here with her. Whatever happens, she won't be alone."

My brows knitted together, I still wasn't exactly sure what had happened to Nikki since I'd left, or why she was being so kind to my mother. I nodded and thanked her quietly, unsure if my voice would crack with emotion. When I stepped toward the center of the room, the guards surrounded me once more. I couldn't bear looking back at my mother, I felt like such a criminal.

"Where's Tosh?" I asked, suddenly realizing she was missing.

"She's already in the Council Hall," Alex replied and I felt guilty for not even realizing she'd left the room.

Without taking one last look at my mother, I breathed in deeply and held my chest up high as I left the library. The Warrior guards in front led us down the stairs that led to the courtyard which was eerily absent of people, but what stopped me in my tracks was the sight of Tosha standing in front of the Council Hall doors with Connor. The circle of guards tightened around me. Tosha looked at me in fear, although Connor's expression was more like cocky disgust. My nostrils began to flare at the sight of them together, the hairs on my arm standing on end.

"Down, boy," Jared said in my ear.

One, two, three, I counted in my head and concentrated on my breathing. Four, five, six, don't break him like a stick. Seven, eight, nine, don't touch what is mine. Ten, eleven, twelve, I can't think of anything that rhymes with twelve.

Alex gave an order for the two of them to go inside. Tosha gave me a guilty look, but then mouthed the words I love you. Alex waved us forward, but Victor stretched his arm in front of me.

"I believe it is best we wait a few more moments," he said and looked down at my arms that were only now starting to lighten in color and the dark hair recede. The guards around me shifted uncomfortably, and I didn't blame them. I wondered if they were on someone's shit list and that's why they got this detail. "Now listen, child, once we are in the Council Hall and you are ready to begin your hearing, you must bow."

"Bow? Like in karate or something?"

Jared snorted and a few of the guards tried stifling their laughs. Thankfully Victor snapped his jaw and all of them straightened up. It was amazing to see the power he still had over them.

"Just a small bow of the head," he replied. "It is a sign of respect that will go far, especially with Julian."

With one last exhale I nodded to Victor that I was in control and our group eventually went through the doors of the Council Hall. In front of us sat Cameron and Devin in tall, regal chairs, while Julian stood just to the side of them. The right side of the hall was scattered with Warriors sitting on hard stone steps that reached the tall ceiling, whereas only Tosha sat on the left side. There was certainly no love coming from the right side of the hall, only dirty looks and whispers.

As we came into the center of the hall, the guards opened up in front but surrounded me like a horseshoe. Only Victor and Jared stood on either side of me. It was the first time I'd ever seen Jared serious and stoic.

Like Victor had instructed, I bowed my head and even opened my hands and arms to show I was ready to begin. When I looked back up I was relieved to see that Cameron had a slight smile, and even Julian seemed impressed. Devin, however, raised his eyebrow and looked in Victor's direction. Victor, of course, gave no hint of his instruction to me.

"Before we begin," Cameron said and stood from his chair, "I would like to point out that we have allowed this to be an open session, and not just a hearing for the Elite Counsel. That said, we expect everyone to behave respectfully as this is a unique situation. Those who disrupt this hearing will be removed at once. Brother?"

Cameron looked over at Devin who then stood from his chair. "Father, Jared, are you choosing to stand with the prisoner?"

"We choose to stand with the accused," Victor corrected, causing a few surprised grumbles. "He is not yet a prisoner, child."

"Retirement has obviously softened your view on things, Father," Devin said pointedly and then gestured to Julian. "Let us begin."

Julian stepped down to stand in front of Cameron and Devin, and my knees began to shake. "State your name."

"Becke…" my voice cracked with nerves, causing a few snickers from the crowd. I cleared my throat and answered, "Beckett Dawes."

"And what class of creature are you?"

"Um…well, that's a little difficult to say," I replied. "Up until a few weeks ago I thought I was human. Then I discovered I was a hybrid, and then I was infected with the lupine virus making me a wolf. So part human, part vampire, and now mostly werewolf."

"How did you become acquainted with the Warrior coven?"

I looked over at Tosha. "Tosh Cushlin saved my life and brought me here."

"And you were not aware you were a hybrid?"

"No. I didn't even believe it at first. I thought you guys were just some kind of goth cosplay group or something."

"What changed your mind?"

I took a deep breath in and replied, "When a vampire named Delia bit me at a party."

There were a few stifled laughs behind me in the stands. Julian, however, wasn't amused. "Prior to recent events, did you have any interaction or association with Garrett Archer?"

"No. The first time I saw Garrett Archer was when he burst through my front door, and abducted my mother."

"Why do you think Garrett chose you? Of all the people in the world, why did he, as you put it, burst through your door and abduct your mother?"

I looked over at Cameron and Devin for permission to answer the question.

Julian cleared his throat. "I'll ask you again, Beckett, why do you think Garrett Archer chose to attack you and your family?" I gave a quick glance down at Victor, and then looked at Cameron and Devin once again. "Do not look at them, Beckett, you will answer my question."

"Well, um…I really can't without permission from Cameron or Devin."

Julian whipped his head around to the coven leaders in their chairs. Devin sighed and replied, "I suppose so. We've prepared ourselves for this moment."

I swallowed hard and Julian turned his attention to me. "Then I will ask a third time. Why you?"

"My full name is Beckett Archer Dawes, named after my birth father Garrett Archer."

Gasps echoed behind me, and Julian's eyes flared. "Garrett Archer…is your father?"

"Birth father. He was a sperm donor and nothing else."

"He is your birth father, and no one thought this was a relevant fact to share with all of us?"

"For his safety, we kept it between a few members of the coven," Cameron answered. "Also, it was determined that Beckett had had no previous interaction or knowledge of his birth father."

"And you expect us to believe that?"

Cameron raised an eyebrow at Julian and answered, "Yes."

Julian took a frustrated inhale and pursed his lips. When he looked back at me, his face hardened. "When did you find out that Garrett Archer was your father?"

"Sperm donor," I corrected, "let's just get that clear. I didn't know until the night Delia attacked me. My mother admitted to me she was with Garrett in college, but left him when she was pregnant with me. My father, Richard, was the man who raised me. I never knew he wasn't my dad."

"Why did your mother leave Garrett?"

"Because she saw Garrett kill a young man," Tosha said and stood from her stoop. "May I, sir?" Julian gestured to the center of the room. "Abby Dawes admitted to me that she saw him kill a young man. Later she remembered that the young man looked a lot like Garrett. We believe that young man might have been another son of Garrett's."

"And when, exactly, did this information come about?"

"A few days ago."

"And Tosha's right," I said and brought Julian's attention back to me. "Garrett has had several sons, all of whom he's tried making a pack leader. But they've either died during the battle, or he's killed them."

"How do you know this?"

"Because he threw it in my face multiple times a day. He also would say that he probably had daughters, but that they wouldn't give him the result he needed, so whenever he found out the baby was a girl, he would leave the mother."

"Douchebag," Jared said under his breath.

"Why wouldn't girls give him the result he wanted?" Julian asked.

"Girls can't be pack leaders," I replied.

"Why not?"

"Misogyny? Sexism?" I shrugged.

"Why did Garrett need his son to be a pack leader?"

"Garrett is building an army, an army of werewolves and vampire, but the wolves are to do most of the work. But only the pack leader can control the wolves. Garrett needs to control the pack leader so he can control everyone else. Only problem is, getting through Vincent has been more challenging than he thought."

"Vincent is the current pack leader?"

"Yes. When Garrett realized I'd betrayed him, he forced me to fight Vincent knowing I probably wouldn't survive. And if I did, he'd be able to control me with threats against my mom and Tosh."

"And how exactly does the pack leader control the other wolves?"

I sighed and felt as though I was betraying the wolves by telling our secrets. "It's a shared consciousness. When the pack leader enforces his will on you, it's almost impossible to disobey. Although, from what some of the others have told me, most leaders don't force themselves on you. You fight for them because you respect and honor your leader. That's not really the case with Vincent, which is why several covered for me so that I could get messages to Tosh."

The Council Hall became very quiet while Julian pondered my answers. It was nearly thirty seconds before he finally asked, "But why wolves? Why has Garrett aligned himself with these creatures when his army would be so much stronger with vampires?"

"Perhaps I could answer that, child," Victor said as he took a step forward. "Garrett Archer, as most of you know, was one of the original members of my coven, before we were officially the protectors of our race. Many centuries ago, there was a summit held to move away from being ruled by the Ancients. Our race had grown so large by then, it was difficult for them to manage, and I believe they had grown tired of it.

"At this summit, we created the very laws we govern ourselves with today. And although we were removing the Ancients from power, we knew there still needed to be a coven to uphold these laws. What many of you do not know, is that there were three covens vying for this responsibility, and each of them very different than the next. Each of the coven leaders had to fight their case, and it was to be taken to a vote.

"At the time, Garrett Archer had a firm belief that we should associate ourselves with the wolves. They were not affected by the sun, and could therefore be our protectors, our guard dogs, so to speak. Initially, I was against it. Werewolves and vampires are mortal enemies, but Garrett was adamant they could be controlled. By the time we were at the summit, I was partially convinced that having them on our side might be a useful weapon.

"However, during the debates, one of the rival covens announced that we had already made alliances with wolves. By the reaction of those at the summit it was clear to me that any association with the wolves would cost us the vote. Therefore, I made it clear that we would never align ourselves with the wolves. My decision is what caused Garrett to defect and betray us. He orchestrated an attack on the summit with the wolves, which we overcame. Obviously, his obsession with the wolves continues to this day."

"And his betrayal is what constituted his execution?" Julian asked and Devin's face hardened.

"Yes," Victor replied. "He should have been the first of my sires to be killed, but here we are."

Victor stepped back behind me. Neither he nor Julian were afraid of making Devin uncomfortable in front of so many people.

"Thank you, Father," Julian said. "All that being said, Beckett, why is Garrett forming a werewolf army?"

"To come after the Warriors."

"Why now?"

"I'm not completely sure."

"Bullshit," someone in the crowd said.

Julian scanned the room, but when no further comments came, he continued, "In the time you were in Garrett's camp, he didn't reveal any of his plans to you?"

"Just that he planned on coming after you. He may have insinuated that you were weaker now."

"And why would that be?" Devin asked.

My stomach dropped as I replied, "Because of the change in leadership." Devin raised an eyebrow at me so I quickly gave another reason. "But it's the first time he had the numbers. Vincent has helped in that, he's vicious."

"The previous wolf…"

"His name is Adam," I snapped.

Julian raised his brows. "*Adam* said there was more than one pack."

"Yes. Some are just outposts, but others were a complete takeover."

"And that doesn't cause dissention?"

I shrugged. "Nothing you can do about it."

Julian paused and licked his lips before asking, "What all did you tell Garrett about us?"

"Nothing," I replied.

"Total bullshit," the same voice said, this time even louder than before.

"Connor, enough," Cameron growled.

Connor stood from within the crowd. "You can't honestly believe that a weakling like him didn't give up absolutely everything he knew about us. Hell, he's even been in the tunnels. Garrett's men could destroy us from the inside out."

"I didn't tell them anything," I shouted.

"Connor, sit down," Cameron said over me. "We know your reasons for objecting. Stop now before you embarrass yourself."

"I'm sorry, sir, you can't possibly be falling for any of this crap."

"I'm telling the truth, I didn't…"

"If you told Garrett what he wanted, did he give you extra treats for being a good dog?"

Arms came around me from all sides as I lunged toward the stone risers. "I was beaten for two days straight because I wouldn't tell him what he wanted. Two days, you son of a bitch!"

Victor placed his hand against my chest and pushed me up against the opposite set of stone risers. "Calm. Your. Self."

My jaw clamped my mouth shut and I forced the breath to go through my nose. Victor's eyes blazed through me. His expression was a mixture of anger and disappointment. Unable to take his stare any longer, I looked over his shoulder and saw two of the guards removing Connor from the Council Hall. At least I wasn't the only one being punished.

Once the tall doors closed behind them, Victor released me, and I was allowed to take my place back in the center of the hall. The remaining guards kept a closer perimeter around me this time. Waiting, I'm sure, for the crazy werewolf to freak out again.

Julian cleared his throat. "Shall we continue?" I nodded. "So it is your testimony that you did not relinquish any information about our coven or headquarters?"

"Yes, sir."

"What sort of things were you asked?"

I sighed while I thought back. "Um...how many Warriors lived here? How many entrances, was there a cache of weapons, what security measures did you have within and on the perimeter, things like that. I told them I only saw the areas for humans – the dining room, the courtyard, and my bedroom. Nothing else."

"And Garrett believed you?"

"No, hence the beatings, but when nothing came of it..."

"But he trusted you enough that you were allowed to leave."

I sighed again. "For recruiting purposes. I was able convince him that I hated the Warriors as much as he did."

"How exactly did you do that?" Julian asked with a smirk.

I'd stepped in it now. I shifted uncomfortably and replied, "Well, I would say things like how manipulative and controlling Victor was." A few grumbles sounded and from the corner of my eye I could see Victor slowly turning his gaze to me. "And I may have said something to the effect of...how could the Warriors be run by...an assassin who couldn't kill who he was supposed to." A low rumble echoed through the hall. Cameron glanced over at Devin who probably wished he had the ability to shoot lasers out of his eyes at me. "It was good to finally put those Psychology classes to good use."

"Nice save," Jared whispered, but I knew he was being kind.

"I did everything I could think of to get him to trust me, knowing full well that the closer I got to him the more he would push me to be pack leader."

"And when did that trust begin to fail?" Julian asked.

"I'm not sure exactly," I replied truthfully. "He might have had suspicions after I met with Tosh. Maybe I wasn't as miserable as I had been."

"And shortly after that he had you followed?"

I nodded. "Garrett's men took me from the motel I'd met Tosha at and informed me that I would be facing Vincent."

"And did you?"

"Yes," I said and a shiver went up my spine at the memory. "Vincent is a monster to say the least, and I was really no match for him, but I held on longer than I expected. It wasn't until he hit me with his signature move did I think I was a goner."

"Signature move?"

"Vincent likes to claw you from shoulder to stomach. Once he does that, he can play with his food, so to speak."

"Yet you survived."

"I was on the ground, I was ready to just let him kill me when Floyd told me that Garrett had gone after my mother."

"Who is Floyd?"

"One of the wolves helping me."

"How exactly did he tell you this?"

I tapped my temple. "Shared consciousness does come in handy sometimes. Once I heard that, I got a second wind or something. I attacked Vincent and injured him enough where I could get away, and then I ran."

"However, you did not go to your mother's home, you went to Facility West."

I licked my lips and sighed. It was a question I was hoping to avoid. "Yes, when I got closer to the city I realized Tosh needed me and changed course."

"How, exactly, did you know Tosh needed you?"

The question seemed to peek everyone's interest. Even Devin shifted in his seat awaiting my answer. I looked over at Tosha and she gave me a sympathetic smile. This was a private matter being made public.

"It's called imprinting," I replied and felt my cheeks get flush. "It's a bond, a connection, between a wolf and someone he loves. You can feel when they're in trouble, or even where they are. In this case it was both."

"And that is when you crashed through the Facility's entrance?" Julian asked rhetorically. "In effect showering the lobby in glass, sending hybrids screaming and running for safety, and covering the floors with your highly toxic blood."

"Um...yeah. I wasn't really in my right mind. I was an animal with one goal. I just needed to get to Tosh."

"To hell with everyone else."

"No! I just couldn't see beyond getting to her. I'm sorry about the Facility. I didn't...I'm sorry for what I did, but I didn't have control."

"Which is precisely why you're so dangerous."

"Julian, move it along," Cameron said.

Julian clenched his jaw and stepped back up to stand next to Cameron. "Give us Garrett's location," he said curtly.

"That could be difficult."

"How's that?"

I sighed. "Since you raided one of their camps, they've been moving every few days. I could tell you where I was, but they won't be there."

"How are they able to move such a large group to different locations so easily?"

"Some of the packs pool their resources to buy land where they can all be together and have a lot of open space for when the full moon comes."

"So give us the locations of all these communal areas."

"I don't know where they are, it's not like they had a map with big arrows pointing to them."

"Then what good are you."

"Julian!" Cameron snapped.

"I'm sorry, sir, but without a location what use is he to us?"

"Um...excuse me," I said, raising my hand like an idiot which made Jared snort. "I still think I can help."

"How so?" Cameron asked.

"I can't give you an absolute location, but I might be able to find them using the shared consciousness."

"Go on."

I swallowed and shifted my weight uncomfortably. "I could direct us in a general area, but to get you right to where they are, I'd need to be in wolf form." Cameron sat back in his seat while others were audibly upset by the idea. "But I would phase back, of course."

Cameron sighed and looked up at Julian. "Do you have anything else, Julian?"

"No, sir," he replied and held his hands behind his back.

"Very good," Cameron said and stood from his chair. "Considering the sensitivity and complexity of this situation, and also to avoid any notion of impropriety, I would like the Elite Council to adjourn with us to the study to decide our next steps. But before we do that, Beckett, I would like to ask you one question. After you became infected, why did you leave us? We would have eventually found Garrett and your mother, it was only a matter of time. Why did you leave our protection?"

I found it difficult to maintain eye contact with Cameron as I replied, "When I first came here, I was told that I was an honorary Warrior by birth, behind closed doors, that is. I was made to feel like part of this family, told of its history and traditions. With everything else in my life going to shit, I felt safe here.

"The first wolf you brought here was put in a cell downstairs, and is still there. When my dad started phasing, you put him in a cell downstairs, where he died. Once I was infected, it was made pretty clear that I wouldn't be welcome here, but even if I stayed, I was pretty sure I'd be stuck in a cell downstairs. In an instant I went from part of the family to being a threat."

"Considering none of us here knew you had even been infected, who exactly made it clear to you that you were a threat?" I didn't answer, but my eyes glanced over to Victor on my left. "I see," Cameron said. "I believe we have concluded this hearing. Julian, your men can secure our guest here, there is no need to bring him downstairs at the moment."

The guards instantly surrounded me and pushed me toward the opposite side of the hall. Devin, Cameron, and several others left the Council Hall and I was suddenly thankful for the guards around me. The vibe in the room changed immediately and all eyes were in my direction.

Jared took position next to me and tilted his head. "They won't get to you, bro, trust me."

"You're gonna stop them, huh?"

"I didn't say that," he laughed. "I'm hoping Dad will step up before I have to."

I smiled, but the only thing that calmed my nerves was Tosha walking toward us. The guards parted and she hugged me tightly around the waist. When I kissed her hair, I snuck a glance at the other side of room and the stares became even nastier.

Tosha looked up at me. "When this is all over, I want you to tell me everything that happened. I don't like learning stuff like this."

"Someday," I replied. "I'm hoping to forget a lot of it."

She tilted her head back and I gave her a gentle kiss. It would have been longer if someone hadn't cleared their throat.

"Child, a word if I may?" Victor asked. Tosha unraveled her arms from around my waist and stepped back through the ring of guards. Victor glanced down at the floor. "Child, I am not used to apologizing," he began and I caught a couple of the guards smirking. "In fact, I rarely regret my actions and therefore don't feel I should have to apologize. However, I feel…" Victor trailed off and eventually looked back up at me. "I did put the lives of my younger grandchildren ahead of yours. I do not deny that, and because they are so young, I do not regret that decision."

"You're doin' great, Dad," Jared said sarcastically.

"I am not finished," Victor snapped. "When I…suggested…that you leave, it was for your benefit." I raised an eyebrow. "Truly. There was no way you would get the knowledge of how to phase or tap into the ways of wolves. You needed to be with your own kind in order to learn. I apologize that you felt as though you would never be allowed to come back. I truly made the suggestion for your own good."

Jared looked over Victor's shoulder at me. "When Dad says he's doing something for your own good, it usually means you're gonna wanna die a few times before it's over."

"That was certainly true," I replied and Victor tightened his lips. "Look, Victor, I made the choice to leave, I knew nothing good was going to happen to me. But you're right, I wouldn't have been able to learn how to be a wolf here."

"You see, there was some benefit to this."

"I wouldn't push it that far," I replied.

"Fine, but now that you're back we can continue where we left off."

"Continue? Victor, they're going to chain me up, there's no continuing anything."

Victor waved me off. "Nonsense. You are far more valuable working with us than being locked away. Trust me, my children will make the right decision."

"Glad you think so," I replied and looked to my left where I saw Tosha speaking to Roberts. He was wearing a black jumpsuit and something seemed different about him. It took me nearly a minute to realize that it was the fact that he was smiling. He had always been so intense that something so simple as a smile made him look totally different. Once Tosha caught me looking at her, she gave Roberts a hug and then stepped back through the circle of guards.

"Everything ok?" I asked and threaded my fingers in hers.

"Yeah," she replied and nodded. "He just wanted to see how I was. I don't think I told you they chose him to be a Warrior. He was telling me they're Turning him once all of this over."

I squeezed her hand. "I'm sorry."

She shook her head. "Nothing to be sorry about."

"Can I ask you something without sounding like a complete jealous jerk?"

"You can ask, but whether you sound jealous or not, well…"

"Why were you talking to Connor?"

Her eyes flinched. "Wow, you went right for it, didn't you?"

"I'm sorry, but yeah, why were you talking to him?"

"He caught me as I was going in," she answered. "He wanted to apologize for what happened when he came to see me. But it didn't get very far since you came around the corner. Feel better?"

"Is it completely out of line if I ask you never to talk to him again?"

"Yes it is," she replied flatly. "How about you trust me enough to make my own decisions about who I want to associate with and not. Ok?"

I lowered my head. "I do trust you. It's just that I…really, I mean really hate that guy."

"Yeah, you made that pretty clear."

Before I could argue with her further, the members of the Elite Counsel came through the doors of the Council Hall.

I looked quickly over at Victor. "That was really quick."

He shrugged. "It doesn't take long when the correct course of action is so simple."

"I'm glad you're so confident," I replied as Cameron and Devin came in and took their seats at the front of the hall. The guards escorted me back to the center of the room and my knees starting shaking.

Devin stood from his chair and the hall fell silent. "Before we begin, I would like to address the elephant in the room. Over five hundred years ago I was Turned by Victor to become a part of his growing coven. Garrett Archer was the only one of my fellow Warriors who even spoke to me. He taught me how to feed, how to avoid the sun, and even how to deal with Father when he would go on one of his rampages." Victor raised his eyebrows and there was soft laughter rumbling through the crowd.

"Garrett Archer was my friend, he was my brother," Devin continued. "When he betrayed us, I thought I was prepared to take his life. When the time came, I failed. I failed in my mission, and in my devotion to our coven. When I lied, I created a cancer that hid below the surface until recently. If I had done my duty, we would not be here at this moment. The loss of innocent lives could have been prevented, and I take responsibility for that.

"Besides the error with Garrett, my record as the Warrior Assassin has been flawless. I don't expect you to believe me, but it is the truth. My kill journals will be available to anyone who wishes to do any further research. For those Warriors that are not here, I will be reaching out to each and every one of them to convey the same message I have here."

Devin took a quick pause and looked over at Julian before continuing, "Once our attack on Garrett is complete, I will voluntarily do a stint on the board and chains with the sentence length to be determined by Julian to prevent any notion of favoritism. What I have done is inexcusable, and I will work to earn your trust back." Devin turned and looked directly at me. "And Mr. Dawes, I am truly sorry for the pain that Garrett has caused you and your family." Devin looked down at Cameron before taking his seat. "Brother?"

Cameron gave him a slight nod and stood from his throne. "Brothers, sisters, this is a unique and uncomfortable situation for us all and we are taking steps to remedy it. But let us get to the heart of the matter - our attack on Garrett Archer and what should be done with Beckett Dawes."

My heart started beating out of my chest.

"Considering Garrett has had several days to pull his forces together," Cameron began, "it is imperative we attack him as soon as possible. Alex, create a team and present plans to us within an hour. You will need to use Beckett's knowledge about how the wolves' camp is usually structured." Alex nodded in my direction. "I know working together with a wolf will be difficult for many of you. Since the dawn of our creation we have hated each other, but we cannot afford that today. Our duty is to protect those who would be harmed by our race, and we must use all resources available to us.

"Therefore, most of you here will stay behind and protect the manor as well as Facility West. We will pull our Warriors from the field to participate in this battle in case Garrett is surveilling us. Beckett," he said and my knees started to shake with nerves, "we will accept your help and allow you to phase into wolf form in order to lead us to Garrett's current location."

The grumbling that had stayed at a steady level became a roar.

"Sir," I said over the noise, "I can lead you to the *pack*. Garrett may not even be there."

"I hope for your sake he is," he replied firmly. "Once you have led us to the location, is it possible for you to phase back to human form?"

"Yes, sir," I replied. "I just need some recovery time. Why?"

"I assume you would want to fight with us," he said and clasped his hands behind his back.

"Y-yes."

"Good. It would probably be safer for you to phase back to human form to prevent any of us from accidently confusing you with the enemy."

"Yeah, I'd like that too," I said and Jared gave a short laugh behind me.

"We will provide more details once we confirm the battle plans. Julian?"

Julian nodded and looked at me. "Beckett Dawes," he began and my jaw clinched, "you are here ordered to pay restitution to Facility West to repair the damage you caused. You will cooperate with us in preparing for our attack. Any information or action on your part to deceive us, rest assured you will be taken down. Is that clear?"

"Yes, sir."

"Very well, we are adjourned," Julian said and took a step to his right.

The Council Hall erupted and Warriors got to their feet. The guards tightened their circle around me with Jared and Victor in front facing the angry crowd.

Devin stood up quickly. "Control yourselves," he said in a loud, forceful voice. The crowd became quiet, although they remained standing. "What is it exactly you have an issue with?" No one spoke up. "Is it the punishment?" Again, no one spoke up. "Or him fighting alongside us?"

"We can do it without him," someone shouted.

"He'll infect us," another said.

"We can't trust an animal!"

This was going downhill quickly. I started to worry if the guards around me felt the same way and would just step aside if someone came after me.

"We are better than this!" Victor shouted over the crowd and the noise died down once again. "There are only a few of us who have even had to battle the wolves. There hasn't been a major skirmish among our kinds in

446 ~ C.R. QUINN

centuries. They make us uncomfortable because they are the rare being that can hurt us. We consider them our enemy because of what they are, but even cats and dogs will form an alliance if the need arises."

Jared looked over his shoulder and muttered, "We know who the dogs are in this scenario."

I forced a smile because I knew he was trying to cut the tension.

"Brothers and sisters," Cameron began, "this was a unanimous decision by your Elite Council. All of us agreed that having Beckett on our side was a benefit to us. Garrett Archer has successfully joined vampires and werewolves to fight on a common side. I would like to think we are higher caliber men and women who could see through the centuries of clouded hatred for the greater cause."

"Beckett Dawes is not the enemy," Devin said and I flinched with surprise. "We have had little luck with trying to track Garrett and his pack ourselves. This is our chance to finally bring him down, and *that* is the only thing any of us need to be thinking about. The werewolf in this room is not the one you need to worry about. He is still part of Victor, a Warrior by birth, despite what has happened to him recently." Devin glanced over at me with stern eyes. "His is aware of what will happen to him if he betrays us. Now we are truly dismissed."

Cameron and Devin stepped down from their platform and I put my hands up. "Wait! Wh-what happens after?"

"After what?" Cameron asked.

"After the attack. What will you do to me?"

Cameron tilted his head and answered, "You will live your life. What else…"

"No cell? N-no prison?"

Cameron sighed. "Beckett, we generally do not jail werewolves just to imprison them. Our current prisoner attacked us and we kept him for information. If we release him now, he could easily give information to Garrett. Your father was brought here for everyone's protection because his phasing was uncontrollable.

"Once Garrett is gone, I truly hope you and your family will be able to pick up your lives and start fresh. And starting today, all of us here will be more accepting. We will do better. Today a new world begins for vampires and werewolves. Does that answer your question?" I nodded. "Good. Once again, we are dismissed."

Devin and Cameron walked down the center aisle and exited the

Council Hall. The guards kept their circle around me until the last Warrior left. When they finally stepped away, I fell to my knees as if they had pulled an imaginary string that had been holding me up. My hand instantly covered my eyes to hide the tears that had formed. Tosha draped herself across my back, whispering in my ear that everything would be ok. I wouldn't be tortured or killed or put in a dank cell, everything was absolutely ok.

I squeezed the corners of my eyes and stood up from the floor. Victor and Jared were still standing in front of me. Their faces held no judgement, only a sense of respect and friendship.

"Thank you," I said, and then swallowed the lump in my throat. "Thank you both for standing up for me."

"Eh, didn't have much else to do today," Jared said with a smirk.

Victor eyed him down and then turned back to me. "The battle hasn't even begun. We need to get you to the planning session. Your knowledge will be vital." I opened my mouth to speak, but Victor put his hand up. "We will be there to ensure nothing happens. If you go in there open, relaxed, and confident, you will begin to gain the trust of the others and they will begin to pass that message down."

I reached back and pulled Tosha's hand in mine. "I want Tosh there too."

Victor nodded. "I have a feeling Miss Cushlin will be more involved than you think."

Chapter Forty-one

Beckett

After my trial, instead of being ushered down to the dungeon, I was taken into a room to help form the Warrior's battle plans. With the exception of knowing I would be phasing in front of dozens of Warriors, I felt high with anticipation on taking down Garrett.

That high, however, disappeared when I discovered that Natasha Cushlin, my girlfriend who almost died a day ago, was being allowed to go on the mission. Needless to say, from the moment I charged into our room, everything went downhill from there.

"Don't think for a minute you can tell me what I can and cannot do," Tosha shouted at me.

"He almost killed you, and you want to go back for more?"

She put her hand up. "I was drunk and unprepared, this is different."

"Different? Yeah, different in the fact that there will be a dozen vamps and three times as many wolves there. All of whom could kill you, infect you..."

"I think I've proven I can fight the disease, Beckett."

"And what about if they rip your head off? That is no place for a..."

"You better be saying hybrid," she growled.

"Of course I was," I lied. "It's too dangerous, why can't you see that?"

Tosha tightened her lips and crossed her arms in front of her chest. Her eyes narrowed as her breath became loud and tense. Finally, "What I *can* see, is that you have forgotten who the fuck you're talking too! *I* was the one who saved you from Garrett's goons that first night. *I* was the one who helped you get away from that bitch Delia. *I* have trained for over a year for this, and I gave it all up for *you*! You go away and suddenly you think you can tell me what to do like I'm some weak little girl, and not someone who could kick your ass into next Thursday, let alone someone you say you love."

"That's exactly it," I yelled and pulled at the ends of my hair. "I almost lost you. I saw you in that hospital bed, I remember the sound of your screams. I can't…there's no way I can…can…" Tosha touched my arm gently, it was in a loving way, I knew that, but it felt like a needle in my arm. My skin was darkening, I could feel the rush of heat and hum of adrenaline. "I need to get out of here."

"Wh-what? Beckett, no," she pleaded as I turned away from her. "We need to talk about this."

"I need some air."

"But…we're on restriction. We're not allowed."

"You think I give a fuck?" I shouted and picked up the new bow and quiver I'd been given. "I've got to worry about my girlfriend getting ripped apart, I have a bow I've never used before, and if I don't get some fucking air then we'll have an even bigger problem here in a minute. Let them try and fucking stop me."

I could hear Tosha's cries behind me as I slammed the door, but I had to get outside and get calm. The corridor was empty. Apparently, all the other Warriors were following the restriction rule and staying in their rooms. It could also be that our room was in a more secluded corner of the manor. For their protection as well as mine, I'm sure.

It took nearly twenty minutes for me to find and setup a target out in the courtyard. The pressure and frustration continued to build within me until I released my arrow. Pffft!

My arrow wasn't near center, but it was somehow easier to breathe. I took another arrow from my quiver, threaded it, pulled it back and released. Still off center. Tomorrow was going to be a nightmare. The bow was too perfect for my defective wrist. I missed my bow. Arrows three, four, and five hit with perfect accuracy, perfect grouping, six to seven inches away from center where I was actually aiming for. But my aim was the least of my worries when the wind brought along with it the smell of a visitor.

"You are aware there is a restriction in effect," Victor said behind me.

I didn't bother turning around as I took another arrow from my quiver and replied, "I heard something about it."

"And you chose to ignore that order for some target practice?"

"Trying to get used to this bow they gave me." I tilted the bow slightly to the left to try and compensate. Pfffft!

"Were you aiming for the corner of the target?" Victor asked next to me.

I threw the bow on the ground. "This is pointless. I can't do this."

Victor raised an eyebrow at me. "What exactly is it that you cannot do?"

"All of this," I replied and started pacing. "The bow's wrong, Tosha's going to get herself killed tomorrow, and I'll probably screw up and lead us to the middle of nowhere rather than where Garrett actually is, then he'll come here and kill everyone, end of days, all of that."

Victor knitted his brows and stared at me for several seconds before saying, "Why is it you have such little faith in yourself and my Warriors?"

"Well, in case you haven't noticed, I'm a bit of a screw up."

He smiled. "You do have a way of making a mess of things."

I laughed and picked the bow up from the ground, laced another arrow, and released it. Pfffft!

"Oh my," Victor muttered. The arrow had hit the upper left-hand corner, rather than the center. "Unless you meant to shoot it there."

I sighed. "Can you fix my bow like you did last time?" I asked and extended the bow in his direction.

"Perhaps I can do something better," he replied and disappeared in a cloud of black smoke.

I threw the bow on the ground again and walked down to the target to remove the arrows that displayed my shame. As I made my way back, Victor reappeared in another cloud of smoke with a bow in his hand. My jaw flinched as he turned the bow lengthwise displaying the awkward grip filed in the center.

"Is that…" I began, but couldn't finish.

"It is your fath…it is Garrett's bow," he said. "The token that Devin brought back to me as proof that Garrett had been killed. I suppose I should have demanded his heart instead. Although I wonder if Devin would have killed someone for their heart, but then of course that is completely against our code of ethics…"

"Uh, Victor?"

He shook his head. "Yes, yes, I'm sorry. I find myself questioning almost everything nowadays. Anyway, this is Garrett's bow, pristinely preserved in my vault, but of course you knew that."

I smirked. "I may have seen it."

"Well now you shall use it," he said and extended it in my direction.

My hands felt heavy as I took the bow from him. As I twisted it up vertically, my hand melted into the grooves that had originally been carved and worn in by my birth father. I hated it. I hated that I shared so many of his traits. Victor must have seen the change in me since he remained silent as I turned toward the target. I pulled an arrow from my quiver, threaded it, pulled it back to my cheek, and let it rip. Pffft!

Dead center.

I sighed and walked to the far corner of the courtyard, putting the target fifty or sixty feet away and at an odd angle. With another sigh I pulled an arrow from my quiver, threaded it, and pulled it back. When I squinted my eye, my vision of the target zoomed forward. Pffft!

Dead center.

After three more arrows, all at different angles, heights, and speeds, all hitting exactly where I wanted them, Victor declared training time over.

"You need rest, child."

"I still don't feel ready."

Victor placed his hand on my shoulder. "When it comes to battle, you'll never feel ready. There will always be nerves and uncertainty, but you must push those feelings aside."

"That's easy for you to say," I replied and tried to take a step away, but he squeezed my shoulder to keep me in place.

"For centuries I have watched my children leave in battle, at my command, and not seeing them all return. On the outside, I show my children the confidence they need in order to do their duty, even though on the inside I may be wrecked with guilt at the fact that I am the one sending them to their potential death. Believe me, child, everyone suffers in these situations."

"What if I can't..."

Victor squeezed my shoulder tightly and brought my face down to his. "You have the training, child. You have persevered time and time again. I have confidence in you." He touched my heart. "There is a Warrior in there, I have seen it, and he will show himself again tomorrow."

"There's something else in there too. A big, hairy something."

"And you will use him as well. You have no choice but to bring the Warrior and the wolf together. But I know you can do it, you are my grandson."

Victor wrapped his arms around me and hugged me tightly. My hands froze for a moment, surprised by the gestured at first, but it was exactly what I needed. But just as quickly as it began, Victor released me and took a step back, straightening up and composing himself as if the moment had never happened. He reached into his pocket and then held his hand out to me.

"I believe this is yours," he said, opening his hand and revealing the small gold Warrior medallion.

Slowly I took the medallion from his hand and began worrying it with my thumb. "Thanks, Victor. For everything."

He nodded curtly and took another step back. "Now go get some rest, and that is an order." I raised my eyebrows at him. "I am still a leader in this coven, I'm allowed to give orders if I want to. Now go, be with Miss Cushlin. You should be with her instead of out here driving yourself mad."

I nodded and stepped past him. After only a couple of steps, I turned around and placed my fist over my heart. Victor gave a tight smile, dipped his head, and put his fist over his heart as well. When I thought for sure I saw a tear coming from his eye, he disappeared in a cloud of smoke.

With a sigh, I turned back toward the manor. The halls were silent except for the sound of my sneakers squeaking along the stone floors. Only the werewolf roamed the halls of the manor full of vampires. My life had become really weird.

When I came to my room, my hand froze on the doorknob. I was scared to go in, and ashamed of how I'd left. The nerves weren't gone, but at least the anger had subsided. Hopefully it was enough to get a few hours of sleep, and I hoped that Tosha would be next to me.

Slowly I opened the door, noticing that the lights had been turned off. I stepped inside and closed the door quietly behind me. "Tosha?" I whispered, and thankfully saw her move in the bed.

Tosha leaned over to the nightstand and turned the light on. She sat up in the bed, her eyes red and puffy from crying.

"I'm sorry," I said. "I'm an asshole. You've told me that several times, so it shouldn't be all that shocking to you."

"I wasn't sure if you were coming back."

"I don't know how to deal with this, Tosha, I don't. If anything happens to you tomorrow…"

"Nothing will happen to me," she said in a louder, frustrated tone. "I have far more skills than you do when it comes to this…"

I put my hands up to stop her. "I am not doubting your skills, Tosha, I'm doubting mine. If I screw up something tomorrow that gets you hurt, I'll never forgive myself. I'm trying to figure out how…how I…" My lungs suddenly felt tight, making me light-headed. I sat down on the edge of the bed with my back to her. The mattress bounced slightly as she crawled across it and wrapped her arms around my shoulders and chest.

"The universe wouldn't have put us through all of this just to tear us apart near the end."

"Where did you hear that?"

"Maybe a fortune cookie, maybe some sappy movie I watched when I was a sobbing, depressed mess when you left, but I think it's true. Why tear us down to then build us back up, only to tear us down again? I would like to believe the world isn't that cruel." She turned me around in her arms to face her. "I need you to have faith in me."

"I do, Tosha, I do," I replied and took a thick strand of her hair between my fingers.

"Because I have faith in you," she continued. "It doesn't matter what bow you have in your hand," she said and pointed to the actual bow I had in my hand and then flinched. "Wait, that's not the bow you had. Is…is that…"

"Garrett's bow, yeah," I replied and leaned over to place it on the chair in the corner. "Victor gave it to me. Apparently, it does matter what bow is in my hand because I was shooting for shit with the other one, and this one magically made me better. Talk about a mindfuck. The only tool that could help me kill Garrett, is his own bow. That's got to be some Greek mythology, Star Wars bullshit." I pulled my fingers through her hair and looked deeply into her dark eyes. "I was always coming back. I'm sorry I made you so upset. I don't like when I make you cry, and I know I've done it a lot lately."

She grazed her fingers above my brow, making my eyes close uncontrollably. "You look tired."

"But not too tired if you want to…you know," I said and kissed her hand. Immediately she tensed. "What? Tosha, what's wrong?"

She swallowed hard, removed her hand from mine, and began

454 ~ C.R. Quinn

wringing it with the other. "Are you sure that's a good idea?" she asked as she rose from the bed. "You should probably get some sleep."

"Tosha?"

She turned nervously. "What? I'm just saying you need to rest before tomorrow. That's what the whole restriction thing is about, so you can be at your strongest."

I stood and stepped carefully around the bed, afraid I would spook her like a frightened deer. "Tosha, there are a bunch of people here doing things besides sleeping. Believe me, I heard them on my way down here." Once I stood in front of her, I realized she was shaking slightly. "Look, if you don't want to…"

"It's not that," she interrupted. "I'm just nervous."

"Nervous? About what? We've done this a couple of times already, remember?"

She shook her head quickly. "Not like this we haven't," she replied.

I sat down on the bed and pulled her by the hips to be in front of me, grazing my thumb under her shirt. "Your new skin?"

"Try new body parts," she replied loudly and flailed her arms out. "And lots of new skin." Her eyes became watery. "I know you liked the scars."

"Only because they were a part of you," I replied.

"You had names for them," she said flatly.

"So I'll find new parts of your body to name." She narrowed her eyes at me. "I'm in love with you, not your scars, Tosha. Don't you trust me?"

"It's not a matter of trust," she replied. "I just can't stress about this tonight. Tomorrow is a big day. Let's just wait until this is over. Ok?"

My heart sank. I wanted her. This could be the last time we would ever be together, I wanted all of her. But, "Sure," I replied and removed my shirt. Her lips tightened as she watched me pull myself across to the opposite end of the bed.

"You're not mad?"

"Of course not," I replied and plunged my legs under the blankets.

Tosha pulled down the blankets on the other side of the bed and ducked underneath. "Your chest looks better, even from this morning."

I nodded. "Hopefully there won't be much left tomorrow."

She gave a tentative smile and placed a hand on my chest. "I do love you, Becks."

"I know you do," I replied and kissed her hand, then stretched over to kiss her on the lips. "Considering the mess we've made, I don't think anyone doubts that we love each other." I gave her one last quick kiss on the lips. "Get some sleep."

She nodded and clicked the lamp off. The room was pitch black. It was hard to tell if my eyes were open or closed. A room with no windows would do that to you. I turned on my side and began sorting through the thoughts that kept circling in my head. Images of the satellite photos of the area I believed the pack might be. Wondering how long I would be down after phasing back. Would someone try and kill me when I was at my most vulnerable? Would I be able to kill Garrett if we were finally face to face?

"You didn't say you loved me," Tosha said out of nowhere.

"Wh-what? Yes I did."

"No, you said you knew I loved you, and that no one could doubt that we loved each other."

"Doesn't that count?"

"No."

"I love you, Natasha. You wanted to follow the restriction, so go to sleep."

I froze for a few seconds, waiting for a reply, but nothing came. The worrying thoughts began to seep back in. Garrett's face coming into focus with Vincent just over his shoulder. I began thinking about all the things they'd done to me. If tomorrow went well, what next? Did I try going back to school? Where would I go for the full moon?

"Tell me about the house in the woods," Tosha said and snuggled up to my back.

"What? I thought you were sleeping."

"The house in the woods," she said again. "You said you would think about us in a little house in the woods."

"Go to bed, Tosha."

"I can't sleep."

"You've literally been trying for less than ten minutes."

"Just tell me again."

"You're not going to let this go until I tell you, are you?"

"Probably not."

I sighed and rolled onto my back. Tosha shifted to allow me room, but then rested comfortably and naturally on my chest. "It's nothing special, just a small house on a few acres of land, two levels, nice front porch to watch the kids running around the yard making a ton of noise."

"We had kids?"

"Mm-hmm. Sometimes girls, sometimes boys, one of each, it always changed."

"But back then I couldn't have…"

"There is more than one way to have a family," I replied and placed my hand on top of hers. "Just the thought of having something helped get me through."

"Ok, what else?"

"Beautiful view, lots of land and woods for me to run around in during the full moon. Maybe even a special enclosure to keep me contained, I don't know. I just liked the quiet, everything so peaceful. And sometimes we'd just sit out on the front porch, having a drink and talking. Our little piece of heaven."

"I like it," she replied. "I like the thought of having peace. I never thought I wanted that. Where should we start looking?"

"Slow down, woman," I said with a laugh.

"What? Why are you laughing?"

"It's a pipe dream, Tosha. There are a lot of things to take care of before we even think about getting there, and one of them is surviving tomorrow. So, sleep?"

She didn't answer, so I started to roll back over on my side when her hand pressed against me. She snaked her arm across my chest and searched my neck and face for my lips. It was so absurdly dark that I got a kiss on the chin, the eye, and then the side of my nose.

"Where are you?" she laughed and my hands found the sides of her face. I pulled her down until the tips of our noses touched and then guided our lips together. Her hair fell like a soft curtain, covering us both with the smell of her shampoo. My hands ducked under her shirt and I had to remind myself I was still with Tosha and not someone else. Her new skin was so soft, and so smooth that my hands glided easily up her back. With one hand, Tosha reached back and pulled her shirt over her head. In an instant, her hot breasts were pressing against me. A wave of energy and heat rushed over me. The wolf was awake. Quickly I pushed Tosha away from me.

"Are you ok?"

I took a deep breath in and began to count down from ten as I exhaled slowly. "What happened to sleeping?"

"I'm sorry."

"Don't be sorry, you just took me by surprise," I said, feeling the wolf inside me begin to retreat. I rolled onto my right side and found the sexy curve of her waist. "I want to see you."

She didn't respond, but I assumed she was sucking in her bottom lip and tightening her jaw. That was her usual expression when she was nervous or scared. To ease her into giving in, my hand traveled down to her hip and pulled at the waistband of her pajama shorts. She placed her hand on top of mine, and I froze. After a moment or two, I pulled my hand away when she squeezed it to keep it in place. Finally she removed her hand from her hip and searched for my face. When her lips once again pressed against mine, I slowly pulled down her shorts until she bent her knees up and freed herself. Her naked body stretched along my side, and this time I breathed through the wolf trying to get out and pushed him as far away as I could, although I knew he would try and rise again.

"I want to see you," I said again.

"Fine," she sighed and rolled away from me toward the nightstand on her side of the bed. With a click, the soft light peeked over her shoulder, casting a shadow across her back, but the blankets had pulled away enough to show the beauty of her miraculous new skin.

Quickly I slid up behind her, wrapping my inside arm around her waist and pulling her back into my chest. Her body twitched as my free hand glided down the curve of her hip to her outer thigh. "Does that hurt?"

She shook her head. "It tickles," she replied with a smile.

A soft laugh sounded in my throat as I began to suck at her neck causing her to release a wonderful moan. As my hand traveled back up her thigh, she reached back and plunged her hand down my pants. The wolf growled in the distance, and I took a deep breath to hold him back while I grew in Tosha's soft and kneading hand. Nervously my fingers ducked between her legs, waiting a moment for any objection before slipping one finger inside her. She gasped so loudly I quickly removed my hand.

"I'm sorry."

She shook her head vigorously. "No, do it again."

I didn't wait a second before slipping two fingers inside of her and almost creaming in my pants at the sound of her orgasmic moan. Together we found our rhythm of my fingers pleasuring her inside and out while her backside grinded up against me. The wolf was begging to come out, nipping at the sides of my consciousness. It wasn't until Tosha's insides spasmed around my fingers, and her moaning came to a fever pitch did the wolf's restraints snap. Another wave of energy and heat rushed over me, causing me to bury my head in the crook of Tosha's neck in order to breathe him back into submission.

"Holy shit," she panted. "That happens every time?"

"Usually not as often as you'd like," I replied and kissed the back of her neck.

Her fingers glided lightly up my arm. "You ok?" I nodded against her. "You look...darker."

"It's calming down. You're safe, I promise."

She pulled my hand into her chest and kissed my knuckles. "I know. You're still in there when you've phased. I've seen it up close."

I lifted my head from her neck. "When was that?"

"At the Facility, remember? You burst into the room, and instantly I knew it was you. To me it didn't feel any different than when you're human. Is that weird?"

"I just don't want you to be afraid of me when I'm...him."

Tosha turned in my arms. We were so close that the tips of our noses touched. "He's you, and you're him. I'll never be afraid of him because he's a part of you. And he's...he's beautiful, Becks."

I shook my head and brushed her hair behind her ear. "No, that's you."

My hands traveled down to her lower back and pressed her into me. She looked deeply into my eyes before kissing me softly. I pulled her outside leg across my hip and she anchored herself tightly against me. The wetness that still lingered between her legs made the blood rush back into my manhood. Tenderly, Tosha reached down between us and slipped me inside her. I tilted my pelvis under and pushed my way deep into the depths of her, causing us both to release a loud guttural moan. Everything about her was different – the warmth and softness, the feeling of natural smooth layers gliding up and down all around me. In some ways I felt guilty that I enjoyed it so much. I could have lived with the scars, but her new body drove the wolf forward from his restraints.

Forcefully I rolled her on her back and began my assault on her breasts. Tosha then wrapped her legs around my hips, pushing me deeper inside her. With each pulse she moaned until she cried out that she was coming once again. I continued pounding myself into her, feeling again her insides twitch and constrict until the big waves of her orgasm came around me. Her body convulsed, her back arched as a high-pitched cry came out of her.

Mesmerized by her pleasure, but not wanting consequences, I quickly pulled out from within her and released myself between us. I laid on top of her, both of us panting and sweating.

"I thought you said it wouldn't happen every time," she said flopping her arm over her eyes.

I laughed. "Maybe I'm better at this than I thought."

She smirked and her hand traveled down my stomach. "I have to remember to tell Nikki that the book was right."

"Book? What book?"

"Just something we found," she replied. "So...how was it for you? Was it...ok?"

I tilted my head back in order to look her in the eye. "Are you serious? Tosha, that was amazing. Why would you ask that?"

Tosha looked down concentrated on her index finger that was tracing circles on my stomach. "It's hard to forget how you would react to my scars, Becks. I know it all felt different to you too."

I tilted her chin up with my index finger. "With or without your scars, whenever we're together, it blows my mind, it's not just physical, can't you feel it?"

She nodded and then her fingers began gently touching my genitals. "How long until we can do it again?"

"Again? Damn, woman."

"What?! I have a lot of time to make up for. And like you said you were pretty good at it."

Chapter Forty-two

Tosh

Trees blurred past my passenger-side window as we made our way north. Devin was driving and ironically singing to "Psycho Killer", while Beckett sat in the front passenger seat constantly tapping the armrest and nervously shaking his leg. With the exception of Devin's random radio singing, not a word had been said since we left the manor. So much was on the line today – Devin's redemption, Beckett's revenge, and proof that the last year of my life hadn't been a waste. Then of course there's the whole worry that this could start an epic war between vampires and werewolves. You know, everyday things.

It didn't help that my nether regions felt as though they had blisters inside and out. If Beckett and I made it out of this, we needed to seriously consider birth control. I could see my smile reflected in the window, it was something I hadn't had to worry about in a long time. But again, we both had to survive.

Cars and trucks from Warriors living outside of the manor had filtered in ahead and behind us for the last couple of hours. By the time we were snaking our way through the heavy forest we were one long chain driving to the rendezvous point.

"How far away are we?" I asked.

"A couple more miles," Devin replied.

A minute later, cars began to peel off in various directions. Some parking on the side of the road, others driving further in to hide their vehicles. This was really happening. Whereas Beckett's shaking became even more pronounced, a sense of calm came over me. I didn't understand why I wasn't nervous, I had everything to lose. But I would be surrounded by the mighty Warriors, and the fiercest of them all, the Warrior Assassin, who was smiling in the front seat.

"This should be good," Devin said and pulled to the side of the road and up through a break in the woods. After cutting the engine, Devin patted Beckett on the shoulder. "You're up." Beckett nodded nervously, but didn't move. "Nervous?"

"That's an understatement," Beckett answered.

"I'm pretty confident it'll be fine."

"And if it isn't?"

"Don't start worrying about all the things that could go wrong. Focus on the first task and nothing else. Once that's finished, then you can focus on the next. One thing at a time. Now get out, you're delaying my timeline."

I smiled and opened my door, taking my backpack and Beckett's new bow, or Garrett's old one depending on how you wanted to look at it. Beckett took a path diagonal from the SUV while Devin walked the opposite direction to gather the Warriors. When I caught up to Beckett he had stopped in a small clearing and was looking up at the sky where all the birds in the area suddenly took flight.

"They certainly have the right idea," he said and looked down at me. "I told you I loved you, right?"

I smiled. "Many times before you became catatonic."

"Sorry, I'm just…"

"Don't be sorry. Are you ready?"

"No," he replied, "but I don't have much choice now." Beckett removed his shirt and handed it to me, but then looked over my shoulder and his face fell. "Do they seriously need to be this close?"

I folded his shirt and looked behind me to see that the Warriors had gathered roughly forty yards away. "Think of it like you're in a locker room."

He raised an eyebrow at me and then knelt down to unlace his boots. "Are you sure you want to watch?"

"I told you I've seen this already." Beckett handed me his boots and I placed them in the backpack along with his shirt. "And Jared will be there to watch over you once you phase back."

He nodded, but didn't make eye contact with me as he undid his pants. "This isn't near as much fun as it usually is when I'm taking my pants off in front of you." I blushed and took his pants from him. He wrapped his hand around the back of my neck, looked at me with his bright green eyes, then kissed me hard. When he rose from my lips he said, "I love you."

"Love you, too. Now drop the underwear, Dawes."

With a loud sigh, he pulled his boxer-briefs off and handed them to me. As he stood back up, he cupped his hands in front of him to cover his private parts. "This is literally a recurring nightmare I used to have."

"This is a nightmare for us too," Jared shouted somewhere behind us.

"Great," Beckett muttered and closed his eyes. "You should step back."

"I'll see you on the other side," I said and slowly backed away, rolling his things into a ball and stuffing them into the backpack. I braced myself for the agony I would see him go through. It wouldn't scare me, like Beckett was worried about, it was the pain I knew he'd be suffering that affected me.

For nearly two minutes Beckett stood tall and naked in the clearing, his face and arms twitched but nothing happened. His skin didn't even darken like it usually did when the wolf was trying to come out.

"Son of a bitch," he panted and wiped the sweat from his forehead. "It's not working."

"Calm down, Beck. Just try again."

He nodded, but turned his back to me. For another couple of minutes only his back muscles tightened and flinched until his shoulders fell completely.

"This is a fucking nightmare," he growled. Quickly I ran in front of him and squeezed his arms. I could see and feel his stress, and behind him the Warriors were getting antsy. "I can't fucking believe this. I start to phase when I don't want to, and then when I need to…what the fuck am I going to do?"

I began to think back at all the times when he started to phase accidentally, and since I couldn't have sex with him at the moment, there was only one other way and that was to make him angry. There was only one thing I could think of that would make him angry enough to phase.

I took a step away from him and said, "Beck, there's something I need to tell you."

He looked up quickly and scrunched his brows together. "Tosha, I don't think this is the time."

"Believe me, Beck, I never wanted to tell you this, but I lied to you."

He stood up straight and narrowed his eyes. "Lied? About what?"

My stomach turned and my breath caught in my throat. With an exhale I finally said, "You asked me if there was ever anything between me and Connor, and I told you there wasn't. That...was a lie." Beckett's jaw tightened, yet no other muscle in his body moved. "For the last year, he and I hooked up off and on, usually whenever he was in a dry spell." Beckett's chest started to move up and down dramatically. "It was never anything serious, which was why I was confused at the fact that he seemed so jealous of you. And then when you left..." I paused at the sight of his skin darkening and took a step back. "When you left, I was mad and hurt and he came to my room." Beckett's breath became very loud as he clinched his fists. "So I thought...I stupidly decided that I would get back at you for leaving me by sleeping with him."

Beckett's skin turned darker than I had ever seen it while all the muscles in his body began to flex and bulk up.

"Natasha," Devin warned but I put my hand up in his direction.

"Connor took one look at my scars and...he's the one who said I was disgusting."

Suddenly Beckett craned his head up to the sky and released a loud, feral roar. In an instant he fell down on all fours, continuing to scream and groan as bones crunched, muscles ripped and stretched, and dark hair grew to cover his body. I watched as the boy I loved disappeared, and in his place rose a tall, dark-haired beast. As he towered over me, his green eyes bore down on me. The wolf took a step forward, opened his mouth, and released a loud roar so powerful that my head flinched back.

"I'm sorry," I replied.

The wolf paused for a moment and then something in the distance caught his attention. He took one last look at me and then leapt past me. The Warriors broke rank and blurred past to follow him. Only Devin remained and he slowly began walking toward me.

"Are you ok?"

I wiped my face quickly and stepped back to where my backpack was on the ground. "Honestly, I was hoping to go to the grave with that."

"Oh?" he replied questioningly. "It seemed a bit strategic."

"Strategic?" I said and threaded my arms through my backpack's straps. "I did what I had to do to get the job done. Beckett may never talk to me again, but I got him to phase. Mission accomplished."

"You truly would have made an excellent Warrior."

"I certainly fucked that all up, didn't I."

Devin nodded and handed me Beckett's bow. "Perhaps we will both have some redemption today."

I gave him a sympathetic smile, knowing my little bit of drama was nothing compared to the embarrassment and shame he must have felt this last month. "Ready?"

Devin nodded and turned his back to me as I slipped the bow over my head and across my chest. After placing Beckett's quiver over my shoulder, I jumped on Devin's back and he caught my legs with his hands.

"Now giddy up," I said and Devin slowly turned his head. "Please...sir."

Devin gave me a sly smirk and leapt forward. For the last time I was going into battle with the Warriors, my brothers and sisters that I had turned my back on, but who would still fight alongside me today. It was more than I deserved.

The Warriors had planned for the several hour drive but not another two-hour run. Devin became even more frustrated when I needed to stop because my legs had gone numb, and another stop for a bathroom break that was just as embarrassing for me as it was for him. My body was thankful when we caught sight of one of our scouts.

Devin lowered me to the ground, but held onto my arm tightly while the blood circulated back into my legs, a lesson learned from earlier in our trip when I just fell on my ass.

"Skylar, what have we found?" Devin asked quietly.

"There's a farm on the other side of that ridge," Skylar pointed ahead. "As of ten minutes ago there twenty-two men gathered outside and started to phase, we're now up to thirty-five. We think they caught wind of us, or maybe they can feel Beckett like he can feel them. Either way, numbers aren't too bad, but it won't be a surprise attack."

"Vamps?"

Skylar nodded. "Another twenty or so."

"Where's Beckett?" I asked.

Skylar pointed to his right. "He's crashed out. Jared's with him. He did well, for a wolf."

I resisted the urge to give Skylar the stink eye and walked past him in the direction he indicated. After a hundred feet or so I found the Warriors gathered with weapons drawn. Several of them pointed further to the right, obviously knowing whom I was looking for. A few feet past the crowd of Warriors, Jared was standing on the trunk of a large downed tree and waving at me.

"How is he?" I whispered.

"Passed out and naked," Jared replied softly. "You're a lucky girl."

"Shut up," I said and climbed the side of the tree. On the other side lay Beckett, face down and bare ass in the air. I had to smile.

"You know what I'm talkin' about," Jared continued with a sly smile. When I ignored him and swung my leg around to jump down to the other side, Jared squeezed my arm. "Why didn't you come to me about Connor?"

"You want to talk about this now?"

"I would have stopped it. I could have helped you."

I took his hand from my arm and squeezed it reassuringly. "I know, Jer. You can't save us all though. The Cushlin girls are good at screwing things up, it's what we do and we have to suck up the consequences."

"Yeah ya do," he smiled childishly.

"You're an idiot. Can I wake my boyfriend now?"

Jared nodded and leapt down from the tree. "By the way, I can still do something to Connor."

"Cameron's taking care of it."

"Good," he replied and took a step away. "I'll still probably do something."

I smirked and landed on the ground near Beckett's head. He didn't stir. Tentatively I knelt down in front of him and gently touched his temple. In a split second Beckett flinched up and grabbed my wrist. It took several seconds for his eyes to focus and realize it was me in front of him.

"Sorry," he said and released my wrist. He looked around at his surroundings and rubbed his face. His voice was low and confused, while his eyes looked tired and out of focus. Finally he stood from the ground, brushing the dirt and dead leaves from his body. I freed myself of his bow and quiver, and dumped out the contents of my backpack. Beckett eyed me as I handed him his pants and underwear, as if he'd never seen them before. Was he still waking up from the grog of his phase, or was he angry? I couldn't tell, but whichever it was, he needed to move faster. I shook his clothes at him again and slowly he took them from my hand. Slowly, unbelievably slowly, he pulled his underwear up his legs.

"We need you to hurry," I whispered. "They know we're here."

Beckett blinked at me several times before putting his pants on. "Was it true?" he said in the same groggy voice. "Or did you lie to get me to phase?"

"It was true, and we can talk about it later, but right now I need you to move faster."

Beckett rubbed his face again and then slapped his cheeks. "What you did before we were together and after I left is none of my business."

"Fine. Put on your shirt," I said and threw his shirt at him. "You said you usually only need fifteen minutes, you've had almost an hour. Are you going to be ok?"

Beckett nodded and tucked his shirt into his pants. He leaned up against the downed tree and began putting on his socks and boots. "They know we're here."

"Yeah, I said that already, which is why you need to wake up," I said, completely unapologetic for my inpatient tone, but it didn't seem to faze him. Frustrated, I shoved his quiver and bow into his hands, and then began fastening my weapons belt around my waist. "Look, if you can't do this we need to know now."

"I need to talk to Devin."

My face fell. I was truly just being a bitch to get him to stop fooling around, but something was truly wrong. "Ok," I replied and together we climbed over the tree trunk. When we landed on the other side, Jared was waving Devin over.

"Is he ok?" Jared whispered nervously in my ear.

"Something's up, but I haven't a clue."

Devin was on us in the blink of an eye. "We cannot delay any further," he said in a low, stern voice.

"I don't think I should go down there," Beckett said, causing all of us to flinch and whip our heads in Beckett's direction.

"Beckett, we all get scared..." Devin began, but Beckett shook his head.

"It's not that. I can…" Beckett threw his bow down on the ground along with his quiver and began raking his hands through his hair. "It's Vincent. I can feel his will on me, it's not strong but it's there. They know we're here because of me. I thought by battling Vincent and leaving, that maybe I'd broken the bond. If I go down there he…"

"Vincent could force his will," Devin finished.

Beckett lowered his head. "If only the bastard had just died. I thought I hurt him bad enough, but obviously I screwed that up too."

Devin sighed. "If you feel you're compromised, then stay back. Provide us some coverage up here if you can."

"There's something else. I…got an image of Garrett with a young boy. I think…I think he found another kid to take my place."

"An image? How…"

"Shared consciousness. Probably my friend Floyd. Just keep an eye out, I guess."

Devin gave a curt nod and turned away from us. Jared patted Beckett on the back and followed after Devin.

"I'm sorry," he muttered to me.

"We'll get him, Becks."

"Find that kid. Garrett will try and disappear with him if he has the chance."

"We will."

"Come back to me."

"I have to," I replied and he cocked his head. "We have a little house in the country to find, remember?"

He gave me a half smile. "Be careful."

"Can't be any safer than with you covering me up here."

He squeezed my hand and gave me a quick, light kiss before picking up his bow and stepping away. By the time I made my way back over to Devin's side everyone was divided and waiting in place to attack. Butterflies fluttered in my stomach as I looked down the soft slope where a small farmhouse was set on the right with a large barn to the left. It was a perfect little picture except for the big pack of werewolves gathering in the foreground.

"Tosh, you and Beckett were supposed to go in first and draw them away so we could come in behind. Do you think…" Devin said and then looked over at Jared and then back to me, "…do you think you can do it alone?"

"I say no," Jared said before I could even open my mouth.

I turned my head to him. "Well, since your name isn't Tosh, I don't think it matters what you say." I turned back to Devin and replied, "Yes. I can do it. And I know Beckett will cover me too."

Devin nodded and gave Jared an I-told-you-so look.

"Don't die," he said and walked away.

"It is good advice," Devin said with a smirk. "We won't leave you out there long, just enough to get them to turn away." I nodded nervously. "You are brave, you are prepared, I know you can do this."

I exhaled nervously. "Wh-when do I go?"

"We'll go off of you," he replied.

I nodded and checked the whips on my belt, and then the knives on my back. "Ok, just give me a minute."

"Very well, but only a minute."

Devin walked away and just like that I was alone. A year of pain and sweat and tears had come to this. When I looked back out at the farmhouse, a sense of calm came over me, covering me like a warm blanket. With a big exhale and a nod to myself that I was ready, I made my way to the ridge and slid down a few feet until I caught some traction and ran down the rest of the way. Once on the ground I made my way through the woods, wincing every time a stick snapped under my foot. Through the trees I could see the lights of the farmhouse and barn. When the edge of the property was only a few yards away, the pack was easily visible, as were the vampires positioned behind them.

"We know you're there," one of the vampires yelled. "Come out or the dogs will bring you to us."

This was it, my make it or break it moment. My hands rested on the handles of my whips as I emerged from the woods. I felt like a sheriff in the Wild West as I stepped onto the property. The wolves flinched and shifted between their feet at the sight of me, but one female vampire stepped through and ordered them to stay. By the slim frame and short hair, I knew immediately who I was dealing with.

"How many lives do you have?" Delia shouted. "Aren't you tired of dying? Because we're tired of killing you."

"I do wish you guys would get it right for once," I replied and Delia straightened her shoulders.

"Well that's something easily remedied," she shouted and turned to the wolves. "Tear her to pieces so she can't put herself back together."

The werewolves leapt to attention, gaining ground as the entire pack ran at me. Quickly I grabbed the handles of my whips and unfurled them like the extensions of my arms they had become. Snap to the left, snap to the right, snap to the left again, cutting through the pack of wolves like a knife down the middle. Only a few seconds went by before I saw the dark cloud of Warriors coming through the weak side of the woods. The pack thinned and spread out while the vampires in back joined the fight.

I kept chopping my way through the pack, losing speed and momentum as I got closer to the center. Snap right, snap left, snap...my arm was suddenly jerked back as a wolf grabbed the whip in my right hand and pulled back hard enough for me to fall on the ground, knocking the breath out of me. Before I knew it, a grey wolf was on top of me, holding my chest down with his knees. My face and neck exploded in pain as his claws tore across my skin. I couldn't move my arms, goddamn it, I couldn't move anything. The wolf's opposite hand started to come down when I heard that familiar and wonderful sound.

Pfffht!

The grey wolf's chest flinched up as an arrow sank deep into his chest. His weight shifted enough that I lifted my hips and knocked him over onto the ground. My head pounded as I pushed myself up to a standing position and picked up my whips. Through the chaos I could see Delia barking orders to those around her. I gave a look up into the trees and knew Beckett was watching me, I only hoped he knew I would need him to clear a path for me.

My feet dug into the ground and then launched me forward through the hoard of vampires and werewolves trying to tear each apart. My whips were flailing around me, hitting anything getting in my way. A wolf leapt in my path, and an arrow instantly went through his neck. A vamp raised his hands to catch my whip, when an arrow went through his shoulder. I snapped my whip forward and it quickly wound around the vamp's neck, the silver coating burning his skin. With a quick yank I pulled him to the ground, unwound my whip, and continued to push through until I reached the outskirt of the battle. Delia instantly locked eyes on me. She deepened her stance and I prepared for her pounce.

Just as I swung my whip around and cracked it loudly, Delia broke out in a run toward the barn. I ran after her and cracked my whip hitting her square in the back. Delia fell forward and crawled into the darkness of the barn. I snapped my whip again and caught her by the ankle. With a quick jerk I pulled her leg out from under her and dragged her through the dirt. In a split second she leapt up from the ground like a cat, pulling me forward and slamming my face down on the hard dirt floor of the barn.

In the second I took to catch my breath, Delia grabbed the back of my shirt and flung me across the barn. Luckily I missed the thick support post and landed in a tall pile of hay. I rolled down to the ground and spit out the bits of hay that were sticking to the blood leaking from my nose and mouth.

"Can't you just stay down for once," Delia groaned, her hands still red and burned from where she had grabbed my whip.

"You don't know me well at all," I replied, unfurling my whips at my sides.

"I know you are a wolf-lover. How did the Warriors take that one? Did his smell on you give you away?" Delia said slowly as she began walking toward me, which was exactly what I needed her to do. "He wasn't alone here, you know. He had some fun getting...acquainted, shall we say, with daughters of the pack." A few more steps, I only needed to listen to her garbage long enough for her to be a few steps closer. "No matter what happens here, Garrett will never let him go. We will hunt Beckett down until he pays for his betrayal. Believe me, Garrett is a patient man when it comes to vendettas. Just look how long it took us to get to this point. Beckett will be hunted down and torn apart limb by limb by those retched animals out there. That's what they do. So if I were you, I'd run. Being with Beckett will only be a death sentence."

"I'll follow Beckett to the grave if I have to."

Delia shrugged and took the last step that I needed. "Suit yourself," she said and went to take another step when I cracked my whip at her, the tip hitting her cheek and leaving a small red mark. Her nostrils flared like a bull, this would be my only shot and I prayed it would work. I cracked the whip in my right hand at her, wrapping it around her left hand. Next, I cracked the whip in my left hand and she grabbed it in mid-air, wrapping it around her wrist. Her hands burned as she pulled back on the silver coated whips. My feet slid across the dirt floor, making me lean back further to create the much-needed tension.

Delia pulled the lines hard, sending me flying toward her. At the perfect arch, I released the whips, reached back for my knives, and as I came down toward her, crossed the knives in front of me and sliced her neck. My landing, however, was anything but graceful and we both fell to the ground in a heap. Thick, dark red blood poured from the cut in Delia's throat, but my knives hadn't cut completely through, and she was left flailing in the dirt like a snake.

I froze. She had caused so much pain, she deserved this. Did I let her suffer? The knives were still in my hands, I could cut her again, or stab her in the heart. Or should I call for Devin?

Just then, the back of my head exploded in pain and I fell to the ground near where Delia still flinched and grabbed at her gaping neck. I looked up to find Garrett standing over me, his face going in and out of focus. The blow to the head left me dazed and I could feel blood running down the back of my neck.

"I swear, if the world ended today, all that would remain would be roaches, and you," he said and walked over to Delia's other side. "Now when I was a Warrior, we were taught to kill without mercy. It's sad Father and Devin don't teach those skills anymore." Garrett reached down and petted Delia's head. In an instant he grabbed a handful of her hair and ripped her head from her body.

"Now," he said and tossed Delia's head behind him, "have you met Vincent?"

Garrett gestured to a large, shadowy figure lurking in the back doorway of the barn. As he drew closer, I could see why he was the intimidating and deadly pack leader. His muscles were bulging from his arms down to his legs, but even through my foggy vision, his yellow eyes pierced the darkness. Garrett knelt down next to me and I tried unsuccessfully to push myself away from him. He grabbed my utility belt and slid me down in front of him. My hands flew at him, but he caught my wrists easily and held them above my head.

"We know he's here," he said softly with a hint of excitement. "And you're going to bring him to me."

"Screw you."

With a smirk he replied, "Trust me, you'd rather me do that than what I'm about to do to you." He looked over his shoulder. "Vincent, toss me that rope."

Vincent picked up a length of rope and threw it over to Garrett. Before I could blink, Garrett wrapped the rope around my wrists and then tied a tight knot. He stood from the ground and pulled me across the rough dirt. I kicked my legs, tried digging my heels in, but it only made Garrett laugh.

"Vincent, the hook."

A moment later Garrett threaded a thick metal hook between my wrists and then I was hoisted up until my toes grazed the ground. My arms and shoulders groaned at my weight.

Garrett squeezed my chin tightly with his fingers. "I need you to scream."

I kicked Garrett in the balls, although it seemed to hurt my foot more than his nuts. In response, Garrett punched me in the stomach and knocked the breath out of me. Vincent tied off the hook's rope and stepped behind Garrett. It was only now that I could see the edges of bandages sticking out from under his collar, and there seemed to be a slight limp in his gate.

"Vincent, should we give the little Warrior princess a taste of her own medicine?"

"With pleasure," Vincent said behind me.

I wiggled back and forth like a fish on a hook. Garrett wrapped his hand around my neck and held me in place. "You will scream for me, and you will bring Beckett to me," Garrett said and then nodded to Vincent over my shoulder. I heard the crack of my whip before the shocking pain burned from my back. "Again."

Another crack and another slash of blinding pain. Tears formed quickly as I gasped, but then clamped my jaw down. Another slash, and then another hitting my back and legs. The pain was so bad I thought I would never use my whips on anyone ever again.

"Again, Vincent!" Garrett yelled and then glared at me. "I will rip you apart if I have to. I will get my scream."

Unfortunately, Garrett didn't have to wait long until he got exactly what he wanted.

Chapter Forty-three

Beckett

I nearly leapt off the ridge when Tosha stepped out into the clearing by herself. How could they let her go alone? They were her friends, her mentors, how could they just let her walk literally into the wolf's den. I'd never climbed a tree so fast in my life, at least on my own. I'll admit, not having Victor as a safety net made me nervous. Falling out of the tree and breaking an arm or my collarbone was the last thing I needed, especially since I overhead some of the Warriors commenting they thought I was being a coward for staying behind. They certainly hadn't been under the will of a pack leader. Vincent's will wasn't as strong on me as on others, but there was enough of a pull that could cause trouble, and the closer I was, the greater the threat.

From my perch, I could see Delia standing in front of the pack, which had grown in the short time I had been away. As though someone fired a starting pistol, the entire pack leapt toward my girlfriend. My immediate reaction was to fire everything I had, but that would give up my position way too early. Drawing the pack away had been part of the plan, and thankfully to the left the Warriors were running at the pack's blindside.

It was amazing to watch Tosha hack through the pack with her whips. But when a wolf tackled her to the ground, I pulled my bow string back to my cheek and waited. When his claws tore across her skin, it was over for him. I squinted my eye and my vision zoomed forward in a flash. With an exhale, I released my arrow and smiled when it sank into the wolf's chest.

Tosha pushed him off of her and got to her feet, seeming a little shaken, but something caught her attention, or should I say someone. Tosha had found Delia and looked back up in my direction.

"I've got you," I whispered and secured myself on my perch.

As Tosha launched herself forward, I reached back and shot two arrows in quick succession, hitting wolves and vamps alike. When Tosha made it out from within the pack, Delia fled toward the barn, but my girl didn't let her get far before those whips were flying and hitting Delia in the arm and back. But then my stomach dropped when Delia ran into the barn and Tosha chased after her.

Quickly I put my arm through my bow and secured it across my chest before climbing down from my perch. As soon as my feet hit the ground I ran to the ridge, but my brain stopped me right before I slid down the slope. By going into the battle I risked being pulled to the other side.

"Damn it, Tosha," I said under my breath and began to pace along the ridge.

She would be fine, she would be fine. Devin wouldn't have let her come if he didn't believe she could handle herself. I peered back over to the barn, even squinting my eyes to zoom in, but all I saw was darkness.

The battle raged on between the pack, Garrett's men, and the Warriors. Several wolves lay dead on the ground. There was only one that I recognized, and thankfully it wasn't Floyd. He'd become a good friend, and in return I sent in the Warriors to kill him. There were only a few other wolves I hoped would survive, but I hoped that Devin ripped the heads off every single one of Garrett's men.

Speaking of, where was Garrett? Where was Vincent, for that matter. For all the talk Garrett did, I figured he would jump at the chance to not only kill some Warriors, but Devin especially. I took another scan of the battle looking for Garrett or Vincent when a pain in my chest knocked me back. The wolf inside me lurched out of the darkness I had pushed him down in. My hair stood on end, my chest and shoulders expanded, all reflexive responses to one frightening fact - Tosha was in trouble.

I leapt off the ridge's edge and slid down the slope. Halfway to the clearing, a scream echoed in my head. I was suddenly filled with gasping pain and fear. My body shook as I forced the wolf back once again. The leash that was holding him was getting thinner and thinner. At any moment it could snap and I wouldn't have the strength to keep him inside. Tosha needed me, and I would have to get through the crowd of vampires and werewolves ripping each other apart.

"You can fucking do this," I said to myself and took an arrow from my quiver. After three quick breaths, I held my bow and arrow at the ready and ran from the woods.

The moment I ran into the clearing, one of Garrett's men was running toward me. He leapt forward, and pfffft! An arrow in his neck. I grabbed another arrow and ran toward the battle. A wolf I recognized from one of the smaller outlier packs began clawing the air between us. Pffft! Arrow in the chest. A gap formed in the middle of the clearing and I ran through it, only to have another wolf leap in front of me. Just as I pulled my arrow back, a black wolf stepped in front of me and launched the other wolf backwards.

"Thanks, Floyd," I shouted as I ran forward, pushing a dueling pair of vamps out of my way. The remaining path to the barn was clear. With an arrow threaded in the bow, I slowly stepped inside the barn, and straight ahead at the opposite end of the barn was a terrifying sight.

"Tosha!" I shouted, leaving all sense behind and running to her. She was hanging by her wrists, the back of her uniform cut open in several places with angry red scars underneath. I dropped my bow and ran around to face her. "I've got you," I said and carefully removed the hook from between her wrists.

Instantly she collapsed in my arms. "I'm so sorry," she cried.

"You have nothing to be sorry for," I replied, cradling her into my chest.

"That's not entirely true."

There was no need to turn around to know it was Garrett behind me. I looked down at Tosha, understanding now why she had apologized. Quickly I grabbed my bow and arrow from the ground, swung around on my knee, and pulled the bowstring back to my cheek.

Garrett tilted his head. "Now that is a sight," he said and took a step forward, his hand reaching out slightly. "I assumed Father snapped her in half, or burned her. How poignant that you bring her back to me."

"You'll need to come and get her first."

He smiled. "You really are my son."

The wolf inside me growled, making my lip curl. "I am the son of Richard Dawes, and I will be until they put me in the ground."

"Well, fortunately for you, that will be sooner rather than later."

At that moment, a hulking mass stepped out of the shadows. Vincent's arms and shoulders were always the most intimidating. It was as though there were mountains on either side of his neck. Even though he was still in his human form, the wolf inside me began to growl and arch his haunches. At the sight of bandages and a slight limp, I guess I had injured him pretty badly since he hadn't fully healed. However, they didn't seem to hinder him too badly since he charged at me.

Quickly I ran into the center of the barn to take this battle away from Tosha, and shot Vincent in the upper thigh. My arrow didn't even slow Vincent down. Before I could thread another arrow, Vincent lowered his shoulder and tackled me to the ground. I could feel his will bearing down on me. The only way to lift it would be to show my intent to challenge him. The wolf inside me lowered his head and bared his teeth, the fur on his back standing on end. And just like that, Vincent's will was lifted.

His weight was crushing my chest, making it hard to defend myself from his punches. When he rose up and pulled his right arm back, I grabbed the arrow sticking out of his thigh and plunged it under his ribs. With a loud howl, he fell back on the ground, allowing me to push myself away. Vincent came up to his knees and I watched as he slowly, and painfully, pulled the arrow out of his body. This guy truly wouldn't die. I was much stronger as a wolf, but Vincent could take me out in the time it would take me to phase. He had injuries, and I would have to use that to my advantage.

I took a step forward and kicked my left leg out, aiming for the puncture wound in his thigh, but Vincent caught my foot and spun me down on my side. In the split second it took for me to catch my breath, Vincent wrapped one of his thick arms around my neck and wrenched me backwards. I tried pulling at his arm, with no luck, and then started to flail my fists around until I hit something that hurt. Finally he grunted when I hit his upper chest. So I did it again, and then again, and when I was on the verge of passing out I kicked my heel back and caught the wound on his leg. Vincent fell to one knee and dropped me to the ground. Quickly I turned around, a little too quickly actually since Vincent was a blur, but I just aimed for the white bandages on his chest and planted my fist into them until the bandages were soaked with blood. Vincent slumped to his side, and I took the advantage by wrapping my arm around his neck like he had done mine. Only problem was he had about fifty pounds on me, so when he pressed his heels into the ground we easily went backwards, his weight crushing my ribs.

I tightened my grip around his neck, interlocking my other arm to help clamp him down. Vincent dug his heels into the ground once again, this time peddling us across the dirt floor causing rocks to dig into my back. I wouldn't last much longer, and my grip around his neck was barely slowing him down.

The wolf was gnashing and jumping against his leash. Even he knew I was done for. In the back of my head I could see him eyeing me, pressing me to let him loose.

We can't phase, I said to him. He gnashed his teeth and pulled at his leash. *I know! But there isn't time.*

Vincent's elbow hit me in the kidney, loosening my grip and allowing him another shot to my kidney.

The wolf growled at me again, sending a shiver through my body. My skin started to darken and the hair on my arm stood on its end.

No! No, stop! I shouted in my head, but instead of him taking over and ripping through my body, he lowered his head with a deep growl. A rush of blood went through my body bringing with it a controlled wave of energy and strength. Somehow, the wolf and I found a middle ground.

The power he had given me was enough to tighten my grip around Vincent's neck until a loud crack sounded. Vincent's body instantly went limp. Quickly I pushed his body off my chest and rolled over to my knees to catch my breath. From behind me I could hear shuffling across the dirt floor. My bow was to my right on the ground a few feet away. Painfully I pushed off the ground and leapt for the bow, scooping it up with my left hand while my right pulled an arrow from my quiver. The arrow was threaded in the bowstring and pulled back to my cheek by the time I turned around. Garrett stood in the middle of the barn holding Tosha by her throat in front of him like a shield.

"Now you kill him? You little shit" Garrett said angrily and shook Tosha by the neck. "So what is your plan now, son?"

"Don't call me that," I said and took a step forward.

"Like it or not…"

"I am NOT your son," I shouted and took another step forward.

"You realize I can snap her neck faster than you can shoot that arrow, don't you?"

"Just shoot him," Tosha struggled to say through Garrett's grip.

Garrett sank his fangs into the space between her neck and shoulder, and I shot my arrow at his face. Within a split second, he spit out a piece of Tosha's flesh and then slapped my arrow down. Tosha screamed as blood ran down from her gaping wound, but Garrett continued to hold her up by her throat.

"Stupid, stupid, child," Garrett growled, just as a shadow passed behind him. "You cannot beat me! Haven't I proved that over and over again? I will kill you as easily as I have your brothers before you. I realize now I need to start their education younger."

Only a few feet behind Garrett, the shadow began to crawl down a support beam and finally I had a glimmer of hope. I threaded another arrow and pulled it back to my cheek. I needed to provide a moment of distraction, but my girlfriend would definitely hate me.

"Your torture of my brothers ends tonight," I said.

Garrett laughed. "And you're the one to stop me?"

"Afraid not, someone's in line ahead of me," I replied and released my arrow low, hitting Tosha in the knee and causing her to fall forward. Garrett lost his balance for only a second before letting Tosha fall to the ground, but it was just enough time for Devin to jump down from the support beam and thrust his fist into Garrett's back and come out through the chest with Garrett's heart in his hand. A little bit of vomit rose in my throat. I'd seen *Indiana Jones and the Temple of Doom* about a hundred times, but it didn't prepare me enough to see this.

Devin pulled his arm back out and Garrett fell limply to the ground. I lowered my bow at the realization that my nightmare was over and ran to Tosha's side.

"I'm sorry, I'm sorry, I'm so sorry," I said and knelt down beside her.

"Get this fucking thing out of me," she screamed and pulled on the arrow which only made her scream more.

Devin nudged me out of the way and plucked the arrow from Tosha's knee. Tosha squealed and then collapsed on the ground. I squeezed her hand and leaned over her.

"Tosha, I'm sorry."

"You said that," she replied in an exhausted tone. "Don't worry, Becks, I would have done the same thing."

"Yeah, but I wouldn't have healed."

"Gotta do what you gotta do," she replied with a smirk.

Carefully I lifted her up to a seated position and Devin knelt down in front of her.

"How did I do, sir?" she asked.

He smiled and patted her uninjured leg. "With the exception of you running in here without coverage, I couldn't be prouder. It saddens me you will not be one of us."

Tosha's eyes filled with tears as she squeezed my hand. "Me too," she said and then looked at me. "But I know where I'm supposed to be."

"Do you think you can stand?" Devin asked and stood up from the ground.

Tosha nodded. "It's healing, but I'll need some help." Devin reached down, but she shook her head. "Make Beckett do it since he shot me in the leg."

I wrapped my arm around her back and took her weight into my chest as she pressed up to a standing position. "You're going to make me feel guilty about this for a while, aren't you?"

"You bet your ass," she answered. "I left the Warriors for you and you shot me in the leg."

"I'll make it up to you. Like, for the rest of my life, I'll make it up to you."

"Yes you will," she said and then kissed me softly.

"If you two are done," Devin prodded and gestured toward the front entrance of the barn, "there is something that requires your attention outside."

I shook with realization. "Oh my god, did we win?"

"Sort of," Devin replied and waved us forward.

With Tosha's arm draped across my shoulder, I helped her limp along the center path of the barn to the outside.

"Oh my god," Tosha shrieked and covered her eyes with her free hand.

At first, I thought her reaction was to the bodies strewn on the ground, losses on all sides it seemed, but then I realized she was most likely reacting to the dozen or so men roaming around completely naked. Since my short time with the pack, naked men walking around wasn't shocking anymore. I had to laugh a little at the fact that Tosha was burying her face into my chest.

"Did they surren…" I started to say when I took a step to the right, but what stopped me in my tracks was the fact that every one of the naked men mirrored my step. With Tosha still in my chest, I took a step to my left, and the same men mirrored my movement once again. "Oh shit."

"What's happening?" Tosha asked, still hiding her face.

480 ~ C.R. QUINN

I looked over at Devin for an explanation, but he simply shrugged. "Suddenly they stopped fighting against us and took out Garrett's remaining vamps. We just stood back and watched."

"Oh shit," I said and felt my heart beating furiously against my ribs. A black man, still naked, walked forward with a smirk on his face. "Floyd!"

"Good to see ya too there, Beckett," he replied and then pointed to Tosha who was still clinging to my chest. "That the girl?"

I nodded and nudged her. "Floyd, this is Natasha. Tosh, meet Floyd."

Tosha lifted her head, but kept her eyes up to the sky while Floyd shook her hand. "Nice...to meet...you."

Floyd laughed. "I'm afraid you'll have to get used to us running around like the day we were born."

"I-I will?"

"Sometimes it's just unavoidable," he replied. "We're not ashamed, believe me. It's just who we are. Eventually you won't even notice the difference."

Tosha finally brought her eyes down to look at Floyd. "I doubt that, but...why would I..."

"Floyd," I interrupted, "what's happening? Devin said you guys just stopped fighting against them."

"Well," he began with a laugh, "we had to follow our pack leader. We changed sides because of our pack leader's will. *Your* will, my friend."

"Nope. No, no, no," I said in a panic and shook my head.

Floyd put his hands up. "You challenged and killed Vincent. You know how it works. You win, you're the pack leader."

My hand instantly raked through my hair. "Oh, shit. Shit, shit, shit. Holy fucking shit."

I peeled Tosha away from my side and began pacing. On the fourth pass, Devin stepped in front of me. "Beckett, isn't this what you wanted?"

"What? Me? No way," I replied quickly. "I just wanted Vincent dead, not...shhhhhit. What the hell am I supposed to do now?"

Devin scrunched his brows together in his well-honed judgmental gaze. "Lead them, Beckett. That's what they need. They are victims as much as you are. Help them find their way through this."

"Who's going to help *me* find my way?"

Devin looked around me to where Tosha was standing. "Seems to me you have a strong woman at your side." I looked back at Tosha who seemed almost as frightened as I was. Devin tapped his finger on my chest above my heart. "You have Warrior blood, Beckett. You are one of us, that will never change."

"Warrior blood," I whispered to myself and then looked back up at Devin. "The kid, did we find the kid?"

Devin pressed the strap around his neck. "Jared, report?"

"I'm literally behind you, bro," Jared replied.

The three of us turned around to find Jared walking toward us from the farmhouse with a young boy at his side. He wasn't the spitting image of Garrett like I was, but similar enough that we could pass as brothers. Shit, we were. Step? No, half. Half-brother, right? Regardless, he looked scared and confused by the naked men walking around the field.

Jared came around to the other side of the boy, trying to shield him as best he could. "Found him hiding in a cabinet in the kitchen. The kid is highly compactable."

"Hey," I said and knelt down to the ground, "what's your name?"

"Brady," he replied shyly as he studied my face. "You look like him."

"Him? You mean Garrett?" He nodded. "Yeah, he was my father."

Brady raised his eyebrows. "Mine too."

"Brady, did you ever see the wolves?" He nodded again. "Did they ever scratch you?"

"No," he replied and I breathed a sigh of relief. "Can I go home now?"

"Yeah," I smiled, surprised at how unaffected he was, "we're all going to go home now."

"Can I get my bow?" Brady asked and pointed back at the farmhouse.

"Your bow?"

"Yeah," he replied as he reached down and touched mine that was dangling from my hand. "Mine has notches like this too!"

I looked over at Devin. "Sorry, Devin, looks like we have yet another honorary Warrior among us."

Devin gave me a strained smile. "Wonderful. Just what we need, another Archer."

"There are worse things."

"I can't think of many," he replied. "Come, Brady, we need to get you home."

Devin placed his arm around Brady's shoulders and ushered him toward the crowd of Warriors. When I turned back around, Tosha was shielding her eyes while Floyd tried having a conversation with her.

"Floyd, give the girl a break, man. Go put on some pants."

Floyd gave me his wide grin. "If that's what the leader wants."

"No, I'm not...that."

"You killed the previous pack leader, that means you're the new pack leader. I'm pretty sure you can't change the rule of our universe, Beck."

"Floyd, I don't know the first thing about being pack leader."

He nodded and thought for a moment. "Start with something simple. Tell us the battle is over, and to put on pants." I looked over his shoulder and opened my mouth when Floyd put his hand up. "Not literally tell us, Beck. Assert your will on us, that's what the leader does."

"But I don't want..." I began, but there was no arguing with him. I hated the feeling of Vincent's will upon me, I didn't want others to have to feel it. When I looked out on the field all their eyes were on me. Oddly I could feel their energy as if they were an extension of me. Floating in the back of my head was the wolf, standing on all fours with his chest high, looking straight through my eyes and finding the wolf behind each man.

Was this what it was like to be pack leader? Or even to be one with the wolf inside of you? We would no longer fight each other, and somehow we both knew it. In my head I told him to let the other wolves go home, we would figure things out later. The wolf howled and the men in front of me began to disburse. The wolf sat and then stretched his front paws forward, resting his head on top of them.

Thank you, I thought to him and he closed his eyes.

Tosha's hand touched my cheek, bringing me back to the present. I looked down at her and asked, "How's the knee?"

"Healed," she replied. "How are you?"

"Honestly, I'm feeling a little beat up," I replied. "Tosha, I'm sorry."

"For what?"

"You didn't sign up for this. I don't know what this pack leader thing is going to entail, or where I'm going to live, or...*how* I live in the real world with all of this."

Tosha knitted her brows together. "What are you trying to say, Becks?"

"Look," I began and took a step away, "the idea of living together was risky enough when I was just a wolf. But now, you put pack leader on top of that? I'm just saying you have a choice here, and there's absolutely no judgement."

Tosha sighed and turned her back on me for nearly thirty seconds before she looked over her shoulder and said, "No judgement?"

Chapter Forty-four

Tosh

It was official. My life with the Warriors was over. There were no more dreams of Cameron or Damon placing a gold pin on my chest, or running alongside my brothers and sisters in battle. My life plan had been so solid for the last year, and in a second it had been shattered. It was freeing yet terrifying at the same time. The only thing sadder than leaving my old life behind was having to say goodbye to the Burke twins. Jack-Jack was clinging to my leg while Olivia hugged me around the neck, neither wanting to let go. I would miss being Toshy. I would miss their cherub smiling faces and innocence, but also their mischief.

"Do you get to be Mrs. Pack Weader, then?" Olivia asked as she brushed away her crookedly cut hair that her brother had taken the scissors to for a second time.

"I don't think that's a thing," I replied.

"Why not?" she pouted.

"Yeah, why not?" Jackson asked. "Santa Cwaus has Mrs. Cwaus? Why can't you be Mrs. Pack Weader?"

"Well, Santa is married to Mrs. Claus, so I think…"

"Then you should marry Beckett!" Livy squealed.

"Burke twins," Brianna said loudly, "leave Tosh alone and give her some love goodbye."

Jackson looked up at his mother. "How can we weave her alone *and* give her love goodbye."

"You are such a stinker," Brianna said with a shaking head. "Give her hugs and kisses and then go play before I throw away every ounce of ice cream that is in this house!"

The twins jumped and tightened their grips around me. "We wuv you, Toshy," they said in unison.

I squeezed them tightly and kissed the tops of their curly heads. "Love you guys, too. I'll see you soon."

"Ok, bye," Livy said and ran back inside with her brother.

"Ice cream is basically their currency," Brianna said and stepped toward me.

"Can't blame them," I laughed. "I'm going to miss them."

"They'll miss you too once they realize you're not in the manor every day. But like you said, you'll see them soon, you're not going far."

"For now," I corrected and sighed.

Brianna put her arms around me and pulled me into her chest. "Moving to the country isn't so bad."

"Yeah, but I'm an outsider living in the country with a bunch of people I don't know and who may not like me because I'm not like them."

Brianna released her arms from around me and looked down at me with motherly eyes. "You've always been an outsider, Natasha. No matter where you've been, you do what you want and you never care what others will think about you. People are drawn to you because of that confidence, honey. You bring the fire, Tosh, don't let your fear extinguish that."

Tears clouded my eyes and I fell back into Brianna's chest. "I'm going to miss you saying things like that to me."

Brianna squeezed me tightly. "You're not dying, Tosh. We have cell phones and video chat and I'll see you at Daddy O's tomorrow night." She squeezed me again and kissed the top of my head. "But I'll miss you too."

"Jesus, you're still saying goodbye?" Nikki said, sounding annoyed as she stepped down from the manor's front steps and continued past us toward the rental car. "We told Mother Abby we'd be there before five."

"Why is your sister calling my mom Mother Abby?" Beckett said.

I looked over Brianna's shoulder to see Beckett coming out of the front door with Cameron. "You told her she could come live at your mom's house, did you think she was going to be normal about it?"

"One could hope," he replied as he stepped down on the driveway. "Ready?"

I nodded nervously and looked up at Cameron. "No Devin?"

Cameron gave an uncomfortable grin. "His words to me were 'I've said everything I needed to say to her, why do I have to say it again?'"

"It's fine," I replied, although I was truly disappointed.

"I am sorry, Natasha. What my brother was really saying is that he will miss you and that he is too upset to have to say goodbye to you in person."

"That's more like it," Brianna muttered.

Cameron turned to Beckett and shook his hand. "Well, young man, we will be talking again soon."

Beckett nodded. "Yes, sir. I look forward to it."

"And I look forward to the peace we can make between our kinds."

"At least between the Warriors and my pack. Not sure we can make all dogs and cats love each other."

"It starts with a spark, Beckett," Cameron replied and patted Beckett on the shoulder.

"Are we leaving today or not?" Nikki shouted from the car.

Beckett sighed and looked over at me. "She was ready to go apartment shopping," I said. "This is all your fault, buddy."

Beckett smirked and switched places with me to say goodbye to Brianna. I stood in front of Cameron and had to bite my cheek in order not to break down in front of him. He wrapped his arms around me and my breath became staggered. I felt like a fool, a crying fool.

"You are welcome here anytime, Natasha," he said in my ear. "You are family, both you and Beckett."

I rose up from his chest. "Not Nikki, I take it?"

"If at all possible," Brianna said and we all laughed.

But when the laughter died down the time had officially come. Beckett placed his arm around my shoulder and turned me toward the rental car. I couldn't wait until my new car arrived and it was just as impractical as my former baby Merc. If I was going to make the sacrifice and live in the country with a pack of wolves, I would be speeding down those country roads to get out when I could.

Beckett opened the passenger door for me, and I was about to step in when someone called after us. When we turned around, Victor was running down the wide front steps.

"I'm glad I caught you both," Victor said and pulled an envelope from his pocket.

"No Roman robes for my last day?" Beckett said with a sly smile. "I'm a little disappointed, sir."

Victor squinted one eye at his grandson before handing the envelope over. "Don't make me reconsider this."

Beckett took the envelope from Victor and lifted the flap. His eyes shot open and looked at me. When he tilted the envelope toward me, I flinched at the sight of a stack of hundred-dollar bills.

"What is this for?" Beckett asked and closed the flap of the envelope.

"I have decided that I like seeing you too much to have you move so far away."

"Um...what?"

Victor sighed in frustration. "Do I have to say it again?"

"Yes, I think so," Beckett replied with another sly smile.

"You living out in the middle of nowhere is not an option for me."

"I don't really have a choice."

"Of course you do," Victor said flatly. "You are the pack leader, you can live wherever you choose."

"I'm not sure I follow."

"I think it's fairly simple. You should live in both places. Have a home here, and another out there where you can stay when needed, especially during the full moon." Victor tapped the envelope. "This should help you with that."

Beckett shook his head and held the envelope out. "Sir, I...I can't."

Victor pushed the envelope back into Beckett's chest. "Of course you favorite, so take advantage of that."

Suddenly the car horn sounded loudly, making all of us flinch. I looked back just in time to see Nikki flopping back in her seat.

"I think we need to get going," I said.

Beckett extended his hand. Victor took his hand and pulled Beckett into a hug, patting his back and then releasing him just as quickly.

"Thank you, sir."

"Yes, yes, now get going before that awful girl honks the horn again."

Beckett laughed and stepped around to the driver's side.

Victor placed his hand on my shoulder. "The best of luck, my dear, although you certainly don't need it. We could put you in the desert and you would find water."

"Thank you, sir," I replied with a blush.

"Take care of our boy."

"I will."

Victor kissed my cheek and walked back up to the step where Brianna and Cameron still stood. I gave them all a wave goodbye and gave one last look at the manor. I didn't hide the tears leaking down my cheeks as I slipped into the passenger seat and shut the door.

"It's about fucking time," Nikki muttered from the backseat.

"Ready?" I sighed and turned to Beckett.

He squeezed my hand and kissed it. "I hope you know I couldn't do any of this without you."

"I know," I replied with a smile.

"Mother Abby is waaaaiting," Nikki whined.

Beckett forced a smile and put the car in gear.

As the car crunched along the gravel driveway, Brianna's and Victor's words echoed in my head. I had been dealt a bad hand time and time again, each time thinking there was no way life could get any harder, and being proven wrong every time. But somehow I always fought my way out to the other side. Perhaps it was all to prepare me for the complicated and hard life Beckett and I would have together. I'd clawed my way back from death on more than one occasion, I'd do it again with Beckett on my back if I had to. I didn't just bring the fire like Brianna had said. I was the fire.

STAY TUNED FOR BOOK FIVE IN THE

Blood-Borne Series

VISIT **WWW.CR-QUINN.COM** FOR THE MOST UP TO DATE INFORMATION ON THE BLOOD-BORNE SERIES AND OTHER PROJECTS FROM C.R. QUINN

Acknowledgments

I'd like to thank the Bravo network for having the best reality TV shows, and having them streaming on Hulu. I could not have written this without *Vanderpump Rules*, *Southern Charm*, and *Housewives of*...anywhere constantly on in the background. I'd also like to thank Frank Beaudry for fixing my brand-new computer whose hard drive crashed in the middle of writing this novel. Without him, you wouldn't be reading this, and I'd still be curled up on the floor crying.

About the Author

C.R. Quinn is a budding author whose prior accomplishments include a bachelor's degree in Biology, surviving the corporate world for over fifteen years, and a singer/dancer/actor/director in community theatre. She lives in Connecticut with her husband, and is lucky to be the stepmother to two wonderful children. C.R. Quinn comes from a family of storytellers whose stories will be showing up in books and plays of their own.

www.ingramcontent.com/pod-product-compliance
Lightning Source LLC
Chambersburg PA
CBHW030747030726
47497CB00001B/174